THE EVER RISING
BOOK ONE

MAGIC FEARED AND FURIOUS

CHANTEL BURNHAM

EVER RISING BOOKS LLC

Book Cover by My Lan Khuc Valle

First paperback edition 2023

ISBN: 978-1-962158-00-8

Imprint: Ever Rising Books

Visit www.chantelburnham.com

This book is dedicated to my best friend, my True Love, the shield
against all my fears, my sounding board, my confidant, my HoneyB.
I love you, Bryan.
Thank you for getting me through this.

PROLOGUE

*C*runch. A lean shape stepped through the ruined doorway of the crumbling, musty cottage. The shaking young man held himself proud, his face handsome. Even with her murky eyesight, she could see that.

Shame he had to die.

She could barely contain the eager anticipation that thrummed through her at the approach of this unwitting mortal. If he possessed magical abilities—even the tiniest potential for the craft—he would be prey indeed.

Hesitant, the young man edged forward, no doubt discomfited over her emotionless, wrinkled face, snarled hair, and the stench that wafted from her tattered clothing. Surely he thought her feeble. Fool.

She stilled, harmless-looking, but coiled to strike.

"Hello?" he croaked. She could practically see the fear rolling off his trembling shoulders. "My name is Brennan Lennox. Are you the great witch that the villagers in these parts speak of?"

The great witch. She had been, long ago. The greatest. The most feared. Had it really been two hundred years since she'd had the opportunity to control the power that now leaked from her? Once, she'd held more power than ten thousand bolts of lightning. She'd brought havoc and fear to entire continents. Nothing had stood against her.

That all changed in an instant, and the world had forgotten all that she had created, all she had done.

All she had conquered.

Now her own body was her prison. She was barely able to move. Though magic—*her* magic—cloaked the entire valley, she was unable to access it. Not without some daft human that came within her reach, and even then, it took great effort just to access their memories without touching them.

She was barely surviving on her dwindling power and the occasional rabbit that was dull enough to stray inside her domicile.

This rabbit looked dull enough to her. He was still speaking to her, stepping carefully around the exposed roots and rocks. Without so much as a blink, she plunged her consciousness into his unprotected mind. She saw him flinch, though he couldn't possibly know where the pain was coming from.

He didn't have a shred of magic in him, though it wasn't outside his reach like most humans.

A pity.

She sifted through the mundane memories of his work on merchant ships and his boyhood terror of the kelpies. Of magic. Interesting, that he came here now. His lack of magical ability made him useless, but perhaps his knowledge could . . .

Her ragged breath caught in her chest as she unearthed from his mind what she'd been waiting for these centuries. It was finally within her reach—a chance for restoration.

For revenge.

With what this boy had brought her, she could leave this hovel and rise from the smoldering ruins of the cottage, powerful, unstoppable.

Whole once more.

The world had enjoyed its peace while she was gone. Now the world would remember.

She heard the faint tinkling of a bell as he continued speaking, and she almost laughed, something she hadn't thought of doing in centuries.

Yes, child, call away. Bring them to me as well, for it will do nothing but aid my ascension.

Giddy, she finally emerged from his recollections enough to see him turn away, glancing behind him, clearly waiting.

She smiled inwardly. He was a foolish boy.

While he was turned, she struck.

PART I

Chapter One

Blood spurted as my fist connected with Ewan's crooked teeth. My torn knuckles burned as Ewan staggered backward, the smell of sweat and blood mingling in the air. I swung again, catching Ewan full in his eye. The jeers from the lads encircling us rang off the trees, but the sound was dulled by my own heartbeat thudding in my ears. Ewan stared at me, his bleeding gob hanging open, his expression dazed as he held a hand up to his bashed eye.

I glared back, anger running hot through my body.

Ewan and his band had followed me as I'd looked for my sisters in the scattering crowds picking blaeberries on the moors, and once I'd entered the woods, his cronies had cut me off from everyone. I could break through the ring and find safety in the crowds of the Blaeberry Festival, but I didn't want to run.

I wanted to show Ewan, once and for all, that even though I didn't go kelpie hunting, I wasn't a witchborn coward.

Like all the lads in these parts, I'd dreamed about the hunts for the giant water horses that roamed the Scottish highlands and dragged victims to a watery grave. Which was uncommon these days, as few were foolish enough to wander the moors alone on autumn nights.

My father had promised to take me during the kelping season when I turned twelve, but then he had died, and my mother had forbade me from ever joining the hunt.

I'd held my temper in check as best I could when Ewan and his gang taunted me for avoiding the "man-making" traditions of our village, but when they started in on my sisters, I couldn't help launching a fist into his self-satisfied face.

He would learn for himself that I could hold my own. He'd never faced me openly before. He usually sent one of his toadies to fight in his stead, but not this time. Folly on his part.

I watched, every muscle taut, as Ewan shook his head like a lazy cow trying to rid itself of flies. Several boys slapped him on the back to bolster him, shouting encouragement.

Wiping his mouth on his sleeve, Ewan shook out his arms and took up the stance again. The lads' cheering swelled as their leader got back into the fray. Ewan took a breath and came hurtling back toward me, fists cocked.

I bent my knees, ready to receive his attack, when someone kicked my ankle out from under me. Ewan laughed as I fell to a knee, then threw a punch at my nose as I rolled away. Not fast enough. His fist got me in the side of my face. The hit wasn't very hard, but the cheers that followed were near deafening. I regained my footing as Ewan rushed me again. He cuffed my mouth, the metallic taste of blood blossoming on my tongue, but I returned with a double strike to his side, and he quickly retreated.

"Is tha' all yeh've got, Lennox?" Ewan coughed, holding his stomach. "Yeh talk like a dandy, and yeh fight like one, too! Yeh're nothin' but the mongrel son of a dead good-for-nothing, and yer witch sisters are the same! Witchborn!" The crowd laughed as Ewan grinned around at the ring of boys.

Witchborn.

The term still bothered me, though there wasn't a speck of truth to the brand. I'd never worked magic in my life. It was common sense not to trust witches or anyone else who used the evil power, but the village priest said that those who were conceived out of wedlock were also not to be trusted, as the sinful act warped the soul of the unborn child, making them witchborn.

While I had known for quite a few years that I had been conceived outside of marriage, my mother didn't know I knew, and my sisters, as far as I hoped, didn't know what a witchborn was.

I ground my teeth, my lip stinging.

Ewan calling me names wasn't what bothered me. If Ewan kept saying my sisters were witches, rumors would start, and then my sisters would be shunned, too.

Anger flared inside me as the crowd continued to laugh, and Ewan guffawed like an old rooster. Clenching my fists, I sprang forward, throwing my shoulder into Ewan's stomach, yelling wordlessly. As I drove him backward, he pounded his fists on my back, trying to stop me. Ignoring the blows, but grunting a little at his weight, I threw him up and over my shoulder, slamming him down onto the trampled grass. There was a collective gasp as I scrambled to my feet and stared down at the motionless Ewan. He stared back, eyes wide, mouth opening and closing like a fish. After a few seconds, he began hacking and gasping. I released my own held breath and took advantage of Ewan's momentary respite.

I leaned over him, baring my teeth. "You can call me whatever you like, Drummond," I snapped over the sound of his booing cronies, "But if you ever say anything like that about my sisters again, you'll have more to fear than just the kelpies." I spit off to the side of Ewan, my body still shaking with anger.

The jeers against me were even louder than the yells of support for Ewan had been as I stepped away from the gasping lad. I wanted to pummel him into a pulp, but it wasn't sporting to attack a stunned dullard. Several lads rushed forward and helped Ewan to his feet. He bent double for a few moments, his breathing ragged, then straightened. I planted my feet, bracing for another attack. He turned to me, his expression snide as he wiped his bleeding lips again. He held up his hands for silence, and the clearing fell quiet. I kept my fists up, ready for more dirty tricks.

Ewan began laughing a wheezy laugh.

"Well, well, Lennox," Ewan coughed, his face red and puffy. "Maybe yeh're not such a craven witchborn after all."

"Ready for another thrashing?" I asked, glad my voice didn't tremble, knowing I would pay for humiliating the great Ewan Drummond. My eyes darted around the circle, awaiting an attack. It wouldn't be the first time Ewan sicked two or three of his lads on me at once. Ewan laughed again, wincing, a look in his eye I didn't like. "Now, now, what say yeh and I let bygones be bygones?" he asked, holding a swollen hand out to me.

"Oh, and why would you want that? Scared of getting a broken nose?" I asked, shifting my feet, trying to look taller as I swiped a few sweaty locks of hair out of my eyes.

Ewan shook his head, chuckling. "Yeh've a wicked fist, I'll give yeh that. It's not easy tae take me down."

I bit my tongue to keep myself from saying something I'd regret. "I know you didn't attack me just so you could compliment my fighting afterwards, Drummond. Either get back to the festival, or let's finish this," I barked, holding my fists up again.

"Now, 'old on," Ewan said, holding up his hands in a pacifying gesture. "I bet a lad that fights like yeh should be man enough tae take down something a little more . . . dangerous."

Chills erupted down my spine as excited murmuring broke out through the circle.

"I suggest a wager," Ewan continued.

I clenched my fists tighter, knuckles searing, now half-hoping for the fight to continue. I wasn't intimidated by Ewan, because even though his father owned half the village, Ewan couldn't boast about much else. Except for the three kelpies he'd downed himself, which he bragged about every moment he could fit it in. Other than that, he wasn't very strong or very smart. He wouldn't want to wager about competitions in the highland games this afternoon—I would easily best him.

If the wager was about me going kelping, I didn't know if I'd be able to resist.

"What do you mean 'wager'?" I asked. If money became involved, things would change. I knew a hard winter was coming. I hadn't been able to work much this year, and my father's debts were surely coming due. I had seen my mother leaving the magistrate's house the other day with several papers in hand, and it looked as if she had been crying, but she wouldn't tell me what was wrong. She was scared we wouldn't survive the winter. I was certain that was the reason for her tears.

Ewan held up a weighty leather pouch, which clinked with coins. I felt my heart drop.

"Here's a wee incentive. If yeh come kelpie hunting with us tonight, and bring down a kelpie, I'll give yeh this whole purse."

I stared at the bag. My family had never had that much money at one time. Before I began to stare too greedily, I snapped my attention back to Ewan, who was smirking as though he had me.

"Are yeh scared yeh won't kill one, and it'll prove how worthless yeh really are?" Ewan asked. "Or are yeh scared of meeting the same fate as your worthless father?"

I ground my teeth. "My father wasn't worthless."

He'd died, taken by a kelpie while on a hunt, before he could pay off the debts of the sheep he'd bought to sustain our family. Because of that, we had to sell the sheep at a loss and were left with the burden of the debt incurred. He'd been a good man, just plagued with having a witchborn for a son.

Ewan waved away my denial. "He wasn't strong enough tae fight off a kelpie," he replied, as if that was a failing on my father's part. "But yeh can prove that yeh do."

He held up the money again.

I looked into Ewan's face, comprehension dawning on me. He didn't want bygones to be bygones. This whole wager was another way to humiliate me. Ewan knew I'd never been kelpie hunting in my life. He and his friends had been out routing the water beasts since they were twelve, as was tradition.

Even though I was fourteen now, I still would be hard pressed to catch, let alone kill, a kelpie on my first try. Besides, I'd made a promise to my mother. Even though kelping was how a boy became a man in our village of Bòidhchead, my mother refused to let me participate. She never did understand the allure of kelping, despite my attempts to convince her. She didn't even like us listening to stories about hunts and near misses by those who trekked across the moors, searching for the giant water horses for sport. It brought bad luck, she said, and we would have no part in it.

I spit again.

I didn't need his money, or the obvious flaunting of his wealth in my face.

"I'm not going to dance your wee jig, Drummond," I snapped, an angry heat rising inside me. "You expect me to believe you'll really give me that money? I'm not that big of a dunce." I started to turn away but Ewan grabbed my arm. I whipped back around, fists up, but Ewan held up his hands.

"Wait, wait, 'old on. We'll sweeten the pot. Come on, lads, give it up," Ewan demanded, turning to the other boys. Grumbling but complying, they began emptying their pockets of coins and other little trinkets: spinning tops, puzzle rings, and buttons. I watched in amazement as Ewan collected the belongings of the other boys, marveling at how they obeyed him without question. Ewan turned to me, the bag in his hands now bulging.

"'Ow about now?" he asked, eyebrow arched in an evil look.

I stared at the wealth that Ewan held in his hands. Something inside me slackened. I honestly would've done it for free had my mother not forbidden me, and it was thinking of her that made me work my jaw and look into Ewan's expectant face.

"I promised my mother I wouldn't," I said, keeping my voice firm.

I expected the laughs, but I wasn't expecting Ewan to wrap his arm around my shoulder, putting his head close to mine as if we were chums. I stiffened.

"Ach, yer mother needn't ever know. And yeh'll have a load of gold tae give tae 'er. I'm sure tha' outweighs any promise, am I righ'? Yeh'd be providing some *real* wages tae help yer family." I ignored the way he said 'real,' as if I didn't already know I had no apprenticeship, and was barely able to get odd jobs in a village as superstitious as Bòidhchead. Such was the luck of a witchborn.

He stared me down, hefting the bulging money bag up to eye level again. My resolve began to waver.

"Why?" I asked, looking Ewan in the face. "Why are you willing to give me such a chance?"

Ewan tilted his head from side to side as if deliberating. "I figure a lad that can throw a punch like yeh shouldn't have tae be afraid of some wee ponies. And besides, I'd rather yeh throw punches *for* me, than *at* me, if yeh take me meaning." The boys around us chuckled. I understood his meaning perfectly. Accept the wager, take down a kelpie, and I'd become one of his toadies.

I was about to open my mouth and give him a colorful answer, but I paused. Maybe being on his good side wouldn't be such a bad thing.

"Besides, if nothing else," Ewan continued at my hesitation, "It'd show yer mother yeh can take care of yerself. And, just maybe," Ewan said, shaking me slightly, "yeh'll prove tae all of Bòidhchead that yeh, Brennan Lennox, are not quite the witchborn they believe yeh tae be."

I licked my lips, hating Ewan for saying all the hopes I'd kept secret in my heart.

"And what would I tell my mother when she asks where I got this money?" I asked, desperate to stump him. But Ewan, ever sly, grinned.

"Just tell 'er yeh won it gambling. She'll scold yeh tae never do it again, and that'll be the end of it," Ewan said with a careless wave of his hand. "And yeh'll be one of me crowd. What do yeh say, Brennan? Will we see yeh tonight?" He hefted the purse in his hands, the jangling coins loud in my ears.

The lean, hungry looks of my three younger sisters came to my mind. I couldn't sit by, letting my mother worry about our money situation and letting my sisters starve, without doing something to help. I might never get this offer again.

"Aye. I'll do it," I heard myself saying.

The boys all cheered and slapped each other on the back. I received a few myself, and despite it, I grinned. My mother would never know. When people in the village started talking about kelpies, she would take her leave. Ewan and his friends were allowed to go kelpie routing without adults; no one would carry the news to her.

We made arrangements to meet on Lookout Hill, a common meeting place outside the village where you could see the whole of Bòidhchead. Thankfully, my house wasn't visible from the hill. I pushed away the guilt I felt with the happy knowledge that I had a chance to prove myself. The lads left the woods, chattering and laughing, and I trailed them at a distance. Part of me worried that Ewan was playing me for a fool, but I figured it would be better to be humiliated than stay home and miss my chance altogether.

Chapter Two

I had just stepped out of the trees, still wrapped up in my own thoughts, when I ran straight into my eleven-year-old sister, Maura, bowling her over. I helped her to her feet, my heart thundering in my chest.

"What are you doing here?" I asked, more worried that she had seen me speaking, not just fighting, with Ewan and his gang. If she had, my mother would most certainly find out about the wager I'd just made to go kelpie hunting. Maura brushed off her dress with a displeased huff and frowned up at me. She opened her mouth to say something, then paused.

"Well?" I asked, holding my breath.

Maura closed her mouth, then shook her head. "We saw you looking for us. We waved, but you didn't see us, so Norah told me to come get you. I'd lost sight of you, and was just coming over to check these woods when you came back out and knocked me over."

I eyed her suspiciously. I'd been in there for some time. Had she followed me in? I watched as she brushed the final bits of grass off her overskirt.

No, I didn't think she had. Knowing Maura, she would've had quite a few words for me about how I was being a dafty for taking Ewan's wager. She hated Ewan as much as I did and trusted him less.

"Sorry," I replied. "I thought you lassies had gone in there, but I couldn't find you."

"That's because we're over there." She pointed out at the moors, toward the thinning crowd. "Come."

As Maura led me back to where she, Norah, and Slaine had been picking berries with their friends, we passed a group of villagers gathered at an enormous clump of berry bushes, where Gordon Brown at that very moment was telling the giggling children about kelpies.

"Aye, giant horses, they are, twenty hands high at least, with green flames for eyes!" Gordon growled, widening his own eyes with a snort, causing a nervous giggle to ripple through the children. Behind the bairns, their parents cast amused glances at each other.

"Fly over the moorlands as though they have wings, they do. Their favorite time tae come out is when the night is deep, and the mists creep through the heather." His voice became so quiet that both Maura and I stopped so we could hear the rest. Our mother hated stories of the kelpies, but my sisters and I couldn't get enough of them. "Beau'iful and dangerous they be. One look from those devilish eyes, and yeh can find yehrself swept up ontae their moss-velvet backs, and yeh'll never be heard from again. For when yeh are snatched up, they take yeh tae their underwater realms . . .

and drown yeh!" He bellowed, lunging out toward the children with curled fingers. They screamed as Gordon roared with laughter.

He caught sight of us standing behind the crowd, and he called toward us, "Ye also need tae have a care about the company ye keep. I hear kelpies are attracted tae magic and witchborns." Everyone turned, curious, and I felt my face grow hot as I locked stares with several distrustful pairs of eyes. I felt Maura slip her hand in mine and give it a comforting squeeze as she stuck her tongue out at the crowd before pulling me away. We joined a throng of villagers that had finished berrying and were heading back to the game field.

We moved down a hill, toward a group of seven or eight lassies sitting beside a large blaeberry bush, their backs to us, their heads close together, talking in hushed tones. I immediately picked out my other two sisters, Norah and Slaine, by the fiery red hair that they'd inherited from our mother.

I was about to call out to them, but hearing the sound of my own name stopped me.

Norah, just a couple years younger than I, was shaking her head at the young village girl who'd said my name.

"Well, Brennan isn't evil," Norah replied, her tone hard.

"I didn't say he was evil," the girl, Peggy Barnes, replied with a heated tone. "I just said he scares me because he's witchborn."

I saw several girls stare at Peggy with open mouths as she continued, "Witches can destroy an entire town if they want. Did you know they get their powers by . . . *human sacrifice*?" The last words were a sharp whisper. All the girls gasped. Maura cast me a worried look, and my stomach flipped.

I'd heard the tales myself. Witches were so feared because they performed dark rituals to obtain their magical powers. In doing so, they corrupted themselves into soulless monsters, no longer human. All magic was feared, but none more so than the magic wielded by witches.

"So, if Brennan *is* witchborn . . . ?" another girl started, her expression awed.

"He brings the bad luck of the witches. He may turn into an evil witch himself at any moment!" Peggy finished, nodding in a superior sort of way. "That's why no one wants to hire him! He's cursed."

"Stop it, Peg," Norah scolded. "This is all nonsense! Brennan is *not* evil!"

Another girl turned to Norah, an exasperated look on her face. "Maybe not right now, but if Brennan really *is* witchborn, what if he *does* turn—"

"Brennan!" Slaine, my youngest sister at age four, called, finally seeing me. There was a collective gasp from the group, and everyone whirled around. The expressions on all their faces were fearful as they saw me standing there. Everyone but my sisters leapt to their feet and scattered, berry baskets in hand.

Feeling sick, I hitched a smile on my face and wandered over to Norah and Slaine, Maura trailing behind me. Norah blushed as I came to stand over them. I ignored her chagrined expression and studied Slaine's basket. It was much emptier than her older sisters'. Slaine looked up at me with a purple-stained smile.

"My, you've nearly cleared the whole bush," I said, smiling down at Slaine, who gave me a proud grin.

"Where have you been, Brennan? And . . . what happened to your face?" Norah asked in a small voice, casting a glance at Maura, who had sat down and was rolling a berry between her fingers, not looking at either of us. I frowned, surprised she wasn't saying anything.

"Mother wants you back at the wagon," I replied, licking my split lip with a wince and ignoring Norah's second question.

There was an awkward silence, then Norah cleared her throat. "Bren, I'm sorry. I . . ." She looked at her hands, shame coloring her cheeks. I gave them all a grave look.

"Do you believe I could turn into a witch?" I asked, unable to keep the hurt from my voice. "That I'm evil?"

"No, no, Brennan, of course not!" Norah blurted as Maura gave a vigorous shake of her head. "Peggy just . . . she . . . I tried to get her to hush! You don't use magic; you're not evil! We're . . . we're sorry." The apology came out as a whimper.

I met their worried eyes, then shook my head. "Well, you best not let Mother know what you were discussing," I replied. "And that's all I'll say on the matter."

"We're sorry," Norah repeated, eyes downcast.

I nodded. "You've all gathered a lot, little birds," I said, admiring their baskets brimming with misty-blue berries, "but it's time to go back."

"Mother said she wanted a lot," Norah explained, "to preserve for the winter."

"Well, there will still be berries here after the celebration," I replied, accepting a sprig of heather from Slaine, "we can pick more then."

"Okay," Slaine said, her tone cheerful as she got to her feet. I had a feeling Slaine had no idea what the older girls had been talking about. I helped gather up the remaining baskets, and we began the hike back toward the heart of the village.

As we entered the green at the center of town, my mother's cart came into view. I spotted my mother nearby, her red hair in stark contrast to the late summer grass of the game field. She was doing brisk business at the wagon, selling homemade blaeberry tarts and jams to those waiting for the highland games to start. A steady stream of people were walking away, eating wedges of tart or carrying loaves of blaeberry bread. She was doling out a slice of pie to an older man, who tucked a coin into her hand and wandered away as we approached. Smiling, she turned to us.

Her smile slipped into a frown.

"Brennan!" She stepped toward me and captured my chin in her palm. "What ever happened?" Her eyes roved over the bruise that was no doubt beginning to bloom on my right temple. I had no desire to tell her what I had been fighting about, so I remained silent.

"I thought we'd been through this. I don't like you fighting," she chided.

"It wasn't me that started it," I began, my tone hot, but my mother cooled my rudeness with a look.

"I don't care, Brennan. You know what I've said about such behavior."

I stood there while she assessed my bloodied lip and swelling temple.

She clicked her tongue and brushed a strand of dark brunette hair off my forehead. "That looks bad, m'love."

"It's not," I lied, pulling my face out of her hand and hiding my kerchief-wrapped hand behind my back. No sense in her worrying over a tiny scratch.

My mother sighed, then smiled again at my sisters, a brighter smile than I'd seen in weeks. She scooped us all into a hug.

"We're doing much better than last year. It's thanks to you all that we were able to make so much with all the berries you've picked these last few days," my mother said, giving all of us a smile.

My mother was beautiful, with dark red curls framing her face and eyes as green as the sea, as my father used to say. She wasn't from the highlands, having moved up to Bóidhchead from Glasgow. We had inherited her more refined speech and were often teased because of it.

"Are you going to be doing any of the games, Brennan?" my mother asked as I lifted Slaine into the wagon bed and boosted myself up onto the cart beside her.

I shook my head, determined to stay near the cart for the rest of the festival, watching the competitions with my mother. I was afraid that if I saw Ewan and his friends again while participating in any of the games, I'd change my mind and back out, especially now that my mother was in view and the guilt was starting to creep into my chest. The deal had been struck, I told myself firmly. Besides, my hands were hurting so much, I wouldn't be able to do much lifting.

"No, I can stay here and help you," I replied.

"Thank you, Brennan," she said with a warm smile.

We ate our picnic dinner in the back of the wagon, watching the games on the green, my favorite being the caber toss. After my sisters finished eating, they wandered back to find their friends. I didn't begrudge my sisters their friends, even though I didn't have any myself. It wasn't considered ladylike for girls to go kelpie hunting, so my sisters weren't shunned for not partaking in the tradition.

The moment we had sold the last of the sweetmeats, my mother began to pack up, insistent that we leave before the sun got too low in the sky. She always made sure we were indoors before sundown, as kelpies came out once dusk began to settle.

She sent me off to find my sisters, and I found them among several groups of girls dancing a reel to a pair of old men playing bagpipes. After saying their goodbyes, we all loaded into the cart. As we were leaving the green, I caught a glimpse of Ewan in the crowds. My stomach twisted, part in guilt, part in a squirm of excitement. My first kelpie hunt. I knew it was against my mother's express wishes, but I was doing this for us, if she would just trust me. My mother's worries wouldn't help me save us from starvation and fear. I needed to show her, show everyone, I was worth more than the circumstances of my birth. I wasn't a wee lad anymore; I was a man. I *had* to make good on my promise to Ewan tonight and prove my worth, or remain branded a witchborn forever.

Chapter Three

By the time we got home that evening, the sun was near setting. Because my father had planned to use the open highlands to raise his flocks of sheep, we lived nearly a mile outside of town. I didn't know where my parents had gotten the money for the cottage and the land, but I assumed that was what all the debts were for.

After putting our work horse away in the barn, I grabbed a length of rope and the mucking pitchfork to arm myself for my first kelpie hunt. I hid the items in a bush outside my bedroom window before going into the house, where my mother was waiting anxiously for my return.

"Finished?" she asked as I came inside after stomping the mud from my boots. I nodded, swallowing against the dry sensation in my throat. "Well then, let's set out the lanterns. Quickly now." She motioned for me to help her gather up the somewhat shriveled tumshies and potatoes, carved with ghastly faces. They would act as sentinels against the dark creatures that frolicked among the highland hills. We inserted coals into each lantern, then placed the flickering faces outside the house. When we were finished, she hurried me inside, double checked the bolted door behind us, then turned to me, exhaling with relief.

"We've had quite a busy day, haven't we? Thank you, Brennan. You've been such a great help." She gave me a tired, but happy, look. I smiled back, trying to ignore the tendril of shame curling in my stomach. My mother, noticing my faltering expression, sighed and placed a gentle hand on my face. "Brennan, I know you've been worried about us, but I don't think you'll need to worry much longer. We'll be quite alright."

"How *did* we do today?" I asked, trying to keep the concern from my tone. The papers from the magistrate and her tears were always in the back of my mind.

"We did very well. Double what we earned last year," my mother replied, a sad smile on her face. Before I could say anything more, she pulled me into a bone-crushing hug, then nudged me toward my room. "Now off to bed with you, Love. It's been a long day."

I hitched a more convincing smile on my lips as I bid my mother goodnight, but my heart felt heavy. Sure, today had been fairly successful, but what about when the money from the festival ran out? I was still witchborn, and there would be more winters. What Ewan was promising me would keep us even longer—and not only because of the money. I couldn't keep second-guessing myself. I would go tonight.

I hurried to my room, where I made a show of changing into my bedclothes and cleaning my teeth with a rag and water before climbing into my bed. My sisters were already asleep, exhausted from the day's excitement. As I settled beneath the covers, my mother came down the hall, peering into our room to make sure we were all in bed before I heard her enter her bedchamber and turn in for the night.

I waited for a good hour to make sure everyone was asleep, my blood roaring in my ears. When the only sound in the house was the wind whispering through the cracks in the window, I slid out of bed and dressed in my hefty work boots, winter pants, and coat. I slid out my window as quietly as I could and took up the pitchfork. Throwing the rope over my shoulder, I picked up one of the glowing turnip lanterns that we'd set around the house and snuck away from the darkened cottage.

I trekked over the hills, a stiff breeze blowing summer away in gusts of frigid mountain air. Every rustle of the brush and mournful howl of the wind turned my blood cold, and the images of kelpies bearing down on me heightened my senses and kept me alert, despite the late hour.

As I hiked, I wished I could've brought a real lantern with me, but I hadn't wanted to creep into the hallway, where the creaking boards would have surely woken my mother. My sisters and I couldn't even get away with whispered conversations about kelpies in the dead of night without Mother descending on us, she slept so lightly.

Soon, Lookout Hill towered above me. As I began the hike up the grassy brae, I watched for the lanterns of an approaching mob of young men. I shivered as the wind began to pick up, and I stomped my feet, trying to keep warm.

After ten minutes of wandering atop the hill with no sign of anyone, I started to feel uneasy. From my vantage point, I could see several miles of moor, with Loch Domhainn a dark blot of ink in the distance. Our cottage, as well as the village, were completely hidden from view by rolling moorland. As I considered going down the other side of the slope to see if the group was waiting there, I heard rustling somewhere off to my left. Though the wind skirled over the moor around me, it wasn't enough to disturb the bushes so. I whirled around, my hair standing on the backs of my arms. I faced the thicket, pitchfork raised, heart beating so fast in my chest it felt as though it wasn't beating at all.

Kelpies.

The rustling grew louder and I braced myself. Fear thrilled through me, but I would fight till my last ounce of strength. I would not be called *coward* again.

"Brennan?" came a small voice from behind the clump of brush. I couldn't believe my ears, and I nearly dropped my pitchfork as a small face peeked out between the branches.

"*Maura?*" I tried to shout, but it came out strangled from momentary relief and bitter cold. My little sister shouldered her way out of the thicket, a small knife from the kitchen in hand. I couldn't decide if I wanted to throttle her, or hug her.

"Maura! What are you doing here? How did you find me?" I thundered, marching over to her, planting the butt of the pitchfork into the spongy earth.

She stepped back, looking determined. "I'm here to help you kill a kelpie."

"Maura, you are going to get *yourself* killed!" My voice cracked. "I can't hunt kelpies as well as watch over you!"

"I have just as much right as you do to be out here!" she insisted. "We need that money. I know Mother's been crying too, you know."

Her revelation surprised me into silence. We stared at each other for a moment, and then I exhaled. "How did you even know I was—"

"I heard you talking to the boys today. I saw you wander into the woods to look for us, but you didn't see us waving." I saw her visibly shiver. "I went to get you, and I saw those boys corner you, so I snuck closer. I heard everything. Nice job whipping Ewan, by the way."

"You go home this instant!" I snapped, pointing over her head in the direction of the house.

"Oh, y-you don't want me to be doing that," Maura replied with a sneer, trying to cover the shivering in her voice. "You see, I'll not be reluctant to inform M-Mother about what you're up to."

We glared at each other until she hefted her knife higher and marched past me. "Stay here if you want, but I'm going. You're welcome to join me."

My mouth dropped open. "What? Join *you*? That's not how it works! *I'm* in charge!"

She gave me a withering look, but I ignored her.

"Yes, I'm in charge, and you're going home right now!" When she continued to stare at me, I exhaled. "I have to do this. If I don't, I'll not only lose the only chance I have to be accepted, but I could lose a small fortune."

"That is why I'm here *helping* you," she replied, rolling her eyes.

I shook my head. "Maura, no. Lassies have no business hunting kelpies. It's a man's job. What would Mother say if you got hurt? I'd never forgive myself." Not to mention the insults I'd get from Ewan's lot if I brought my *sister* along.

She glared at me, and I glared back.

"Come on, I'm taking you back home," I snarled.

"Are you going to stay at home as well?" she asked, eyes narrowed in suspicion. When I didn't reply, her face darkened. "I don't want you getting hurt either. We do this together or not at all."

I cast my mind back to the lads I was going to meet. They hadn't shown up yet, but delivering my sister back home would take a lot of time. If they came and I wasn't here, they would probably leave me behind, marking me off as a bad job. My insides curdled at the thought, but it couldn't be helped now. It wasn't even a question, leaving Maura out here. My mother would never forgive me.

"We'll see. They probably won't be there if I come back, anyway. You've just lost us a great deal of money, coming out here. Why didn't you leave well enough alone?" I snapped.

"They probably wouldn't give you the money anyway." Maura scowled. "I bet Ewan isn't even going to show."

I clenched my teeth and didn't reply as I grabbed her shoulder with my free hand and began marching us back toward home at a quick pace.

My first-ever kelpie hunt, ruined by an eleven-year-old girl. She was probably right about Ewan not showing up, but I didn't want to think about the consequences if she was wrong. Once I got her inside, I was coming back here. Maybe I could make it. I would wake Norah and tell her to keep an eye on Maura.

We hurried across the moors, the stars and moon occasionally disappearing behind thick black clouds. Gusts of wind whipped at our clothing, and my fingers began turning purple from the cold. I could feel Maura grab at my tunic every time something rustled in the bushes.

"I told you that you shouldn't have come along," I scoffed.

She replied by punching me in the small of my back with a hissed, "Haud yer wheesht!"

I grunted at the blow. She was stronger than I thought. I frowned at her use of the village slang. It seemed gossip wasn't the only trait she was picking up from her friends.

The wind became more and more biting as we neared our house. Maura's teeth were chattering as the whole night sky became one large blanket of clouds, black as pitch.

"D-do you h-hear that, Br-Brennan?" Maura chattered, and I looked down to see her clutching tightly to the threadbare cloak wrapped around her shoulders. Through her thick auburn hair blowing in her face, I could see that her lips were turning blue. She stumbled as she walked, and I was amazed she had followed me so far in the dark. I stripped off my coat and slung it over Maura's shoulders while straining to hear any threatening sounds over the whistle of the wind. Maura gratefully trembled her bare arms into the coat sleeves and gave me a small blue smile. Listening hard, I finally heard a faint shout.

"That sounds like your name, Maura," I said slowly, as the call came echoing on the wind again.

"M-Mother," she replied, glancing up at me, and my heart sank. We were in for it now. I definitely wouldn't be able to sneak out again in time to meet the lads.

As we neared the road that led to our house, we could see a white figure pacing anxiously in front of the dark house, occasionally calling our names, her voice hoarse with fear. As soon as she saw our glowing lantern, she began to run toward us.

"She m-must have heard me get the knife f-from the kitchen," Maura chattered.

I was about to give her a sharp rebuke when we heard an unnatural, ear-piercing shriek behind us.

Maura whipped around and stared into the blackness as goose pimples prickled the nape of my neck. I turned, my stomach full of ice, following her gaze. Out of the black landscape, an even darker shape was charging in our direction.

The form became clear as the sound of thunderous hooves resounded in our ears. In an instant it was upon us: a beautiful, sleek stallion, its coat gleaming like green lightning despite the starless night. It turned a cruel eye on me, the whites rolling in its head. The gigantic stallion screamed again, rearing onto its hind legs. The smell of moss and mud filled my nose as it towered over us.

I heard Maura scream, but neither of us could move, our legs frozen as the enormous beast fixed us with an icy gaze.

My mind was clear, though terror lapped at my consciousness. Unwittingly, I reached a hand toward the kelpie's neck. Horror washed over any coherent thought as I tried to stop my hand from moving forward, but the power of the kelpie's gaze was too strong. I took a step toward it, Maura following.

I had heard of the power of the kelpies, but I hadn't known how compelling the pull of the creature actually was. I was about to be tugged onto the back of the kelpie with my sister, to be taken to our death. I closed my eyes as I took another step, despite my straining to pull away.

Something hit me hard in the shoulder, and I found myself knocked from my feet as the beast shrieked again. I tumbled and skidded to a stop, face down in the mist-wet grass. The lantern in my hand rolled away, the coal tumbling out of the turnip and winking faintly in the blackness. I raised my head and saw Maura lying a few feet from me, sobbing uncontrollably. Groaning, I turned to see my mother standing before the kelpie, both arms outstretched, hair and cloak snapping in the sharp wind.

"Take me!" she bellowed, her tone giving me more chills than the kelpie's screams had. The kelpie snorted and dipped its head low, circling ever closer toward the reach of my mother.

"Mother, don't!" I tried to scream, but the wind snatched away my voice. We didn't all need to die. I was sure once it collected my mother, it would come for Maura and myself. I could still feel the freezing effects of the kelpie as it towered over my mother, but now its full attention was focused on her. I wanted to move, but I could barely keep myself supported enough to see what was going on. My mother reached her shaking hands toward the slick, velvety back of the kelpie.

"Brennan, take Maura and run," she called, her voice trembling but determined as she placed her hands onto its powerful shoulder. With a squeal, the kelpie reared and flung my mother onto its sturdy back with its strange magic. The demon then turned toward us, but my mother, her eyes fierce, kicked the flanks of the kelpie with all her might. With an unearthly shriek, the kelpie reared and bolted off into the night.

My mother's scream echoed off the highland peaks.

As soon as the kelpie was out of sight, the eerie immovability lifted and I rolled to my hands and knees, groaning at the pain in my shoulder where I had landed.

"Mother!" I cried out into the pitiless darkness. I stumbled to my feet and helped Maura stand. Her face was white as milk, and she was gasping for air through her wild tears.

"Get inside, bolt the doors, and don't leave!" I shouted, turning her to face the darkened house. All the lanterns we'd placed around the cottage had gone out. They would be no use to me.

"What about Mother?" Maura sobbed.

"Go *inside*!" I shouted, pushing her toward our home. I spied Maura's knife and snatched it up; my pitchfork would be too heavy to carry while running. I made sure Maura got inside, then ran in the direction the kelpie had taken our mother.

All thought had fled except the drive to find her. I needed her. I couldn't even think about returning to our cottage and facing my three young sisters without her. I didn't care about other kelpies or bogles or cat sìths or any other kind of dark beast that wandered the shadowy highlands. I *had* to save my mother.

Unbidden, unwanted thoughts raced through my mind as my feet carried me over the rippling hills. What if I was delayed by a kelpie or some other night creature? What was a kelpie doing so close to the house? What would happen to the four of us if I couldn't reach Mother in time? The last thought haunted me and spurred me to run faster.

As the night deepened, the wind began to pick up and whipped me so ferociously that I had to keep my head down and fight against the dust blowing into my face. The cold began to numb my feet and hands as the dark clouds raced overhead.

When I didn't come upon any lochs after an hour of running, I realized I must've gotten lost. I had no idea where I was, but I continued on, panic making my voice shrill across the barrens as I called for my mother.

My strength finally gave out from the exertion, and I fell to the ground on my hands and knees, my chest heaving for breath. I sat up, shivering on the cold, misty moors, unsure of which direction to go.

I had assumed the kelpie would head to the nearest body of water, probably Loch Domhainn, but I'd lost sight of it in the dark. My heart froze as I thought of all the other lochs that surrounded our village—all the other lochs the beast could have taken my mother to. I'd lost her.

I fell backward into the grass and began to sob. She was gone. This couldn't have happened. My mother couldn't be dead. I had lost my father, but somehow that didn't hit me with the same force as the knowledge that my sweet mother had been taken from me and cruelly drowned.

Tears chilled my cheeks. My body ached, and I was so cold I couldn't think straight. I didn't even know where I was. I cried until, slowly, reason returned. If I died out here, my wee sisters would be left all alone. They wouldn't have any idea of what happened to me. I had to get back home.

I rolled to my side and tried to sit up, but exhaustion pulled me back to the wet dirt. I stared up at the sky.

The wind had swept the threatening clouds over the mountains and out of sight, leaving cold starlight blazing above me. My breath caught in my throat as I stared at that endless ocean of glimmering stars, feeling as though the yawning heavens would swallow me whole.

I was so caught up in the view that at first I didn't notice the green, purple, and yellow lights that began rising from the tall grasses beside me. Only when one floated in front of my eyes did I realize I was surrounded. The glow of the creatures was so vibrant that I couldn't make out their shapes as the multicolored lights pulsed and twirled, dancing with the blades of grass.

A fyre fairy thicket.

The small lights, no bigger than my thumb, rose silently into the sky. I watched in wonder as giant clouds of the glowing creatures swirled and drifted lazily upward, untouched by the icy winds that caused the grass to ripple and my tunic to flap. The fairies blotted out the stars and lit up the darkened valley as the lights filtered away toward the distant mountains. One fairy landed on my nose, the touch calming my anguished mind. Through the blinding gleam, I thought I could make out the shape of a small person inside the dome of light just as I dropped unconscious in the night's chill.

Chapter Four

S omeone shook me hard with a gruff, "Eh, lad, dinnae ye fall
asleep, now!"

I jerked awake. I was still lying on the cold grass of the moors,
the stars glimmering above me. An eyelash moon hung low over the
highland hills. The shimmering lights of the fyre fairies were just
colored specks in the star-filled sky, disappearing within the blink of
an eye.

A dark man was kneeling before me, his large hands on my
shoulders, propping me up. Beside him sat an enclosed woven reed
basket, many colored lights floating inside. Behind him stood a
woman holding a burning torch that cast a circle of light around us.
Her hooded robe and flower-and-weeds circlet were familiar.

"Druids," I choked, scrambling to stand, but my weak limbs
collapsed under me. I panted as I stared up at them, trying to catch
my breath.

I recognized the druid woman. She was slim, with thick ebony
hair lightly streaked with silver. She carried a wooden staff with a

twisting horn of bark at the top. Not much was known of druids, as they usually kept to themselves, their haunts hidden out on the moors. Though everyone knew they were magic users, one particular coven of druids had been coming to the village for many years. They were allowed to enter town only because they didn't try to sell magical talismans or potions. No honest man would touch magic, even if it promised safety against the kelpies. Everyone in the village alleged that druids were akin to witches, and everyone knew that witches were not to be trusted. If the druids let slip even a hint that they were offering magic for money, they'd be run out of town.

Instead, the ones near our village only sold the meat and fur they gathered from the moors, selling to those who were too poor to frequent the regular shops. My mother bought goods from this woman's stall when she came to market—the druid's meat was cheaper than the butcher's—and the druid woman was often alone. I'd never seen the man in the village.

I always got shaky when I saw magic users like druids, and not only because the village saw me in the same distasteful light. Magic scared me more than I liked to admit. Whenever I passed the druids in town, I could feel the aura of magic around them, and people said that if you were in contact with magic for too long, it would change you into a witch. I was already witchborn; I didn't want to risk becoming one entirely.

My vision tilted as I tried to stand again.

"Aye, careful now, laddie," the man rumbled, his voice deeper than a mountain loch. "Easy."

"What are you doin' out here?" the woman asked, her tone stern. "Hunting for fyre fairies? All alone? The Ever keep you, you're lucky not to have been taken by a kelpie!"

"Aye, he is at that. Leprekin, perhaps?" the man asked the woman behind him, his tone faintly amused.

"Quite unlikely," she replied. Their voices seemed to be growing further and further away as my vision began to spin.

She slapped the man on the shoulder. "Oh, quick, Daimh, give him this. He looks ready to swoon again, he does." She plucked several petals from her circlet, wrapped them around something small and dark she pulled from her robe, and handed it to the man.

"Eat this, lad," the man commanded. I felt so light-headed that I didn't even consider that I was accepting something suspicious from a pair of druids. I took it with clumsy fingers, put it in my mouth, and bit down. Sharp, bitter flavors flared on my tongue, awakening my senses, and the dizzy sensation left immediately. The strong flavors mellowed into the comforting taste of rabbit meat, seasoned with something peppery and delicious. As I finished chewing the jerky, the man cleared his throat.

"Now, tell us why ye're out here lad, before my wife badgers the truth out of ye."

The woman gave another playful slap on her husband's shoulder. I stared up at the druids, their faces cast in long, flickering shadows. I was told magic users had darkness in every facet of their being, but these just seemed like normal people. I looked between them, deliberating on whether I really needed to fear them, when the scream of a kelpie seemed to echo inside my head. The pair glanced behind them.

"My mother!" I cried, fear battering against my ribs. The scream hadn't been inside my mind. There was a kelpie out here, and it had my mother!

I stood and moved to lunge past the pair, but the man was quicker. He gripped me tight, pulling me to his chest, and whispered, "Don't move, lad."

I stopped fighting against him as terror lashed me in place. Out on the moor ahead of us, I saw the enormous shape of a kelpie approach. For half a heartbeat, I imagined it was the one that had my mother, and I was ready to run out toward it, but its slick back was empty.

The kelpie was nearing, so close I could hear its hateful breath, feel its hooves shake the ground. The woman raised a hand. With a flick of her wrist something dark and wispy, almost indiscernible from the darkness around us, shot out toward the approaching beast. With an ear-shattering shriek, the water demon turned tail and thundered away from us, its squealing fading into the night.

"Let me go," I panted, struggling against the man's grip, watching the beast go. "That monster had my mother! I have to save her!"

The man didn't let me go, but the woman turned toward me, the torchlight deepening the frown on her face.

"You came out here, chasing a kelpie that took your mother?" she asked, her voice faint.

"I can still reach her! I know I can!" I wrested free from the male druid, but he caught my arm again.

"Lad, I'm sorry, but if a kelpie took yer mother . . . I'm sorry, but there's nothing ye—"

"No! She is *not* gone! She's not—*I can save her*!" I shouted. As the words left my mouth, they turned sour. I had been running for a long time, and I hadn't come upon the loch. Any loch. It was too late . . . It was as though someone had punched me in the stomach. I put a hand to my mouth, feeling sick.

The druids watched me, silent, their faces dim but readable in the light of their torch. I turned away from their pity, searching over the highlands.

"She's out there. I'm going to find her!"

"Son—"

"Thank you for your kindness and your help," I interrupted, determined to hold onto whatever foolish hope still remained in my mind, "but I need to go find my mother." I turned to march away, but I was yanked back again. I glared at the man and tried to jerk my arm out of his grasp, but his grip was impossibly strong. "I have three sisters that depend on me! If I go back now, I'll have to tell them that their mother is . . . that my mother is . . ." My voice died, and I gripped a handful of my hair, trying to stop the fire in my throat.

The man still held my sleeve, and I gave up tugging against it.

"I can't tell them that she's gone. I can't do that!" I looked back at the druids with burning eyes. The man's expression was sorrowful, while the woman held a hand to her mouth, eyes bright. My chest rose and fell with rising speed, their expressions making my emotions churn faster and faster, and I felt I would be unable to hold them back. "My mother's greatest fear is the kelpies, for her to have been taken by them . . ." I fought against the truth that battered against my desperate hope. "She can't be dead, because if she is, it's my fault!"

The realization struck me like a punch in the face.

"It's my fault she's gone," I said dumbly, hot, shameful guilt replacing terror and despair as the truth burned into my mind. "If I hadn't gone out for that idiotic wager . . ."

We would've all been inside, asleep, safe from the kelpie's gaze. I had brought this on us.

I really was witchborn. Cursed.

I looked up at the couple.

"I was supposed to protect them," I replied, my chin quivering. "All of them. I'm responsible. I should've been taken." With a whimper, I dropped to my knees, the man letting go of my sleeve. I turned my face to the sky, my throat and nose burning with anguish.

The stars above blurred together in dazzling splashes of light as tears spilled from my eyes. She was truly gone. Forever.

What was I going to do now?

I let it all go, and I knelt there in the cold grass, sobbing like a wee babe. My mother with her sweet, peach-round smile. Her hands, roughened from hard work but still gentle when she stroked my hair or hugged me close. Her diligent trust in me to help run the household. The way she scolded me when I acted below what she expected of me. Her fears of the kelpies. Her fierce love for her children and worry for their protection.

Now we were left to find our way, alone.

I cried all the pain and hopelessness and loss into that cold ground. I didn't want to think about going home and telling my sisters, feeling their blame. I didn't want to think about the fresh responsibility of raising my sisters, when I still felt like a small lad myself—a small lad who had wanted to prove himself a man.

I didn't want to be a man anymore.

I wanted my mother to be here, loving me, taking care of me, scolding me for punching the sense out of lads in the village. I wanted to taste her tarts, to hear her sing.

I would never hear her voice again.

Slowly my weeping stopped and I sat back on my heels, numb, and noticed how much the stars had rotated their positions in the night sky. The druids still stood there in the dark. I hadn't noticed them, silently watching over me as I grieved.

I didn't even feel embarrassed as I stood, my back and knees protesting at the lengthy time I'd been crouched in that position. The sharp night wind had died down to a gentle breath that barely tickled the grass.

Without looking at the druids, I brushed off my knees.

"I must get going," I croaked. "I left my sisters alone." My breath caught with alarm as I thought of the three girls huddled, scared, wondering if anyone would come back.

"You better wait with us until daylight, lad. Kelpies are in full force at witching hour," the woman said, her tone brooking no refusal. "Not to mention any bog you might fall into in the dark. Our coven isn't far from here."

I shook my head. "My sisters are home alone," I pressed, the image haunting me. "I need to get back."

"But the kelpies, it's dangerous—"

"I don't care," I snapped. I half wished I would meet another kelpie, so that I could drive Maura's small knife into its brain. "I'm going back. My sisters probably think I'm dead, too."

We stood quietly for a moment as I surveyed the hills, trying to get my bearings. I had no idea where I was.

"If that's how ye feel, take this," the man said at last, pulling a rattling necklace from around his throat. His wife began to protest, but he ignored her as he held the leather cord out to me. Several animal teeth and a colored stone hung from the necklace.

"Take it," the man said again, the offered necklace sitting in his outstretched palm. The polished rock was bright green, swirled with white veins. A sooty, swirling pair of symbols I didn't recognize were painted on the face. I felt chills erupt on my skin as the stone neared my arm. I stepped back from his proffered gift. The man didn't lower his hand, but fixed me with a serious expression.

"Lad, this will shield ye from any creature that wishes to harm ye."

"Daimh, no," the woman implored, "it took years to find that for you, you cannae—"

"He needs it more than I, now!" Daimh growled and brandished the amulet at me again. I eyed the stone warily, fear pattering inside my chest.

Magic was dangerous, bringing calamity upon all those who sought its power, and no honest person would use or wear magical charms to protect themselves.

The magical amulets that the village men spoke of were described as so black they drained the color and heat from any living thing around them, and smelled of sulfur, like the devil.

This rock, however, was the brightest green I'd ever seen besides the grass and trees, and, if anything, it seemed to glow slightly in the dark. It looked harmless, cheerful even, though the hairs on my neck stood on end as the stone swung toward me.

Despite myself, I reached out for it and touched it, expecting to feel the unnatural iciness I'd heard about, but instead, it felt warm and comforting. Emotion swirled in my chest. I felt a hand on my cheek, and looked up to see the druid woman looking at me with a kind, sorrowful expression. Gently she wiped away the tears I hadn't realized had slipped from my eyes.

The woman took the necklace from her husband and, before I could protest, looped the cord over my neck, where the rock rested on my chest, warming my cold skin.

"You take good care of this. It's worth more than you know," she whispered, her voice gentle but firm.

It was magic. If anything, it was more dangerous than I knew. But I didn't say anything, and we stood in silence for a moment, the couple waiting for me to regain control of my emotions. The man cleared his throat.

"Takes a mighty brave young man to shoulder such a responsibility."

I glared at him through the darkness.

"If I were braver, I could've saved her," I said, my stuffy nose making my claim sound childish, even to my ears. What was worse, if I'd been braver, I wouldn't have feared the comments from the village lads.

"You cannae blame yourself, lad," the woman insisted. "Ever knows, it's a part of life out here, living with the kelpies. Aye, we druids have noticed that the kelpies seem to be worse of late, but it's the cycle of life. It is not your fault."

Cycle of death, I thought, swallowing hard.

I pushed my guilt away, realizing that wallowing in my folly wouldn't help my sisters. They needed me to be strong. I had to put my selfish desires behind me. Now, more than ever, my sisters and their safety had to come first, above everything. We had nothing else but each other, after all. And it's what my mother would have wanted from me.

"I'm so sorry, lad," the woman whispered. She sounded like she truly meant it. I nodded, about to walk away when I realized I had no idea which direction to go. I was too exhausted to be prideful about finding my own way. I turned back to the couple, and the man, sensing my intent, pointed over his shoulder.

"Town is that way. About four miles. Just keep going straight over the hills and ye'll come to the road. Ye can make it from there, aye?"

I nodded again. The woman broke in.

"You sure I cannae convince you to stay with us till first light? We have plenty of room at our hearth."

"I'm sure. Thank you for everything," I said, impassive.

"Think nothing of it, lad," Daimh replied. "I wish ye good luck. And be careful."

Without another word, I started off across the moon-lit slopes, leaving the druids and their torchlight behind. Strange lights danced across the sky, and I heard the occasional shriek of a cat sìth as I charged across the moors. There was no room for fear in my heart—only determination to get home to my sisters.

By the time our small cottage came into view, the distant horizon was graying with the approaching dawn. I slowed, my legs trembling as I reached the walls of my home. Glancing in a window, I saw my sisters huddled next to the darkened fireplace. My heart wrenched at the sight, knowing they must have been sitting there for hours. I hurried to the door but stopped right before entering, trying to prepare myself for the responsibility that now was mine.

I wiped the cooling sweat from my throat, trying to steady myself, when I felt the leather necklace warm against my hand. As I stood there on the stoop of my house, aching with loss, I realized I couldn't tell my sisters about my meeting with the druids, for fear they would think me a changeling, not truly their brother returned to them. This talisman would raise questions. Besides, the stone was a reminder of what a curse magic was upon the world. Upon me.

I took the necklace from my neck, feeling colder as the stone left my skin, and hurled the stone as hard as I could into the waning darkness. The relic glinted as it soared upward, then went dark as it sailed out of sight.

Good riddance to all magic.

I tried the handle, and, finding it locked, pounded heavily on the door. In an instant, it flew open, and Norah stood on the threshold, her face drawn and white. Beyond her, Maura was holding Slaine on her lap beside the unlit fireplace. She and Slaine stood and hurried to my side, throwing themselves into my arms with renewed tears. I was too spent to cry, so I gently stroked their heads, hot and cold emotions waging war inside my chest.

My poor mother, all alone except for her demonic steed, plunging into the black depths of a murky loch. I jolted myself to stop thinking those dark thoughts. As I hugged my sisters, I could feel the coldness of their skin through their nightdresses, and my eyes stung.

"We should get to bed, little birds," I croaked, wanting to escape the sorrow for at least a few hours. Looking down at my sisters, I felt as if I had aged ten years. I couldn't be a fourteen-year-old anymore. I would have to be a real man now.

"Brennan," Norah whispered, her voice trembling, as we filed into our bedchamber. "Can you sleep in our bed with us?"

Without hesitation I nodded. The lassies slipped under the covers, holding each other tight, and I sat on the edge of the mattress, knowing I wouldn't be able to sleep. Nightmares were sure to await me. Instead, I sang soft, choked songs to the girls until their weeping slowed. When all were soundly sleeping, cold tears glinting like stars on their cheeks, I went to the window, staring up into the silent heavens. We were alone.

Chapter Five

Word spread quickly throughout the village that our mother had been drowned by the kelpies. Over the next few days, our house was flooded with well-wishers and do-gooders. While our clothes were laundered and our house was cleaned, those acts of kindness were nothing compared to the gifts of food we received. We were overwhelmed with fresh vegetables, bread, and packets of tea, as well as other luxuries that we would never have been able to afford ourselves, like delicate sugar candies, butter, and a small slab of fresh beef wrapped in paper from the butcher. Though I may have singed it a bit, we felt like royalty as we tucked into that beef steak, with a side of sweet confections and butter on our bread.

There was talk around town of separating my sisters and me into different houses or even sending us away to different villages. I was determined to keep us together—I would run away with my sisters before I let them divide us. Being separated wasn't an option, not just because I wanted to make sure my sisters were well taken care of, but because I knew as soon as the lassies were settled in with other families, I would be sent away, possibly to work in factories in the city. No one was offering to take *me* in. I'd heard horror stories of men who had lost hands in the machinery.

Besides, I'd never see my sisters again, and I wouldn't know if they were being treated well. So although some kind families offered to take in my sisters, I refused. I would show them all I could raise my family on my own.

To my dismay, almost a month after my mother's death, the magistrate of the village stopped by our home as I was preparing to head into town with my sisters. I made sure that I had odd jobs to do nearly every day. Staying busy kept my mind off everything, and I hoped to earn the town's confidence. It wasn't going well.

As I watched the magistrate arrive in his chaise, I felt my heart flutter. This was it—he was delivering the news we were to be separated.

With a grim face I met the magistrate at the door. He was a rail-thin man with extremely bushy eyebrows, which were contracted in thought as he stepped inside. After declining the offer of tea and giving the girls a small parcel with goodies, he turned to me.

"Now, Brennan," the magistrate said, taking off his hat. "I have some business to speak to ye about."

"You can't take us out of our house, sir," I blurted out before he could say another word.

"Yer mother would not want ye to be living alone," he said, his voice steady.

"She wouldn't want us separated, either!" I snapped.

The magistrate nodded his head, "I agree." I stared at him, holding my breath, waiting for him to finish with, *but that cannot be helped.*

"Did yer mother ever mention her family in Glasgow?" he asked instead.

I frowned, though my heart remained constricted. "No," I replied. "All I know is that our father was from further north and that he met my mother in Glasgow when he went there to look for work. Mother said they settled here because they wanted a fresh start."

"Aye, lad, but there's more to it than that." From inside his cloak, he brought out a letter. "This came for yer mother last night. An express. Since I am a civil servant, yer mother entrusted me to handle the letters she received from her relatives in the south. For the past few months, she's been in correspondence with her brother, and a few days before she passed, yer mother visited me about a certain letter she'd gotten, containing some distressing news."

My mind flashed back to seeing our mother in town, and the papers she had been reading the night I found her crying.

"What news?" I asked, worrying that perhaps we didn't have a house to live in anymore. The debts were sure to be due.

"Her father had fallen very ill, and her brother had written to her, explaining the situation. She came to ask me for advice about details in the letter and some other items of business, and had me post a letter in return. This came for her last night, via my address. I told yer mother I'd let her know when it arrived. She wanted to keep her correspondences a secret until the final news. So now this falls to ye, as head of the household. If I'm correct, what's contained in here may be the answer to yer concerns."

I took the envelope from his offered hand and stared at the wax seal. I'd never opened a letter before. Did one just peel off the wax? I ran a finger under the flap that was sealed with an M inlaid into the wax. The seal popped free with little work. With trembling hands and my sisters looking over my shoulders, I unfolded the paper, where neat, masculine handwriting covered the page. I was thankful my mother had insisted we all learn to read and write—it would've been embarrassing to ask the magistrate to read the letter to us.

The letter was dated five days ago.

Dearest Lorna,

As to my previous letter, I stated that Father may not survive to see the next month, and I'm relieved to say, I was correct. He passed away this very morning, leaving the entirety of the estate to me, including the house in Glasgow, Kedlefield Hall in Perthfordshire, and a few other properties.

While I know our father did his best to uphold the family estate in reputable esteem, he did not do his best by you. For this reason, and because he is no longer suffering, I am glad of his passing, and we can hope that he is with Mama and our Maker.

As Father did indeed leave the estate to me, I am only too pleased to fulfill the promise I made to you, and welcome you back with open arms. Lorna, I would greatly desire that you will bring your children to live with Alana and me in Glasgow. I hope to be able to work out the details of your inheritance when you arrive.

At your earliest convenience, write to us and we shall send you a carriage.

With great affection, your brother,
Douglas McFayden

I read the letter twice, not understanding some of the words but grasping the significance of the news. I lowered the paper, meeting the magistrate's eyes. He held out a hand.

"Yer mother shared with me her other letters. May I see this one, please?"

I handed it over without a word, and watched as his eyes trailed down the page, then nodded as he folded it up and handed it back to me.

"As I suspected. Yer mother, too, believed that her father would pass away in short order."

I stared at the letter, a clenching pain in my chest growing stronger with every word. I tried not to think about the terrible truth that lurked in the back of my mind, but I couldn't help myself. My mother had known the possibility of moving away from here. Back with her family. Away from the danger of the kelpies.

Only the news had arrived too late. Had I known, would I have taken matters into my own hands to try and protect my family? Would the knowledge have been enough to save her? I shook away the horrific thoughts and their ensuing guilt and looked up at the magistrate.

"Did she want to move to Glasgow?"

The magistrate paused, considering his words. "I believe that after yer father's passing, she began to miss her family."

"Why didn't our uncle write beforehand with the invitation?" I demanded, anger and sadness making my hands shake. It sounded as though my mother and her brother were very close. Why did she leave him and the only town she knew to come out to the highlands, where the winters were hard and there wasn't always enough to eat?

The magistrate sighed. "In previous letters, your uncle explained that he did not present the offer earlier because their father was in good health. Your uncle sent your mother money from time to time, but your grandfather caught him and halted it." He paused. When he spoke again, it was as if he was considering whether he should share any more. "It appears that once yer grandfather passed, yer uncle was able to extend the proposition to your mother to move back. Yer mother told me that she wanted to move back to the city so that her children could grow up with the birthright they should have had."

"Why didn't we grow up in Glasgow?" Maura interrupted.

The magistrate exhaled, long and slow. "I don't wish to cause ye any more pain, but I suppose ye must know the situation ye're to be heading into. There were . . . complications involving yer parents' marriage. It seemed yer grandfather was against yer mother marrying yer father, and so he . . . cut her off," the magistrate said, turning his hat in his hands, not meeting my eye. The sharp sting of guilt and embarrassment pierced my heart. My mother was pregnant with me before they married. It wasn't the marriage my grandfather had been ashamed of.

"But that is in the past," the magistrate said, clearing his throat and looking over all of us. "What ye now have to decide is, do ye want to move all yer sisters and belongings to Glasgow to be with family, or do ye want to stay here and possibly be separated?"

"Why can't we stay here and *not* be separ—" I began.

The magistrate held up a hand again. "'Tis not seemly for ones as young as yerselves to be raised alone clear out here. 'Tis dangerous, and the village cannae stand by and watch ye struggle. There are several families willing to take the younger girls in."

I noticed he didn't mention a willingness to take in a fourteen-year-old boy. No one wanted a witchborn lad that had no schooling and no apprenticeship. My willingness to work hard wouldn't be worth two straws if I couldn't make a living.

"I've already written to yer uncle and explained the situation of yer mother's passing. I have a feeling the offer still stands, especially under the circumstances. Now, I will allow ye to stay here, under supervision of yer neighbors, while we await a response. I'll be back once I receive word from your uncle. If yer family decides to take you in, I hope ye take them up on that offer." He pinned me with a look, and I had a feeling he knew my thoughts about running away. Fear of having to leave our home and worries about being rejected by our newfound family danced around my mind, but despite my fear, I gave a small nod. What else could I do?

"Very good. Now, I see that ye were heading out to town. Can I give ye a ride?" The magistrate swept up his hat and gestured toward the door and carriage beyond. I shook my head.

"I thank you, no. Our cart is already hitched."

"Very well, then. We'll speak again when I have news." With a nod of farewell, he left the house.

We watched him climb aboard his two-wheeled carriage and start off down the road before I shepherded my sisters toward our cart.

As I drove to the village, I contemplated the letter and what it meant for us. My sisters were quiet too, and I knew they were considering our choice as well. There was no choice, really. We'd been given a miracle: a way to protect my sisters from hunger, danger from the highlands, and from being separated.

What would become of us in the city? Maybe I could leave the status of witchborn behind. No one—well, no one besides my family in Glasgow—would know about the circumstances of my birth. I could start over. The kelpies wouldn't be a danger to my family anymore. The haunted dreams I had of the water demons could truly become just nightmares, a part of our sad past, left behind.

"We're going to live with them, right, Brennan?" Norah asked, interrupting my thoughts. I turned in my seat and looked between the three of them.

"You all agree we should go?" I asked.

As one, they nodded, and I exhaled. "Very well."

I felt a thrill as I said the words.

We would be stepping into a new world, but we would be going together.

A fortnight later, the magistrate delivered another letter informing us that our relatives were more than willing to take us in and would come gather us within a week. The magistrate looked relieved when we told him that we would go to Glasgow.

In short order our house was boarded up, our scant belongings packed away in the barn, our animals sold. We spent the last few days saying goodbye to those in town and out on the moors, but we were always careful to come back to the house well before dark. The highlands looked more beautiful than ever before, as if they were trying to convince us to stay. I saw Ewan once while in town, but he steered clear of me. I never did learn if his gang ever came to Lookout

Hill that night, but I didn't care to find out. I was just glad to be leaving him and his lot behind.

Soon the day came when our aunt and uncle arrived to take us back to Glasgow. My sisters were nervous, as was I, but I had to remind myself that we would be together, no matter the circumstances or how we were treated.

I found my uncle a kind though somber man, while my aunt was lively and gentle. My uncle was a merchant, having already started his business by the time my mother was banished, leaving him to inherit. The moment we'd been introduced, plans were made for our future; tutors, music lessons, and an apprenticeship for myself as a merchant were all discussed in a whirlwind of packing up a few of our belongings, as we were leaving much of our things in the cottage. Everything happened so fast, and I felt like I couldn't catch my breath. My sisters began to cry as we were loaded up into the carriage, and with one last look at our childhood home, the carriage pulled away.

"Now, now, no tears," my aunt Alana replied, pulling out a handkerchief and handing it to Maura. "Everything will be alright. You'll see."

I grasped Norah's and Maura's hands, with Slaine sitting on my lap, and we looked at our aunt and uncle.

"Yes, I'm sure we shall," I replied. My sisters squeezed my hands back.

"I'm going to make a respectable man out of you yet. A man you can be proud of. That your mother would be proud of," my uncle Douglas said, looking me in the eye.

We stared at each other in silence for a moment, some unspoken understanding passing between us as the carriage swayed and creaked. My uncle nodded and leaned back into his seat, ending the moment.

"You'll get started on your apprenticeship the moment we return to Glasgow. I have a feeling you'll do grand. I won't go easy on you. I'll work you harder than anyone in my employ, but only because I want you to succeed. And I feel you shall." My uncle chuckled.

I nodded, taking a deep breath. "Thank you, sir."

"Very good," my uncle said with a laugh, and he gave me a kind look that strengthened my resolve. I would do this. I would work harder, learn faster than any apprentice he'd ever seen. I wanted to prove myself to this man, to this family. They were all I had now, and I couldn't let them down.

"Good, good," my uncle murmured, sitting back into the carriage seat and looking pleased. "We'll make sure to keep you busy. Get your mind off these dreadful past few weeks. Now all we need to do is get you back to Glasgow."

The carriage fell into silence once more, and I watched the knolls and lochs of my childhood slip out of sight.

PART II

Chapter Six

Five Years Later

I stared at myself in the small mirror, glaring at the crimson bead of blood that rolled down my throat. Of course this would happen. Today I was to see my family again after nearly a year of being away from them, out on the open sea as I sailed my uncle's ship, and I mar myself. How could I have been so careless?

Growling, I took a rag, dipped it in the water basin, and cleaned around the cut my razor had made, making sure no blood stained my unbuttoned white shirt. When I was satisfied the shirt was unblemished, I chuckled. My sisters probably wouldn't notice the knick under my chin, but Emilia would.

My stomach leaped as I thought of Emilia. I'd never known a year to stretch on as long as this, I had missed her so. The last time I had a mark on my face—from breaking up a fight on the docks—she'd scolded me for ruining her "handsome view." I could only imagine what response she would have to the cut. She always could get me to laugh. She acted demure when we were in public, but her sense of humor was as sharp as the razor in my hand. I exhaled. And I would be seeing her today.

Shaking my head, I quickly cleaned my razor and finished shaving and dressing—tossing the pink-stained water out my small cabin window to the river beyond—then hurried to the top deck. We would be docking in Glasgow soon, as the stiff wind filling the sails made our ship slice across the river's surface like an oiled seal.

After acknowledging the greeted shout from the helmsman, I walked to the railing and watched as the welcoming, green landscape slipped by as we made our way up the river, Glasgow a smoky haze in the distance.

I had done it. I had successfully completed my first voyage without my uncle. Sadness twisted up along with the pride inside my chest. I wished he could've been here to welcome me home.

My uncle had contracted a bad cough a little over a year ago. He thought nothing of it, playing it off as merely a passing cold, but within a few days, he was gone. My aunt believed it was something he got from traveling on the brisk winter oceans. His death left us all in a state of shock for several weeks. I was left alone to run the business, though I'd had some help from my aunt, who knew the operation well.

I desperately wanted to prove myself an asset to the company, which my uncle had already made a success, to show everyone that I had learned well by my uncle's side for the last five years. It had been a challenging and difficult road.

True to his word, my uncle hadn't coddled me in my boyhood years, pushing me to my utmost limits and beyond. However, I was grateful for it, as it made me sure in my abilities and eager for more challenges. I had confidence that I could take anything on, and persist in that course until I found solutions. I owed it to my uncle's memory to do all I could to continue growing our success and ensure my family's comfort and livelihood. I had no worries about my future.

It was an odd feeling. As a boy, I had worried constantly about starvation and acceptance and kelpies. Everything was so different now.

And I would not take it or anything else for granted, especially my family. They were the reason I was doing all of this, and they were waiting for me just beyond the port.

After what felt like ages in my agitated state, we pulled into the harbor and up alongside the wharf, the ship's mooring lines secured. Leaving instructions with the first mate, I took a deep, fortifying breath of Glasgow air and stepped off the gangway, my legs unsteady on the solid dock after months on the swaying deck of a ship.

The familiar sights and sounds were like a balm after so many months out in the salt and spray. The town was much larger than it had been when I first arrived as a frightened boy all those years ago. Now, the docks were bustling with activity, and even more shipyards were being built further down the river, next to the mouth of the sea.

Being without my uncle on this last voyage took me back to that tempestuous time when we had arrived in Glasgow as children.

Staring out at the city now, I recalled how I had felt as that boy. My sisters and I all felt as though we would get lost in the hurry and bustle of this great port city, that we would choke on the very air, so filled with smoke and dust. I had felt helplessly stupid, trying to learn my uncle's trade: countless figures, maps, and types of wares. I had felt as though I was suffocating. During that time, my uncle had assured me that all things here would become as known to me as my own face. I had clung to that assurance as a drowning man clung to a rope thrown to him on a tempest-tossed sea.

I was happy to see that my uncle had been right. After much striving, I was able to overcome my childhood fears and learn to trust myself and my abilities. Now everything about living in Glasgow was second nature.

I had worried that my past would follow us to Glasgow, that my aunt and uncle would treat me differently because of my witchborn status, but I came to learn that the city didn't care much about the traditions and superstitions of the countryside. Most barely knew the names of many magical creatures, and some believed them to all be myths. My aunt and uncle didn't treat me any differently than my sisters, and though I once heard the servants whisper about me being a witchborn, I was never really bothered with the stigma again.

I sighed, remembering how I felt for the first time in my life that I belonged as I worked and learned by my uncle's side.

And now, I would have to continue on without him.

"Brennan!" I heard the shout over the crowd that had gathered to meet their returning loved ones, and I turned to see my three sisters hurrying toward me, ribbons and skirts billowing. Behind them, the most beautiful woman in Glasgow followed at their heels. I drank in the sight of Emilia, her playful smile and bright eyes following my movements.

As one, Norah, Maura, and Slaine flung themselves into my arms, and I tore my gaze away from Emilia, surprised at my sisters' unladylike behavior. I laughed and encircled them all into a gentle hug, chuckling as I saw tears shining in their eyes.

"We just heard your ship was in port!" Norah said, wiping her cheeks with the back of her hand. I stepped back to admire my sisters. They seemed to have grown so much while I was gone, even though it was only eight months. After kissing them all hello, I turned to the woman I had been courting, who stood a little behind my sisters.

"Welcome back, Mr. Lennox," she said, her voice breathless, a warm blush coloring her cheeks.

"Miss MacCowen," I said, and she smiled, which lit up her already-brilliant eyes. My heart stuttered in my chest, and I felt embarrassed at the state I was in. There wasn't much I could do about my long, wild hair until I saw a barber.

"Thank you for coming to meet me," I said, my tone formal, though I wished to scoop her up into my arms.

"We were having Emilia over for tea when we heard your ship was in port," Slaine explained, smoothing her rose-colored dress as she spoke, "And we all wanted to come see if you were still at the dock."

"I'm so glad you all did, little birds," I replied with a chuckle.

"Oh, Brennan, we have so many things to tell you!" Norah said, smiling. "And Slaine has something she wants to show you!"

I turned to look at my youngest sister. "Do you, now?"

Slaine smiled, a blush of excitement blooming on her face, and from behind her back, she thrust a pocket handkerchief at me. "I won first prize for the best stitched pocket handkerchief at finishing school," she said, aglow with pride.

I took the handkerchief, admiring the neatly sewn swans with delicately arching necks, and the vibrant purple thistle blossoms in the corners. I looked down at Slaine, who was watching me carefully, tremulous hope in her face, waiting to see if I was proud.

"This is wonderful, Slaine!" I exclaimed, studying the kerchief again. "I'm not surprised at all that you won. I think it might even be better than the one Maura did that won first prize a few years ago." I looked to Maura, who rolled her eyes as I winked at her.

"I made it for you!" Slaine said, beaming and bouncing slightly on her toes. I pulled Slaine into a hug, kissing her cheeks.

"I'll always carry it, Slaine, thank you. I'm so proud of you," I said, tucking the handkerchief into my trouser pocket.

"She deserved first place," Emilia said, smiling at Slaine as we broke apart. Slaine stepped back, and Emilia encircled her arms around my youngest sister and pulled her back into her chest, giving her a squeeze. "I was one of the judges," Emilia continued, looking up at me. "Don't worry, she won by her own merit, not because I'm courting her brother." Emilia winked at me.

I laughed, and Emilia shook her head and looked up at the ship's masts before her. A few stray locks of Emilia's honey-colored hair had pulled loose from her bonnet and seemed to glow in the sunlight. Emilia and I locked eyes, and her blush deepened. She released Slaine, who scurried past us to watch a crowd of men hoisting barrels of rum off the ship.

"Will you be able to walk home with us, Mr. Lennox?" Emilia asked, stepping a bit closer, and my heart rate increased.

"I have a few matters to take care of with the captain and orders to issue concerning the merchandise, but I'll be along shortly," I promised.

I saw her gaze alight onto the gash, just as I knew she would, and she reached out a hand, gently probing the cut area. "I know you were excited to see me, but you mustn't lose your head, sir," she whispered. I grinned at her as she giggled. Maura interrupted us with an impatient, "We'll hold tea for you." She flashed me a teasing smile. "If you hurry."

"I promise I'll do my best," I assured them. After one last hug to my sisters and a formal nod and smile to Emilia, I watched as they meandered back through the crowd, arms linked. Emilia glanced back briefly before the crowd swallowed them, and I exhaled at the sight.

Not wanting to miss tea, I oversaw a few of the items being unloaded, sought out the captain to relay the instructions about taking the goods to their respective warehouses, then hurried home.

As I entered through the front door, our butler Peter was quick to take my hat and coat from me, murmuring, "Welcome back, sir. Mr. Campbell is here to see you. He's in the study."

"What?" I turned to see Peter's expression, which was its usual unruffled mien. "Has he been waiting long?" I asked, handing him my gloves. I had been intending to send him a letter as soon as tea was done, to inform him of our return.

"No, sir."

"Very well. Thank you, Peter," I said, straightening my collar. "My trunks will be arriving from the ship in a few moments. Will you see to them?"

Peter bowed with a small, "Yes sir," as I moved toward my uncle's study. While the desire to join my sisters and Miss MacCowen at tea was strong, ignoring my uncle's lawyer wouldn't do.

I stepped into my uncle's bookroom, where Mr. Campbell, a tall, graying man with a heavy jaw and straight back stood waiting for me, staring out the window. My aunt was sitting in a nearby chair doing needlepoint, and she stood and embraced me as I entered.

"Welcome home, dear," she said, giving me a warm smile.

"Thank you, Aunt. It's wonderful to be home. John," I said, stepping toward him, a smile alighting on his lined face.

"Ah, Brennan," Mr. Campbell said, shaking my extended hand. "How was your voyage from the West Indies?"

"Very good, sir." I briefly relayed our success in acquiring the sugar and cotton from the islands.

He nodded. "Fine, fine, that's all very fine. And you didn't meet any problems with any American trade or war ships?" Mr. Campbell asked.

I shook my head. "None, sir. Though there is news that the Americans are aiming for a fight, upset at the duties they have to pay to England to trade with France."

Mr. Campbell sighed. "Yes. The Americans don't realize that Bonaparte needs to be curtailed. Their neutrality on the war with France is their own undoing." Mr. Campbell shook his head, his brow crinkled with a frown. "Are you worried about seizures on the open ocean?"

"It might be difficult," I conceded, "but we're ready to weather any problems we might face. We have good crews and we deal honestly with our partners, so I'm sure everything will come to rights."

Surely what was to come wouldn't be any worse than facing a storm on the open ocean or as tiresome as dealing with Bonaparte.

Mr. Campbell smiled. "Well, Brennan, I must say, you're the only one I've spoken to that has a positive outlook on the coming conflicts. And, from what I hear, you have made excellent decisions with the business in the Indies. You would've made your uncle very, very proud."

I dipped my head in thanks, though my smile deflated a bit.

"I felt his absence greatly on this last voyage," I said, wishing my uncle was here to welcome me back from my first voyage alone and to see me put into effect all that I had learned from him.

Everything I had been working toward for five long years was soon to come to fruition. I had proven myself to my late uncle with my dedication to the business. My sisters were well adjusted and considered some of the most eligible ladies in Glasgow. The two eldest were very popular and attended more social parties than I could count, while wee Slaine, still too young to be out at social gatherings, was blooming into a young woman. I myself was courting the most kind and beautiful girl I'd ever met. Just thinking of her made my stomach squirm in excitement. I had no doubt she was the one I wanted to marry, and I was planning on asking her father for her hand when I was certain I was financially stable.

Which I hoped was the reason for Mr. Campbell's visit.

"Yes, your uncle was a great friend and man. He is greatly missed."

"Yes. I thank you. So, to what do we owe the pleasure?" I asked.

"Quite so, to business. Now, I'm sorry it's been so long, but I finally received the finalization of your uncle's will a month before, and the moment I heard your ship was in port, I hurried over here, as executor of his affairs, to read the will."

I glanced at my aunt as I took a seat beside her, and she gave me a small smile and nodded.

"Very well. We're ready," I replied. Mr. Campbell shook out the papers in his hand.

"Fine, fine. Now, as he was unable to produce an heir of his own, Douglas Walter McFayden has named you, Brennan Alban Lennox, as heir of his estate and proprietor of his business."

I felt as if my heart had stopped beating in my chest for a moment as I stared in awe at the lawyer. I had some idea that I would receive some sort of monetary inheritance, as my uncle had been eager to make amends for how my mother had been treated. My uncle told me that he had secretly given money to my parents so that they could buy the cottage and land in Bòidhchead, and, once they took us in, my uncle paid off all my father's debts to his creditors. My uncle Douglas was one of the most honest and generous men I'd ever met, but I never suspected of being named heir and proprietor. My aunt grabbed my hand, smiling at me with misty eyes.

"Your sisters will each receive a substantial dowry at the time of their marriage, and provisions have been made to provide for Mr. McFayden's widow," he continued, nodding to my aunt, who was dabbing her eyes with my uncle's handkerchief.

"He always did take such good care of us," my aunt whispered. I nodded, gripping her hand as my heart ached at the memory of my dear uncle. Not only did he care for us as if we were his own children, he had saved us from both poverty and the magical denizens of the moors.

My aunt beamed at me. "Congratulations, Brennan."

"Thank you, Aunt. And thank you, Mr. Campbell, for coming here and sharing this news," I said, standing and shaking hands with him again.

"Not at all, not at all, sir. Congratulations. Well," he said, taking up his hat and cane, "I shan't keep you from the rest of your day. Here is the will, and we'll talk again soon."

"Thank you, sir," I said, trying to keep my composure, but I couldn't stop smiling as Mr. Campbell took his leave. Once we bade him goodbye, both my aunt and I hurried to the tearoom.

My sisters and Miss MacCowen made room for us as we joined them for tea, and my aunt told everyone about Mr. Campbell's visit and his announcement: that I was named heir. My sisters all broke out into excited tittering, but my eyes sought Emilia's face, who was seated next to me. She grabbed my hand, beaming at me.

"I'm so glad for you, Mr. Lennox," she whispered.

Her hand remained in mine as the subject turned to the coming conflicts with both France and America, and my thoughts drifted. Tomorrow I would be able to spend all my time with Emilia. My stomach flipped at the realization that very soon I would be able to call on her father for her hand. The sentiment warmed my face, and for a moment, I imagined how happy my mother would be for us.

Chapter Seven

The next afternoon, after returning home from overseeing the materials at the warehouses, I washed up in preparation for my stroll with Emilia. As I came down the stairs in a fresh tailcoat and gloves, I was stopped by Peter, who had a stack of mail. Peter ordinarily took the mail straight to my aunt to be processed; however, he handed me a letter from the stack. It was addressed to me, care of my aunt and uncle, from Bòidhchead.

I paused. Who would be contacting me, and why? I hadn't thought of our old childhood village in years. Surely people there had forgotten all about us. We were just another bunch of children sent off to distant relatives as a result of kelpie attacks. Such a practice wasn't unusual in a small village like Bòidhchead.

I took the letter, and with an expression of bemusement, tore open the wax seal.

There wasn't much to the message. The old magistrate, the one that had written our relatives so long ago, had been taken by a kelpie. The new magistrate, Angus McByrd, was writing to tell me that the old magistrate had looked after our residence outside the village during his time in office, but, as new magistrate, he had no desire to continue doing so. The letter requested that my relatives, to whom the property belonged, come to set their affairs in order, and either sell off the house or hand it off to someone in the village.

I read over the letter twice. Why on earth had the old magistrate kept an eye on the cottage? There was nothing of value there, except perhaps the land. My uncle had fronted the money to my father to build it so long ago, and when my mother died, ownership had passed to my aunt. Would she want possession of it now?

I stepped into the drawing room, where my aunt was chatting happily with Maura and Slaine as they trimmed bonnets and parasols, while Norah sat reading.

I held the letter out to my aunt. She set down the ribbon she had been pinning to the brim of her bonnet, giving me a questioning glance.

"What is this, Brennan?" Alana asked, taking the offered letter. She studied the missive, then looked up at me. "I had almost forgotten about that old place," she said, lowering the paper.

"I gather that he wants us to sell the property so he doesn't have to watch over it in our name," I replied, tossing my coattails out of the way as I sat down beside Slaine on the settee.

"Well, I doubt there will be many people who want to buy it. It must be quite decrepit by now," Alana said, folding up the letter with a shake of her head. "It can't be worth much."

"I don't know, someone might want the land for farming, or to keep sheep," I said, my merchant mind beginning to mull ideas around. "You could get some of your money back that you lent my father."

"Probably not even enough to bother with," Alana replied.

"Maybe I can sell it," I said. It would be another test in my mind: if I could sell a property that had been abandoned for years, for a good price, I could sell anything. "I'd like to try," I pressed again. I would need her permission to act in her name; it was her property, after all.

"Are you certain? It was your childhood home," my aunt said, watching me carefully.

I nodded. "I haven't thought of that place in ages. Our home is here."

My aunt shrugged. "Heaven knows I don't care about that place. But if you want to try to sell it, you have my permission."

"Excellent." I stood and left the room, returning with ink, quill, and a piece of parchment, on which I quickly wrote down the terms of acting on her behalf, and had her sign her permission.

"Thank you, Aunt," I said, looking over the contract as she finished signing it. "I suppose it would be nice to visit, to see the old place again one last time," I mused. Out of the corner of my eye, I saw my sisters visibly perk up. "But then we can be done with it for good," I finished.

"A visit? Back to Bòidhchead? Can I go with you, Brennan?" Maura asked, setting down her parasol.

"It will be a business trip of sorts, Maura," I said, taking the letter back and folding it up with the contract my aunt had signed, slipping both into my coat pocket. "The next voyage isn't until next month, and I'll be back before then."

"Oh, please, can we go?" Slaine pleaded, rushing to my side and placing an imploring hand on my arm. "I don't remember much of that place."

"It would be nice to visit with everyone," Norah pointed out, setting down her book.

"Besides, we haven't been on a holiday in so long," Maura said with a sigh. "I want to see more of the north."

"Again, it won't be much of a holiday," I reminded, keeping my tone patient. "It will only be a week or so, to set our property and affairs in order."

"But it sounds so droll, to visit our little village," Slaine said, her eyes shining with excitement.

Norah stood and came over to me. "Please, Brennan. We haven't been able to spend time with you in so long. You're always gone. This would be the perfect little holiday for us."

"Oh, please, please, please, Brennan!" Slaine begged, and I smiled down at her. For a moment, I saw the little child, holding up a sprig of heather that she had found in the grasses of the highlands, looking for praise.

I remembered how much pain we'd suffered back there, and my desire to shield them from it rose within me. However, the fervor of my sister's pleadings made me think that maybe they'd be alright. The painful memories didn't seem to bother them at all as we spoke of our childhood village.

"I suppose I could take you ladies along. A short visit wouldn't hurt," I finally relented. I was a grown man now, I reasoned, and I would be able to protect them from any dangers that came along. The highlands were surely nothing in comparison to the many dangers of the open oceans.

Slaine and Maura squealed and hugged me, while Norah's pleasure was evident in the wide smile she shared with me.

"I'll write to the magistrate to tell him of our coming," I said. With a few final hugs, my sisters hurried out of the room, discussing what to pack and what they would see up in the "wild north."

While I was discussing with my aunt the initial amount my uncle had bought the land for, Peter walked in, announcing Miss McCowan. With chagrin, I realized that in light of the letter we'd received, I had forgotten about picking up Emilia at her home for our afternoon stroll.

I stood and turned as Emilia entered with her governess, Ms. Gillies, acting as chaperon. I bowed low to Emilia's curtsy and, ignoring Ms. Gillies' cold expression, rushed to take Emilia's hand and kiss it. Emilia clicked her tongue in reproach.

"You've neglected me, Mr. Lennox," she said, a smile hiding in her eyes. I disregarded Ms. Gillies' soft snort of derision. Being from a small village like myself, Ms. Gillies knew of the customs and beliefs of the highlands and had no doubt learned of my witchborn brand from the gossip of servants when I started courting Emilia. She didn't approve of Emilia's choice in me and let me know as often as she could in glares and disdainful sounds.

"I decided to come here myself in search of you, as you failed to call upon me." Emilia smoothed her skirts and gave me a playful look.

"Oh, Brennan," my aunt said, reproachful.

"I'm terribly, terribly sorry," I said, taking Emilia's hand and pressing another soft kiss to her gloved knuckles. "Certain business detained me. I only now just remembered. Please forgive me."

"I daresay you'll have to do better than that to earn my forgiveness," Emilia replied, winking at my aunt.

"She's right, Brennan," Alana laughed. "This will require a grand gesture."

"Of course," I said, bowing slightly to my aunt, who knew of my plan, as anxiety twisted in my stomach. "Would you stay for supper, Emilia?" I asked, and Emilia hooked her arm around mine, giving me a warm smile.

"I'll consider it. But shall we? It's such a beautiful day. I'd hate to miss our walk," Emilia said, squeezing my arm.

"Of course, I'll not detain it any longer. Aunt, we'll return in time for supper," I replied, glancing at my aunt, who had come to stand beside me.

"Very well," Alana said, giving me a smile. "I'll tell Cook. Enjoy yourselves." My aunt spared a small, narrow look toward Ms. Gillies.

Emilia's whole family knew of my witchborn label, no doubt from Ms. Gillies' lips, and Alana was still resentful toward the governess for it. Thankfully, Emilia's family had brushed off the old woman's claims as superstitious nonsense, allowing me to continue courting Emilia. I had no doubt that my uncle's wealth had something to do with her family's willingness to accept me. That fact only made me even more grateful to my uncle for taking us in.

Ms. Gillies stepped out of the way as I led Emilia toward the front door. We stepped out onto the busy avenue, heading toward the park a few streets away. The park was small, but the trees helped dampen the hustle and noise of the busy merchant city.

Leaving the busy roads behind us, we fell into easy step, though my heart pounded at a rapid pace as we walked the paths. The day was beautiful for early April, the shadows from the newly budding trees dappling the ground in the weak spring sunshine. I had wanted to take this stroll with Emilia to ask her a very important question, and I felt even more foolish that I had allowed something as trivial as that letter to distract me from my design.

I cleared my throat, hoping to keep the tremor out of it.

"Emilia."

"Yes?" she asked, her voice soft.

I looked to her, where she was admiring the paths through the parkway, a contented smile on her face. Looking at her cream-colored skin, her honey curls framing her face, my breath caught.

She was the most beautiful woman I'd ever seen, and I'd grown up among some of Glasgow's finest beauties. But it wasn't only her beauty that made me feel like a king every time we went out into the street: her kindness toward my sisters was what truly made me fall in love with her, and my sisters in turn adored and admired her.

"Do you recollect the first time we met?" I asked. I distinctly remembered the first time I'd seen her. She was on the arm of one of the captains stationed in our district. In our gentlemen circles, we knew the captain to be a gambler and a bit of a cad. To see him imposing himself into the company of well-bred ladies as if he were a gentleman made indignation flare inside me. I was determined to do something about it.

Emilia turned to me, her eyebrows quirking up in that playful expression that made my knees go weak. "If I recall correctly, you purposefully spilled punch down Captain Williamson's coat, just to dance with me." Her lips twitched, hiding a smile.

"Terribly clumsy of me," I replied, looking ahead and keeping my expression solemn. Emilia laughed and squeezed my arm tighter.

"How did you know that would work?" she asked. "He'd been harping after me for weeks to dance with him at the Blair ball."

I chuckled and shook my head. "A bigger dandy I've never met. I knew if there was one thing that was more important to him than your hand in a dance, it was his apparel. And thus he proved what a fool he was, too, because I was there to take his place." I looked sideways at her, and she laughed again, her cheeks pink.

"I'm so glad you were. I can't believe I ever agreed to dance with him. The things he called you, in front of everyone! Disgraceful behavior," she said, her voice full of disgust.

I had won her favor, thanks to the ugly comments the captain had said to me, and we danced together as many dances as was appropriate for the rest of the evening.

We began courting soon thereafter.

"Yes, he acted a buffoon in an attempt to make me look bad," I said. I had been angry then, but I was grateful now at how terribly he had acted. "He didn't go after what he truly wanted. If he'd been more well-mannered, he might have won you after all. He didn't understand that he has to see things all the way through if he's to accomplish his designs."

"And I suppose you always do such things?" she asked.

"Always," I replied firmly. I stopped walking as we came beneath a large tree, and she looked up at me, her brow furrowed in a question. "And I intend to do such a thing now." I turned to face her, sure she would be able to hear the thudding of my heart in my chest. I took a deep breath.

Bravery, man.

"I have business to attend to in the north on my aunt's behalf. I'll only be gone for a fortnight at most, but," I cleared my throat, "I hope that when I return, I will be able to speak to your father."

Emilia's face flushed scarlet, her smile growing. Encouraged by her expression, I hurried on. "I know we're young, but now that I've been made heir, I . . ." I paused. No, not like this. Emilia deserved to know my heart, and though I feared laying it out before her, she deserved to hear my feelings.

"Emilia, you're the only woman I've ever loved. The moment I saw you, you snatched my heart," I said, trailing my finger along a honey lock of hair that curled over her cheek. Her eyes were bright as they met mine, and I clasped both of her hands in my palms. "And it will never belong to anyone else. My life will not be happy unless you are in it. I promise to treat you as the angels in the heavens. You would want for nothing, and I would want for nothing, if you would just be mine. Will you do me the great honor of accepting my hand, and become my wi—"

"No!" came an angry outburst behind us. Ms. Gillies, who had been following us rather closely, now came up between us, her face flushed with anger as she looked daggers at me before turning to Emilia.

"No, I cannae stand by. I held my tongue when ye began courting, but I cannae allow this to go on any longer! Miss Emilia, ye cannae join yerself with *this*," she blustered, jabbing a finger at me, "this intolerable, sinful—"

"Fina, you overstep your bounds," Emilia snapped, eyes flashing as she pulled closer to me.

"Miss, ye cannae marry him! He carries the weight of magic, which no human should possess! He's sinful bad luck!"

"How dare you—" Emilia began but was cut short as Ms. Gillies latched onto Emilia's elbow and dragged her out of my arms.

"Yer coming home with me this instant," Ms. Gillies snarled, yanking Emilia several steps away. Anger at Ms. Gillies pulsed through me, not only for intruding on the special moment between myself and Emilia, but for treating Emilia as though she were some street urchin. I marched after the arguing pair just as Emilia, face red and blotchy with fury, tore herself out of her governess's grip.

"I am not a child to be pulled about!" Emilia shouted, while Ms. Gillies tried to shush her, for we were drawing attention, and I saw more than one scandalized expression from those around us. "How dare you treat me thus! Go home this instant, Fina. I'll have words with my father about you when I return home!"

Emilia's eyes sought mine as I enveloped her to my chest. Her eyes were furious, her limbs trembling as she clung to me, and my anger increased. How dare this old woman make Emilia feel this way? I met Ms. Gillies glare with my own, and her mouth took a disdainful upturn.

"Ye cursed beast," she hissed. "Magic in humans should be forbidden, not paraded about in good society!"

The desire to scold and shame the older woman into silence filled me, but I remained quiet, allowing Emilia to take command of her own governess. Emilia glared at Ms. Gillies, who was still standing rigidly before us.

"Go!" Emilia ordered. Ms. Gillies made a crossing motion at me and then spit at my feet, and Emilia gasped.

"Bad luck!" Ms. Gillies shouted before stomping away. The crowd that stood around observing us quickly stepped out of her way as she passed. Emilia glowered at those who were watching us, and the crowd dispersed in a flurry of buzzing, no doubt whispering about the scene. I led a panting Emilia to a nearby bench and sat her down, where she began to weep. I pulled out my handkerchief that Slaine had stitched for me and held it out to her. She accepted it and began to dab at the tears trailing down her cheeks.

"Brennan, I'm so, so sorry," Emilia whispered, her body trembling in my arms. She took a few fortifying breaths, then looked up into my face. "You know I don't see you as cursed or evil. You know that, don't you?"

"Of course I do," I soothed, unsure if I could hold her as closely as I wanted in such a public place. "I just hope I didn't cause any irreparable trouble with Ms. Gillies—"

"That contemptible old hen," Emilia snapped, pulling out of my arms to shake her head. "She has no more sense than a brick wall. I will be speaking to my father about her behavior. Especially since he's so fond of you." She looked at me again, and I ran a thumb over a stray tear on her chin, suddenly aware that she was without a chaperon.

"Perhaps we should head back—" I began to stand, but she pulled me back down.

"No, let us stay a while longer. Please?" she sniffed, wiping her eyes. "I . . . don't wish to upset your aunt with my appearance." She placed a hand on her cheek, where the redness was rather becoming.

"You look beautiful. Nothing amiss," I said, placing my hand on hers. She smiled, then tears filled her eyes again, and she ducked her head.

"Forgive me . . ." She paused, sniffling. I sat there, wishing there was more I could do to comfort her.

"There's nothing to forgive. I . . . I'm sorry if courting me has caused you any other instances of censure," I said, feeling a hot flare of anger. The power of gossiping servants was no secret, but my witchborn brand was never brought up, at least not in more civilized circles. I'd hoped that my good manners and fortune were enough to prove to everyone that there was nothing to the rumor. However, if others had said something scathing to Emilia because of our courtship . . . My fist tightened at the thought.

"Well," Emilia replied, casting her eyes down for a moment, "If I have, it doesn't matter. Those who do are fools, and I care not what they think. I love you, Brennan," she whispered, her expression fierce for a moment as she looked into my eyes. Color flooded her face as we both realized what she had just uttered.

My lips curled into a grin at this unprecedented declaration. We stared at each other, Emilia biting her lip, her face blooming red.

"I love you," she said again.

"I love you. Dearly," I whispered. We sat in silence, staring and smiling at one another, until the silence became awkward, and Emilia let out a breathy laugh to clear the embarrassment.

"Besides, Fina is intolerable," Emilia said, looking up at me. "She blames everything on superstitious drivel, and it might be time for her to find another post."

I was holding back the urge to kiss the lips she was now pursing in an indignant expression. She loved me enough to send her childhood governess away, enough to ignore the rumors, and declare herself to me.

"So, I may still speak with your father when I return?" I asked. No more waiting, I realized. We loved one another, and I could provide for her. There was nothing to hold us back.

Emilia's smile grew so big she bit down on her lower lip to contain it, and she nodded. My heart thrilled against my ribs, and I took her hands, running my thumb over the back of her knuckles.

"You're certain it can't be before you leave?" she asked with a small laugh.

I shook my head. "Unfortunately not. I'll be busy preparing documents and a leave of absence for my journey. But now I have a greater incentive to hurry home," I replied, pulling her hand to my lips and pressing a kiss to her smooth knuckles. She laughed, and heat flooded around my ears as I watched her smile and shake back the curls around her face.

"Then I shall have to be patient," she replied with a sigh. She glanced around, and I followed her gaze. At the moment, no one was within view of us. I turned back to face her just as she leaned forward, her face close to mine. "I will be your wife, Brennan Lennox," she whispered, then pressed her rose-petal lips to mine.

I closed my eyes, my heart stuttering in my chest, a swooping sensation in my stomach as I felt her lips move, soft and gentle, and her body seemed to relax into me. I felt her hand on my cheek, and I was about to cup her chin and kiss her more deeply when I heard approaching voices. We quickly pulled away from one another as a strolling couple came into view. Looking at each other, breathless, we laughed. I stood, holding my arm out to her. She wrapped her arms around my elbow, her cheeks flushed.

"Perhaps I'll cut my trip to only a week at most," I mused. Emilia gave a vigorous nod, flashing me a coy smile. "See that you do, Brennan Lennox. I fought Fina off for you, see that those efforts were not in vain." She bit her lip as I pressed a promising kiss to the palm of her hand.

Chapter Eight

Our childhood village rose up before me as I maneuvered our carriage over the crest of the final hill that overlooked Bòidhchead. The few lingering clouds from a recent rainstorm were riding out on the stiff breeze that whipped my cloak and tugged at my hat. From my vantage point, I could see another storm riding in on the same wind. I pulled my hat more firmly onto my head and flicked the reins. Our aunt had been kind enough to let me use a pair of steeds and a carriage so that I could bring my sisters. I'd driven plenty of carts in my day, so I was comfortable driving the carriage myself, despite the distance. During the first part of the journey, I made sure to arrive at each waypoint town long before dark every evening, the memories of the dangers of this place spurring me to be overcautious. Though, when no threats presented themselves after the first few days, I felt myself relaxing and enjoying the beauty of the moors.

My heart beat at a rapid clip as we neared the main road that passed through the middle of Bòidhchead. Now that we were back,

I realized how much I had missed this place. Returning, I felt awed by the rough beauty of the moors, the glittering lochs, the highland peaks. I felt alive out here. It was similar to the feeling of being out on the open ocean, but being here felt like home. I took a deep breath, the air fresh and wet from the rain, and for a brief moment, I didn't understand how I had been able to leave all this behind.

I shook my head. What nonsense was I thinking? There was a lot that we had left behind: poverty, danger, and memories that needed to remain buried in the past. Our childhood home had been an unfortunate loss but one I was happy to give up for the life we now lived in Glasgow. I had to remind myself that the purpose of this trip was just to come collect a few more of our parents' belongings, try to make a deal with the town concerning our house, and return to Glasgow. Our real home.

Over the sound of the horses' hooves, I could hear my sisters' excited chatter as we passed well-known places from our childhood. However, as we passed houses and shops, moving toward the heart of the village, something felt different. I realized that there weren't as many people out, and hardly any children were in the street, which was odd, considering the rare break in the rainy weather.

The few people going about their business on the street stopped to stare as our carriage passed. I nodded respectfully to women and men I knew from my childhood but didn't receive much of a greeting in return. After receiving blank stares from several passersby, it struck me that they didn't recognize us. Five years was a long time to be gone, and though there were a few new houses, it felt as though nothing had changed about the town except us.

"Can we *please* stop now, Brennan? We've been trapped in this carriage for hours!" Maura complained out the window. Over the creaking of the wagon wheels, I could hear Norah rebuking Maura that complaining wasn't ladylike. Maura made a clipped answer in return that I couldn't quite catch. Poor, motherly Norah, she didn't stand a chance when it came to cautioning her spirited sister. Maura's sharp tongue was something of a legend among her friends and was sure to put her future husband into an early grave.

With a chuckle and a shake of my head, I pulled the carriage to a stop in front of Clyde's Tannery. People across the street at Merl's Goods gawked as I hopped down from the driver's seat to lower the carriage steps and help my sisters down. With sighs of relief, we all turned and took in the sights and smells of this simple loch town.

"Everything is so small," Norah said, looking up and down the street.

"The houses look like doll houses," Maura agreed, stretching her arms behind her back with a sigh.

While the town had grown, there were no towering cathedrals, no opera houses, no masts of docked ships piercing the sky.

"What's that smell?" Slaine asked, holding a handkerchief to her nose with a grimace. I filled my lungs with a deep breath, taking in the sharp smell of freshly tanned hides.

"We're in front of a tannery," Norah said, pointing toward a few workers who were scraping the fat and meat off a cow hide strung up on a line. Slaine looked at the hides with a wrinkled nose. "Not very pleasant, is it?" she asked, glancing at me.

"Can we move?" Maura asked, coughing.

"Let's head to Merl's," I said, offering my arm to Norah, while Maura tucked her hands into the crook of my other elbow. "I wrote him a letter a fortnight ago, asking him if he would be interested in buying things from the house. He hasn't replied, so I want to speak with him directly."

Slaine took Norah's free hand, and we started across the muddy road. I looked toward the green near the center of town, and frowned. When I was younger, the green would be brimming with boys and young men playing and training for the highland games that started in late spring. Today, however, the field was nearly deserted, with only a few young men out practicing tossing cabers.

"Why is it so quiet?" Norah asked. "I don't remember it being so quiet."

"I don't know," I replied. "Perhaps the war with France has finally affected this place," I replied. The breeze shifted, and the delicious smells of yeast and sugar wafted into the street.

"I'm hungry," Slaine whispered, shying away from the prying eyes of a group of old men passing by with fishing poles over their shoulders.

"Carson's bakery is a few doors down from Merl's," Maura said, nodding toward the well-known building where my mother used to sell some of her baked goods. "We could stop for some pastries."

I reached into my pocket and pulled out a few coins.

I'd brought enough money to spend two weeks here while we were on our errand, but I thought it more probable that we'd only stay for a few days. Knowing my sisters, they were sure to become bored with such a tiny place as soon as they remembered that there were no parties or social events to attend here. With my own work and Emilia back in Glasgow waiting for me, I had no desire to stay more than a week.

"Buy us some pastries, and then we'll head to the house. Merl might want to come along to see the inventory. Stay together," I said, giving the coins to Norah. Smiling with excitement, my sisters hurried from my side.

Nodding to two young women who passed me by, I entered Merl's Goods.

Merl himself was busy showing a man some animal feed, so I decided to look at some new bits for a harness until Merl was finished with his customer. I was engrossed in comparing the prices here to the ones in Glasgow, when angry shouting at the front of the store interrupted the tranquil murmur of people out on the street.

Dropping the bits and moving to the door, I saw Merl shouting and shoving a petite woman with wild hair out of his store. The woman tried slipping past him back into the shop, but he shoved her again and grabbed at a wooden broom standing nearby.

I ran to the door and ducked in front of the woman just as Merl brought the broom head down, the wooden handle cracking across my face, the bristly head of the broom slamming into my shoulder. I took a few staggering steps backward with the force of the blow but remained standing in front of the defenseless woman behind me.

"What's going on here?" I barked, wincing at the stinging on the side of my face and holding out my hand to stave off another blow. Merl straightened, his face crumpled in confusion at my interference. I took the broom from his hand to avoid getting hit again. Merl gave it up without much fight, his mouth open like a freshly-caught brown trout. After a moment, he puffed up, indignation coloring his face.

"Who the ruddy 'ell are yeh?" Merl thundered, looking me up and down.

"Don't recognize me?" I asked, giving him a grimacing sort of smile. Hopefully he would remember me before he decided to put a fist in my face.

Merl stepped back, and it was a moment before his frown dissipated to recognition. "Gor blimey. Brennan Lennox, is tha' really yeh?"

"As I live and breathe," I said, handing the broom back to him. He took it with a dumbfounded expression.

"I didn't get yer letter but yesterdee! And 'ere yeh are. I ain't 'ardly recognized yeh! The last time I saw yeh, yeh were a mere boy. Well yeh've grown up now, 'aven't yeh." He took another appraising look at me and then shook his head. "None of us 'ere ever thought we'd lay eyes on yeh again. It's good to see yeh, lad." He held out a hand. "And sorry 'bout tha'." He nodded toward the red, tender mark on my face.

Squinting through my injured eye, I reached to take his hand. "It's good to see you as—"

Someone grabbed me from behind and pulled me sideways. I found myself staring into the face of the petite woman Merl had been shouting at. She was a good head shorter than me, and her hair was ebony black streaked with silver. Her greenery-wreathed circlet was a little askew on her head, but she didn't seem to notice.

I instantly recognized the druid woman I'd met the night when my mother had been taken. She hadn't changed a bit in five years. She stared at me as though I had been raised from the dead, and she gripped my shirt and pulled me closer, her eyes raking my face.

"Lad. Lad, it *is* you!" she whispered, her voice hoarse, her eyes wide.

"*Yeh let go of 'im, yeh witch*!" Merl roared, raising the broom again threateningly. The druid turned to look at Merl with a disdainful expression.

"If I were a witch, you'd be the first I'd curse, Merl MacDermott."

"Get out of me store and away from 'ere!" Merl shouted. The druid gave him one last withering stare before turning back to me. I held out a hand to Merl, who was threatening to bring the broom down on us again.

"It's alright, Merl," I said, giving him a reassuring nod before turning back to face the druid who still held me tightly on the front of my shirt.

"Lad, you're back. Oh, how I need you now," she whispered, her face solemn. "You could be the only one, now."

"I . . . I don't know what you mean," I replied, uncomfortably aware that Merl and half of the thoroughfare outside was listening in. I had no desire to dredge up how I knew this woman in front of the whole street.

"We aren't staying long," I called, hoping to send people on their way. "We're just here to take care of the business in selling our old house, and then we're headed back to Glas—"

"I'll meet you there," the druid whispered. As quickly as she had grabbed me, she released my shirt. Without another word, she slipped down the street and out of sight. Merl came to stand beside me, planting the broom handle onto the floor with a huff.

"I'm sorry about tha', lad. Tha' old witch 'as gotten more and more barmy as the years 'ave passed. Quite lunatic, now."

"Lunatic how?" I asked, rubbing my throbbing face. The last time I had met her, she hadn't seemed a lunatic at all, though I had been afraid of her kind.

Merl shook his head with a weary expression. "Tha' mad spellcaster is trying to convince boys to go out kelpie routing alone."

I turned to look at him, incredulous, and he nodded.

"What? Just one boy trying to catch a kelpie by himself?" I asked, anger bubbling inside me.

"Aye. It's got people downright nervous, what with the kelpies gettin' bad and all," Merl continued, his voice heavy. "And our jack o'lanterns aren't even doing the trick of keeping them out of the village proper anymore. We've doubled our lantern count, but tha' doesn't seem to deter 'em."

I had stopped listening to what Merl was saying. The news that the druid, who had probably saved my life so long ago, was now actively trying to put boys in danger made me feel sick. She had saved me that night from a kelpie. What did she mean by it?

"And 'ere she is, tryin' to get young, inexperienced boys out by themselves. She's tried to convince my own grandson, as well as several of 'is friends. A few older men said she's approached them as well, but they wouldn't even listen to her. Shooed 'er off right sharpish, they did. She won't say why they need to go out alone, just tha' they need to go out there. She's gettin' to be dangerous."

"She can't be *that* dangerous," I said, shaking my head in disbelief.

"Yeh can't trust witches, boy!" Merl said heatedly. "Or 'as yer time with swanky city folks made yeh forget tha'?" Still puffing and grumbling, Merl turned to shoo away onlookers who had gathered to see the commotion. I stared after where the druid had disappeared, frowning.

"Well?" Merl called to me, "Are we going to talk business or are yeh going to stand there like a tattyboggle?"

I walked out of Merl's a half hour later with the agreement that tomorrow Merl would bring his wagon to the house and we would look over what we wanted to sell to him. He warned me as we shook hands goodbye that I wouldn't find anyone to buy our cottage and land. It was too far out of town, he claimed, despite the quality of the acreage. People didn't want to risk living outside the safety of the village limits. I had thanked him for his concerns, but I was sure I would be able to find a buyer.

My sisters were waiting for me beside the carriage when I stepped out of the shop, a few pastries for me in their hands. Eager to see our house, they climbed inside the carriage, and I drove the well-remembered path out of town toward our home.

Chapter Nine

I pulled the carriage to a stop in front of our cottage and, still considering what Merl had told me of the druid, sat back in the seat with a sigh.

Why would she be trying to lure young men out for kelpie routing? It didn't make sense. Druids kept to themselves, not to mention they didn't partake in kelpie hunting at all. No one knew what they did, and no one cared to ask for fear that they'd be touched by magic or worse. The fact that one was now actively stirring up trouble in the village was puzzling.

And the kelpies.

Merl's news was frightening, but people had always claimed that the kelpies were getting stronger and more populous, though the claims were mostly used to scare children. Besides, exaggerations in tales about kelpie routing was a tradition, though I knew firsthand how deadly the beasts could be. More likely there was an obvious explanation. The kelpies were enjoying a boom in population, like the rabbits did every couple of years when we were children: they abounded in the field so much so that you couldn't take five steps without stepping on one. Of course, the kelpies were more dangerous than rabbits, but I was sure that their numbers would dwindle down when the season ran its course, and then our property would be saleable again.

"Brennan?" Norah called. "Are you alright?" Her voice shook me from my reverie, and I hurriedly tied the reins to the armrest of the driver's seat and jumped to the sodden April turf.

I helped Maura, Norah, and Slaine down from the interior, and we turned our attention to our cottage.

"Oh, my," Norah whispered.

"It looks bad, doesn't it, Bren?" Maura asked.

I nodded and pushed the hat off my head so that I could get a better look at our inheritance. The once familiar home was now hidden by creepers and climbing weeds. The planks over the windows were mere shards now, some of the slats missing entirely. The heavy rains and cold winter winds seemed to have done quite a job on our beloved house. Thistles and grass grew high, tickling the windowsills, and budding heather covered the thatched roof.

"What a mess," Slaine said, taking Maura's hand.

I quickly unhitched the horses, knowing we'd be here a few hours, and staked the steeds a few paces away. Then, together, we moved to the house. Corrosion had set into the latch, but after a few moments of wiggling, the bolt loosened. I shoved open the door, which squealed on rust-dry hinges, and we stepped inside. Dust floated in the shafts of light that shone through the board gaps of the windows and the now-open door.

"We really came all this way for this?" Maura asked, striding into the house and looking skeptically around the small sitting room.

Norah put a hand on my shoulder. "We'll never be able to sell it, Brennan."

I sighed and rubbed a hand over the stubble on my chin. "Maybe not the house, exactly, but perhaps the land. And we still have some belongings here. We'll see what Merl wants. Perhaps I can sell the house and land for a pittance, just so we don't have it under our name anymore."

"Can we go back to Glasgow now?" Slaine asked, gingerly side-stepping a pile of animal droppings on the floor.

"Come on," I laughed, a surprising flash of nostalgia filling me. Happy memories seemed to flood my mind as we stood in that tiny house. "You don't remember the fun we had here? This is where Mother would make her famous pies and tarts." I placed a hand on the dusty countertop that overlooked the back, boarded-up window. "We'd read Father's books by the fireplace." The memories filled my mind's eye. Father showing me how to roast apples, Mother reading in her soft, sweet voice. Norah rocking baby Slaine. I felt the love in that memory curl around me.

"Look at this tiny hall!" Maura called over her shoulder, breaking the spell. "How did mother ever fit down here to check on us? Oh! Our old bedroom!"

We followed Maura's voice down the hall, though I had to stoop down to enter it. Slaine and Norah followed Maura into our old room, but I stopped outside the door, placing my hand on the dusty latch. My sisters wandered the room, looking out the window and peering under the two beds.

The rickety nightstand still stood beside the bed, more canker-ous and dilapidated than ever. Everything looked so forlorn, it hurt my heart to see all our possessions crumbling and worn with disuse. Nostalgia for our simpler life, warm and longing, filled me again.

"You used to tell us kelpie stories in secret while we lay in bed," Maura said, turning to me. "That seems so long ago."

"Should we sleep here tonight?" I asked on impulse, half serious. Maura and Norah exchanged glances, while Slaine wrinkled her nose in distaste.

"I don't think so, Brennan. Those mattresses are sure to be full of vermin," Norah said with a grimace. Slaine sidestepped away from the beds.

"We have money to stay in an inn," Maura reminded. "Besides . . . the kelpies . . ." She fell silent, biting her lip. I looked between my sisters, realizing that they had heard the same thing I had about the kelpies being more numerous than usual.

"I don't want to sleep here, Brennan. It's filthy," Slaine finally said, seemingly unaware of what we were discussing. Norah gave me an apologetic look as she nodded in agreement with Slaine.

I wondered at my sisters' eagerness to leave so soon. I realized that perhaps I was the only one that felt nostalgic. I had lived here the longest, after all.

However, my sisters could not be denied their comforts, so I nodded. "Very well. Let's bring the things we'd stacked in the barn inside and go through it all. We'll place everything that we want to keep in one pile and the items to sell in another. Merl will come tomorrow to take what he wants."

With relieved smiles, my sisters agreed, though I felt sorrowful at their obvious disgust toward our family home.

We all headed back to the barn. It, too, looked ragged. The garden was overgrown with unchecked carrots and potatoes. The shed smelled of rotten hay, and we could hear mice moving around in the corners.

It took only a few minutes to haul all of the wooden crates back to the house, as Maura and Norah were not adverse to a little dirt and hard work. Slaine, on the other hand, made sure to stay far away from the dusty crates, for fear of bugs. As I was piling the last of the boxes in the middle of the sitting room, I heard a soft, "Hello, hello?" coming from out front. My sisters gave me questioning looks at the voice. Clapping the dust from my hands, I went to look out the front door.

Standing slightly concealed behind our carriage was the druid, watching the house with a curious expression on her face. When she saw me peering out the door at her, she beckoned me over with a hand and a brisk, "Lad! Come, come!"

I turned back to my sisters, who had begun gingerly working the lids off the crates with their fingertips, grimaces on their faces.

"Stay here. I'll be right back." I left the house and made my way over to where the druid was waiting. As I approached, I saw her bend down and pick a small flowering plant. As she wove the plant into the wreath around her head, she stared at me, sizing me up.

If rumors in town were to be believed, I didn't want her staying around. Her reaction to my return piqued my interest, and I was curious as to what she wanted from me, but I was also wary of her intentions.

When I reached her side, she grasped my hand and squeezed it tightly.

"It's good to see you back, lad." She gave me a warm smile. I didn't return it. I didn't have anything to do with this woman. We had never really conversed, except for that horrible night. I didn't know what she was playing at, acting as though we had a long history.

"What's the matter, boy? You look as grave as a loch leech."

"How did you know where to find me? You've never been to this farm before," I said, making sure to keep my tone light. She was a magic user, after all.

"People in town do talk, lad."

I thought for a moment before I spoke. If she was deranged, I wanted to speak carefully, so as not to set her off. "People in town say you're dangerous. I just want to make sure you don't mean my sisters any harm. We are strangers, you and I."

"Oh, we're acquaintances, boy," she said, her tone brisk. "And dinnae mind what those fools in town say. They know nothing and understand less."

I frowned. "So then why have you been trying to coerce young boys to go kelpie hunting with you, unaccompanied?" I tried to keep my anger from shining through, but it was difficult. Having her near put me on edge.

The druid raised an eyebrow at my tone.

"Sounds like an underhanded scheme you're trying for," I continued. "People have lost loved ones as it is. You're not helping your reputation."

"Oh, hang my reputation. It won't change people's minds, and I dinnae care. Now, we have things to discuss. First of all—"

"But you can understand why people are upset, can you not?" I interrupted. The last thing I wanted to do was get into a discussion with her.

"Of course I can, lad, but it doesn't matter if it upsets people. It has to be done!" She paused, her voice going quiet. "You did it once. Went out, all alone."

"If you remember, I was half-crazed with loss at the time." I got shivers at the memory. I had been a fool to think I could save my mother. I could've perished, leaving my sisters alone. "No one in their sane mind would do what I did."

"Well, of course not. Not if they didnae understand what I'm trying to accomplish. But with you back, and that relic we gave you those years ago, you may be able to help me."

I shifted uncomfortably, unwilling to discuss her gift that I had thrown away.

"And what are you trying to do, exactly?" I asked, glancing back toward the house, making sure none of my sisters were listening in. I didn't want to upset them with this talk, or even have them see me speaking with a magic wielder. Ever since that night, we hadn't spoken of magic, and we hadn't discussed what had happened to me out on the moors.

Turning back to the druid, I saw that her easy-going air was gone, replaced with a grave expression.

"Lad . . ." she paused. "What people are saying in town is true. Kelpies are becoming more and more frequent, and are even becoming so bold as to come out during daylight hours, not just once the sun goes down."

"How can that be possible?" I'd heard the rumor often since we'd arrived, but it was so fantastical that I shook it off. "Kelpies cannot change their ways and whims, just as the seasons cannot change their order."

"And yet, sometimes snow may fall in late spring," the druid responded.

I shook my head. She was turning my words to suit her purpose, and I didn't want to hear it. Besides, was I going to trust the word of a *druid*, not to mention a druid that was bordering on madness?

"Well, it isn't possible for kelpies to suddenly *not* have an aversion to sunlight."

The druid was silent, biting her lip. "I have a few theories about that, but we can discuss them once you promise to help me."

"Well, I don't reckon that will ever happen," I retorted. "I have my sisters here with me. I need them to be safe, and what you're doing, who you are, is the opposite of safe."

She looked me up and down, her expression furrowed.

"What if I told you there was a way to eradicate the kelpies?" she asked.

I paused, then laughed to cover my frown. "I don't understand what you mean. People have been hunting kelpies for decades, and if what you are saying was true, it's apparent that they haven't made a dent in the population."

"I can." Not a hint of a smile played about her lips. Her expression demanded belief.

I stared at her almost in wonder. She really was mad. No sane person would believe they could wipe out the kelpies entirely, especially alone. If whole groups of men couldn't do it for ages, how could one woman do so?

No, I couldn't get involved with this woman, no matter how desperate she seemed.

"I'm sorry, but I cannot help you."

"You owe me this." Her grave demeanor changed for a brief moment, clouding over with grief and anger.

"I beg your pardon?" I bristled. "I owe you what?"

Her expression shifted, her face now apologetic. "Nothing, I'm sorry. I just mean, if you understood what's at stake for all of us, what is truly going on around you in the world of magic, you—"

I felt angry now, and annoyed. This woman thought I owed her something? I owed her nothing, and I especially didn't owe the magic world anything: it had taken my parents away from me.

"I want nothing to do with magic, do you understand me?" I asked, my voice almost a snarl. "Magic is evil, and I'll have nothing to do with it, or with you!"

"Magic protected you all those years ago, boy, when my husband gave you that relic!" she bit back. I took a deep breath. I didn't want to fight with her, it would risk provoking her to use magic in her deranged state.

"I'm sorry, but I can't help you. This place . . ." I looked around at the rolling hills, sprouting with spring flowers and buzzing with insects. "It's not my home anymore. Kelpies aren't my concern any-more."

"Boy, this *concern* is much larger than just the highlands. If they are multiplying and becoming more fearless, dinnae you think they'll start attacking the larger cities?" she asked, a little angrily now. "This problem isn't what you think it is. It goes much deeper."

"Kelpies, glastigs, boobries, red caps, what is the difference?" I asked. "Every creature has bad and good, and every creature has seasons of population growth and seasons of decline—"

"You've been gone too long, lad," the druid said, shaking her head, her expression sorrowful. "The creatures you've mentioned have begun to disappear. They've gone underground, I expect, from the wars across Europe, and . . . never mind. But kelpies are not doing so, and killing them isn't helping, even the men around here no longer feel happy about a kill—"

"You're right. I've been gone a long time. I'm not the young boy you met, and kelping isn't alluring to me anymore. I don't need to prove myself a man by how many kelpies I kill. I can provide for my sisters. I live with my family. I'm a prosperous merchant. I don't need any of this highland nonsense." I turned to walk away, but she grabbed me and whipped me back to face her. I grunted in surprise at her strength.

"But kelpies aren't what they seem! Are you not hearing me? Do you see ceasgs attacking homes? Or goblins? Red caps stay in their swamps; they don't come out and steal people away by the hundreds! What I have discovered could completely undermine everything we know about kelpies, but no one will believe me. But you, you are different!"

"Different because I've lost both parents to them?" I asked coldly.

"They took my husband," she snapped, her voice ringing with grief. I paused, noting the almost wild look in her eyes, and pity crept into my stomach. I remembered well that anguish in her expression.

"I'm sorry," I said, meaning it.

"A few months after I met *you*. He was taken by them." Something in her tone made it seem like she blamed me. I felt myself bristle.

"Well, I'm sorry, but I don't see what that has to do with me."

"You understand what it is to lose family! You can understand why this needs to change! And it can!" The druid opened her mouth to continue, but I cut her off.

"I've let go of the past and moved on. I'm not a part of this place anymore. Kelpies are no longer a concern for me. Did you know, in the cities, hardly anyone knows that kelpies exist?"

"Of course they don't, because they're too blinded by their fancy parties and frilly nonsense," she said, angry tears clinging to her lashes. "But it won't remain so. Lad, please, just come with me, and I'll show you what I've discovered!"

I stepped away, holding out a hand. I wasn't going to be dragged into this. I would not muck about in the past. There was nothing that could be done for it.

"I'm sorry, I cannot. I'm here only a few days, and then we are returning to our real lives, back in Glasgow. I'm sure the kelpies had a fertile year or two. But come hunting season, the men will take care of that. Nature sorts itself out."

"Haven't you been hearing me?" the druid said, pleading. "Hunting isn't—"

"I'm sorry," I replied, backing away, tired of the repetitiveness of her pleas, and fearful of her growing agitation. "Please, don't harm me or my sisters."

Her shoulders slumped, and I turned to move away, but she called, "Wait. Where is that relic my husband gave you? The stone," she clarified.

I stopped a few feet from the front door and turned back to glance at her. She stood, expression hopeful, her skirts rippling in the wind. Would she want retribution for the stone? Would she take it from my own flesh? But I couldn't lie. I wouldn't.

"It's gone," I confessed, regret twisting in my stomach. "I'm very sorry. I have to go, now, I have—"

To my surprise, instead of puffing up with ire, I watched as she fell to her knees, her face in her hands, shoulders shuddering. I felt my fear and annoyance melt away and pity well up inside me as I remembered she had suffered losses as well.

I moved toward her, but before I could reach her, she stood up, gave me a tearful look, and hurried away.

"Wait!" I called. But she didn't stop or look back, and she was soon swallowed up by the hills.

I stood where I was for several moments, guilt flooding my heart. While I didn't regret my decision to turn her down, I berated myself for my callousness. But with magic, it was best not to take chances. I sighed. The sooner we finished our business here, the better.

As I looked over the budding moor, I realized I had lied to the woman. That cursed stone wasn't gone, exactly. It was just out in the field somewhere. I had been so eager to get her away from my family that I had misspoken.

Remembering that night many years ago, I walked in the direction I had thrown the necklace. As I had been a young boy, though I had been strong, it couldn't have been thrown too far. Maybe I could find it and return it to her, perhaps giving it back to her would get her to leave me, and any other village boys, be.

I scanned the grass as I walked in the vicinity where I had thrown it. After a few minutes of searching, I shrugged. Well, I had tried somewhat, and I didn't want to waste all my time out here looking. It was possible someone might have picked it up, or it might've sunk beneath the soil after so many years of rain, snow, and wind.

As I walked back to the house, still surveying the ground, something impossibly green glinted on a base branch, in stark contrast to the yellow flowers, of a highland gorse. Walking toward it, I knew what the green glimmer was before I even reached the shrub. Careful of the wicked thorns of the bramble, I pulled the necklace free of the tangled bush. The stone was warm in my hand, despite having been in the wind and shadows.

The strap was worn but still intact, the inky, drawn-on symbols still clearly visible on the stone, with the animal teeth barely clinging to the leather. I studied the necklace in my hand for a moment. It *was* beautiful, but that warmth about it was off-putting. Magic.

I would return it to the owner, and maybe doing so would absolve me of whatever fault the druid held against me. It had been her husband's, after all. It was only right that I returned his talisman. I slipped the necklace inside my trouser pocket and headed back to the house.

Entering the house, I twisted the bolt shut before turning to my sisters. They had all laid out their cloaks on the floor and were sitting on them to keep the dust from their dresses. They looked up at me with questioning expressions as I came to stand over them. Not wanting to get into what I had been up to, I quickly clapped my hands together.

"So, what do we have in these boxes?" I asked with a forced smile.

Chapter Ten

We sorted our past into two piles: possessions to sell and possessions to keep. The former was overflowing. It had taken less than an hour to go through everything. Our mother had owned a lovely set of china dishes that we were holding onto, as well as several dresses that Norah and Maura wanted.

"They're out of style, but perhaps Maura and I can add some alterations to bring them up to date," Norah said, smiling as she piled the dresses neatly in the corner.

"And this coat was Father's, I imagine," Maura said, holding up a patched, dusty looking overcoat. "Do you want it, Bren?"

I took it from her hands. It was thick, with a few faded patches on the elbows. The fabric was midnight blue and double breasted. Shaking it out and holding up, it looked rather refined, if a little dirty.

"Yes, I think I will keep this," I said. "I don't have anything that was his."

After everything was sorted, we stood back and looked at our piles. We didn't have much to show for our childhood.

"Well, I'm famished," Maura announced, dusting off her hands and her skirts. "Can we go to the inn now?"

I looked out the window. The sun was still high in the April sky. We had plenty of time to reach the inn before dark.

"Yes, we can go," I said, stretching the kinks out of my lower back. "I'm sure the inn will start serving supper soon. I'll load up everything now so we don't forget anything."

Stowing everything into the carriage only took a few minutes. When I was finished, I jumped to the grass, the late afternoon sun warming my dirt-smudged face. I inhaled the clean breeze, a smell very different from the air of the inner city.

"It is beautiful here," Maura sighed, turning her face to the sun as well.

"There's so much space, but it's too quiet," Slaine replied, and I realized the difference between here and Glasgow would be the starkest for her. She had the fewest memories here.

"Maybe. But it's beautiful days like this that make it hard to go back to the city," I said. I was about to un-picket the horses, but Norah, wandering a few paces from the house, made me pause.

She stood with her back to us, looking over the landscape. "I remember days like this, going to town with Mother to pick out bolts of fabric for new clothes. Merl would slip us small candies, usually the ones that were old and wouldn't sell," Norah said, her voice soft.

"Peppermint or licorice," I recalled.

"I adored the peppermint drops," Norah sighed.

I glanced out at Norah, who continued to look out at the vast expanse of hills painted with budding flowers.

"Norah?" I walked to stand next to her.

"This is beautiful country. I do miss it sometimes," she said, her voice thick.

"I do too," I murmured. Slaine and Maura came up beside us, and I put my arms around all of them. This place was a distant part of us, and soon we would be leaving it for good.

"Mother loved this time of year," Norah said in a whisper as we overlooked the landscape, splashed with yellow gorse and early blooming heather in the spring warmth. Beside me, Maura began sniffling. I turned to her and saw her eyes brimming with tears.

"Maura?"

"I've been missing her a lot lately," Maura sniffed. Slaine leaned up against my side, and I squeezed her shoulders. Understanding softened my frown as Maura continued.

"Being here makes me wonder . . . If we had known earlier about Glasgow, maybe that night . . . wouldn't have happened," Maura choked, ducking her head. "I wouldn't have followed you, Mother wouldn't have followed, and whether or not you had won that money, she would still be—" She ceased speaking, her shoulders shuddering.

My heart wrenched as I realized that, like me, Maura felt the guilt of our mother's death, yet she believed the guilt to be on *her*. I grabbed her shoulders and turned her to face me.

"Listen to me, it wasn't your fault," I asserted, struggling to keep the conflicting anger and guilt from showing in my tone.

"But it was!" she demanded, face twisted in pain. "I shouldn't have followed. If it hadn't been for me—" Maura began, but I cut her off.

"I don't blame you in the slightest. You believe me, don't you? All the blame rests on my shoulders. Mine alone," I insisted. "I could've walked away from Ewan and his money, from his jibes. We both know he wouldn't have given me the money anyway. I knew it then, yet I went anyway. It's *my* fault. Besides, if Mother hadn't been there, we would have *both* been taken away. She saved our lives, and we need to behave in a way that honors her. You are not at fault, do you understand?"

Maura still didn't look convinced as more tears spilled down her cheeks. I pulled her to me and kissed her forehead. "You are not to blame. You aren't. It's all on me," I whispered.

Norah pulled Maura into a hug. "Maura, I like to think that Mother is with Father now, and both are happy that we're not poor and alone," Norah said. "We have our family, and we have the life they wanted for us. We shouldn't be looking behind us. This place is a part of our past; there's nothing to keep us here."

"These feelings will go away as soon as we're back in Glasgow and you have the harp in your arms once again," I said, squeezing her hand.

Maura nodded and wiped at her wet cheekbones.

"Will you be alright?" Norah asked, wrapping an arm around Maura's shoulders.

Maura nodded again. "It's just this place. Like Brennan said, I'll be better once we're back home," she said, giving us a watery smile. Slaine wrapped her arms around Maura's waist, and Maura hugged her back.

We sat in silence for a moment before Slaine made a clicking sound with her tongue and broke away from Maura's embrace. "Can I wash my hands?" she asked, looking in disgust at her palms, gray with dust. We broke apart, the tender moment between us ending. I brushed my own dusty hands on my dirty trousers as we moved back into the house, and I pointed to the back door.

"There's a stream out behind the barn," I said.

"Only a stream?" Slaine asked, frowning. I smiled. With the luxury that our home in Glasgow afforded, Slaine had forgotten that water had to come from somewhere and didn't just appear in her morning wash pitcher.

"Here, I'll show you. I need to wash as well," Norah said, striding toward the back door. "You coming, Maura?"

"In a moment. I'm going to go put my cloak in the carriage first so it doesn't get wet," Maura said, checking her hair in a small, cracked mirror that was lying on the table. I pushed a few of the items that had escaped the sale pile back into place, listening to the faint sounds of Norah and Slaine giggling and splashing in the small brooklet.

"I hope the business here concludes before the week is out," Maura said, giving her hair a final look over. "Margaret Benning is having an evening party on Saturday next."

"I'm sure we'll be home long before then," I replied with a laugh. "But you best get washed up, Maura. You can look at yourself as long as you want back at the inn."

Giving me an annoyed look, Maura plucked up her traveling cloak off the kitchen table and marched out the front door while I chuckled. As Norah and Slaine came back in, cloaks draped over their damp arms, I picked up my hat and coat that had been lying on the table, readying to step outside and hitch up the horses to the carriage.

"Do you think they serve Yorkshire pudding at the inn?" Slaine asked.

"I don't know. Shall we go find out?" I asked, and Slaine nodded, grinning.

"Very well," I replied, clapping my hands together, "Let us—"

A high-pitched squeal, the sound that had haunted my dreams, shattered the calm outside the house. Another distant screech followed, and I heard Maura screaming.

Without hesitation, I dropped my hat and coat and bolted out of the house. The carriage horses were rearing and squealing, their tethers keeping them from running off. I dashed past the carriage that blocked the view from the door and skidded to a stop.

A waking nightmare loomed before my eyes.

Just beyond the carriage, Maura was holding her hands outstretched toward not one, but three enormous black stallions that towered above her. In the daylight, I could see their eyes. A cold fire seemed to burn inside their gazes as the three bore down upon my sister, their coats reflecting green in the sun, though the hides were a deeper black than the darkest night. Their wild manes seemed to ripple as if in a high wind. The animals were stunning in their terrifying beauty. The beasts bucked and nipped at one another, jostling for position to get at Maura first, who stood there, back rigid, arms outstretched.

"Maura!" I shouted, sprinting toward her. Common sense bellowed that I would be taken away with her if I kept moving toward her, but I didn't care. I couldn't *not* try.

Within a heartbeat, one of the kelpies lifted Maura up onto its moss-slicked back with its strange magic. Maura turned and looked at me for a half second, her eyes wide with terror, before the demon horse reared up with a scream and started toward the distant hills.

"Maura, *no*!" I bellowed, skidding to a stop, Maura's scream echoing inside my head as the other two kelpies turned their attention to me.

A vision of my mother on the back of a dark horse on a starry night flashed in my mind's eye. I shook the image away and shouted over my shoulder to Norah and Slaine, who were screaming just inside the doorway.

"Norah! Lock the door!" I roared, wanting to save my two remaining sisters from having to see me be pulled by that overpowering magic onto the moss-velvet back of a kelpie. I steeled myself for the inevitable as Norah slammed the door shut.

As I turned back to the kelpies who were moving toward me, sniffing for me, they suddenly reared back. With guttural screams and rolling eyes, the two remaining brutes charged away from me in different directions.

I didn't take time to wonder what had happened. More memories of that horrible night threatened to overtake my mind, drowning out all logical thought, but I pushed those memories away. Panicking hadn't helped me all those years ago. I needed to act, but in a smarter fashion than when I had been a boy. I could still see the kelpie that had Maura as it charged across the knolls. I could catch up. But running wouldn't do it, despite my longer legs and my stamina from working ships.

I took off instead toward the crazed carriage horses. Careful of their agitated bucking, I wrenched the picket of one of the steeds from the ground and heaved myself up onto the frantic horse. Not taking time to calm the beast, I urged it into a gallop after the black speck that was the kelpie.

It wouldn't easily outdistance me this time.

Tracking the beast's direction, I calculated that it was heading toward Loch Domhainn, and that spurred my determination. I wasn't a helpless boy anymore, it wasn't dark this time, and I had a steed of my own. I could make it.

After several minutes, the kelpie had disappeared from sight, but I charged on, running the horse as I had never run one before, heedless of the danger of pushing a panicked animal. My own breathing was ragged, as if I were the one running so fast my heart would burst. I shuddered as my mind tried to get me to see reason. There was no way I could make it in time. She was gone. The kelpie was too fast, even if I was on my own steed. The kelpies had won. Again.

I tried to banish the negative thoughts, but they came in such a strong force that tears began to stream down my cheeks as I flew across the moors. I should never have taken my sisters with me. They should've stayed in the safety of the city.

Despair began to weaken my resolve and strength. But I didn't slow the horse's relentless pace, not if there was a *chance.* The few miles melted away beneath the pounding hooves of the frothing horse. It felt like an age before my charger burst through the trees that lined Loch Domhainn. I found myself looking over the glassy water that reflected the oncoming thunderheads, the horse shuddering beneath me. Somewhere out in the hills, I heard a distant screech. Another kelpie nearby? Or was it the brute that had taken Maura? The sound faded, leaving me in silence to scan the storm-darkening shores, my chest heaving. I could neither see nor hear the kelpie or my sister, and the waters were calm in the silence that preceded the stormwall. Had the beast gone on to a different loch? Only the sound of the lapping waves on the shore echoed in my ears, thunderous in the otherwise still surroundings. I urged my horse along the thin, pebbly beach, my eyes searching, my ears straining, my heart nearly bursting.

I couldn't give up. I couldn't give up.

As I hurried along the shore, a large thicket of weeds and bushes blocked my path, and the horse refused to go into the water to get around it. Cursing the stubborn animal, I launched off its back and charged into the shallows to get past the obstacle on foot. As I waded toward the other side of the brush, I tripped over something hidden beneath the surface and I fell to my hands and knees in the shallow, frigid water. I didn't rise, my body heaving with grief.

She was gone. It was just the same as before. I had failed to save my mother that night, and I failed to save Maura.

I was no longer a boy, but I felt one at that moment. I was still helpless against the power of these highlands. Of the kelpies. No matter how far away I lived, I realized I would never be able to escape them. They would hunt me down until they utterly destroyed me.

"*Why?*" I bellowed out at the shadowed waters, wind now kicking up small white caps along the surface. My horse behind me whinnied at the sudden savage sound. "*Why are you so cruel? Damn you!*" I pounded a fist into the lapping waves, my knuckles shrieking as I struck a submerged rock.

"Damn you," I choked.

Hand throbbing, I sat back on my heels, gripping my hair as hot tears burned my cheeks. I didn't care that I was resting in a kelpie lair. They would be foolish to come for me right now. I felt as though I could rip one in half this very moment.

Cold seeped through me that had nothing to do with me kneeling in the icy loch.

Maura.

She had been so full of life, so ready to see the world. Now she would see nothing more. Her wit and sharp tongue had kept our family laughing, even when times were hard. How would we ever laugh again?

Thoughts I didn't want to dwell on pushed and pulled within my mind, forcing me to realize what I had done. I was responsible. Again. My family was being taken away from me one by one. Was I destined to lose them all?

I shook myself free of the raging thoughts, coming back to my surroundings. The rumbling thunderheads that spilled over the horizon brought premature twilight to Scotland, and night creatures of the loch were coming to life with croaking and buzzing. I couldn't sit here. I had my two remaining sisters waiting for me. I had left them alone, terrified. Again.

Fresh tears followed the salty trails on my face, guilt welling inside me for leaving them. I splashed freezing loch water onto my face, washing the tears away. I had to be strong for Norah and Slaine. I had to protect them as best as I could, no matter what. They were all I had left.

I stood, my knees and ankles groaning as water streamed down my legs, my skin chilled from the blasts of storm wind, and I felt my sorrow harden into resolve. That was it. I would leave this cursed countryside and never return. We were leaving tomorrow, sale or no sale. And we were never coming back.

I sloshed back to my steed, who was snorting and flicking its tail in agitation. I calmed the horse and climbed back on, my heart aching. I never dreamed I'd feel this horror again, the memory reserved only for my mother and father. But with young Maura . . . It was all too nightmarish.

I pushed my mount into a trot, leaving the loch behind me.

Night creatures screamed and howled between the hills as I pressed the steed into a gallop. My blood seethed with energy, and I wasn't afraid as I traversed the moors. Dark shapes in the shadows stayed out of sight, slinking away at my approach as the wind rippled the grass.

Lightning crackled above in the billowing storm clouds as I pulled the horse to a stop outside our house. As quick as I could, I buckled the now-calm horses into the shafts of the carriage, securing the traces, and then went to the house, where dim light shone through the grimy glass of the boarded-up windows.

With a shuddering breath, I knocked so my sisters would let me in. Norah opened the door, her face drawn, and Slaine was at the kitchen table, her head buried in her arms, sobbing quietly. Norah stood back as I entered.

"Why did you leave us?" Norah's voice cracked, her eyes and nose puffy. "We didn't know if you'd ever come back!" Her voice ended in a shout.

Tired, I hung my head. "I had to try to get her back. If I hadn't tried, I'd be just as worthless as the men in the village think I am, just some useless city boy who never went kelpie hunting in his life because he was scared."

"Brennan, we know you are braver than all the men in the town put together," Norah said, choking on her words, "But what if you had been taken too, leaving us here? You are not divine! You couldn't have stopped those kelpies. There was nothing—"

"*Don't*," I barked, feeling heat flare up in my chest. "Don't say there is nothing we could've done. Don't you say that. Ever again."

The room was silent save for the sound of Slaine weeping in her chair, her shoulders shaking.

"I had to *try*," I pressed. "I will *always* try, for you, for Slaine . . . Or forever hate myself."

"I'm sorry," Norah said, fresh tears spilling from her eyes. She stared at me, silent, and I pulled her into a rough hug, her body shaking against mine.

Outside, rain began falling in heavy sheets. Slaine hurried over to us and I wrapped an arm around her, my clothing still damp from the loch. We stood without speaking for several minutes, just listening to the torrent of rain outside. My heart felt numb. I had no more tears left in my eyes. I stood gravely with my weeping sisters in my arms, just as I had after our mother died. After nearly a quarter of an hour, my sisters' tears slowed, and I looked down at them.

"Let's get into the carriage and get back to the village," I said, my voice ragged as my sisters broke the embrace. I felt exhausted but resolved as I began blowing out the warped candles my sisters had lit. We came here for a reason, and I would see it through, but we would not be staying a week.

"We're leaving tomorrow." The storm outside had been merely a cloudburst, as the deluge slowed to a mere sprinkling in the few minutes we stood in the house. But the storm outside had been nothing to what was raging inside my heart.

Norah merely nodded. Gathering up their cloaks, and with a protective arm over Norah and Slaine, I hurried them out to the carriage in the softening rain.

Chapter Eleven

It was completely dark by the time we got to Bòidhchead village. The rain-driven streets were empty of people, but once I handed the horses over to a stable boy and we entered the inn, we found that it was full of bright lights and the loud chatter of people seated in the dining area for supper.

I sat my sisters down at an empty table. Striding over to the bar, I flagged the barman's attention. "I need two rooms for the night and a meal for fou . . . For three." I nearly choked on the words, but I kept my composure, although my fingernails cut grooves into the wooden bar. The barman gave me the number of two adjoining rooms, and I hurried back toward my sisters, who were staring at the tabletop with blank expressions. When I sat down, they both looked up at me, their faces drawn and ghostly pale.

"Do we have to be here, Brennan?" Norah whispered as more quiet tears began to stream down Slaine's face. "We have no appetite, and we just want to go up to our room."

"You both need to eat to keep your strength up," I replied, although I myself felt like vomiting.

"But—" Harsh laughter erupted from a nearby table, making Norah jump. Slaine buried her face into her hands to hide her tears.

"Brennan, we can't be here right now," Norah pressed. "I feel ill, and Slaine needs rest."

The chatter of the crowd pressed in on my ears and pipe smoke burned my eyes. I understood her needs. For me, however, the relentless babble felt a welcome relief. Silence allowed horrible thoughts and guilt of my failure to dominate my mind.

I got to my feet and held out my hand. "You're right. This isn't acceptable. I'll take you to your room and bring up your supper."

"Thank you, Brennan," Norah said, her voice shaking. We hurried out of the dining hall and up the steps to the second floor. Opening their bedroom door, I ushered them inside.

"Keep this door bolted," I instructed. Norah nodded.

Though I knew no one here meant them harm, I still waited until I heard the latch slide before I headed back downstairs. After nearly half an hour of waiting, I was finally handed a tray of food. I started up the stairs, my heart growing heavier with every step. Norah opened the door, and without a word, I stepped inside and set the tray down on the washbasin.

"Wait, Brennan," she said, as I turned to go back downstairs. "Aren't you going to have any?"

I looked at the tray of steaming food, and my stomach turned. Eating was the last thing on my mind. I needed a distraction, and being here with my sisters as we ate silently, with what had just occurred pounding in our heads, was more than I could bear.

"I'll eat downstairs while I'm taking care of some business," I rasped.

Norah gave me a narrow look.

"I'll be back to check on you lassies in an hour," I said, ignoring her silent rebuke. "Bar your door." Norah looked like she wanted to argue, but hearing Slaine's weeping, she hurried to her side with the tray. I shut the door and returned downstairs.

The loud, crowded dining hall was perfect for my current state, and I sat at an empty table near the loudest people there. Anything to distract me from my own thoughts. People came and went as they finished their supper, and soon it was only men in the dining hall, all filled with hot food and ready to drink and swap stories. I listened to farmers and butchers tell jokes and recount tales, often of victory over the kelpies that were slain during the killing season.

I didn't feel like sharing in the conversation, and I had no desire to share the loss that had just transpired with anyone here. They didn't recognize me, and even if they did, I was still witchborn to them. They would consider my sister's death a result of my bad luck.

I was only half-listening to a man tell a story of how he and his band had killed two kelpies in one night, just to have a third beast spirit a good friend of his away, when I saw a familiar figure in her tell-tale circlet of flowers and grasses slip through the tables. She ordered a tankard of something at the bar, then took her drink and settled herself down in a distant corner, to the disgust of several people sitting nearby. I tore my eyes away from her, sick of feeling guilty, listening even more intently to the story beside me.

"That man was one of the best men I ever knew," the storyteller was saying, his voice gruff. "He killed more of those wicked beasts than I could count on my fingers. Heaven knows what's happening to this country." His comments were greeted with nods and grunts of agreement. "It's gotten to be that I dinnae feel safe letting my children out of my sight anymore. The missus goes near mad if they go outside alone."

"It's a scourge, to be sure," another man said, his grave voice slurred with drink. "Sometimes I feel kelpie routing does no good. Those demons from 'ell are doubling their efforts. It's enough to make any man lose sleep o'er it."

Cedric, who worked in the tannery, slammed his drink on the table. "Didn't ye 'ear? I was making a delivery two days ago up north, and I 'eard tell that nearly 'alf of Kinlochleven was taken during one of their spring festivals last week."

I started in horror at that. Kinlochleven was a small village a few miles north of Bòidhchead. I'd run a few deliveries there for Merl when I was a boy. Spring festivals took place during the day. Kelpies coming out in broad daylight was unheard of, but I'd seen it with my own eyes. If I had known . . .

More people groaned and muttered, an air of sadness pressing in on us all like the cold ocean depths.

"It's bad enough that we 'ear them every night now, just outside the village limits," Henry McBaird said, "But according to poor Merl, it seems that those brutes are no longer afeared of the jack o'lanterns, did you 'ear about that?" There was a murmur of nos, and so Henry settled into his chair. "I noticed Merl was acting pretty broken up these last few weeks, so I go over to talk to 'im about it, and apparently last month over twenty men over in Blackwater, along with Merl's son-in-law, went kelpie routing, and not one ever came back. Over twenty men. And they 'ad two lanterns for every man. I s'pose Death is no longer afearing the lanterns."

"Well, we all knew that!" someone called, laughing in his drunkenness, "We see them passing our windows every night, and there are lanterns all around the village!" He then roared with laughter while others clicked their tongues in disgust.

"Well, it's worse, because I even heard," the barkeep interjected as he handed out more drinks, "That some folks in the outskirts of Edinburgh hae been taken by kelpies." There were a few exclamations of disbelief at that.

Over the whispers, someone burst out, "Seems to me like we should start hunting kelpies all year round. Those southern cities don't know beans about killing kelpies. I heard they think they're just children's tales." There were more grunts of assent, and someone in the group said, "Heaven help us."

I sat, rooted to my chair.

Edinburgh, I thought, the knowledge freezing my heart. A large city.

Glasgow could be next. It *would* be next.

Emilia. My family.

Before I knew what I was doing, I was across the room and standing before the druid's table. She looked up at me, her face tranquil but her voice cold. "Well, lad, here I thought we'd seen the last of one another—"

"Why do you need me?" I cut across her, pressing my palms against the surface of the table, leaning toward her. She kept her eyes locked with mine as she took another drink from her tankard. By her expression, she was still upset with me for how I'd treated her. I *had* been out of line, but I didn't care about that right now. I needed answers.

When she didn't say anything, I exhaled.

"You said you had theories and perhaps a way to finish off these devilish creatures once and for all. Why do you need me?" I demanded.

"Lad, I'm not sure you're up for this," she said, her tone icy. "A city lad like you?"

I slammed my fist on the table, causing the room to fall silent for a moment before the noise picked up again. The druid stared me down with narrowed eyes as I glared back, breathing hard.

"Don't mock me," I said, panting. "I've lost more than I can say to this business, and if I can, I want to help end it."

"Why the change of heart?" the druid sniffed.

Pain bloomed in my chest, and the woman across from me became blurry. I blinked the tears away, though my heart still ached. I looked around the room, realizing that this woman was the only one I felt comfortable sharing my most recent loss, and failure, with.

"They took my sister," I whispered, my voice strained. "Those devils . . ." I sat down wearily in the chair across from the druid, my shoulders heavy. "This afternoon. In broad daylight. Three of them. There was nothing I could—" I paused, biting the inside of my cheeks to keep the anguish at bay. Tears wouldn't answer questions. I looked back up at her, smothering my emotions.

The druid's features softened from knife-like to sympathetic as I continued.

"It happened right in front of me. Again. Maura . . ." More tears blinded me, and I looked away, grinding my jaw.

"What do you need from me?" I asked, feeling as though I was choking on the very air. The druid reached across the table and gently patted my hand.

"There, there, lad. It will be alright." Her expression shifted from sympathy to curiosity. "But, tell me lad, if there were three kelpies, how . . . how did you . . ." Her voice dwindled to nothing as I shook my head.

"Survive? I don't know." I replied in an exhale. "They were coming for me, and then they just turned and ran away."

The druid stared, dumbfounded. "Lad, did you lie to me? Did you keep my relic?" she asked, her voice breathless.

Remembering the leather necklace I'd found in the grass and now carried in my pocket, I reached in and pulled out the polished stone, warm and bright. The druid gasped as I set the amulet on the table, the animal teeth clicking against the wooden surface.

"I thought you said it was gone," she rasped, snatching the necklace up off the tabletop, inspecting the gleaming stone with wide eyes, running a gentle thumb over the symbols.

"I thought it was. I had thrown it away, but searched it out and found it in the brush after you left," I replied. "I was going to return it to you if I saw you again."

Eyes shining with tears, the druid slipped the necklace in her pocket. "Well, thank you for returning it to me. I'm . . . so grateful."

"So, magic protects one from kelpies, then," I murmured, the realization not bringing any life to my numb heart.

"The common folk don't wish to know, so we don't tell them," she sighed, settling back into her seat, her expression more lively now. "Doing so would've brought death to my kind."

"Please," I said, wanting to get back to the matter at hand. "If there is anything I can do to help, I'm your man," I said, my voice hoarse. "Glasgow doesn't matter now. Nothing matters now except the safety of my family. I cannot sit and worry anymore. I have to act. And what you said is true, about the boldness of those beasts coming to the cities, and I believe it after seeing what I did today. All of the United Kingdom may be in danger of being overrun, and if I can't stop it before they reach the cities, then I'll have nothing to go back to. And so *this*," I said, jabbing my forefinger onto the tabletop, "is my business now."

The druid leaned back into her chair, a strange expression on her face. "Well, lad, you've exceeded expectations already."

I waved her away. "Just tell me: Why do you need me, and what is it you need done?"

The druid leaned forward, opening her mouth, then paused and glanced narrow-eyed around the loud, crowded room.

"Don't like to be overheard," she muttered.

"No one will overhear us," I said. The room was so loud I could barely hear the words that were leaving my own mouth.

"Oh no?" she asked, an amused smile curling on her lips. "McIntyre!" she said, not loudly, but with enough force that the elderly man at the table beside us jumped and looked guiltily over at us.

"Dropping a nice eaves on us, were you?" the druid asked him, lifting her tankard to her lips and taking a careful sip. McIntyre and his friends turned away, looking chagrined.

"You seem to have forgotten that village folk love gossip just as much as the city folk do," the druid chuckled as I stared around the room. I locked stares with more than one pair of eyes, and I realized that I had drawn a large amount of attention to us by coming and sitting with a feared druid. I realized she was probably given service here because they were afraid of her cursing this establishment.

"Gossip flows freely, especially among the drunken night owls. Doubly so when a stranger is speaking to the town outcast. Makes for interesting talk." The druid rolled her eyes.

"So what do you suggest?" I asked, barely moving my lips to keep my voice muffled.

"Well, if I'm to understand, you ordered rooms here for the night, did you not?"

When I raised an eyebrow, she smiled. "It's right sweet how you've forgot how attentive country folk can be."

I huffed out an annoyed sigh. "Come along then," I grunted, moving to stand.

"I'll come up in a bit," she said, sitting back in her chair and taking another drink from her tankard. "I don't want folk around here getting unwarranted notions about us, me following you upstairs to your room and all."

My face flamed at her insinuation, but I nodded. "Right," I whispered. "It's—"

"I know the room," she whispered, so soft I barely heard her. I turned on my toes and waded through the tables, aware that several people watched me exit the dining room.

I climbed the stairs to my room and sat down heavily on the hay mattress.

I had only been gone five years and already forgotten the dangers of this place, lost in the luxury of my new life. The events of today had been a cruel reminder.

Silence was a battering ram on my mind. I took a deep breath and shut my eyes tight, willing the horrid memories echoing inside me to go away.

Chapter Twelve

The knocking on the door interrupted my tortured thoughts, and in relief I sprang to my feet, flinging the door open. The druid stood there, holding a tray of food in her hands.

She stepped inside and shut the door behind her with a foot before I could react.

"No one saw me, if that's what you're wondering."

"How?" I asked, eyeing the tray. She would've caused a lot of kerfuffle ordering food and moving upstairs.

"You really dinnae know much about magic at all, do you?" was her simple reply.

"Aye, that'd be the truth," I responded, still a little wary.

"Well, that will be remedied before our time together is through. Anyway, I brought you supper."

The druid set the tray of food on the washstand as I sat down on the bed.

"I already ate," I lied. Looking at the tray—laden with chicken, fried onions, a thick slice of bread, and a tankard of ale—was making my stomach turn.

The druid, who had been in the act of pulling up one of the rough chairs next to my bed, straightened and nodded.

"Here," the druid said, pulling several small, purple flower petals from her circlet. "Hold out your hand." She dropped the petals into my outstretched palm and shook back her hair. "Put those on your tongue and suck on them. They'll calm your stomach so you can eat."

I looked at her, amazed at her perception. I slid the petals onto my tongue. They were slightly bitter, like the milk of a dandelion, but as the petals dissolved away, the painful gurgling in my stomach ebbed and my nausea stopped. I looked at the druid with an awed expression.

"Handy having a druid around, isn't it?" she said with a tired smile.

"I suppose it is," I said, rubbing at the stubble already coming in on my chin. "Thank you."

"Not at all. Now eat up. We have some things to discuss."

I stood as she sat down. "One moment. I promised my sisters I would look in on them." I left the room and knocked on my sisters' door.

Norah opened it, face blotchy and red, but her voice steady. "Slaine is already asleep. We'll be alright, Brennan, we're safe here. You needn't worry."

I gave a curt nod. "Very well. Please try to get some sleep."

"You as well, Brennan," Norah said, her tone soft. She squeezed my hand, then bid me good night as she shut and latched the door.

Back in my room, I sat down on the bed. Taking the tray into my lap, I began to tear away pieces of the bread, soaking them into the juice of the chicken. The bird was flavored with sage and pepper, and my appetite was now roaring.

"Now, lad." The druid paused, her head cocked. "Your name is . . . Brody?"

I shook my head and swallowed. "Brennan," I said, realizing that I didn't know her name either. "And yours is?"

She smiled. "Rhetta."

"Rhetta," I repeated. "Pleased to finally know your name."

"Likewise. Right," Rhetta said, clapping her hands together. "I'll keep you awake for a bit longer, so you understand what you're getting yourself into. But I warn you, it's no easy task, so if you want to withdraw—"

"I'm not going to withdraw, no matter what danger," I said, my voice tired. I had made my decision. The kelpies were a force to be reckoned with, but I'd seen the power that magic had in driving them away. If this magic user had an idea on how to stem the tide of darkness, I'd follow her anywhere. "So, why do you think you can stop the kelpies, and how?"

"Well, lad, I'd rather not tell you everything I know," Rhetta said hesitantly, "until we see if the first part of my plan will work."

I raised an eyebrow, a chicken bone paused halfway to my mouth. She saw my expression and held up a hand. "Now, I know what you're thinking. I intend to tell you *everything*, but I want to ease you into this."

"Because of magic?" I asked, goosebumps rushing up my arms at the word. I assumed she would be using at least some magic to tamp down the kelpies' pull, and I'd have to learn to get over my fear.

A wry smile quirked at the corners of Rhetta's lips.

"Yes, magic is part of it. But not all, and some things must be verified first."

"Well, you must understand my situation," I pressed. "You're asking me to leave my betrothed, my sisters, and my livelihood to try to eradicate an entire species of animal. I'd say I deserve some explanation as to what I'm getting into."

"I understand. Do you trust me?" she asked.

I nearly laughed. We'd only spoken three times in our lives, and on top of that, she was a being with magic woven into her very soul. She was the embodiment of everything I'd feared since I was a small child.

I considered myself a level-headed man, but magic still frightened me, and there were reasons it wasn't to be trifled with. Legends of calamities coming upon towns where magic users resided were based on facts, and they had ingrained in me a healthy fear of the wicked power. Just considering the kelpies was proof enough that magic in any form was dangerous and evil.

However, as Rhetta sat patiently, awaiting my reply, I caught sight of the rock talisman hanging around her neck. The green stone, bright in the dark room, brought back the memories of when I first held it in my hand that night. I had felt warmth where the common folk said I'd feel coldness and evil. It had made the beasts I'd felt powerless against flee like frightened rabbits.

I looked up into Rhetta's face. I couldn't place her age because her face was still young. Studying her more thoroughly, it seemed as though she hadn't aged at all since I'd seen her last, though she did look more tired.

I remembered the pity she had in her face when I'd lost my mother and, just now, my sister. People said magic users couldn't feel human emotion, but when she heard of my loss, that pain that showed in her face was real.

Besides, she seemed to trust me. Trust had to go both ways. Perhaps this plan was going to be dangerous, and she needed to have trust in me to stick with her. Perhaps I needed to show trust to receive trust, and then everything would be revealed to me when the time came.

"I don't trust magic," I heard myself saying, "But I trust you. For now. I expect more explanation in the coming days, though."

Rhetta inclined her head. "Thank you, lad. I shan't take your trust lightly. I just hope you understand that I'll keep some things to myself until you're comfortable with me, and with magic."

"Very well," I replied, taking another hearty bite of bread.

"Good. And as to your assertion that you're giving up your trade and family," Rhetta said, smiling, "I'm happy to announce that if all goes well, Ever willing, you'll be back with your family in a few short weeks."

I started. "What? A few *weeks*?"

"Yes. Once we have everything we need, you can go back to your family. But if, after a few days, you're not convinced that this plan will work, you can leave me at once. How does that sound?"

I didn't know what to say. I had expected months at the very least. How could she expect to stop the kelpies in a few short weeks?

"I . . . I suppose I'm confused. Why so short a time?" I asked.

"Well, it *may* take longer than that," Rhetta admitted. "But if you feel this isn't working out how you imagined, you can leave. I will understand. But remember, I'll explain more when you're more comfortable with . . . my kind."

"Very well, those are agreeable terms. And so I guess we shall see after a few weeks." I shrugged and took a large gulp of ale.

"Excellent. Because our first task is to capture a kelpie."

I choked on my drink and accidentally spat out a mouthful. "Capture? *Alive?*" I coughed, staring at her as I set down my drink and wiped my chin.

She inclined her head again. "Aye. All magical creatures have weaknesses that can be exploited, and we need to find the kelpies'."

I stared at her, wide-eyed. "Is this why you needed young lads to go with you?"

Rhetta nodded. "I need a kelpie alive, and I cannae catch it without help, but no one in town would help me."

"What about your coven?" I asked. "Surely this is something they'd want to help with?"

Rhetta's face hardened. "Those of my coven were too afraid of the task, and after the kelpie took my husband, my coven journeyed farther south, hoping to steer clear of them. I stayed behind because I wanted to do something. I *had* to do something."

I understood how that felt.

"I knew outrunning the beasts would be in vain," she continued. "It's not a threat that can be ignored now. It's a moving, growing danger. So I needed help from common folk."

"But young lads?" I asked. Rhetta's angry expression turned wry, and she chuckled.

"Most young lads know how to bait and hold off a kelpie long enough to kill one, and they're more agile than all the old toads in town. I know how to keep a person from being taken. It would've been a perfect pairing, except I need the creature alive."

"Well, I don't know how to bait and hold off a kelpie. I've never done it before," I confessed.

"Well, that doesn't matter, really. I just need someone *non-magical* to attract the kelpies. And I can keep you safe."

"With your amulet?" I asked.

Rhetta shook her head. "Not exactly, but that's part of it, now that I have it in my possession once more," she replied, though she didn't meet my eye.

After pushing her further as to what exactly her plan entailed, she gave me a quick summary of her strategy. Even though she would be there, using magic to pull me off the kelpie, the venture still sounded like madness. But we had to start somewhere. She sounded confident in her plan, and I had decided to trust her. We wouldn't find out anything until we tried.

"Have you asked around in other towns?" I asked.

"Nay. I decided I would start somewhere I was relatively known, figuring those here would give me some trust. I was foolishly optimistic. Most people here not only mistrust me but fear me outright. These are perilous times, and a stranger, let alone a druid, doesn't garner much confidence. Everyone here now believes I've gone mad and, even though I've mentioned I can help with the kelpies, they're afraid they won't come back if they go with me. Which, considering the circumstances, is all too possible." She fixed me with an honest look and sighed.

"Lad, you must know, you may not come back. This is a dangerous business, and I won't have you going into it thinking you will be safe and protected. I'm sure of my methods and plan, but still, things can go awry. Being aware of that, are you still willing to come with me?" She gnawed her bottom lip, awaiting my reply.

I considered the task she was asking of me. I'd chased after two kelpies so far and was unable to stop either one from getting to their lochs. But I was still alive. Being able to capture one alive would be a feat not many, if anyone, had heard of. Just capturing one alone would be enough to help unlock some of the mysteries of the kelpies.

I looked up at Rhetta.

"How long have you been working on this?" I asked.

Rhetta chuckled in a tired way. "A long time. I had no idea where to begin. I just took every avenue I thought of, and I made some victories and a lot of failures to get to this point. But I think this is as much as I can tell you: once we capture a kelpie, if you're still willing to go on, then I can share more."

She had been working on this alone for years, and she was still alive. That alone was a testament to her protection and resilience. I had to trust that she knew enough of what she was doing to keep me safe, though I would make sure to keep a knife on me at all times. If I did get taken, I could stab the beast in the brain.

So I would either kill my first kelpie, or we'd capture one alive to unlock its secrets. Either way, I needed to get to the bottom of this.

"I understand the risks, and I'll do it," I replied, grim. "As long as you're willing to take along someone as blighted with bad luck as me." I tore another bite from the chicken.

"Hold on there, boy," Rhetta frowned, holding up her hand as if trying to shoo away my words. "What's this you're saying?"

I bit the inside of my cheeks. "It's my fault my mother and sister died. I failed to save them. I'm not afraid to take the blame, I just want you to know, I've had bad luck with these beasts before. I'm witchborn, and I may curse your endeavors now."

"Oh, lad," Rhetta blustered, "*witchborn*? Honestly! There's no such thing! What rubbish. You cannae think that any of these circumstances are your fault!" Her expression turned a little angry. "You are not a failure, and you're not guilty of their deaths. Has everyone in this village rescued a loved one from a kelpie except for you?"

Her words struck me with such force that I couldn't breathe, and I looked down at my lap. I had never thought of it in that way. I had focused so much on how I couldn't reach the kelpies in time to save my mother and sister, when in reality, I was in good company.

"Lad, even *I* couldn't save my husband, and I can use magic!" Rhetta exclaimed. "But I dinnae blame myself. I am trying to do something about it, and you are as well. If anything, I'd say you've done more than those who have been killing kelpies their entire lives.

"I've been around a while, and I've heard plenty of kelpie stories. The villagers dinnae understand the meaning of real courage. The men here may talk big, but none of them will go out in a group of fewer than ten. And even then, they set off running away when one of their comrades gets snatched." She paused, taking a deep breath. "But you, you're different. You have gone out into the black, and you will again. You have courage unseen. I've never heard of anyone running after a kelpie like you did that night we met. Imagine my amazement when we found you out there, searching for your mother, just a young boy. That struck me deep in the heart. You're not failing your sister or your mother. You're honoring them by protecting others." I looked up at her, and she smiled at me in encouragement.

"I have been combing the highlands for the last several years, trying to find a man with such courage as you showed, and I couldn't find one. You are the only chance we have, Brennan."

I nodded my head, swallowing hard. For the first time in all my days, someone from out here in the moors—besides my family—didn't see me as a cursed failure or a coward.

"That's settled, then. Send your sisters off in the morning, and then we will depart as well. Get some sleep, and—"

"Oh!" I said with a start. "My sisters. I told them we were leaving for Glasgow together tomorrow!" I had forgotten them during the course of this discussion, and I felt shame curl in my stomach, but I pushed it away. I had a good reason for my forgetfulness. I had been through hell, after all.

"Hmm," Rhetta said, tapping her lip with a finger. "Why don't you hire a boy from the village to accompany them back home, while you stay here for this? They—"

"No. I am not letting them out of my sight on the moors until they're back in Glasgow," I said firmly, standing and stretching out my back. "I did that once. I won't do it again."

"Lad, I'm sorry, I know things are delicate and painful right now, but this is bigger than you and me," she urged, following me with her eyes as I returned the tray to the washstand. "Or your sisters. If you go back with them to Glasgow, you'll be swept up in your life back in the city."

"You don't know that! My sister is dead! I can never forget that." My voice broke, and I half turned away.

"But the city has a strange way of making the country and its problems seem distant," Rhetta countered, her voice soft. "Rely upon it. If you leave, you will not return. And I need you. You're the only person who has listened to me in five years."

I stared at her. I knew this druid was a very perceptive woman, and I felt that I could trust what she said. If she said I wouldn't come back from Glasgow, I thought grudgingly, she was probably right. Upon arriving in Glasgow, we would plan a service for Maura, and I would be reunited with Emilia, and my trade, and my life would continue. I wouldn't *want* to come back.

"Very well," I said, clenching my fists. "But I'm hiring *two* men from the village to go with them. Do you know any trustworthy people? I've been gone so long, I don't know anyone anymore."

"I know a few men," she said, nodding. "I'll scout out possible ones for the job and let you know tomorrow." She paused, then cleared her throat and dug out a small, polished burl of wood from her robes. It had the same curling symbols as Rhetta's stone. "I know you dinnae care for magic yet, but put this in the back of your carriage, and it should give your sisters some measure of protection on their journey." My heart hurt at the thought of sending them home, but I appreciated Rhetta's care as I took the knotted wood.

"Very well. Do you have a place to sleep tonight?" I asked, looking longingly at my bed, hoping that I wouldn't have to give it up for her.

"Oh, don't be silly, lad. I'll make it alright. You sleep here," she said.

"Are you sure?" I pressed, yawning.

"Yes, yes. I have a few places I can hole up in and not be disturbed. I'll come to you in the morning."

She was out the door before I could say another word. I stared blankly for several minutes at the door she had closed behind her.

I didn't want to think about tomorrow. I couldn't imagine how I would explain all this to my sisters, especially sending them off with the news of Maura to my Aunt Alana, without me accompanying them. What would Aunt Alana think of me when I didn't return with my sisters? That I was shirking my responsibilities, running away from my sorrows? I imagined her and my sisters, sitting at home, wondering if I'd ever return. I knew they'd be angry and confused, but that couldn't be helped. I was staying for the greater good, even if they could never understand. I barely understood it myself.

I had forgotten about the treachery of these hills, the dangers that lurked around every brae. Because of my laxity, tragedy struck. I needed to absolve myself of my mistakes.

I slipped out of my pants and shirt, blew out all the candles, and slid under the blankets. The lumps in the mattress didn't even bother me as I instantly fell asleep.

Chapter Thirteen

A loud knocking woke me from the darkness of sleep, and through the gray light of pre-dawn I squinted toward the source of the sound. A sheaf of parchment sailed into the room from the gap under the door. With a pounding head, I heaved myself out of bed and scooped up the paper, grunting. Taking the parchment to the window for more light, I squinted at the words on the page.

It was from Rhetta, recommending the Dunbar brothers, who worked at the tannery, as those trustworthy enough to take my sisters back to Glasgow. She also instructed where to meet her after I got my sisters on their way.

Sitting heavily on the edge of the bed, the parchment crumpling in my hand, I fought against the memories of yesterday—was it really only yesterday?—as they threatened to crash over me.

I stood abruptly to avoid stewing inside my own mind and went to the washbasin. I splashed my face several times with cold water and then ran my wet hands through my hair, making it stand on end. Bracing myself against the wash table, I watched the water drip off my chin back into the basin. I stared at the ripples that bounced around the bowl, distorting my dim reflection. I reflected that my future, too, was now distorted and uncertain. Unnerved, I combed my damp hair down and dressed back into my clothes from yesterday, tucking the parchment from Rhetta into my trouser pocket as I left my bedchamber. I had to get my sisters up and on their way as soon as possible. The less time they spent here, the safer they'd be.

I also wanted to shield them from the prying eyes and whispers of the townsfolk. News was sure to get out about our loss, and I didn't want my sisters bothered with provoking questions. Despite my reluctance to send my sisters back to Glasgow alone with the sorry tale of our loss, it was better than them staying here. I buried the regret. I had to. I had work to do here.

Though the sun was not yet up, for the next hour, I was a whirlwind of feverish activity. At the stables, I ordered our carriage to be prepared, then sent a message to Merl, telling him he was free to take whatever he wanted from our cottage. Afterward, I went to see the Dunbar brothers—grown men that I vaguely remembered from my boyhood—and commissioned them to escort my sisters home. I offered them a hefty sum for their services, and they agreed to my terms—including my implicit instructions that they not speak to my sisters about anything related to the kelpies, though they gave me some peculiar looks for that.

I began to realize how my mother must have felt after my father died. Shame curled in my stomach at how I had ignored her wishes to avoid talk of the kelpies as a boy. She tried so hard to shield us from the ugliness, despite us wanting to run face first into it.

When I settled up with the Dunbar brothers, I headed back to the inn and ordered breakfast. While I waited, I wrote letters to my aunt and Emilia, detailing different truths as to why I had stayed behind. The letter to Emilia was the most difficult to compose.

My pen paused after writing Emilia's name. My teeth were clenched so hard that they hurt as I stared down at her inked name seeping into the parchment. Would I ever see her again? It was a possibility that I would never see *any* of my family again. I had so much going for me back in Glasgow if I left this mad conquest behind. I had accomplished much after such hardships. How could I give up all that I'd earned to simply endure more hardship and pain?

And yet, if kelpies were to continue their rampage, my future wasn't safe. If by some miracle we did accomplish what Rhetta had in mind and I survived it, then my return home would be even more sweet, and my future even more secure. I knew I couldn't sit idly by if there was possibly a way to end this growing menace. I had to do something, because no one else would.

My resolve hardened at the thought, and I felt a slight measure of peace settle over my heart. Yes, this was the right thing to do, imminent death or not.

My thoughts returned to Emilia. Could I give her hope of my return? Or would I have to tell her not to wait for me? Could I bear the pain of losing her? I shook my head, feeling sick at the thought. No, I couldn't. My hand would not write the words. Instead, I would write a third letter, foretelling of my death and freeing Emilia from our engagement. I would entrust it to Rhetta. She had been chasing kelpies for nearly five years. I was certain she would survive even if I did not.

With that hopeful thought, I completed my communications, telling Emilia that I had been called away on an important matter that would secure our future together, and I would return as swiftly as possible.

I was sealing the last of the letters just as the serving girl brought me my tray laden with bowls of porridge and plates of sausage links, eggs, tattie scones, and a pot of tea. Giving her several coins, I took the tray and hurried the food back upstairs to my sisters' chamber.

Telling my sisters that I was sending them off, without me, was more difficult than I ever imagined.

Slaine burst into renewed sobs as I explained I wouldn't be going with them, and Norah stared at me, her face white as a sheet as I handed her the letters.

"You're going to leave us when we need you most," Norah said, her voice hard as iron.

I exhaled, closing my eyes. "Norah, believe me, I don't want to leave you, but necessity has made it impossible for me to go back just yet."

Slaine, with her lip quivering and her eyes shiny, asked, "When will you return?"

"It may be some weeks. I'm hoping not more than a few months. I'm not sure. This business is strange. I cannot share what it is, but please know I will return." I was resolved not to make my words lies.

"The way you're speaking sounds as though you don't expect to return at all," Norah said, looking horrified. I sat between them on the bed, putting a comforting arm around each of them.

"I'm sorry, I don't mean to frighten you. Of course I mean to come back," I replied, forcing a cheerful note in my voice as I squeezed them tight. "I just don't want you to worry. Everything will be alright. It's just some other business that has come up. But I want you lassies to be safe, so I'm sending you home without me. Please see that those letters are delivered." We sat in the quiet of the darkened, shuttered room, holding each other until I couldn't take the silence anymore. With a final squeeze, I smiled at both of them. "Come, we must get you off."

I could tell Norah wanted more information, but she let me be. After breakfast was eaten and trunks were packed, we left the inn.

We arrived at the carriage just as the Dunbar brothers showed up, each carrying a knapsack over their shoulders, one of them bearing a long Baker rifle slung across his back.

I introduced my sisters, then gave the brothers a stern look.

"I want you to the next inn well before sundown," I commanded, and the brothers nodded, though in my heart I knew that wouldn't guarantee their safety. Kelpies could be out there even now, roaming the hills this early in the morning. My only consolations were the protective knot of magical wood I had snuck into the back of the carriage and the thought that back in Glasgow, they had even more protection because of the size and population of the city.

While the men were busy readying their items, Slaine latched onto my hand and looked up at me with a pleading expression. "Must you stay?" she asked, chin trembling.

"Yes. And you must be off now, little bird," I murmured. As she looked up at me, silent tears dripped from her chin. I crouched before her and gently swept away the wet trails on her cheeks with the handkerchief she had given me. It felt as though a horse had kicked me in the chest as she held my gaze. For an instant, it was like looking into my mother's face. In a heartbeat the moment passed, and I spoke kindly but firmly, almost reassuring myself as much as her.

"I'll be safe. I know you don't want to go alone but you must be brave. I'm doing this so you'll be safe too. I'm doing this for—"

"For Maura?" Slaine asked in a whisper, so only I could hear it.

I clenched my jaw and swallowed hard. A look of comprehension brimmed in Slaine's tear-filled eyes. She understood more about my business than she ought.

"Yes. For Maura. And for you and Norah. And Emilia. I wish I could come back home with you, but I have to do this."

Slaine bit her lip, her eyes misty. "You're trying to protect us."

"With all that I am. For all my little birds."

"Will *you* be safe?" she asked, wiping her eyes with her cloaked arm.

I considered the letter I had tucked into my bag, the one that explained everything just in case something did go horribly wrong and I never made it back to them.

"I'm going to do everything I can to be so." My throat wouldn't stop burning as I stared into her face.

Slaine gave me a fierce hug and held onto me for several moments. With a soft, "I love you, Bren," she broke away and ducked into the awaiting carriage, sobs loud and heartrending. Norah stood apart, looking at me with a hard expression.

Her hug was cold, but like Slaine, she held me for several moments before kissing my cheek and slipping into the carriage. I shook both brothers' hands before they climbed up into the driver seat. Nodding to me, they cracked the whip and the carriage lurched into motion. My two sisters, with tears on their cheeks, waved to me out of the window as the carriage rolled away. I waved back until the carriage passed out of sight.

Chapter Fourteen

I stood, silent and watching, several minutes after the carriage disappeared behind the rolling hills. The brisk breeze tickled my hair and made gooseflesh rise up on my arms, but I did not take it as an omen. I *would* see my family again. This venture would not take me from them, I vowed.

With a sharp exhale, I turned and marched back to the inn. I gathered my small knapsack, paid our dues, and then started toward the north end of the village in search of the druid. The hills that surrounded Bòidhchead were like rising sentries, keeping the village inside a protective bowl, vibrantly green in the spring months. Crossing the stream that fed Loch Bòidhchead, I hurried toward the road that led north out of the town.

As I left the last houses behind, I turned to hike up the nearest hill, which was soft and slippery with mud, searching for the druid. Approaching the road that led to Kinlockleven, I noted how overgrown the path had become. Evidently, no one wanted to brave the dangers of the open highlands. Not far off the road, I saw Rhetta standing against a tree, reading over a heavily creased paper. When she heard me approach, she hurriedly tucked the paper into a pocket of her homemade robe.

"Got your sisters off?" she called, brushing off her hands. I nodded, and she smiled. "Excellent. Now you can focus on the important task at hand."

"Where are we headed?" I asked, unable to shake the somber mood of my recent goodbyes.

I reminded myself that, after a few weeks, if I wasn't convinced of Rhetta's plan, if this whole scheme turned out to be nothing but a mad dream, I could leave. I could return to my life back in Glasgow.

However, most of me hoped as I'd never hoped before that it *wasn't* a mad dream. Because if this plan all came to nothing, I didn't know how I could keep my family safe from the kelpies, aside from moving us all to the West Indies. I'd seen the beasts' growing power, their changing behavior, and if nothing could be done, we would all be doomed.

"We're heading up north. The kelpies originated there, therefore they're more numerous and active the farther in that direction you go, so we'll have more luck finding one in good time. Besides, I dinnae want anyone around here knowing what we're up to. I've caused quite a ruckus around here, and the villagers would try to disrupt our work and drive us out." She led me toward a small cart where a sturdy Highland pony was hitched, munching tender spring shoots.

Climbing aboard, Rhetta plied the whip to her pony. I turned in my seat and watched as the hills slowly swallowed up the noises and sights of my little childhood village. So much sadness and heartbreak had occurred there, yet still people stayed. If you were to even suggest that they leave, you'd most likely get a fist in the face. The beauty of the lochs, the vales, and the rolling hills were enough to stave off any fear they had of the dangers of living in the highlands. They'd grown up here. Their parents and their grandparents and their great-grandparents had lived in these hills, passing down land and traditions, and most wouldn't leave it for a wagonload of gold; even with the increased danger the kelpies posed.

With a sigh, I settled deeper into the bench, facing forward. Rhetta was an expert at handling her fat pony, and we were soon traveling at a brisk pace through the moorland hills.

As a boy, I had never traveled further than the small village of Kinlochleven, and I watched the landscape pass by with curiosity. The landscape flattened out a bit, groves of trees speckling the countryside. In the distance I could see towering spires of rock, some draped with the fragile lace of late snows on their peaks.

I didn't speak for the first few hours, as anxiety about our trek and my sisters kept me subdued. However, as the day wore on and the wooden bench beneath me grew harder and harder, I turned to Rhetta. I was ready to learn, and to be distracted from the ache growing in my backside.

"So where are we headed, exactly?" I asked. Rhetta smiled and gave me a kind look. I got the impression that she had been waiting for me to speak, not wanting to intrude on my thoughts until I was ready to discuss everything.

"There's a tiny town a few hours north called Dèanta Suas. It's not heavily populated, but there are plenty of lochs nearby that will work for our purposes," Rhetta replied. I watched as she twiddled the stone that hung around her neck as she spoke. With a frown, I noticed the symbols on it were different than before.

"What is that, anyway?" I asked, nodding toward her amulet.

"A relic. It took us years to find one like this. I had my husband use it because he was always out in the wild."

"But what is it? What does it do?" I asked, shifting on the wooden bench with a suppressed grimace. It was one thing to travel for hours in a carriage with a padded seat. This trip was going to be long.

Rhetta looked at me, eyebrow raised, mouth quirked into a smile. "You sure you want to know? It's about magic—I know how you feel about magic."

I gave a sharp nod. "Whether I like it or not, magic will be part of my life for the next little while. Besides, that thing saved my life. I reckon I should know more about the powers that be."

Rhetta nodded. "Very well. Let me see . . ." She was quiet for a moment, sucking on her lower lip. "Most magical creatures create and exude magic, like a musk. Druids can too. It's what many mages use to cast spells. Mages draw upon the magic excreted from fantastical beasts and use it for their own ends. Many sentient magical beings such as nymphs, ceasgs, leprechauns, selkies, dunnies, and the like," Rhetta said, waving her hand in the air, "are aware that exuding such magic is dangerous. It makes you prey to those who *can* use the magic. Most sentient or humanoid magical creatures realize they have to find a way to hide their magical trails, so they search out special stones or other natural materials that can absorb magical power."

I nodded to show her I was following her explanations so far. She continued. "Humanoids or those who are thinking, reasoning creatures will wear these natural materials, or relics, around themselves to hide that they are magical. One can change the function of a relic with drawn-on symbols. This symbol, for example," she said as she held out her stone for me to see, "keeps my magic close to me, drawing it into the stone for future use, and hiding most of my powerful aura." The symbol on the stone was square, with a dot in the middle. "The symbol that it had before, the swirling one, sent out magical signatures, to scare away other animals. You can alter relics to do many things at once, like shield yourself, withdraw from others, and so on." Rhetta's pony began to slow, and so she cracked the whip again, earning an annoyed whinny from the sumpter, but he picked up his pace again.

"The stone or metal relics—or wood from the wych elm trees, in a pinch—will absorb the magic for years," Rhetta continued. "If the creature with a relic dies, they leave the relic behind, now full of many years' worth of magical power.

"Witches, sorcerers, druids: we're always looking out for relics. They're very rare, as magical creatures are long lived, and don't usually die out in the open. We obtained this one," she touched the stone again, "in the lair of a very ancient ghillie dhu."

"A ghillie dhu?" I asked, a giddy sort of shiver running through me. "Really?"

My father had told me the story about how, as a young boy, he had gotten lost in the woods one evening, and a ghillie dhu had found him. My father had said the stout creature had fed and cared for him that night in his burrow and had led him home the next morning. Upon his return, the village had been terrified that the creature would come after them. No matter how much my father had tried to explain that the little fairy man meant them no harm, the villagers had hunted the woods for days, desperate to exterminate the magical threat, but to no avail. The ghillie dhu had disappeared, never to be seen by my father again.

Could it have been the same one? It was unlikely, but the thought left me with a lingering ache for my father. I imagined he would have been proud of me for talking with a magic wielder about mystical creatures. He hadn't feared magic as most did.

"Aye. Not many left of them out in the world, unless they're all in deep hiding," Rhetta said with a sorrowful tone. "The poor elfin creature was on his way out when we found his lair, shown to us by several children who had received gifts from him through the years. The ghillie dhu recognized us as druids and gave the relic to us as a show of good faith. I tried to save the wee man, but it was fruitless in the end." She fell silent as the sun disappeared behind a blanket of darkening clouds.

At that moment, a chorus of shrill screams broke through our silence, and sweeping chills rushed down my body. I twisted in my seat toward the sound at the same time Rhetta did. Rhetta's pony didn't seem bothered by the frightening shrieks.

Across the valley, unmistakable in the sunlight, was a band of seven kelpies, charging together across the heath.

"Dinnae worry, lad. You're with me. Besides, this is enough to protect us," Rhetta said, clasping the stone around her neck. At that moment, I saw the symbol etched on its face shift. It changed from the square with the dot, to the swirling pattern again, signifying that magic was now radiating around us like a protective veil.

We watched as the kelpies stampeded across the moors, trumpeting and squealing, their manes and tails rippling green in the sunlight.

"Now that's not a sight you see every day," Rhetta breathed, her voice tight with emotion. "Kelpies oft travel alone, unless they sense prey and are fighting to get there first. More proof the kelpies are evolving, traveling in bands like true wild horses."

The sight continued to send chills down me as we watched the beasts prance and charge, until they disappeared behind a moorland hill. I exhaled, long and slow. My hairs were still standing on end, and I rubbed my arms, trying to chase away the sensation. I hated how entrancing the steeds were, how beautiful and alluring, when I knew what they could do. What they had done. My mind flashed with the memory of fiery eyes and mossy-smooth hides snatching away Maura, my mother, and my father.

"So . . . so you draw magic from that stone, then?" I asked, pointing to the relic, desperate for anything to keep the tide of fear and sadness away from my mind.

"Aye, and other sources. We use the magic from all natural things. Plants, animals, and even certain minerals have magical properties. Those fyre faeries Daimh and I captured the night we met you were to be used to imbue more relics for our safety." She gave me a sad smile. "Power can even be drawn from malevolent creatures, like the shellycoat or beithir, if you can get near enough. But we druids only use magic naturally acquired, to help heal, grow, and cleanse."

"A beithir?" I spluttered. Recalling the tales of those unfortunate enough to be stung by the draconic beast. "You've seen one? How are you still alive?"

Rhetta smiled at my awed expression. "I've personally never collected magic from the great wyrm, but I've heard stories of those who have."

"Isn't its magic evil?" I whispered.

"No," Rhetta replied, shifting in her seat. "Magic is merely a source of power, neither good nor bad, but can be used for both. The creatures' evil disposition is what makes the magic seem evil. Darkness isn't a property of magic. Most animalistic creatures are not deliberately evil; they just act according to their nature, which can be dark or light, and so the magic reflects this. Collecting the magic doesn't hurt the creatures, because magic is a secretion, like sweat or poison."

I tried to imagine how one went about collecting magic from a mythical beast. Was it like milking a cow? I tried to put the mental image of milking a beithir out of my head.

"So, do the creatures attack you if you try to take their magic?" I asked.

"No, not usually, especially since most creatures like that cannae *use* their own magic for themselves. Do you understand?" She must have caught my frown of bemusement as I tried to follow her explanation.

"So, creatures like a nymph cannot cast spells?" I asked.

"To an extent. They cannae cast spells like humans can, such as turning someone into a toad, but they can enact magic that is part of their nature; magic that is singular to their species. For example, nymphs are extremely persuasive, and can make you do things against your will. Selkies have magic to turn into a human and back to a seal again. That's magic. Humans are the only creatures that can draw magic from other entities and use it to cast any spell."

"So then, is there a difference between witches and druids? Why are witches so universally feared if they use the same magic druids do?"

Rhetta sighed. "Witches are a difficult issue. The process one goes through to become a witch is what sets them apart from druids, or from any human that can wield magic, for that matter. Choosing to become a witch can make a person dark, and they get even darker if they allow themselves to slip further down the path of evil." When she saw my bemused expression, Rhetta laughed.

"We druids are humans, born with a flurry of magic in us. Of course, many humans can *learn* to use magic if they have the ability to hold magic in them. And if they do, they become sorcerers. A witch or warlock, on the other hand, was once a human that had no capacity for magic, no magical spark in them whatsoever. To use magic, they have to become an entirely different creature. No longer human, really. Witches become darker, more evil, more cunning because of what is required of them for the transformation."

My breath caught, remembering the tales from my boyhood. "Human sacrifice," I whispered.

Rhetta nodded, her knuckles tightening on the reins. "Yes, some witches, the very darkest ones, perform human sacrifices. There can be good and pure witches and warlocks, but they only become such after making amends for the horrible acts they committed. Others have to be blessed by mythical creatures to gain their powers, which is incredibly rare.

"However, no matter what way they obtain power, they leave the human race behind, as magic has entered unnaturally into their essence, and more often than not has left them warped. There were many, many witches centuries ago, but most have been wiped from the face of the Earth by each other, vying for power."

"Witches have wars?" I asked, amazed.

"Oh, aye. Witches are known for destroying one another and hoarding the knowledge that they obtain, wanting to be the most powerful. Not all witches, mind you," Rhetta said quickly, "but there's that stigma for a reason." Her face turned sad. "It has sent magical progress back into the dark, so not even we druids know what all can be done with magic. Much knowledge has been lost concerning the power, and only now that nearly all the witches have killed each other off has some magical knowledge come back into the world. But its reemergence has been slow, because, well, we're all afraid. Afraid of being preyed upon. There are still people out there, rare as they are, that will kill you without a moment's notice, for your magic."

"So you don't use your magic?" I asked.

She tipped her head from side to side. "We use it as little as possible, only when we need protection. Many creatures dinnae like feeling other creature's magic, for fear of being hunted. Even dull, animalistic creatures shy away from magic that isn't their own."

"Which is why you couldn't catch a kelpie before and need my help?"

"Just so. The magic made the devilish beasts avoid me. Even a relic as good as this one wouldn't be able to shield all my magic. This one is small compared to other, more powerful relics, like those of pure crystal or of metal."

I bit my lip, my mind whirling. "So if magic can be felt, and witches have wars to kill for magic, what about druids? Have they been nearly wiped off the face of the Earth by infighting?" I asked, thinking about the fear her coven had when Rhetta told them of her husband being taken by the kelpies.

Rhetta shook her head. "No, no, we're not so ambitious as those who become witches and warlocks, and we've been able to keep relatively hidden from the interest of other, stronger covens and individuals. Besides, more humans than you'd imagine have the propensity for magic. But, again, as magic is so feared, most don't even know it."

We were quiet for a time, and I watched the blooming gorse pass as I mulled over everything that Rhetta had said.

I had been thrown into a confusing, dangerous world of magic and the supernatural, one I'd actively avoided most of my life. Now, in this campaign to end the kelpies, I would need to immerse myself in this world. I would need the knowledge to help destroy the kelpies.

As I mulled over our impending task, the ridiculousness of what we were trying to accomplish finally hit me so hard I chuckled aloud.

"What?" Rhetta asked, smiling.

"I just can't believe we're going after an entity that has been around since the dawn of time," I replied, shaking my head.

"Oh lad, you don't think we'd be so foolish as to accomplish something like that, do you?" Rhetta asked, plying her whip to her slowing pony.

"Isn't that what we're doing?" I asked, amused.

"Lad, kelpies haven't been around since time began. They haven't even been around for two centuries." She cast me a sideways glance, and my smile dropped into a frown of confusion.

"What?" I asked, clenching the side of the bench.

"When I was a young girl, kelpies were mere myth. And that was more than ninety years ago. They've expanded aggressively. Before that, no one really knew what a kelpie was."

I stared at her, startled into silence. As shocking as this revelation was, something she had said was even more striking.

"You're ninety?" I blurted. Rhetta glanced at me and smiled at my flabbergasted expression.

"Ninety-nine. I look good for my age, aye?" she asked, casting me a wink.

"How . . . how . . . ?" I sputtered.

"Magic, lad! How else?" She laughed, snapping the whip again as I pondered this newest revelation.

Magic. I'd been so fearful of the power, I never considered what could actually be accomplished with it. To think, living beyond your natural years and still looking younger than forty? My mind whirled.

We lapsed into silence again, Rhetta driving her wagon into the distant, darkening horizon.

Chapter Fifteen

F or the next hour, we passed occasional squares of land where farmers had hacked out a living for themselves between the small thickets and rolling hills.

We had come around a small knoll when a large loch, far in the distance, came into view. The loch was bottlenecked on either side by two large highland cliffs. On the very narrow bank, I could see lights shining in the hazy darkness of the storm, signifying a small settlement nestled up against the hillside.

Rhetta stopped the wagon and my heart began a drumroll in my chest.

"Here we are. This should do well. These other lochs should have kelpies in them," she said, pointing to two smaller lochs in the distance, "they're far enough away that they won't all have been butchered from living so near a village."

Rhetta hopped down from the driver seat and began fishing something out of the back of the wagon. The breeze had turned chilly, and I could smell rain on the air. I took a deep breath to steel myself and jumped to the grass. Clenching my trembling hands, I hurried to Rhetta's side where she was pulling two heavy coils of rope from the wagon bed.

She held out one end of the larger coil toward me. "You take this end to tie about yourself; I'll take the other end," she directed as I took the rope in my hands.

It was coarse, yet thin enough that I could easily tie knots in it. I hoped it was stronger than it looked. I quickly lashed the cord around my upper chest and under my arms, securing it with a knot. All my time on ships had given me confidence so far as knots were concerned—this knot would not come loose until I wanted it to. I noticed as I ran a finger over the braided fibers that my shaking hands had calmed. Surely a kelpie wasn't as bad as a storm-tossed sea, where never-tiring waves threatened to pull you under to the creatures that lurked below.

"I'm sorry, lad," Rhetta said, interrupting my thoughts, "but I'll have to move far away, else I'll frighten any potential prey."

I nodded, feeling less frightened than before of the task ahead of me, though my heart still beat against my chest in a rapid cadence. I exhaled sharply, hoping that any remaining fear wasn't showing through my determined expression.

"Dinnae fight the beast as it pulls you onto its back, lad. I dinnae want you to be injured before we've even begun," Rhetta instructed. As I beheld Rhetta's tiny frame, I worried that she wouldn't be strong enough to overcome the blasted beast's mysterious pull before it took me to a watery grave.

"Remember, we need hair, and you need to try to pin the beast to the ground once it's knocked off its feet," Rhetta admonished. I nodded.

"Right, well, off you go," she said, looking out across the wind-whipped hills. I turned to follow her gaze, and I could see a black curtain of rain billowing toward us. "Dinnae forget your knife and the other rope."

I took another deep breath, gripping the short but freshly sharpened knife in my hand, and flung the other heavy coil of rope over my shoulder.

"Good luck, lad," the druid said, her tone solemn, barely intelligible over the rising wind. Without another moments' hesitation, I set off toward the uninhabited loch, steel gray and choppy. Rhetta followed me at a distance, uncoiling the rope as I trekked away. I turned as I heard Rhetta's shout of, "Hya!" and watched her cart trundle away, trailing rope as it went.

Climbing up the nearest knoll, I saw the glint of village lights visible off in the distance. They quickly disappeared as the rain hit. As the fury of howling and lashing rain pummeled me, I stood on the flooding grass, waiting. Within moments I was drenched, shivering in the gathering darkness, every gust of wind a banshee, every rumble of thunder the pounding of kelpies' hooves.

I turned the cold, dripping knife over in my hand, shifting my weight from foot to foot, rope draped over my shoulder, trying to ease the pounding in my chest with deep breaths. I was sure a kelpie could feel my quaking heart from across the valley. I tried reassuring myself with thoughts that I'd faced storms worse than this, on a ship that nearly sank. This wouldn't be nearly as frightening as the maw of the ocean opening to swallow me whole.

I pivoted in a circle, watching the horizon on all sides, all the while making sure the rope around my chest didn't tangle around my legs. I hoped Rhetta had time to find a tree strong enough to help her pull me off the kelpie, because I doubted she would be able to hear me in this tempest.

I strained to see beyond the rolling hills, searching for any spectral shape. For a brief moment, my mind went to my sisters. They would be at an inn by now—at least I hoped they were—and soon they'd be home. Safe.

A screech broke my thoughts and I turned, my heart nearly bursting at the sound. Somewhere in the distance, I heard echoing screams as hooves, methodical and heavy, surged toward me. Coming out of the rain like some terrible thunderhead, the kelpie loomed over me, roaring and snorting.

My mouth went dry as I met its gaze, and I felt the tell-tale sign of its power as my feet began involuntarily moving toward the panting beast. White mist gusted from its nostrils as it bucked once before ducking its beautiful demon head toward me. Before placing my hand on the beast's hide, I jerked hard on the rope around my waist, doubting that Rhetta felt it.

My heart pounded a deafening beat in my ears, visions of the past flashing before my eyes as I placed my hand on the kelpie's shoulder, its silky black hair slick and mossy. My feet left the ground, and I was thrown up onto its back, the beast snorting and bucking, trumpeting now that it had its prize.

Gripping its mane, I glanced back in the direction I had come for one brief moment. The rope appeared slack. The next second, the horse screamed again, rearing up on its hind legs.

I shouted, "Now!" with all the power of my lungs, hoping I was heard as the demon horse darted down the knoll, the thunderous hoof beats crashing in my ears.

I fumbled with my knife, my hands tangled in the thick mass of mossy-black hair. My vision swam, flashes of colors and faces interrupting my sight. The galloping nearly upset my grip, and for a few frightful seconds I thought I had dropped the knife, losing it in the heavy, wild mane. After several frantic heartbeats, my hands grasped the polished handle as it slid toward the blurred ground. With two swipes, I cut a few locks of hair free from the beast.

I uncoiled the rope around my shoulder, my movements jerky as the horse pounded closer and closer toward the wind-tossed loch. I was unsure if the howling was from the speed of the dark horse, or from the beast itself. Making a quick loop in the rope, I moved to hook it around the kelpie's neck.

At that moment, as the rain and wind pummeled me, the jolting feel of the horse speeding into a sprint beneath me, memories from long ago flooded unbidden into my mind's eye.

Wind howled. I hauled on the rope, my legs burning, arms straining as another wave bashed against the side of the ship, throwing up an icy spray, drenching my already soaked skin. I was so used to the sloshing waves on deck that my eyes no longer stung from the salt.

I was too afraid, too tired to be seasick. The storm had come up unexpectedly, and the sails needed to be raised. I slipped on the wet wood of the deck, colliding painfully with the base of the mast.

"Lennox!" the captain shouted somewhere behind me, hidden by the rain and waves, "Get yer sorry hide up!"

Gritting my teeth, I staggered to my feet and hauled on the rope with the other shipmates, raising the sails up to those who lashed them to the yards above.

I'd never been so physically drained as I was at that moment. The cold did nothing to numb the pains that burned in my body like fire.

A shout went up, unintelligible over the roar of wind, and a wave smashed against the side of the ship, knocking me clean off my feet. I slid into the rail, fighting against the rush of water. I heard someone shouting as I felt my body tip over the railing, falling toward the heaving ocean below. I hit the icy sea and the lifeline tightened around my belly.

Sharp, intense pain jerked around my middle, an ear-shattering squeal broke the vision behind my eyes, and the world snapped upside-down. The air was knocked out of me as I was wrenched off the kelpie. I was suspended in the air for a brief moment before I slammed into the muddy grass. My vision flashed black and yellow as somewhere beside me the ground shook as the kelpie was knocked off its feet.

A shrill ringing drowned out all other sounds as I rolled onto my back and lay on the rain-soaked ground, mouth stretched wide, but no air entered my lungs. My vision threatened to black out entirely, but after several terrifying seconds, I inhaled the chilly air, my vision no longer swimming. I sucked in greedy breaths, my entire body searing with pain as I coughed on the rain spilling into my mouth.

Within a few moments, the ringing began to recede, and I heard more screaming over the wind, though it seemed to be growing fainter and fainter before disappearing entirely. I lay gasping in the noise of the storm, wind whipping my soaked shirt, icy rain coursing down my skin, not caring if the kelpie was coming back for me or not.

More shocking than the pain thumping through my body was the realization that I had ridden a kelpie and survived. The thought almost took my breath away again.

After a few moments, I heard the murmuring of voices nearby. I tried to sit up, but my body didn't respond. I contented myself with remaining supine, though the cold was now tempering the heat of my aching body and seeping into my bones. A few moments later, I could hear Rhetta's words. She wasn't alone.

"Do you think it worked? Do you think we pulled him off?" I heard Rhetta call, her voice thick with worry.

"Well, the rope is still here," I heard a second, unfamiliar woman's voice reply. "The question is whether the kelpie is still here, too? Or did it escape?" The new voice was brisk and hard.

"I reckon we would hear the kelpie if it was still here. But what if the rope wasn't strong enough and it broke—"

"Oh look, what be tha'?" the new voice interrupted, and I heard running footfalls approaching.

"Brennan?" Rhetta called. I raised a trembling hand, wondering if I could be seen in the darkness, as I was still unable to speak. I lowered my arm as two figures, just dark shadows in the shroud of rain, loomed over my sprawled form.

"Oh, lad!" I heard Rhetta gasp, falling down beside me. "Thank the Ever, you're alright!"

I merely grunted.

The darkness fled as a flameless orb of light burst into being in the rain above us, revealing a soaked Rhetta kneeling and staring into my face, and a younger woman standing behind her.

"I got the hair," I wheezed.

"Well, it's pretty useless since we dinnae have the kelpie tha' goes with it!" the stranger replied, exasperated, and I frowned.

I had just survived riding on a kelpie. I didn't think my contribution had been completely useless. But I didn't say anything aloud.

It would take too much air, which I was still desperately trying to catch into my lungs.

I took one final deep breath, praying that my body wasn't actually torn in half before forcing myself to sit up. I groaned, wincing as pain lanced down my side.

"Careful, now," Rhetta called over the lashing rain, "You've just accomplished something no one has ever done before. Take things easy. We dinnae know if there are any side effects from riding a kelpie and living to tell about it. Magic and all that."

"Well, besides almost getting broken to bits, I feel well enough," I coughed, my vision spinning for a moment as I sat up straight. The cold rain was helping to numb the pain throbbing in my body.

"Let us see the hair, lad," the stranger said impatiently, holding out her hand to me. I looked up at the newcomer, squinting to see her features through the rain. The light above us illuminated her face. She was smaller than Rhetta, with a young, very pretty face. Long auburn hair was plastered to her body with the rain, and her deep blue eyes seemed to crackle with fire. I slapped the soaking blackish-green hair into her hand.

She took it, rubbing a forefinger down it. "Well, now tha' we know one can get off a kelpie and survive, we may get to the bottom of this yet. Ever preserve us."

Rhetta helped me to my feet, and I stared at the pretty stranger.

"Who are you?" I asked, trying to keep the groan out of my voice.

"I'd rather not stand here in the rain and discuss it," the new woman said with a hint of irritation. "Come, let us go back to me cottage. We'll make introductions there."

Together the three of us made our way back toward Rhetta's wagon, the new woman gathering up the rope as we went along.

"So, tell us lad," Rhetta said, turning to me and shouting over the hiss of rain, "What was it like?"

"Riding a kelpie?" I asked, hobbling alone behind.

The stranger snorted. "No, she's asking about having tea with the king and queen. Dunce," she muttered.

Ignoring the woman, I shook the rain out of my eyes and looked to Rhetta. "It was strange, I . . . I was taken back to when I was a young boy, back on my uncle's sailing ship."

"A memory?" Rhetta asked.

"Aye, from my first voyage. It was so real, so clear. I truly felt I was back there."

The two women were silent for a moment as we reached the wagon, and the stranger heaved the sodden rope into the back of the cart.

"An effect from the kelpies?" Rhetta asked the woman, who shrugged.

"Perhaps. Maybe it's how they keep their prey docile while being taken to the loch."

"Intriguing. We'll have to study more of this," Rhetta said, getting up into the wagon. "Anything else out of the ordinary?"

I shook my head. "Not that I recall."

"Well, let's discuss this more at me house, please," the stranger snapped, and we all climbed into the wagon, eager to get out of the rain.

Chapter Sixteen

The storm was still raging when Rhetta pulled her wagon up to a cottage, hidden in a copse of trees beside a steep highland cliff that blocked out most of the sky. I recognized the hill as one of the cliffs that bottle-necked the loch on the opposing side, where the settlement resided. The new woman and I hopped out of the cart, my movements slow and hobbling, and Rhetta maneuvered her wagon into a small shack set behind the cottage.

"Come, come," the stranger clicked, ushering me out of the rain and into the cottage, where embers smoldered in the hearth. The woman hurried to the fireplace, and the fire danced to a blaze, casting flickering shadows over the furniture.

The woman set a kettle on the flames, then busied herself lighting candles around the room. In a few moments, the cottage lost its eerie atmosphere, becoming cheerful and warm.

While the woman was busy clattering dishes, I studied the room in which we stood. The kitchen was small, smaller than the one in my childhood cottage, but its many windows made the room feel larger than it was. The room also held a table that would seat four as well as a cupboard tacked to the wall above a rickety counter for prepping food beside the fireplace. Looking up, one could see the roof thatching between the rafters.

I rubbed my hands together, hoping to get some warmth back into them as I kept silent. We didn't say anything for several minutes. I stayed beside the door, looking anywhere but at the woman. It was highly unseemly for us to be here together without a chaperon, as this woman looked about Norah's age.

Rhetta came bursting through the door, her lips blue but smiling. Shaking her dripping hair out of her eye, Rhetta asked, "Is there tea?"

At that moment, the stranger was pouring boiling water from a kettle into a teapot.

"In a few," the woman said, setting out saucers and cups, a half loaf of pound cake, and a few dry biscuits.

Rhetta shed her dripping cloak and placed it over a chair beside the fire. "Goodness, lad," Rhetta said, pulling out a chair for herself, "Come sit down. You look dreadful."

I could imagine so. I was soaking and covered in mud from my fall.

"Aye, dinnae worry about ruining my chairs with your filthy clothing," the new woman said, rolling her eyes.

"Perhaps introductions should be made," I replied. I looked to the woman, straightening. "My name's Brennan Lennox of Glasgow. What is your name, miss?"

"Ooh, *miss*, is it?" the young woman said with a sneer as she turned to stoke the fire. "Where did you find this *fine* city *gentleman*, Rhetta?"

Rhetta clucked her tongue as she took a slice of pound cake, casting me an apologetic expression. "Dinnae mind her, lad. She's just—" Rhetta began.

"I can introduce myself, Rhetta *dear*," the woman snapped, straightening from the fireplace. She turned to me, an almost defensive look on her face. Clearly she wasn't happy I was there, though I didn't know what I had done to cause her offense.

"Me name's Eimhir," she sniffed, crossing her arms, fire poker still in hand. "And I wasn't expecting some too-good dandy to be in me kitchen, demanding information from me."

"Don't be so cross, Eimhir," Rhetta chided. "I told you this morning that I was bringing him."

I turned to Rhetta, confused at how she could've told this woman this morning that I was coming, but Eimhir interrupted me before I could ask any questions.

"Yes, but did you tell *him* where you were bringing him?" Eimhir asked with an arched brow. "I asked you in me note if he knew about me. So, *did* you inform this—" her eyes flicked me up and down, "fine-looking man who *I* am? I dinnae need the Ever-hating villagers to discover me and come and drive me out if he gets frightened and tells people where I live."

Something clicked in my mind as she watched me from across the table.

Rhetta hadn't wanted to tell me what we were doing, and she certainly didn't tell me if there were others involved in our cause. I had a feeling Rhetta would have told me there were others to help us, unless that person was someone even *more* undesirable than a druid.

Which meant this woman . . .

I stepped back, a sick feeling rising in my throat.

The woman before me put her hands on her hips, staring me down. I took in her appearance with new eyes, now that I knew what she was.

I'd never seen a witch before, but I'd heard the stories, the myths. Yet all of them didn't prepare me for the truth as it stood before me. I hadn't expected witches to look so . . . young. And quite beautiful. I felt wrong-footed just looking at her.

Her youth was making me most uncomfortable. Witches were supposed to be old, unkempt, and evil to the core. They were supposed to live in swamps, curse you on sight, and smell of sulfur. But this young woman had an air that commanded respect. Her home was tidy. Comfortable, even. Witches were not supposed to be organized, serving tea and pound cakes on patterned dishes like a lady. Everything I had heard of witches was crumbling in the face of this woman, and I had no lifeline to hang on to.

I had a feeling I would become more disillusioned with this journey, but for now, I had to remember that witches weren't to be trusted. And yet, Rhetta had brought me into the home of one. I took a deep breath, trying to keep my voice calm, but I heard it shaking as I addressed Rhetta.

"You spent most of the time on our journey up here telling me how terrible witches are, and now you're working with one?" I breathed. "And brought me to her abode?"

"Ever knows I certainly didnae ask for you to come," Eimhir snapped, and Rhetta shot her a quelling look.

"I said *most* witches, lad, remember," Rhetta replied, her voice stern. "Some witches have goodness in them."

Eimhir snorted. "Thank you for the glowing compliment, Rhetta dear."

I looked to Rhetta, who was nibbling her pound cake, her eyes darting between me and the witch. The witch didn't take her eyes off me.

"Rhetta, how could you work with . . . with a . . ." My voice died in my throat as I tried to say the word.

"*Witch*, lad," Eimhir sniffed, folding her arms over her bosom. "A witch. 'Twon't curse you to say the word aloud."

"Fine," I said, trying to keep the tremble from my voice, "A *witch*." My lips curled into a snarl at the word. Eimhir's own lips twisted into a narrow smile as we stared each other down.

"She's been helping me over the last several years," Rhetta hurried in. "I'm sorry I didnae tell you earlier, at the inn," Rhetta explained, her expression sheepish. "I was afraid you'd abandon the cause if you found out a witch was involved, before you even saw what was possible tonight. Just think about what you've done! You survived riding a kelpie! That has never been done before. I wanted you to see some successes before we brought, well," Rhetta glanced at Eimhir, "witches into it. I was afraid you'd refuse to help."

"Yes, I probably would have. I still might," I said, clenching my fists to keep from running out the door that moment.

All the stories of villages getting razed by witches resounded in my mind. Where a witch went, destruction followed.

"Rhetta, may I speak with you in private, please?" I asked through clenched teeth.

Rhetta looked to Eimhir, who was looking more and more contemptuous.

"Eimhir, would you give us a few moments, please?" Rhetta sighed. Eimhir, rolling her eyes, marched from the room into her bedchamber, slamming the door behind her.

I turned to Rhetta, anger blazing. "What are you thinking, working with her?"

Rhetta held out her hands. "Brennan, remember how you thought druids were dangerous too? And I'm not! Now, while witches are . . . more dangerous than druids, not all are pure evil. There are all types, and Eimhir isn't so bad. Besides," Rhetta paused as I made a disparaging noise, "she's willing to help us!"

"Oh, and why is that?" I asked. "I don't trust her willingness to help with anything unless she has something to gain from it."

"She does," Rhetta said, "The same thing you do. Her family."

I hesitated, a snide comment freezing on my lips. Rhetta patted the seat beside her, and against my better judgment, I sat.

"Witches don't have families," I replied blankly as Rhetta poured us tea.

"Aye, most do not that they care about, 'tis true. But a few do, and Eimhir did." Rhetta took a sip of her tea and sighed.

"Are the members of her family witches too?" I asked, fear turning my insides cold.

"I cannae tell you that. It's her story to tell." Rhetta set down her teacup and looked me squarely in the eye. "Brennan, please, if you listen to her story, you may change your mind."

I snorted, and Rhetta pressed on, her tone patient. "Lad, aye, it's true that witches are more volatile than any other magic user, but witches are scarce in these parts. And though our magic protects us for now, she knows as well as I that soon it might not be enough to protect us. The kelpies are growing in such strength that they can come out in daylight. It won't be long until they're immune to their fear of magic, too. And then those of us with magic will be in danger of being taken as well."

"Good. Let all the witches be killed off. So much the better," I snapped.

Rhetta's expression turned sad. "Magic, as weak as it was, didnae protect my husband. Or Eimhir's loved one." We stared each other down, not speaking until Rhetta sighed.

"Oh, lad, put aside your naive prejudices and listen to her. Aye, she's cunning, and rather barbed sometimes, I won't lie about that. I myself didnae trust her for a long while, but I dinnae think we have to worry about her," Rhetta said, glancing toward the bedroom door that Eimhir had shut herself behind. "I am not ignorant about witches, lad, dinnae think me a fool on that account. If she were any other witch, I wouldn't trust her, but she *is* different. And, well," she glanced again at the shut door, her voice dropping to a whisper, "Eimhir isn't strong in magic at all."

"What do you mean?" I asked, my eyebrows contracting so much I could see the dark line of my brow just above my sight-line.

"When one wields magical power," Rhetta began, "one can tell the amount of power in other magical people. In her, it's basically nothing. Her magic is only a little more than a decade or two old."

"How do you know? What if she lied about her magical strength?" I asked.

"One cannae falsify the amount of power one has in themselves, whether it's pretending you have more or less than you really do," Rhetta explained, "especially from someone who is magically stronger than you. Yes, magical creatures can shield themselves from everyday magic seekers with relics, but once a magical creature's power is exposed and targeted, their amount of power can be discerned, and they cannae diminish the amount they have."

My head spun, not totally understanding what she was saying, but I let her continue without interruption.

"I was able to inspect Eimhir's power fairly easily, as I'm older and stronger than she, and she is barely a witch. But she has motivation, and she's very clever. Besides, magical power isn't just about casting spells. She's a very good potion maker, stronger than I am in that regard, but I dinnae fear potions. They're used by those who cannae do real magic," Rhetta said, her tone a little disdainful. "If anything, she shouldn't trust me, yet she does. And she has suffered loss like the rest of us. For that reason, she's willing to help us."

"Help us how?" I asked, still wary but intrigued. What about this whole business would make Rhetta turn to a witch for help, no matter how weak in magic the she-devil was?

"Well . . . we need a witch's expertise, because . . ." Rhetta began slowly, sucking on the inside of her cheek.

"Because the kelpies are a witch's creation from long ago," Eimhir interrupted, stepping out of her bedroom.

"*What*?" I barked.

Rhetta cried, "Eimhir!"

Eimhir brushed Rhetta's accusatory glare away with a careless wave. "'Twas agonizing to wait in there, while you were dancing about the subject," she snapped, "and the boy needs to know. Might as well be now. He's already disgusted, a little more disenchantment 'twon't hurt him." She fixed me with a look, matching my horrified expression with an equally defiant one.

"The kelpies are a witch's creation, and who better knows the mind of a witch than a witch?" Eimhir sniffed. "I know how they think, and I've been working with Rhetta to make a counter-curse to this plague. But it's been taking too long. Only now have we been able to get the hair from a kelpie, so we can finally move on to the next step."

My thoughts were snarled in a mess of questions, not only about my own morality in talking with this witch, but also with curiosity at their plans. I grabbed the first question that came to my mind, hoping that answers would start to sort out the tangle of emotions inside me.

"Why would a witch do such a thing?" I asked, ignoring my cooling tea and resting my forearms on the table. "What would they have to gain from such a creation?"

Eimhir slid into the seat across from me with such grace I could almost imagine she was a refined young lady of society. Eimhir shook back her hair and mirrored me, resting her forearms on the table.

"Witches, despite popular belief, like to create, not just destroy. We are constantly searching for ways to make a spell more potent, a potion more long-lasting." She gave me a twisted smile, "Or a curse more horrible, if you like. We are also creatures of emotion. The dark rituals to become a witch deepens our feelings, so what was a minor slight before becomes a major insult, and jealousy can turn to an outright murderous rage if you give in to it. It's a temptation tha' I fight every day, especially now tha' me—" She cut herself off, hurt dashing across her face.

"Especially now that what?" I asked. Eimhir looked away, refusing to say more.

I turned to Rhetta, trying in vain to keep the anger out of my voice. "If what you're saying is true, then I need to know why we are agreeing to trust you." I looked back at Eimhir, but silence met my question. Rhetta glanced at me, then at Eimhir, who was refusing to look at either one of us as the storm lashed the windows.

I frowned at Rhetta.

"It's her story to tell." She shrugged, her tone apologetic.

I exhaled, realizing I wouldn't get anything more out of Eimhir about her past.

"Fine, if you won't say any more about that, how did you two meet?" I asked the room.

Rhetta looked to Eimhir again, impatient this time. "His questions all concern you. Do you want to tell him?"

Eimhir glowered at me, her lip curled, and she replied, "No. I'll not share my most distressing details with this . . . *well-born* gentleman." She said the word "well-born" as if it were a curse.

I laughed, the sound humorless and brittle. The irony was only apparent to myself. It seemed I couldn't get anyone's trust, as I was either considered witch-born or well-born.

"What distressing details?" I snapped back. "You claim to have deep emotions, but I don't reckon witches can feel *anything*."

Eimhir's look of disgust curled into a smile that sent shivers down my spine.

"Oh, that's enough, you two!" Rhetta replied, interrupting our heated glaring. "Fine, Eimhir, we won't share that story until you're comfortable with Brennan and he's comfortable with you, alright?"

Eimhir looked me up and down one last time, something suggestive in her look, and I studied my teacup, feeling hot around the ears.

"Very well," Eimhir replied, a suppressed laugh in her tone.

Shaking her head with a sigh, Rhetta turned to me. "Brennan. Just trust *me* for now, won't you? Keep asking questions. We'll answer them as they come."

"Very well," I said, repeating Eimhir, avoiding her gaze. I looked around the house, wondering what else to ask. "How long have you been working on this problem, Rhetta?" I asked, my voice barely audible over the thrashing rain. Rhetta sighed, sorrow now etching in her expression.

"Ever since my husband was taken, which was about six months after I met you. My coven left shortly after, and I traveled north alone for a few years, trying to find someone to help me, and I ran into Eimhir, where we struck a deal to help one another find a cure for this plague."

I stared at the kelpie hair Rhetta had placed on the table, uncomfortable. "So, you only needed me to get you some kelpie hair?"

Eimhir replied, "Yes," just as Rhetta cried, "No!"

Eimhir rolled her eyes and continued. "We tried speaking to villagers who killed kelpies, asking them to give us some of the hair or hooves or anything, but ye ken how superstitious mortals are about kelpies," Eimhir said with a roll of her eyes. "They want to touch the kelpie as little as possible, and cutting off a keepsake—"

"It's bad luck," I finished, the memories from my boyhood surfacing.

No one kept the hooves or heads from the kelpies in their houses. The moment a kelpie was killed, it was tied down with stones and sunk into the lochs. Bobby Reid once kept a few strands of hair from his first kelpie kill, and his house caught fire a week later. No one was killed, but it reminded everyone that kelpies scourged anyone who handled their remains heedlessly.

"Precisely. Humans think horrible things will happen if they disrespect the kelpie's dead body, so we were unable to progress.

But now we can move on because you're here." Eimhir didn't look pleased.

Ignoring her glower of disapproval, I asked, "So, what's the hair for?"

"We needed the hair to add to a potion tha' will strip away the spell—" Eimhir began.

"Revealing whether the witch cursed a real horse, or made the animal out of thin air," Rhetta interrupted, making Eimhir cast her the glare she'd been reserving for me. "We won't know until we add the hair to the potion Eimhir made and test it on a kelpie," Rhetta finished, glancing at Eimhir, who rolled her eyes. I sat back in my chair, thinking hard.

They'd been working for years on this, yet were unable to work directly on a kelpie, which made me feel uneasy. They were basing everything on conjecture, and I couldn't, in good conscience, remain working with a witch simply on wild guesses.

"How do you know for certain that kelpies are a witch's spell?" I asked. They had yet to show me any concrete evidence, and my hope was dwindling that this scheme would bear any fruit.

"Well, all mythical creatures create magic, but kelpies do not. That's one way we think it's a witch's curse . . ." Rhetta said slowly, glancing helplessly at Eimhir.

"But how do you *know*?" I demanded.

After a quick glance at Rhetta, Eimhir stood, her chair groaning against the wooden floor, and she gestured toward the door. Rhetta also stood, and both women looked down at me.

"We'll have to show you," Eimhir replied simply.

Chapter Seventeen

I trusted Rhetta enough that I decided I would see what they had to show me. But I warned them as I stood up from the table that if whatever they showed me wasn't enough to allay my fears of working with a witch, and didn't prove that whatever plan they had would yield results, I was walking out that very night.

Eimhir laughed at my declaration and strode out of the house into the pouring rain, taking the kelpie hair with her. Rhetta gave me a pleading look and gestured for me to follow. Steeling my nerves, I hurried after her.

Outside, the howling wind, pounding rain, and the distant cackling of creatures seemed to swirl around us. We hurried to follow Eimhir's figure through the darkness as she came to a stop at the steep hill. Bending down, Eimhir pulled up on a large, leafless bush. The bush was resting on top of a large plank of soil-covered wood that hid a long tunnel entrance. Propping open the hatch, Eimhir summoned orbs of light from nowhere and then ducked into the tunnel, Rhetta following without hesitation. I watched their progress as the lights got smaller and then disappeared, leaving the entrance in total darkness.

"Shut tha' door after you!" Eimhir called, her voice resounding up from the black burrow.

Courage, man.

I entered the tunnel, taking out the long pole Eimhir had used to prop up the door as I did so. The trapdoor fell shut, truly settling me in the pitch black. Running a hand along the wall to navigate the tunnel in the darkness, I was surprised to find that the walls were not the texture of loose dirt, as I had imagined them to be, but were as smooth as the marble floors of the entrance hall in Emilia's family home.

I followed the hallway until the wall curved, and I could see a dim light around the corner. I turned, following the brightening light until I stepped inside a large domed room, carved in the center of the hill. A few hand-sized holes peppered the ceiling above, and though they were choked with shrubs, they allowed fresh air and some rainwater from the torrent outside to seep in.

Inside, two long tables ran down the center of the room, and innumerable shelves placed into the walls were stacked with cauldrons, clay pots, bound herbs, animal skins, glass bottles filled with mysterious liquids, and a few hand-bound books. Three areas in the room bore the scars of cook fires. One of the fires was lit, with a heavy metal cauldron sitting in the embers. The two women went to the cauldron on the orange coals, and I followed behind. Inside the pot, a reddish-brown concoction steamed.

"What is this?" I asked, stepping away. It looked a lot like old blood. Memories of the gruesome wounds that sailors had sustained on the high seas passed through my mind.

"Give us a moment, and you'll see," Rhetta replied. "Dinnae touch it."

"Aye, you dinnae need to drink a potion for it to affect you," Eimhir called at my disgusted look. "If you get it on your skin, it can still work its magic on you, but more slowly and painfully."

Eimhir and Rhetta had placed themselves at the table nearest the cauldron and were pulling out a few earthen bowls. The other table held a large, rusted birdcage that was filled with several grouse. I wandered over to the shelf that contained the handmade books, which were merely stacks of papers bound together with leather strips and thin sheets of wood as covers. Curiosity besetting me, I opened one. Inside, handwriting and sketches traveled down the pages.

"My journals," Eimhir called from across the room, where she was setting down a few of the items in her arms. "I've written them all myself. Everything about every potion, spell, and curse I've created, especially notes on things tha' didnae work. I dinnae have much written down, because I haven't done much," she replied, her tone sour. I felt ill as I stared at the book in my hand. This represented the fruits of witchcraft. What was I getting myself into?

Eimhir, who had been watching me, seemed to read my thoughts and called, "I needed a place to work my magic, and I wasn't going to do it in me house. If the villagers ever discovered what I am, they would try to burn down my home, and I didnae want any of my items damaged. It took me years to accumulate all of this—years of travel—and it wasn't easy collecting most of it. Now, put tha' down, boy, and get over here," Eimhir called. I frowned. Eimhir looked even younger than me, and I didn't appreciate being called a child when I'd accomplished far more than Eimhir ever had.

I slapped the cover shut and went to their table. When I reached their side, Eimhir looked me in the eye.

"Rhetta and I have been working on this specific potion for the last three years, testing it on those birds," Eimhir said, motioning toward the birdcage. "It's only been the last few weeks tha' I got it perfected, and tha' was when Rhetta went back to Bòidhchead to find us a witless apprentice such as yourself."

Rhetta clicked her tongue, her brows drawn together, and looked at me, hands twisting together.

"So, ready to test it?" Rhetta asked.

"What, now?" I sputtered.

Eimhir snorted at my tone. "Oh aye, do you have a fancy ball you must get to this evening?"

"So this potion will end the whole curse of the kelpies?" I asked loudly, ignoring her jibe.

"Dinnae be a daft tumshie, we're not nearly there, yet," Eimhir replied. "But one dose will take the curse off the one water horse we feed it to, if I've done me work right. Which I have," she added, as if afraid I'd question her abilities.

I did question them, not believing a potion could do such a thing, but then again, I was here to learn, and contradicting a witch didn't seem like a great idea.

"Very well, if it's ready, I'm ready, I suppose," I said, wincing at the welt around my middle where the rope from earlier this evening had burned into my skin. I would be worse for wear before this night was over.

The storm still raged outside Eimhir's cave. Although the thunder and lightning had stopped, sheets of rain still plummeted from the ebony black sky.

Screams echoed through the torrents, but Eimhir and Rhetta kept with me as we went out to the hills, their magic staving off any premature kelpie that wanted to come upon me before I was ready. Rain dripped down our faces and turned the landscape into a dark blur. We picked a spot, and I helped the women set snares to the bases of the sturdiest bushes and saplings we could find around where I would be standing. Their hope was that the snares would make it easier to bring down and restrain the demon so the potion could be administered.

"Now, here's your rope and knife," Rhetta shouted over the downpour. "Only use the knife as a last resort. If we dinnae bring down the kelpie and cannae pull you off, stab the beast in the brain to kill it and keep it from taking you away. Hopefully the snares will do their job and the knife won't be necessary. Then you must keep the beast down until we have time to work the magic."

I merely grunted, too anxious to reply.

By the time the ropes were all set, the wind had picked up, and rain had begun to fall even harder. Rhetta wished me luck, and then both women departed to hide, disappearing from view through the gray curtains of rain. I brushed my wet hair out of my eyes and scanned the horizon for signs of approaching demons, holding the soaking rope, my hands blue with cold. I steeled myself mentally, not wanting to be distracted by my boyhood memories again.

The two women were barely out of sight when I heard the pounding of hoof beats and the panting squeal of water demons.

I turned toward the noise of the creatures, and two beasts came bearing down on me, smaller—but only just—than the one I'd faced only hours before. The pull toward the kelpies had yet to begin as I unwound the rope from my shoulder, and my eyes locked onto the nearest beast. It bowed its head, sniffing for me, and I jumped up onto its back without waiting for the magic of the animal to compel me up.

The animal froze to an almost statue-like stillness as I landed hard on its back, no doubt in surprise at how willingly I had jumped on. Taking advantage of its bewildered state, I whipped the rope down the animal's side, around its belly, and up the other side. Catching the end with fumbling fingers, I quickly tied a knot as the demon got over its surprise.

The second kelpie shrieked and darted off into the night. I tightened the rope hard, and the animal backed up, squealing in pain. As it retreated a few steps, I felt the great beast stumble. Hoping its foot found purchase in a snare, I took advantage of its confusion to loop another part of the rope over its rain-slicked neck as I clung to the thick mane, draping the cord down to encircle its legs, rain blurring my sight.

Flashes of memory from the first time I went fishing with my father threatened to swarm my mind's eye, but now that I knew this was the kelpie's doing, I focused harder on my task and my anger, pushing away the flood of memories. I was here to bring this beast down.

The beast bucked, trying to bolt away, but the ropes around its legs made it stumble. While it tried to catch its footing, I hauled myself to the side as if trying to heave myself off the animal, keeping a tight grip on the rope around the great beast's belly. The kelpie, wrong footed and unsteady, screeched and tottered, and with agonizing slowness, finally fell onto its side.

I bellowed as the great beast toppled, and with desperation, I wrenched my leg out of the way, narrowly avoiding being crushed as the beast landed on its side. As the kelpie hit the ground with an earth-trembling thud, I found myself freed from its back. Rolling away from the flailing beast, I got to my feet as quickly as I could on the slippery grass and pulled the rope, trying to keep the animal down and confused as it thrashed its legs, trying to right itself.

"Hold him, lad!" a voice shouted off to my left. I never took my eyes off the animal as it tried to stand. I jerked the rope around the beast's middle, my sore muscles screaming against the strain, and the kelpie rolled back onto its side, wildly fighting against the tangle of lines.

In a heartbeat, the witch and the druid were standing over the flailing kelpie. Rhetta threw herself onto the kelpie's neck, pressing her hands to the rain-slick muscles of the beast, chanting unintelligibly. The kelpie suddenly appeared to be moving through thickening air, its flailing hooves slowed, its rocking body barely moving. Despite being almost frozen in motion, the kelpie's squealing intensified with panic. Eimhir got to work, tossing more ropes over the kelpie to tack it down to the moor. There were moments when the storm drowned out Rhetta's chanting, and the kelpie would kick its hooves for a brief, ferocious instant before slowing again.

"Move, lad! Help us!" Eimhir shouted, a wild, dark look in her eye. I leapt to the witch's side, careful to avoid the sharp hooves of the kelpie as it regained another burst of strength to resist Rhetta's spell. The kelpie continued to scream relentlessly as I helped Eimhir pry open the kelpie's mouth.

Holding open the demon's jaw required all my strength and concentration, as the horse tried to jerk away and bite us. I had no desire to lose fingers. Though Rhetta's spell helped slow the kelpie's movements, the beast was still powerful, requiring me to fight against its strength until my muscles burned.

Eimhir added fresh kelpie hairs to the urn that held the potion and poured the steaming concoction into the kelpie's mouth, which I kept pried open, my fingers cut and bleeding against the demon's teeth. The kelpie choked and squealed, trying to fight against our hands as Eimhir fed more and more potion into its mouth.

"Hold, Rhetta!" Eimhir shouted as the kelpie gave a vigorous shake of its head, knocking me backward. With a growl, I leapt back and wrestled the beast's mouth open again while Rhetta kept herself pressed to the kelpie's neck, her chanting now a shout.

When the last dregs of the potion finally disappeared down the beast's throat, Eimhir and I stumbled back, afraid of getting brained by the frenzied beast that was regaining its strength, while Rhetta continued her chanting. I waited with bated breath for the potion to take effect. Rain poured down, and Rhetta's voice was lost in the rain and screams of the kelpie as it fought against its tangled bonds.

I stared down at the beast, studying it in the light that I only now noticed above us. Eimhir must have conjured it the moment she appeared.

I'd never seen a kelpie for this long before. Despite being a demon, it was a beautiful creature. Its hair shined, powerful muscles rippled beneath its hide, and its large eyes rolled with what I imagined was fear and rage.

With a final shout, Rhetta threw herself away from the twisting beast and rolled to her feet. Steam began to issue from the mouth, nose, and ears of the kelpie, and the frenzied animal's screams only increased. I had to clap my hands over my ears, but it seemed to do no good, the sound battered against my skull and into my very being. I felt the noise would rend me apart. I closed my eyes, not wanting to watch for fear I would be sick.

At that moment, the witch grabbed my arm and my eyes snapped open.

"*Look*, lad!" she bellowed, pointing. I looked at the kelpie, and through the rain saw that the beast looked smaller. The kelpie before us began to shrink, the mane and tail shortening, the hair turning from a black-green to a light brown, and the body turning from black to translucent white. With a final shriek that became more of a wail, the kelpie slumped and stopped moving.

But it was no longer a kelpie.

Before us, lying wet, pale, and naked in the soaking grass, was a woman.

Chapter Eighteen

The storm had tapered off to barely a drizzle as we sat, silent, inside Eimhir's cottage. A fire snapped in the fireplace, filling the room with its comforting warmth. I felt nothing but numbness as I studied the woman seated before me, my emotions too close to the surface to really speak. I ran a hand over my trembling mouth, feeling sick as I stared at her.

Human.

Kelpies were *humans*, trapped in a cursed form. My hair stood on end as I considered the truth sitting before me. The implications of such truth . . . my sister, my mother, my father . . . I shook away those thoughts. If I dwelled on them, I would break down. Instead, I focused on the curse itself.

I had always known that witches were not to be trusted, but in light of this newly discovered depravity? I felt . . . I couldn't name what I felt. Waves of warring emotions threatened to overwhelm my concentration, so I pushed them far down, wrenching my attention back to the kelplie-turned-woman.

She was middle-aged, with barely visible silver streaks in her curly brown hair. Her skin was unnaturally pale, and she had a body shaped like a pear. Rhetta had dressed the strange woman into some of her own clothing, draping a shawl over her shoulders to help hide the snugness of the dress. The woman's damp hair hung limp down her back, her eyes distant and hollow. She seemed not to hear Rhetta trying to coax a response from her.

Rhetta and Eimhir had been busy plying the woman with hot stew and lavender tea, practically forcing food and water into her unresponsive mouth for the last half hour. After successfully getting some nourishment into her, the woman started to come out of her stupor.

Rhetta was patting the woman's hand, asking questions, though the woman remained unresponsive. I looked to Rhetta, and then to Eimhir, who was standing beside the fire, watching the woman with a frightening intensity.

Had both women known that kelpies were humans? Why wouldn't they have told me?

The woman made a strangled sort of noise that broke me out of my accusatory thoughts, and my attention snapped back to her.

"That's it, dear," Rhetta was encouraging. "What is your name?"

I watched as the woman's eyes darted around the room, her expression a bit wild, though she didn't make another sound. Rhetta sat back in weariness. She had been beseeching the woman ever since we got her out of the storm. *If this woman could come back, if she could be saved, maybe . . .* No, I couldn't think about what this might mean for my family. Right now, I needed to focus on getting answers. And for that, we needed to break through this woman's dazed mind.

"What is your name?" I asked, putting a gentle hand on hers. My deeper voice made her jump, but she locked eyes with me. In them, I saw the pain of unthinkable horrors, but some of the fog seemed to clear from her pale green eyes. Rhetta caught my attention, nodding in encouragement to speak again.

I patted her hand softly. "What's your name, ma'am?"

"Me . . . Me n-name . . ." she said faintly. "Me name is Maighread." Her voice was barely a whisper, and the look on her face was one of wonder, as if she couldn't believe she had a voice. "Maighread," she said, and in the same breath she said, "and me 'usband's name was . . ." She paused, her face working as she struggled to remember. "Ramsay," she choked, tears spilling down her cheeks.

I gave her hand a reassuring squeeze, though my heart was fighting to beat out of my chest. "It will be alright."

"Where are you from, dear?" Rhetta asked gently. Maighread looked to her, the unshed tears in her eyes reflecting the firelight.

"Er . . ." she gurgled, her eyes darting around the house. "I'm from . . . from—Morvich. Near Loch . . . Loch Duich." Her voice nearly gave out.

"Tha's a little north of here," Eimhir whispered, taking a seat beside me.

"Aye, Morvich," Maighread said with more conviction, and a light seemed to grow in her eyes as her voice gained strength.

"Maighread," Rhetta began, her voice breathless, "do you remember where you were before you came to us? Do you remember what happened to you?"

The light in Maighread's expression went out immediately, and her eyes grew round and fearful as she shook her head, closing her eyes tight.

"Maighread?" Rhetta soothed.

"No . . . No, no, no," Maighread muttered.

"Maighread, you're safe now. You're alright. Please," Rhetta urged, but Maighread sank deeper into her seat, a spasm of terror crossed her face, her eyes still pinched shut. My heart twisted at her expression. It was obvious she remembered at least some of it.

Rhetta looked at me, pleading. I scooted closer to the frightened woman.

"Maighread, it's alright, you don't have to be afraid anymore," I murmured, lifting her trembling hand and wrapping it in both of mine. I could feel the fear, the terror, in her small, cold hand. She kept her eyes closed, but her hand flexed under mine. She uncurled her fist and gripped my palm as though she were afraid I would disappear.

"Maighread," I pressed, careful to keep my voice gentle despite my impatience for her answers. "Please. We need your help."

With labored slowness, she opened her eyes, her brow still furrowed in fear.

"Just think," I urged, keeping my tone light. She was our greatest well of knowledge about how to end these creatures. "Take your time. Do you know what happened to you?"

Maighread took a deep breath, gripping my hand for strength.

"I remember . . . now that . . . now that I'm no longer . . ." Her voice caught, and she let go of my fingers and buried her face in her hands, her shoulders trembling with sobs.

Rhetta wrapped an arm around her shoulders, murmuring soft, kind words and handing Maighread a handkerchief. "Tell us what you remember, dear. You're safe now."

Maighread took a shaky breath. "I'm . . . I'm terribly sorry. I dinnae remember much. But, I do remember always feeling so lonely I thought me 'eart would break. Now that I'm no longer . . . *it*, I do remember what 'appened to me. But while I was . . . *it*, everything was kind of a blur, just darkness and hunger." I watched as she took a drink of her tea, on her own this time, and she breathed in a steadying breath. "I just 'ad this drive, this need, to find someone, anyone, and keep them with me. Nothing else mattered. I felt I'd die if I went back . . . back to the loch alone." She exhaled, long and slow, as a few tears escaped from her eyes.

"Can you tell us what happened the moment you were taken? Please," Rhetta pressed, and Eimhir made an impatient noise that Rhetta quelled with a look.

"Well, I was taken . . . What year is it?" Maighread asked suddenly, looking up at me.

"Eighteen hundred and twelve," I replied.

She gasped, her face draining of what little color had been there.

"Maighread, are you alright, dear?" Rhetta asked. It was a moment before Maighread spoke again, her voice hollow.

"I was taken in the autumn of seventeen 'undred ninety-four. I 'ad been out late on accident, and . . . Eighteen years," she whispered, and she felt her face, pulled her hair over her shoulder, and looked at the wispy ends. She then looked to the window, where her reflection stared back at her from the dark glass. "I was forty-six when I was taken . . . 'Ow am I still forty-six . . . after *eighteen years*?" she asked, her voice strangled. Eimhir made a small sound, and

I looked to her, where she was gripping her hands together and pressing them to her mouth, her eyes shiny with tears. When Eimhir caught me looking at her, she quickly stood and made herself busy at the fireplace.

"Magic, my dear," Rhetta whispered.

"Ma-Magic?" Maighread gulped. "'Ow . . . 'ow was—"

"Dinnae worry, we're not here to hurt you," Rhetta assured, interrupting her. "What else can you tell us?"

Maighread took a deep breath. "I was taken to Loch Duich. The kelpie plunged in the water, and then . . . I remember my body changing, my mind changing, and then, I just remember wandering the moors, looking for someone, anyone, to comfort me. To be with me. When I found someone, I dinnae ken why, I couldn't 'elp but bring them back to the loch, any loch. But once they . . . changed . . . it was as if I was alone again. So I'd search out someone else. It was never-ending sadness."

I shook my head. Her existence sounded like hell. To have no control over her actions—to have her power to think and act for herself warped—she was just as much a victim as those she'd lured away. Driven by magic, she had been a slave to these devilish whims and emotions.

Anger, hot and quick, churned my stomach. It wasn't the kelpies' fault, I realized. Whoever had cursed them was to blame. Whatever *witch* had made them was no human, had no proper feelings or compassion. We had to end this curse. Half of my family was stuck in this twisted state, lost and alone, reaching out for someone to help them. Before tonight, there had been no one to help them. But even now, no one but the witch who created them and the four of us sitting in this cottage knew the truth.

The thought made my vision blur with tears. I blinked them away before anyone noticed, but my resolve deepened. I wouldn't stop until they were all freed. Maura had only just been taken, but it made me ill to think of her suffering. I realized that despite the enormity of our discovery, our efforts to change back all the kelpies would never be enough. Only the three of us were working on this against an army of thousands of kelpies. We had to find some way to speed up the process, for not only were people in danger of the kelpies, the kelpies were in danger of the villagers.

I rubbed a hand across my brow, a headache forming as I thought with horror about the kelpie hunts. Kelpies were sure to be hunted all year 'round, now that they were coming out during the day. What would happen when the country learned what the kelpies really were?

"Do you know why the kelpies are becoming more bold?" I asked. I felt bad for making Maighread re-live her pain, but we needed to learn all we could. "Why are they coming out during the day, and no longer keeping to the highlands?"

Maighread bit her lip. "I dinnae ken. Daylight 'urt me eyes when I was *it*, but me desires became so strong that I would brave the sun's rays and go out searching anyway."

Rhetta turned to me, whispering to keep out of earshot of Maighread. "The spell must be strengthening over time. Or perhaps the witch is doing it out of pure vindictiveness."

We all fell silent, contemplating what we had learned. Rhetta refreshed Maighread's teacup.

"'Ow did you . . . change me back?" Maighread asked.

After a look of trepidation, Rhetta smiled. "We'll not bother you with such information," Rhetta replied. "That's not important. What is important is that you're safe."

Eimhir, who had returned from the fireplace with her composure intact, sat down across from Maighread and looked her in the eye, her expression hungry.

"Tell me, Maighread," Eimhir began, glancing at Rhetta, who nodded, "Have you heard of any powerful witches or warlocks up where you lived? Anything at all?" she pressed.

Maighread, who had been taking a sip of her tea, shook her head. "No, why?" she asked, looking between all of us.

Eimhir seemed to deflate a bit, and Rhetta shook her head in warning at Eimhir.

"No reason. Well, will you be able to get home?" Eimhir asked, her voice tired. Startled, I sat up in my chair.

"What do you mean?" I began, "We need to question her some more—" Eimhir cut me off by standing and leaving the cottage, walking out into the night. I looked to Rhetta, who gave me an apologetic smile.

"Don't we need to ask her more questions?" I asked, glancing at Maighread, who was looking around the cottage with curiosity.

Rhetta shook her head and whispered to me, "She's given us all we can use." She turned to Maighread. "We can take you to an inn for tonight. Will you be able to find your way home from there?"

I stared open-mouthed at her. I had so many questions for the poor woman. Surely we should keep her around for a few days? Not only to see if more of her memories came back, but also to see if the spell held and she remained a human.

Maighread shook her head, her expression fearful. "I dinnae ken if I still have a 'ome. Me 'usband was taken a few years before I was." Maighread's eyes suddenly widened, and her cheeks flushed. "Could ye 'elp 'im come back?" Rhetta leaned away as a panting Maighread reached out, clawing at Rhetta's dress. "Can ye 'elp? Can ye get me 'usband back?" she urged.

"My dear," Rhetta said, laying a hand on Maighread's shoulder and pressing her back in her chair. "That is what we are trying to do. But I'm afraid it's a very difficult road ahead of us to bring everyone back. The kelpies have been expanding and taking hundreds, thousands of victims for decades, and we cannae just turn each person back one at a time. We'd be turning people back for the rest of our lives and beyond, and the kelpies would still be taking people. We wanted to get to the source of the problem, which is—"

"None of your concern," Eimhir interrupted, coming back into the cottage, dripping wet and carrying a small vial in her hand. "However, you've been a great help. Ready, Rhetta?" she asked, coming to stand beside Maighread.

Rhetta nodded, looking resigned. "We wish you all the best in finding your family, Maighread," Rhetta replied, standing.

"Ready for what—" I began.

"Now!" Eimhir commanded. Plucking a hair from Maighread's head, Eimhir slipped the long strand into the vial of potion in her hand. The potion bubbled.

Rhetta pinned Maighread down, and Eimhir forced the confused woman's lips open and tipped the vial into the woman's mouth.

"What are you *doing*?" I shouted, standing and charging toward Eimhir, but both women had already let go of Maighread. Rhetta held out a hand, stopping me in my tracks.

"I'm sorry, lad. It's the only way."

"Only way for what? What are you doing to her?" I demanded as a blank look came over Maighread's face. Rhetta leaned forward and whispered things into Maighread's ear, too quiet for me to hear.

"We've erased her memories of when she was a kelpie. She'll have no recollection of ever being one," Eimhir replied.

"You erased her memories? Eighteen years of her life?" I nearly shouted.

"They were not pretty memories, lad," Eimhir sniffed. "We erased all knowledge tha' she was a kelpie from her mind, and she can go on with her life."

"Why are you doing this?" I whispered, staring at Maighread, who still had a dazed look on her face as Rhetta stepped away.

"She could give us nothing more, and we cannae have her going around touting about turning kelpies back into humans," Rhetta said, her tone apologetic. "Eimhir and I discussed it for many weeks, and we decided that erasing their memories is the best way to avoid any human interruptions."

"But what about her family? What will they think when she turns up from the dead?" I demanded, feeling sick as I watched Maighread look around the room, her eyes glazed.

"Lad, if people find out kelpies are humans, magic users will come under even more scrutiny," Eimhir snapped. "We'll be chased off or chased down by those who want their families back. You saw Maighread's reaction when she found out what we were doing. Imagine the entire country behaving so. We gave her ideas as to where she might have been, and she can essentially choose the one tha' fits best, and she'll make her way home and explain it to her family. Tha's the most we can do."

I opened my mouth to argue, but Rhetta put a hand on my shoulder.

"We cannae focus solely on one person. There is too much work to be done for that. Hopefully once we find the remedy, we can put everyone's memories right."

I stared at Maighread, who was sitting motionless, seemingly unaware we were there.

"How . . . did you erase her memory with just a potion? Why did you put her hair in it?" I asked, unable to keep the disgust out of my voice. "Why not use a spell?"

Eimhir sighed, then glanced at Maighread. "She won't be lucid for a few minutes more. I suppose I have a moment to explain to this dullard about potions."

She settled in her seat, seemingly uncaring that the woman beside her was as blank as a slate.

"Potions can be quite powerful magic, but they're very difficult because the ingredients are the hardest things to come by. Especially fresh pieces of someone you're trying to focus the magic on, which is why most witches and warlocks dinnae rely on potions. But I have to.

"No doubt Rhetta explained how weak in magic I am," Eimhir said, glancing at Rhetta, who nodded. "I've worked most of me magic this way, since, well, me strengths are not in me physical spell-making.

"This potion I gave to Maighread was nearly ready to go. It's raw power tha' will do what I brewed it for, it just needed the final connection to be made, usually with pieces of magical animals or a person, depending on what the potion is for. It's a method I use on most of me potions, because they can be tailored however I want them, at a moment's notice. As this is a memory-erasing potion, I needed a bit of the person whose memory will be erased, and add it immediately before consumption. But the hair has to be very fresh for it to work, which was why we didnae use the very first kelpie hair you brought us. Once we got back to the cottage, it was worthless."

Maighread shifted in her seat, a small sound escaping her lips. As she slowly came to herself, I noticed her eyes were less hollow, her expression less weary and weighed down. When she spoke several moments later, there was no hint of trauma, or hurt, or memory. The pain of the knowledge of her previous existence was gone, and so were the nightmares that no doubt would have haunted her the rest of her life.

"Well, thank ye for the lovely visit, dearies," Maighread murmured, rubbing her eyes as she slowly came back to herself. "I—" She paused, again looking confused.

"Dinnae worry," Eimhir whispered to me, for I had been gripping the tabletop as I watched Maighread come out of her stupor. "She'll be right soon enough, once she latches onto a memory idea."

"I'll take you to town, dear," Rhetta soothed, helping the woman stand from her chair, "We'll give you some money for an inn and on the morrow, you can commission a carriage to take you where you want to go."

Maighread nodded. "Thank ye, love. Very kind of ye," she replied, bustling over to wait by the door.

"We can't let her go out in this!" I hissed, standing so quickly my chair clattered backward. I saw Eimhir roll her eyes.

"There's no use in waiting for the rain to stop. It'll be raining like this for the next several days," Eimhir replied. "Best get her on her way now."

"I have some rain screens. We'll be alright," Rhetta added. Maighread seemed oblivious to our discussion, her expression going slack every few moments.

"At this hour?" I demanded as Eimhir handed Rhetta a small leather bag that clinked.

"I'll knock at the inn until someone wakes," Rhetta reassured, tossing a heavier shawl around Maighread's shoulders. "Dinnae worry, laddie, I won't leave her alone until I know she's well looked after."

Before I could say another word, Rhetta took some rain screens that hung on hooks beside the door and ushered Maighread out into the rain, taking a lamp from the wall as she left the cottage. I stomped to the open door and watched as they climbed into the wagon that sat inside Eimhir's barn, where the pony was still hitched up. With a crack of Rhetta's whip, they faded into the sheets of rain.

I worked my jaw, glaring into the night.

Eimhir came up beside me, sighing. "Time is of the essence now tha' we've made progress. As Maighread didnae know of any witch or warlock, we need to move on, busy ourselves changing back someone who *will* know of a powerful witch near where they lived."

"How can you be sure that people will know where witches reside?" I asked, failing to keep the scorn from my tone. The late hour and the shock of our discovery was making me more ill-tempered than I'd been in years.

Eimhir smiled another snake's smile at my angry expression. "Trust me, a magic wielder with enough power to make this curse would be well known by those he or she lives near."

I took a deep breath, trying to further calm my tumultuous emotions. I hated this feeling of not understanding this world of magic and monsters that I'd been thrust into.

"Why do we have to find the witch? We already have an antidote."

"This is *not* the antidote," Eimhir scoffed, gesturing toward the now empty urn that had held the potion that changed back Maighread. "This is a potion tha' reveals the true form of the creature who consumes it. The potion is powerful enough to dispel whatever curse was holding it in a false form, but it's a single dosage, it takes a long time to make, and it will not solve the entire problem of the kelpies."

"Can't you just make the same spell that the witch made?" I huffed. I struggled to calm myself, but my face flushed with anger and impatience. I leaned against the doorframe, taking deep breaths from the cool, rain-washed breeze from the open door. The familiar smell helped soothe my heated temper.

Eimhir shook her head, chuckling. "I forget how ignorant you are. It would be impossible to find the exact replica of the spell the witch used to create the kelpies, and making one of our own wouldn't fit our needs. It's possible tha' a spell wouldn't be strong enough to keep the kelpies human. Every witch has their own style of spell-making. We need the spell exactly as it was cast, directly from the one who made it. Otherwise we'd be using my potion to turn kelpies back into humans for the rest of our lives, and we want to change them all back, all at once, if we can. The fastest and most reliable way would be to find the witch and get the exact spell from her."

I grumbled, remembering the time and effort it had taken to change back just one human. It would be impossible to maintain this method and hope to turn all the kelpies back in a reasonable time.

"So how would we do that; find her, and get her spell?" I demanded, eager to stop being "ignorant."

"Well," Eimhir sighed, plopping down into a chair, "if most witches are like me, they write down their spells and works in journals. We could look for a cache of journals we could steal from, but tha's an improbable way to go about it. More likely than not, we'll have to try to steal the information directly from her mind."

I started, mouth falling open. "You can do that?"

Eimhir nodded with a slight grimace. "'Tis looked down upon, breaking into someone's mind, but if she will not cooperate with us, she's our enemy, and it must be done."

"Is there any chance at all that she would honor our request to lift the curse?"

Eimhir chuckled. "Very, very improbable. Nay, it's more likely she'll try to strike us down just for bothering her."

"Then how on earth are we even going to approach her?" I groused, throwing my hands up and accidentally knocking an enormous bundle of dried bog myrtle off its hook on the wall. I caught it before it fell to the floor and cast a glance at Eimhir, who didn't look amused. "Sorry." I fumbled with the plant, finally hooking it and turning back to Eimhir. "So, how *will* we approach her?"

"Well, the biggest problem is finding her," Eimhir sniffed.

"That's our biggest problem?" I asked, incredulity slackening my jaw.

"We have no idea what witch could have done this," Eimhir declared. "She may not even be in Scotland anymore, for all we know. Tha's why changing back kelpies is crucial. One of them may be an original kelpie, as they don't appear to age, or they may have heard of a powerful witch near where they lived. We can work on finding them from there."

"Wouldn't it be faster to just travel from town to town, searching for witches?" I asked, staring out at the rain again. The darkness beyond sent a prickle of fear at the back of my neck.

Eimhir snorted. "Aye, you go out and ride around the entire country, searching every forest, every valley, every home, for a witch tha' might not even be in this country. Not to mention the danger we would be putting ourselves in facing every witch in Christendom, despite us being few in number. Witches hide for a reason, and they dinnae talk willingly," Eimhir said, "but a witch's *reputation* is harder to hide. People who know of her will be a better source of information, hence the kelpies she's turned. We can spend years of our lives traveling around, or we could use tha' time to turn people back from the darkness while searching for hints of the witch. If after a few years, no kelpies yield results, we might have to scour the country for a witch of such repute, but for now, we focus on the kelpies. Now close tha' door. It's getting cold."

Pulling the door shut, I fell into a chair and ran my hands through my hair, trying not to think of the monumental task before us, and how much of it would be grasping at straws. It seemed almost impossible that we'd find the witch in this lifetime.

"Dinnae fret so, lad," Eimhir laughed at my despondent expression. "Like I said, a witch as old and powerful as to make this curse will have a reputation. We needn't focus on young witches like me, untried and weak." Eimhir made a face like the words left a bad taste in her mouth, then she sighed. "We'll find her, eventually. There aren't many truly, truly old witches around, so she won't be too hard to find."

The enormity of the task still left a pit in my stomach. But Eimhir and Rhetta seemed fairly certain it wouldn't be terribly hard, and so I decided to trust their optimism. We could do this.

"What will we do when we *do* discover the location of such a magic wielder?" I asked, folding my arms across my chest.

Eimhir shook her head. "We'll dwell on tha' once we find them. For now, we focus on finding them, and turning people back."

Feeling more exhausted than I'd ever felt in my life, I leaned my forearms against the kitchen table and stared into the fire, watching the flames spit and sputter in the grate.

Chapter Nineteen

It seemed an age before Rhetta finally returned. I had been dozing at the kitchen table when she came in, and I jerked awake as the door swung open.

"Well, Maighread is settled at the inn, with a carriage commissioned for her in the morning," Rhetta said, hanging the umbrellas up on a hook beside the door.

I stood, rolling out my shoulders and blinking away my sleep, and planted myself before Rhetta. "You knew they were humans," I demanded. Their lack of shock at Maighread's appearance was proof of that. Rhetta's eyes flicked to Eimhir, who had come back into the kitchen from her bedchamber.

"You didnae explain while I was gone?" Rhetta asked Eimhir over my shoulder.

I didn't turn around as Eimhir replied, "You didnae tell him my story. I wasn't about to tell him yours."

Rhetta nodded, her eyes growing misty as she locked stares with me.

"I knew it when my Daimh was taken," she said, her voice trembling.

"How?" I insisted. "I thought you said that kelpies stayed away from druids because of their magic."

"Daimh wasn't a druid," Rhetta answered with a trembling smile. "He didnae have any magical potential in him. He was pure human. That was why it was so important to me for him to have a powerful relic, so that he could always be protected from any magical creature that wished him harm."

I remembered Rhetta's accusatory look when I had told her I didn't have the relic anymore. Guilt sparked within me for taking the relic from her husband, but I smothered the regret. What was done was done.

"Daimh was taken outside our home, near sundown. He no longer had his relic, but we thought he would be safe because it was too early for kelpies to be out. He was gathering up herbs he had laid out to dry in the sun, far away from us all, so no one would tread on his work.

"I heard the kelpie just as Daimh started yelling. I ran out of our camp in time to see Daimh get swept away. I remembered you, lad, in that moment," she said, looking to me, her lower lip trembling at the memory. "How you chased down the kelpie that night. I thought I had a better chance at getting Daimh back because of my magic, so I flew along behind them, careful to keep my distance. I should've tried to pull him off before they reached the loch, but I was too afraid of the kelpie, and I never imagined . . ."

She took a shuddering breath. "I figured I could at least get to the loch, and pull my husband out of the water before he drowned. Once we got to the loch, the kelpie plunged under the surface, and

I . . . dove in after them, using my magic to see and breathe." She shuddered anew, her hands trembling in her lap, "Daimh was far, far beneath the surface, still on the kelpie's back, but I noticed the kelpie's legs had turned into flippers. Daimh was thrashing around, and I thought he was trying to get off the kelpie. I swam toward Daimh, but I noticed that he, too, began to transform . . . his body began to sprout horse hair, and he lengthened, and . . ." She gasped, now sobbing freely. "He turned, right before my eyes. He became this hateful beast. Once he was fully transformed, he swam toward the surface, and came straight for me. I shot out of the water into the sky and hovered in the safety of the air, watching as my beloved Daimh and the kelpie that turned him left the water. Their flippers turned to regular horse legs and they ran off into the darkened countryside. I saw his eyes, his face . . . he seemed to no longer have a single human emotion in him, he didnae recognize me, he . . . he was a monster." She was silent for several moments and Eimhir stood to get her a cup of tea.

"Forgive me. Retelling the story always brings me to tears," Rhetta sniffed.

"Not at all," I replied, passing her the handkerchief Slaine had made me and giving her a sad smile.

"I went back to my coven that night and told them what I had witnessed," Rhetta continued, accepting a teacup from Eimhir. "They were terrified, because they knew what Daimh's transformation meant: a curse was in force. And because it was a curse, a witch was responsible. A powerful one. They didnae want anything to do with witches, especially one that would do this. I tried to convince them that we needed to fix this. Only those with magic could, but they were too terrified." Her face hardened into anger. "They left the next morning."

"So, just because the kelpies turn humans into other kelpies, how do you know it's a witch's curse?" I asked, feeling acutely my lack of magical knowledge as I watched Eimhir roll her eyes. "How do you know it's not just the power of the kelpies themselves that turn the humans?" I pressed.

Sighing, Rhetta dried her eyes with the handkerchief. "Like nature and science, magic has universal rules as well. It is well known in magical communities that animals, magical or ordinary, cannae turn humans into creatures like themselves unless a curse is involved. At first we imagined that the kelpies just took and drowned humans. The fact that kelpies *change* humans into kelpies is proof that they are cursed."

"Like a vampire?" I asked. Growing up, I'd heard the stories of vampires, that they were individuals cursed by God, doomed to live among humans as monsters for eternity. But if kelpies were a witch's curse, were vampires also victims of a witch?

"Aye, vampires. Werewolves, too, are examples of such curses. Most believe their curses are from God, but it's possible they were made from a cursed artifact or a djinn. We dinnae worry too much about them, they've been around for millennia. They also restrain themselves because they understand that they would be hunted down if they started turning humans by the hundreds."

"Besides, vampires are more likely to eat the humans than transform them," Eimhir replied, giving a cold chuckle.

Rhetta made a face. "Really Eimhir, please."

"What? It's the truth. The lad's not so squeamish, is he?"

Rhetta shook her head. "You're so morbid at times, Eimhir."

Eimhir grinned a chilling smile back.

Rhetta shook her head and continued. "We know kelpies are a curse because they are relatively new, and they just burst into being."

"Ye also cannae draw magic off of them," Eimhir interjected. "All magical creatures excrete magic, but kelpies do not."

"Well, what if it was a djinn that changed the first kelpie?" I asked.

"Be thankful it wasn't," Rhetta shuddered. "The fact that a magic potion turned the kelpies back into humans makes us certain it's a witch's spell. If it was God or a djinn, a potion wouldn't have done anything."

"Very well. It's the work of a witch or warlock," I agreed. "Now to find them." I tried not to feel panicked at the thought.

Outside, I noticed that the sky was beginning to lighten, even though the storm clouds were still sending down rain.

I couldn't believe everything that had happened, everything I'd learned, had all been in one night. It felt as though three weeks had passed since yesterday morning, when I sent my sisters back to Glasgow.

Stretching, Eimhir stood. "Well, we'll not be finding them tonight. We best get off to bed." Rhetta also stood, bid me goodnight, then headed for the back door.

"Wait, Rhetta, where are you going?" I asked, getting to my feet as well.

Rhetta smiled at me. "I sleep in a small room in Eimhir's barn. Dinnae worry, it's much more comfortable than where you'll be sleeping."

"Shouldn't I take the barn? You know, for . . . propriety's sake?" I asked.

"Oh, for Ever's sake, lad," Eimhir burst in. "Are you afraid the town gossips will learn about this? Nonsense. Rhetta is fine in the barn, and as she said, it's more comfortable than your room."

"Just imagine you're giving up a lovely bed for a lady like myself. Propriety restored," Rhetta said, smiling. Giving me a tired wink, she hurried out into the rain.

"Well, come on, lad, hurry up. I'm tired." Eimhir gestured, and I followed her to the second door, which she opened to reveal a narrow room with a small hay pallet in the corner. Eimhir handed me a blanket and a ragged pillow.

"This is all I have. Get some sleep. We have much to do on the morrow."

I threw the blanket and pillow onto the pallet, aware that Eimhir was still watching me. She leaned back into the room, hand on the latch.

"I hope you're ready, lad, for what's ahead of us. Tonight was just the beginning." With a significant look, she shut the door behind her, leaving me in the brightening darkness.

Chapter Twenty

I awoke to dawn bursting over the hills and golden light streaming through the small window. I sighed, blinking at the sudden brightness.

Summer was in full bloom, and it was hard to believe that I'd been here with Rhetta and Eimhir for nearly three months. Every day, we focused on capturing kelpies and changing them back into humans. Even though I had to keep fighting off recollections of my early life and had ended up with a wide variety of bruises, I was getting fairly good at it and felt proud that the odds of me dying or getting changed to a kelpie became less and less as my skill improved.

Once those I wrangled were turned back into their own human skins, we would bring them to the cottage for refreshment and questioning. We inquired for any information they had on witches or warlocks that they knew of before sending them on their way, dazed, with memories of their time as kelpies wiped from their minds. The process was slow-going, and while I kept a diligent record of everything we were learning, we were no longer obtaining new information from those we saved. The work was becoming monotonous, dulling the excitement of discovery.

Only a handful of people that we had changed back knew of witches near where they lived, but once they described them as doing paltry tricks for food or a few coins, Eimhir would end the interview. The first time she ended an examination in such a manner, she explained that the witch we were looking for would be so powerful they would not stoop to pleasing humans the way these charlatans did.

And so the search continued, day and night.

I sent letters to my sisters and Emilia every so often, but kept them bland and insignificant, afraid of revealing too much. Every letter was painfully short, merely telling them I was fine and would be home as soon as I could. Empty words that I hated sending.

Rhetta had offered to enchant my letters so they could fly to Glasgow within a day or so. She explained that she and her husband, and now Eimhir, had used such methods to keep in contact when their searches for magical items separated them for days or weeks. As Daimh couldn't wield magic, Rhetta would enchant the letters to return to her unopened if Daimh never got them. If she never received them back, she knew he was safe. Using magic, Rhetta showed me how she folded a piece of parchment into the shape of a swallow that could fly against the breeze. She entertained me by folding parchment into various objects, my favorite being the delicate, detailed sailing ship that I kept by my bedside. Though the idea intrigued me, I knew I could never send magical letters to my sisters, who would panic at receiving such a missive. So I sent my communications by post in the nearby village, trusting my sisters received my letters and felt comforted by them.

I wasn't comforted, however. Several months of turning back kelpies was all fine and good, but it wasn't enough. Kelpies were taking humans by the dozens every day, while we could only change back two or three people at most. Such slow progress reminded me of time spent on my uncle's sailing ships, when no wind blew and our vessel sat listless in the water for ages.

I shifted on the small pallet in my corner, noting that the constant aching I had felt at the beginning of our work was now gone. My body had hardened, and I was even stronger than I had been from working on the ships. I now knew that kelpies were stronger than any storm-filled sail.

I was about to fall back asleep when I heard weeping from outside my door.

Remembrance of last night's argument with Eimhir made my stomach squirm. Eimhir and I butted heads more often than I'd care to recall, driving Rhetta mad. I didn't know how we were going to get past our differences. Eimhir thought I was a child, and deemed to treat me like one, and I still got thrills of horror whenever I turned around and she was there, staring at me. Our latest spat had been particularly cutting, especially once she threatened to kill me just to get rid of me, and I suggested to Rhetta that we leave Eimhir behind and work without her, now that we knew what we were looking for.

Eimhir had screamed curses at me before storming from the cottage, and I figured during the night she'd gotten over my empty threat. But as I listened to the sobs beyond the door, memories of my mother's own heartrending tears she had shed when she thought no one heard her flashed in my mind. I got up, quietly slipping on my trousers and a shirt, and eased out of my bedroom door. Eimhir was sniffling as she washed a teacup. As I moved closer, a creaking floorboard fractured the silence and Eimhir whipped around, tear trails on her cheeks, a furious expression on her face as she caught me staring at her.

"How dare you sneak up on me!" she cried, raising the soapy teacup above her head, ready to hurl it at me. I sprang toward her and snatched the cup from her hand before she could throw it. She had already broken several dishes over me in the last several months—whether in fits of rage or annoyance—and I wasn't about to let her do it again, especially so early in the morning.

Shock froze her features as I set the teacup down away from her and glared back. "A simple 'good morning' would suffice," I rebuked. I expected her to shout at me, but instead, Eimhir lowered her hand, her face shifting from shock back to sadness.

"I-I'm sorry," she replied, tears again welling in her eyes. "It's just been a difficult . . . never mind."

She turned away from me without any more reproach on my intrusion. She didn't even hiss at me for taking away the enjoyment of shattering porcelain over me. Confused, I reached out a cautious hand to touch her shoulder, but she shifted away from my touch. I dropped my hand, feeling foolish. This wasn't my mother. In fact, this woman wasn't someone with whom I could relate to on any level.

I turned back to my room, muttering, "And here I thought witches didn't *have* emotions."

The teacup exploded on the wall beside me, and I whipped around to see Eimhir facing me, her fists clenched, her face blooming an angry red. Fear flared inside my chest, and I cursed myself inwardly. I'd become too complacent. I forgot that, even though she was much weaker than Rhetta, she could still use magic, and provoking her was foolish.

"Do ye know what it's like, being a witch?" Eimhir fumed. I could only stare at her, frozen. "It's horrible," Eimhir spat when I didn't answer. "I became a witch because of . . . well, my own reasons, but not all witches are the same. Some are darker, and some have more light," she snarled, her words coming out in a rush. "I felt like I had more light because of my daughter, but she . . ." Eimhir's face crumpled, and she turned and began to sob into the wash tub.

I felt myself relax, though I was still wary she might turn on me. I mulled over her words as I stared at her shuddering shoulders. Maybe I was wrong. Maybe we did have more in common than I imagined.

Compelled by the tears she shed, I eased over to her and, despite the danger of her ire, put a gentle hand on her shoulder again. This time she didn't jerk away, but instead flung herself into my arms and sobbed into my chest, stunning me into stone.

I didn't know what to do with my arms, which I held up away from my body as Eimhir continued to sob into my tunic. We stood there for several moments. I finally gave her a gentle embrace, and heat crept into my face. Feeling more foolish than ever, I very carefully led her over to a chair and helped her sit. To give myself something to do besides sit and stare while she cried, I took the now-cooling kettle she had filled that morning and put it back on the embers. Then I handed Eimhir a tea towel. She took it, burying her face into it.

I stared at her in wonder as she wiped her eyes, hiccupping. I'd seen that type of heartbreak. I'd *felt* it. Could witches really suffer so?

When the kettle steamed, I fixed her a cup of tea as her sobs slowed, and she accepted it with a choked thank you. I tentatively sat down across from her with my own cup. I knew she was a witch, but seeing her tormented with so much pain made me wish there was something I could do or say to ease her suffering. Perhaps I looked as genuinely concerned as I felt, because she looked up at me, eyes puffy, and her face softened.

"I had a family, once. I felt love, once. I wasn't always a witch. My husband and I had a beautiful baby girl, Ismay," she whispered the name with reverence. "We were happy. Or so I thought. Then, a few months after Ismay was born, I learned tha' my husband's heart was being stolen by another." Her face crumpled with pain. "We had a daughter, how could he do this to her? To me?" She shook her head, wiping her cheeks again with the towel, and took a shuddering breath.

"I was desperate. And so . . . I turned to magic, anything to get him to come back to me." She sat, biting her lip, then laughed humorlessly. "The thing was, I didnae have a drop of magic in my blood. Nothing like Rhetta, and so I knew I would have to take a darker path. But I was desperate enough tha' I did it anyway. I learned how to become a witch. I did it for me daughter, and for me. But it was all in vain," Eimhir whispered, shaking her head. "By the time I was strong enough to try to bring my husband back, he had fled with his new lover. *Catriona*." She spat the name with such venom I shifted in my seat, uncomfortable. Eimhir sighed, wiping at her nose. "It was just me and my daughter, left alone to live our lives after tha'. I had no hope tha' Gawen would return." She fell silent again.

I ran my thumbnail along a groove in the wooden table, unsure if she wanted a response from me.

She continued. "Ismay was the light of my life. She kept me from going black, blacker than most witches. She saved my soul. And our life was happy."

I knew what was coming. I didn't ask, but she continued on anyway.

"Then, one day, my Ismay was out playing among the trees just outside. I was out back, hanging laundry. 'Twasn't near dark enough for kelpies to come. When a kelpie came upon her, in the brightness of day, I panicked. I tried to save her with me magic, but it only fueled the flight of the kelpie away from me. And tha' was when I met Rhetta." Eimhir looked up, locking eyes with me. "She was driving by in her cart and saw the whole thing. She helped me back from the brink. She told me everything, about how the kelpies were really humans, trapped by a witch's curse. She explained she was working on a way to bring the kelpies back to their human shapes. Of course, it took some time for us to trust one another, us being rival mages and all, but we had the same goal, and I believed her. I had to. It meant there was hope to bring me light back into me life." Eimhir sniffed, looking away from me with a pink face.

"I'm . . . I'm so sorry," I replied honestly. That pain of loss was something that never went away. "How long ago was this?" I asked.

"Almost three years. And now we've had a breakthrough," Eimhir breathed. "I'm so happy, but I'm also terrified. We've changed back so many, and yet none of them have been me little girl yet. What if . . . what if she's—" The trembling of her lips stopped her speaking, and she quickly drank down her cooling tea.

"Don't think like that," I replied, placing a hand on hers. I was surprised that she gripped my hand back. "We have to have hope. My mother was taken five years ago, my father before that, and I'm just hoping that, since the kelpies have become so numerous, they've had a greater chance of escaping the grave. We've turned back folk who have been kelpies a lot longer than your daughter or my father," I reminded her.

Eimhir nodded. "Aye, you're right. But it's just tha', sometimes . . . I get scared."

"I understand. And we'll keep working until we change every single one back. I promise. We're in this together, after all."

Eimhir looked at me, a smile trembling on her pale lips. She clutched my hand, her eyes locked with mine. "Though I dinnae like to admit it, you're a good man, Brennan Lennox."

I nodded in thanks, and we pulled our hands apart. An awkward silence filled the space between us, so I cleared my throat.

"Where's Rhetta?" I asked.

Eimhir shook her head. "No doubt out doing whatever fool things druids do."

We fell silent again, and Eimhir refreshed our cups. I considered what she had told me. When I first met Eimhir, she had refused to tell me her story, and now I understood why.

It's a very intimate thing, losing a loved one. She trusted me with her story. Perhaps I could show her the same sort of trust.

"I also lost my sister, Maura . . . a few months ago," I whispered, throat tightening with the familiar pain. "Now it's just my other two sisters left in Glasgow."

Eimhir reached out, surprising me as she grabbed my hand again, grasping it gently.

"What are your sisters' names?" Eimhir asked, her expression soft.

"Norah and Slaine. They're all I have left in the world. Well, and my aunt Alana. And Emilia," I added, my mind going to her with familiar longing.

"Who's Emilia?" Eimhir asked, a small smile tugging at her lips.

"The woman I'm courting," I replied, very aware of Eimhir's hand in mine. But I didn't want to pull away, for fear of insulting her.

"And have you asked for her *hand*?" Eimhir asked, squeezing my hand playfully. "Or did fear stop you from doing so?"

I ducked my head. "I was going to, officially, but then Maura . . ." I stopped, and Eimhir's smile disappeared.

"Oh, I understand. I'm sorry . . . Brennan." I looked up as she said my name, and, realizing she still held my hand, she unclenched her fingers and pulled her hand out of mine.

"But," Eimhir continued, "I'm glad you have some people left. If this venture doesn't work out like we want, at least you'll have someone to return home to." She swallowed hard, her knuckles white as she clenched her fingers into fists.

"We'll get your daughter back," I insisted.

"I certainly hope for it every day," she said, biting her lip and looking at me with welling eyes. I smiled back, and I saw her flush pink. Coughing, Eimhir stood abruptly and began busying herself with gathering her teacup. "Where in the blazes is tha' Rhetta?" she huffed, bustling away from the table.

Chapter Twenty-One

A while later, Rhetta burst through the door, holding up several bundles of thorny gorse in her apron. "It's such a beautiful day, Eimhir," Rhetta trilled, and, seeing me sitting there, she smiled at me. "Ah, good morning, Brennan."

"More gorse?" I asked, staring at the spiny branches. "Does that mean . . . ?" I paused, looking to Eimhir, who nodded.

"We're taking the day to make more potion. Brennan, you serve Rhetta some tea while I head to the cavern to begin prepping the ingredients," Eimhir commanded. I had a feeling she wanted to get away from the awkwardness that had come between us now that I knew her story. Scooping up the gorse, Eimhir stepped out into the sunshine.

I stood and pulled out a chair for Rhetta. As she sat, I poured her a cup of tea, then pulled out a plate of biscuits and set them before her. She gave me a sweet smile of thanks as she tucked into her tea.

"So, Eimhir shared her story with me," I said, glancing out the window as I sat beside Rhetta. "About her daughter."

Rhetta swallowed her mouthful of tea then beamed at me. "Beginning to get along, are you? It's about time," Rhetta laughed, her eyes crinkling at the corners. "I'm glad to hear it. I wish she would've shared it earlier, but Eimhir is so very private, sometimes I wonder," she said, shaking her head. "But I'm so glad she finally has. I thought you would understand her a little better once she told you. It was a difficult time for her, when her daughter was taken."

"She said you saw it happen," I prompted.

"Oh, aye. Heartbreaking, it was. I'd been working alone for two years after Daimh was gone, with nothing to show for it." Rhetta sighed. "I knew approaching another mage was foolish, but I needed magical help, and no druids would accompany me. All the hope I had left was with witches. I'd heard whispers of a witch near this village, and I wanted to see if she could help in some way. It was dangerous, I know. But I was desperate.

"I was riding along in my cart when I saw a kelpie leave these trees with a child on its back, Eimhir chasing after it." Rhetta gave me a sheepish look. "Though I felt pity for her, I knew that this would be the perfect opportunity for me to get help from a witch and not be killed. Thankfully, she was so distraught that I could get near enough to explain everything to her, and she was eager to join my crusade. We've been working together ever since. Unfortunately, us both being magical meant we could never capture a live kelpie until we recruited a non-magical being, and you were the first in three years to offer aid. We're both grateful to you, though, Ever-knowing, Eimhir will never show it."

I thought about the almost intimate interaction I had just had with Eimhir and decided to keep it to myself.

"What's the 'Ever'?" I inquired instead.

Rhetta sprayed a bit of tea across the table. "*What*? Oy! Forgive me!" she cried as I blinked at the tea that had speckled my face, and she tossed me a tea towel. "I'm sorry!"

"You're always invoking the Ever," I said, blotting at the tea staining my tunic. "What is that, exactly?"

"Blimey, I hadn't realized you'd picked up on that."

"What is it?"

She sighed, wiping her mouth. "The Ever is the realm beyond our own. It's where magic originated. Magic used to be more widely acknowledged, ages and ages ago, and there used to be millions of magical creatures in this world." She shook her head. "But something, maybe the conquering of the world, has diminished the mythic creatures here, or maybe something happened to the Ever, I don't know, but there are not as many creatures now, even from what I remember from when I was a girl. Maybe most have all gone back into the Ever. I've never tried to go there. From the stories passed down from druids who have ventured into the realm, it's not a pleasant place."

I sat back in my chair, disturbed. There was a whole realm of pure magic, just beyond our sight? What would happen should those who dwell there—should they be logical, human-like beings—come charging in, desirous to take over? If there were even ten creatures that had more magic than Rhetta, I couldn't see any hope for humankind. But something had happened to it? I shuddered thinking about there being more magical creatures roaming about than there were now.

Rhetta said nothing more about it, and I didn't voice my worried thoughts, forcing them from my mind. I had to deal with the problems of here and now.

After Rhetta had polished off two cups of tea and several biscuits, we traipsed out to the cave.

"Here, you're on shucking duty again," Eimhir said, handing me the enormous, dried husk of some scaly beast's clawed flipper. The chunk of flipper was a bit longer than my forearm and three times as thick, covered in hundreds of thousands of tiny, pearly blue scales, ending in two dangerous looking claws. I wouldn't wish to meet the creature it had belonged to.

Eimhir sounded as irritated as I felt as she recited a list of ingredients she was gathering up from her stores. This was our third potion-making day since I'd arrived. We'd spend the entire day creating the concoction. While I appreciated the reprieve from kelpie wrangling, the task kept us from changing back more people. I felt more useless on these days, as I was nothing more than an assistant. I would go out foraging for plants the women taught me about, peel ingredients, skin animals, and tend the fires, which had to be kept at a fairly constant size of flame or the potion would either burn or not cook properly.

It was such a warm day that the thought of being stuck in the stuffy, hot cavern was torturous. As I looked at the scaly flipper in my hand, a thought struck me. I pointed to a small table in the corner that the women weren't using.

"Would it be alright if I took this outside to work?" It was a beautiful day, I would be able to work without worrying about getting rained on, and if I was out of sight, I wouldn't be asked to do more of the disgusting or laborious tasks.

"I s'pose. But make sure you dinnae get any impurities in the scale powder, or you'll regret it," Eimhir warned. I promised and lugged the table, mortar and pestle, and flipper outside. Standing in the shade of a tree, I enjoyed the clear breeze and clouds shifting shapes in the sky as I pulled scales off the desiccated flipper to be ground into powder, grateful that I'd left the smoky, dank interior of Eimhir's cavern.

I grimaced as I pried more scales from the withered claw. The scales were fairly easy to remove, but it never failed to make my skin crawl as I dropped the dull blue flakes into the mortar.

As I considered popping inside the cottage to grab a slice of bread and perhaps take a short break from standing hunched over the tabletop, something rustled in the bushes ahead of me. I looked up just in time to see several men burst from the brush, weapons of all sorts in hand, shouting in wordless roars as they overwhelmed me.

I was knocked backward by a fist to my jaw, and I nearly fell to the ground. Two men leapt to grab me, and I stumbled sideways, whirling away.

"*Get 'im!*" one of the men bellowed over the clamor of raw shouting, and as I gained my footing, I saw another group of men flood the clearing on horseback, bearing torches and heading toward the cottage. One man grabbed my arm as I watched them overturn my worktable, the contents sliding to the ground, and then put a torch to the table for good measure. I yanked my arm out of the grip of my captor and sent him sprawling with a lunging punch, then ducked as a man lashed a torch at me.

"Die, yeh *witch!*" the villager snarled, swinging his torch at me again as if trying to ward off a charging cat sìth. The crackle of fire filled my ears, the heat causing pinpricks of sweat to break out on my face as I jumped back, dodging the blows. As the man over-swung his torch, I jumped past his guard and tackled him, trying to wrench the torch from him. We tumbled into a nearby tree, his head making a sickening crack against the trunk as I fell shoulder-first into the roots.

Leaving the unconscious man where he lay beneath the tree, I stood, my shoulder aching, and turned just in time to see another man raising his musket at me.

I spun away as the gun went off, and sharp, hot pain flared in my side. Ignoring the wound, I charged at the man with the gun, grappling for the weapon as he backpedaled, trying to reload. Ripping the musket free from his grasp, I knocked the butt of the weapon against his head, then turned just as I heard another crack of gunfire. Searing agony blazed through the side of my leg. I staggered, looking up to see another man begin reloading his gun, the smell of gunsmoke and blood staining the clear air.

I glanced down to see a bloody hole in the side of my upper thigh. My heart caught in my throat when I realized there was no exit wound, but I hoped that meant the bullet would help staunch the bleeding, at least for the moment. Right now, I had to get the gun away from the villager before he could reload.

Picking up the musket I'd taken off the unconscious man, I charged at the rifleman as he tried to get the ramrod down his weapon's muzzle. My thigh shrieking at the effort, I lunged at him. He got his gun up too late, and I knocked him senseless to the ground. I straightened, panting, to take in my surroundings through my swimming vision.

All around me was a chaotic blur of noises: shouting men and the whinnying of horses, crackling fire and breaking glass. No one else seemed to notice me as the mob ran to the cottage, trying to set

Eimhir's roof aflame. I swayed, realizing they had to be stopped, but I couldn't go on much longer with my injured leg.

I'd seen gunshot wounds to the leg before, and I knew I'd lose a lot of blood unless I bandaged it up at least a little. Working quickly, I ripped off one of my shirt sleeves and knotted it around my leg as tightly as I could without impeding my movement. I then scooped up an abandoned munition pouch that had spilled some of its paper cartridges of gunpowder and bullets on the ground, and charged toward the house.

"Rhetta, Eimhir!" I bellowed as I ran forward, my injured leg slowing me. It had felt like an hour had gone by since the beginning of the attack, but I knew it had only been minutes. Rhetta and Eimhir, being so deep underground, might not have heard the commotion as of yet.

A man came out of nowhere and tackled me to the grass, trying to put a knife through me. Sweat poured from my face as I struggled to get the knife from him, my side wound gushing warm blood down my side, my hands slick and bloody. He straddled me, using the weight of his entire body to try and plunge the knife into my face. Bellowing, I worked my feet under him and, using all my remaining strength, I kicked him off. My leg gave out as I did so, and the man was able to get a good cut along my arm as he tumbled away. I clambered to my feet and moved to bring the rifle down onto him, but he screamed and rolled away. I watched as he scrambled to his feet and ran back into the safety of the mob.

Pain lanced through me as I staggered to the shelter of a tree, favoring my injured leg and trying to keep myself from retching. For the moment, I was left alone with my pitching stomach. Thinking of the cures for seasickness I was taught as a boy, I took several fortifying breaths and tilted my head the way my vision was tilting until the nausea passed and I came to myself again.

Around me, men shouted and fired their guns into the air as they surrounded the cottage. I saw licking flames inside the door. Energy bloomed inside me, erasing any pain I felt. I charged toward a man on horseback who was shattering a window, readying to throw his torch inside.

Half leaping, half falling, I barreled the man off his horse with the help of my new gun, and then pulled myself into the now-empty saddle. Riding kelpies for so many weeks had accustomed me to jumping onto horses, and in comparison to mounting a ferocious kelpie, handling a broken beast such as this was practically effortless.

Wheeling the horse around, gritting my teeth as my bleeding wounds sang, I fired my rifle at an oncoming member of the mob. He fell with a cry, and I steered the horse around the cottage, trying to scare off men with the charging animal as I loaded the musket again with the paper cartridges, the reins clamped in my teeth. I kicked out at a man who was throwing a burning torch onto the roof, my thigh screaming at the effort, and I aimed and fired again, dropping another man that was aiming a gun at me.

As I went to reload once more, a shock wave of *something* reverberated around the clearing, causing the horse to rear backward.

The weeks of kelpie wrangling hit me in that moment, and I felt I was once again on the back of a water demon. My reflexes took over. Dropping the gun and gripping the mane, I leapt off the beast, using my weight to wrench the creature's head sideways and down. With a squeal, the horse was pulled off balance and we toppled to the ground.

I landed hard on my injured leg but somehow kept my feet. I stood there panting and shaking as energy from the struggle zipped through me, the sharp pain in my leg bringing me back to the present.

There was no kelpie, and there wasn't any danger of me being dragged to a loch, at least not at the moment. I watched the horse flail about, trying to right itself, and remorse welled up in me. The poor creature didn't deserve the rough treatment I had just given it. I backed away, watching the horse right itself and bolt out of sight in a flurry of trumpeting and bucking.

Once the horse was gone, I realized the clearing had fallen silent. Turning, I saw that every man that had been in the glade was lying on the grass, motionless. Those that had been on horses had also been thrown and their horses had scattered. I looked toward the cave to see Rhetta standing at the mouth, her arms up and out, a snarl on her lips. Eimhir rushed toward her cottage with a bucket of water in hand to put out the small fires.

Biting back the groans of pain, I hobbled toward Eimhir to help her put out flames as Rhetta descended on a prone man nearest her. As I approached Eimhir, she was easily extinguishing the smoldering fires that were failing to spread on the damp thatched roof. Catching sight of me, Eimhir called, "Leave off, boy. Go help Rhetta. I've got this sorted."

I switched directions and limped to Rhetta's side, who was kneeling beside a man that was just coming to.

"Who are you? What are you doing here?" Rhetta demanded, her tone harsher than I'd ever heard her speak.

The man trembled as he looked up at her, his face green. "P-p-p-please, d-d-dinnae hurt me, p-p-please—"

"How did you find us?" Rhetta snapped. "Speak, and I will spare you."

The quaking man looked between Rhetta and me, swallowing several times before speaking. "We-we noticed yeh b-bringing strangers into t-town," he gasped, his eyes still dancing between us. "For s-several weeks, n-n-now, and all the people yeh brought d-d-didnae have no m-m-memories of why th-they were h-here, or where they c-co-come from. We realized yeh must b-be witches, and we w-wanted to drive yeh out."

Rhetta cursed, glancing at me. "I didnae think about that at all."

"What do we do?" I rasped, glancing between her and the fallen man. With a sigh, Rhetta took the man's face in her hands. Alarm contorted his features and he tried to shy away. Rhetta's eyes were half closed as she murmured something under her breath. Chills crawled up my arms. The warm, tingly feeling that I had come to recognize as the flow of magic surrounded us, and the man's expression went blank. Rhetta sat back on her heels as the man got to his feet, still in a daze, and began to wander back the way the mob had come.

"Did you erase his memory?" I panted.

Rhetta nodded, her mouth a thin line. "Since the memories are fairly recent, they're easy enough to nudge in a different direction without a potion. Hopefully it will be enough to keep them from attacking us again until we can wipe the whole village." Rhetta stood, then glanced at me, her eyes going wide.

"Heavens, lad!" she gasped. "Why did you not tell me about your injuries immediately?" I looked down at myself as she grasped my shoulder. Half of my shirt was drenched red. The sight made my vision swim.

"I didn't—" I rasped as I collapsed to the ground.

"Fool boy," Rhetta hissed through her teeth. "*Eimhir!*"

I felt as though I was weightless, floating in an ocean of muted sounds in a timeless void. I lay there, staring at a blurred blue canopy, not feeling much until a sharp twinge in my side jolted me from my stupor. Eimhir was kneeling over me. Rhetta had rolled up her sleeves and lifted my shirt as I lay on my back. A bloody line lashed across my side, but it didn't look too deep. However, I'd seen wounds of this mildness during a few skirmishes with pirates in the China Sea, and more often than not, they turned septic.

"Do you think there's a doctor in town?" I asked through gritted teeth, and I was surprised when Rhetta and Eimhir laughed.

"Lad, druids are nothing if not healers," Rhetta chuckled. "Now lay still while I clean out your wounds. Eimhir, will you fetch us some clean cloth?" She inspected my side and arm first and claimed them to be nothing more than shallow gashes, then turned to my leg.

"Do you mind if I . . . ?" she asked, gesturing to my pant leg. I nodded. Using the hole as a starting point, Rhetta tore off my pant leg and began inspecting the wound.

"Oh, it seems the bullet took some fabric with it. No exit wound, that's good for faster healing."

"But the bullet and the fabric, it could cause infection—" I slurred, but Rhetta shushed me.

"Lie back and hold still. This will hurt."

She pressed a hand over the bleeding hole in the side of my thigh, and closed her eyes. Chills erupted across my skin, and agony ripped through my leg.

Biting back the shouts of pain, I watched through half-clenched eyelids as Rhetta withdrew the bullet and a small fragment of cloth with magic, then pulled several different leaves from her circlet, chewed them in her mouth and placed them into the wound.

"These will speed the healing process, lad."

Eimhir returned with several strips of cloth she kept on hand for my kelpie-wrangling injuries and sat down beside us. Rhetta took the cloth and began to bind my wounds.

"Thank you," I panted.

"The bullets missed all vital parts. You were very lucky, lad," Rhetta said, casting a warm smile at me.

Eimhir snorted. "More probable these fools were all drunk and couldn't hit the vast face of a mountain if they tried."

"I believe I got this lad under control now. Eimhir, you take care of these beasts," Rhetta growled, waving a hand at all the men that were still lying senseless on the grass.

"With Ever-loving pleasure," Eimhir snarled, stalking away. As Rhetta worked on my other wounds, I watched as Eimhir began feeding men the memory-erasing potion mixed with their individual hairs. When she came to the men I'd shot, she quickly patched them up before feeding them the potion. Soon all the men had left the clearing, leaving us alone once more.

Rhetta finished tying off the last of the bandages on my arm and side, and then helped me stand.

"Take it easy, lad, until we can get things cleared away. You lost a lot of blood, and you're paler than an Irishman, you are."

I trailed behind Rhetta to assess the damage the mob had caused. As we were inspecting the half-ransacked cottage, we heard Eimhir shouting. I hobbled after Rhetta to where Eimhir stood, staring at where I had been descaling the leathery flipper. What remained of the scaly leg was a twisted, burned lump of charcoal beside the cinders that had been my worktable.

"The entire flipper, gone," Eimhir growled, kicking at the charred remains of the table and cursing under her breath. Rhetta crouched down, looking sorrowfully at the unrecognizable claw.

"What do we do now?" I asked, wanting to skip any awkward arguments about who was to blame for the destruction of the scales. I had wanted to work outside, so it was my fault that the flipper had been lost, but I hadn't been counting on getting mobbed by witch-hunters.

"We need to harvest another," Eimhir said, fists on her hips, her lips pursed. She looked up at the cloudless sky, eyes half-closed in thought. "Full moon's in three days, what do you reckon, Rhetta? Think we can make it in time?"

Rhetta was sucking on her lower lip as she stood, brushing away the soot from her fingers. "I dinnae ken, Eimhir. I . . . didnae feel right about it last time, and I dinnae this time. You said we wouldn't have to do it again."

"Well tha' was before the entire blooming village came and burned half of our ingredients!" Eimhir snapped.

"We barely made it out alive last time," Rhetta argued. "And the only reason we did was because we took it by surprise. It might recognize the trap again and be more wary."

Eimhir snorted. "It's a dumb brute. It cannae think. Besides, this time we have the help of an industrious young man," Eimhir said, giving me a significant look before turning back to Rhetta. "We need those scales if we want to continue our work. Or do you think by some miracle we would be able to hunt down some crossbreed we can harvest from in this lifetime?" Eimhir scoffed. "You know the Taboo. Hybrids are killed."

Rhetta nodded, her expression solemn. "We would never find one."

"Tarragons are the only creature we can reach in a reasonable amount of time tha' has the power to sever enchantments, and you know it, Rhetta."

"I'm sorry, what are you discussing?" I asked with a grimace as I shifted my weight, looking between the two women. Rhetta didn't answer, so Eimhir turned to me.

"You've had plenty of practice capturing kelpies. Ready to capture a water tarragon?" Eimhir asked, a knowing smile on her lips.

Chapter Twenty-Two

The wagon creaked underneath us as Rhetta directed her pony up a large, steep hill. The trip had taken three days, and I was tired of riding in the back, wedged among the many items stacked with me.

Eimhir had insisted that we bring most of the supplies from her cave, just in case something went awry. She said she didn't want to waste time gathering ingredients, but I suspected it was because she worried the mob would come back, find her cave, and destroy everything she had.

The journey northward to the loch that held the mysterious water tarragon had been fairly uneventful, except for the evening our wagon was set upon by a pack of pech: brawny, human-like creatures that barely reached the height of my knee but liked to fight with Scotsmen.

The diminutive pech had wanted our supplies, but they were driven off without much trouble. Eimhir said we'd still arrive at the loch on time, despite the delay in retrieving our pilfered provisions.

"Why do we have to go so far to find a water tarragon, anyway?" I asked, grimacing as I worked my leg free and draped it out the side of the wagon. The tickling feeling of pins and needles began to crawl along my leg. During the past three days, my wounds had healed miraculously fast, so much so that I wasn't bothered by them. Maybe magic wasn't so bad.

"Water tarragons live in deep lochs, often near the sites of standing stones, so tha's why we have to go so far," Eimhir explained as she reached out to steady an urn that had worked itself free with the wagon's jostling.

"I've not heard much of tarragons," I replied. I'd heard passing myths of magical creatures when I was younger, mostly by adults who wanted to scare us into being good. Growing up in a village as small as Bòidhchead, the stories only focused on creatures that were considered a part of, and a threat to, our everyday life on the moors: kelpies, witches, and the occasional cat sìth or bogle.

"No, most people wouldn't have. Not much is known of them," Rhetta said over her shoulder.

"They're very elusive, staying deep beneath the waves of their lochs. They're the most active on full moons, when magic is heightened for those who use it. He will be out," Eimhir reassured.

"Lad, look, you'll enjoy this. It is quite a sight to be seen," Rhetta called from the driver's seat as the wagon finally reached the top of the hill.

I shifted my attention to the front and felt my jaw drop as we crested the ridge. The moors spread below us like a colorful blanket, a loch filling the right half of the view, surrounded by a forest that gave way to gentle, treeless hills splashed with colors. Rhetta stopped the wagon so that we could appreciate the prospect. But the magnificent loch and the beautiful purples, reds, and yellows of the landscape weren't what caught my eye.

In the middle of the dense forest that surrounded the loch was an enormous clearing, and in that clearing was an immense array of standing stones, more than I'd ever seen in my life, and more than I could count from this distance.

Most of the stones stood upright as if hoping to pierce the sky, but some had fallen, lying against their fellows like resting giants. The stones seemed to outnumber the very trees, a forest of monoliths rising from the ground.

"Welcome to An Coille Cloiche. It translates to 'The Stone Wood,'" Eimhir said, glancing at me and smiling. "Fitting, no?"

"It's beautiful," I breathed.

"Aye, beautiful. And powerful, they say. Those strong in magic come here to feel the energy of this place. It might be something in the rocks themselves, or the way they are set up tha' just gives off a soothing sensation for those who use magic," Eimhir mused.

Rhetta clicked the reins and we started off, heading not toward the standing stones but the glittering loch. The water appeared innocent and unassuming, yet I knew a creature just as awe-inspiring as the megaliths swam beneath its depths.

We set up camp near the shore opposite the forest of monoliths, and the women spent the next several hours preparing the ropes to make them strong enough to hold the beast, while I was sent off to snare several rabbits to use as bait. By the time I arrived back at camp, a sackful of rabbits and a few game hens slung on my back, the women had a fire going. Fish were roasting beside the fire on sticks thrust into the soft soil of the loch's bank. Upon seeing me, Eimhir smiled and patted the log they'd rolled up beside the fire. Smiling back, I sat and we waited for the full moon to rise above the trees.

"And all we need are these rabbits for bait?" I asked as Rhetta handed me a second helping of fish. "Won't the tarragon swallow them in one bite or, I dunno, when it sees us, let go and not fall into the snare?"

"Like all dumb beasts, loch monsters are very stubborn, and the tarragon will want its prize," Eimhir said with an air of arrogance. "It won't let go."

"Won't your magic scare him off?" I asked, staring into the flames of our fire that sputtered in the breeze.

Eimhir snorted. "The beast doesn't fear magic, and it fears humans even less."

"Eimhir means that it usually eats whatever creatures it can catch from the shore, magical or mundane. Magic doesn't bother its stomach," Rhetta replied, tucking into a second helping of fish as well. "Plus, there aren't many creatures that can stand against it. They have nothing to fear because they are so large."

"Except us," I said, my tone wry.

"Except us," Eimhir agreed with a self-satisfied smile.

We sat in silence for a time as I tried to calm my drumming heart. This creature would be much larger and more dangerous than a kelpie. And if it didn't fear magic, how could we possibly stand against it and hope to win?

"It's time," Eimhir said, looking over my head and getting to her feet. Glancing behind me, I saw the pale face of the full moon peeking over the treetops, casting us in a pearly light.

Gathering the ropes and the brace of rabbits, we headed down to the shore. After tying the rabbits to the end of the rope, we passed the bait through the noose that would ensnare the loch beast's neck, and then Rhetta used magic to hurl the rabbits far into the loch. The bait sank into the depths, taking the trailing rope beneath the waves.

Eimhir and Rhetta then set up the rope with the noose, making it float on the water's surface several yards from the shore and enchanting the cord so that it appeared nearly invisible on the water. The goal was that when we pulled up the rope containing the rabbits, and hopefully tarragon, the noose would slip over the head of the beast as it rose to the surface. Thus we'd be able to pull the beast to shore more securely. Eimhir said it had worked properly last time, so I was hoping for a repeat of their previous success. Though I prepared myself for several hours of waiting there on the shore of that silent, moon-glazed loch, we didn't have to wait long.

After only about fifteen minutes, the rope with the rabbits began to unwind from its coil.

"Told you he'd be about tonight." Eimhir smirked. With a flick of her wrist, the cord stopped mid-uncoil, and the rope that disappeared into the water pulled tight.

"Get ready to pull!" Rhetta warned. Eimhir and I got on either side of the rope that held the rabbits, while Rhetta took charge of the noose rope. As one, Eimhir and I began to haul the bait rope out of the water.

Though we were aided by magic, it was still a demanding task, pulling on the rope that lay beneath the silent loch. What made it even more taxing was knowing what was at the end of the rope.

The moon rose high above us, and yet we continued to pull, my arms straining, sweat rolling down my back, my feet braced in the stony shore.

Something disturbed the surface of the water, a quick flash, like the flick of a shark's fin on the ocean, and then all at once, the loch erupted with a lowing growl into churning white water.

"Pull! Pull!" Eimhir panted as we hauled on the line, towing the rope—and the monstrous, dark form—toward us.

Folly, the thought burst through the emptiness of my mind caused by intense focus on the task at hand. *This is pure folly.*

Of course, I had first imagined riding kelpies to be folly, and now I could do so with barely any uneasiness. Besides, it wasn't folly to free those who were kelpies—which was why we were towing an ancient loch monster toward us instead of running like any rational person would.

However, steadying my thoughts did nothing to still the giddiness that had entered my middle, fear and anticipation jangling my nerves.

The loch fell silent for a moment, then the chaos struck the water's surface again. The magnitude of the beast rose up before us as its head came through the noose and up out of the water. It loomed over us as it stood in the shallows, the rabbits crushed between its teeth.

My courage nearly failed me.

Every Scotsman has heard rumors of the great loch monsters that dwelt beneath the waves, but seeing one before me, in all its magnificence, made tears spring into my eyes. The length of the beast's neck was nearly four times my own height, and its small, needle-like teeth were bared through its grip on the rabbits. The scales were a silvery blue in the moonlight, a much deeper, richer color than the dull, dead scales I was used to seeing. Its long, thick tail thrashed in the water behind it. Vibrant yellow eyes stared down at us, water streaming over its scales like some fairy fountain. Its jaws were clamped down on our bait, the other rope looping around its neck.

Rhetta pulled hard, and the noose tightened.

The beast then seemed to realize what was happening.

With a muffled blow through its nostrils, still wanting its prize, the beast began to flail against the noose that Rhetta held steadily, her magic giving her and the rope strength.

"Pull!" Eimhir cried. "We need it further ashore to reach a fin!"

As we hauled the thrashing beast onto the shore, aided by magic, I could see that part of one of its flippers was missing. The sight made horror curl in my stomach.

"Heave!" Eimhir cried. "Lad, get near the water, be ready to cut a flipper off!"

The thought of hacking off a piece of a living animal, especially one so majestic, made me feel queasy, but who was I to question these methods? Leaving the hauling of the rope to the women and their magic, I neared the beast as it was pulled onto shore. The beast was nearly as long as my old cottage, and half of its body was now out on the bank. It floundered, nearly helpless now that it was so far out of the water, its flippers digging into the mud to no avail.

The beast snorted and fixed its eyes on me, an almost intelligent look in them as I neared, knife in hand. It gave a mournful bellow through its nostrils as I approached. As I raised my knife to hack away a part of the exposed, undamaged flipper, I paused.

I was about to cut into a creature so old and ancient, even the myths were difficult to come by. What was the purpose of saving those who were trapped in the curse if I hurt other creatures? Creatures who, like this loch beast, had intelligence shining from its mournful eyes? I always thought magic was evil, and though I couldn't use magic myself, I was doing something evil anyway. I didn't want to hurt him. It didn't feel right.

I began to slowly lower my knife, and I saw the beast's eyes flash in fear. He roared, let go of his prize, and began bucking, splashing muddy water into my eyes, blinding me. I stumbled away, not wanting to be crushed by the floundering beast while I couldn't see. I slipped and fell to my knees just as I heard Rhetta cry out, "*Lad!*"

I cleared an eye just in time to see the tarragon flick his tail above my head, snapping the rope around his neck. He was free. The beast turned and began lumbering back toward deep water. I didn't have time to move before the tail swooshed back toward me, catching me and flinging me with incredible force into the water.

Disoriented, I flailed under the surface until I felt a scaly hide ram into me. Grabbing onto the raised scales that traveled down the beast's spine, I held fast to him as he bucked and roared, catching a breath when I could. When the beast finally reached water deep enough, he dove beneath the waves.

I clung on, holding my breath, terrified he would drag me to the bottom of the loch, but I was back up and out of the water again as the beast surfaced and writhed beneath me, trying to shake me free. The shoreline quickly became shrouded in darkness as it fell away, the moonlight blinding me as it glanced off the water flowing across the scales of the tarragon, turning every wave, every splash of water, into molten silver. The fiend dove again, and the force of the water pushed me sideways so much that my grip failed and I slipped. I fell through the water for a second before latching onto the hind flipper of the monster.

Through the water, I saw the giant beast crane its neck, its head turned to look at me, its eye like a glowing coal under the surface. The creature gnashed its teeth with a menacing roar. The air left my lungs in a whoosh of bubbles, but I clung on. The creature would have a harder time reaching me if I stayed close to its body rather than out in open water.

The beast dove deep, then turned upward and increased its speed until it breached the surface. Leaping clear from the water, I felt my stomach rise to my throat as we sailed through the air and then plunged under the water with a magnificent splash that nearly ripped me free again. I clung on with one hand, battling against the rushing force of water, struggling to grab hold again with my other hand. A muffled roar reverberated through the water as the tarragon bucked again, finally shaking me free from its clawed flipper.

The water swept me underneath him. I scrabbled against its rough-scaled underbelly, lungs crying for air, desperate to cling to anything. I was finally able to grab the end of its long, muscular tail, thin enough for me to get my arms around. As I clamped down onto it, desperate for breath and about to let go, I heard the beast bellow anew and felt him make a sharp turn. In an instant, I was out of the water again. The tail flexed beneath me, whipping so fast that my grip snapped free. As I fell through the air, I saw the reason for the beast's sharp turn: we had come upon the opposing shore, and he had used the momentum of the turn to shake me loose. I flew over the rocky shore, landing hard on the ground and skidding to a stop in the undergrowth.

I lay there, stunned, breathless, and immeasurably grateful I was alive and on dry land. The thought of floundering somewhere out in the middle of the loch where that monster could have made a quick meal of me made me shudder.

I took a few moments to calm my clamoring heart, still incredulous that I was alive. The ordeal felt like it had simultaneously taken an eternity, and yet no time at all. Coughing on water and air alike, I sat up. Grimacing, I ran my hands through my dripping hair, pushing it out of my face. I stared around, trying to get my bearings.

I glanced behind me toward the loch, and my heart almost stopped beating. The loch monster's head was poking out of the water near the shore, its eyes on me as I sat there in the brush. Our eyes locked, and as we stared one another down, I felt another wave of guilt wash over me. I gazed back, barely breathing as it seemed to stare into my soul. A low rumbling sound echoed from within its chest, never taking its eyes from me.

Swallowing hard, I very slowly and carefully got to my feet. It continued to watch me, unmoving. I was far enough away that I could easily run if it tried to attack, but I felt like it was waiting for something. For me to speak to it, perhaps?

Licking my lips, I whispered, "I'm sorry. I didn't *want* to hurt you."

The beast gave a sharp exhale, as if disapproving.

"Truly. I'm sorry. I just . . . I need to stop the kelpies."

It huffed again, softer this time. Emotion, unbidden, welled up inside me. Could it truly understand me? Was it so intelligent?

"We'll just have to find another way," I said. "I won't help do magic if I'm asked to do this. I'm sorry you were hurt before."

A low hum came from its chest, and the tarragon tilted its head for a moment, watching me. Suddenly, the loch monster jerked its head upward, staring over my head toward the trees. Its hum became a growl, and it bobbed its head upward a few times before it withdrew from the shoreline and slipped beneath the surface.

I watched the waves for a time, relieved that I hadn't cut into his flipper. I was surprised at the emotion I felt for the enormous creature. I didn't know how we were going to find a substitute for the loch monster's scales, but I was resolved we would not cut into that magnificent creature again. Exhaling, I wiped my eyes on my sleeve and turned toward the forest.

Through the trees, moonlight dappled down on me, making every shadow a hiding place for goblins and bogles. I made a quick check over myself to make sure nothing was severely injured and grimaced as I saw I was caked with mud from my landing. I scraped off as much as I could before creeping through the brush, not eager to startle any creature that roamed the nights.

As I paused in the trees, trying to get my bearings, I heard a faint scream on the soft breeze. I stilled, heart galloping. My mind instantly went to kelpies out of habit, but I'd dealt with enough of the water demons to recognize that this wasn't one of their shrill screams. Besides, no kelpie would live in this loch, not with that tarragon in there. A bean-nighe, perhaps? The scream came again, and this time I knew it was no bean-nighe nor cat sìth. It was a woman. I hurried through the underbrush, trying to pinpoint where the increasingly urgent screaming was coming from.

I came to the edge of the clearing. Through the bushes, in the full moonlight, the giant standing stones we had passed earlier that day cast dark shadows across the moors, majestic in their silence.

But the clearing itself was not silent. Several poles topped with fire ringed the inside of a nearby section of the standing stones. Inside the ring of torches, I saw the figures of a woman, a man, and a young girl who looked no older than sixteen. The girl was dressed in a white shift, and she was the one screaming, pleading to be let go. Ignoring her, the woman and the man were tying the girl to one of the fallen stones.

My blood froze as I looked upon the sight.

Human sacrifice.

These two were witches. Or rather, people trying to become the twisted monsters.

I looked around, hoping that maybe Rhetta and Eimhir had followed the course the tarragon had taken me and were coming in my direction. Even if they weren't, I wouldn't have time to fetch them before this girl was killed.

The couple finished tying the girl off and then held hands, their backs to me, staring at their captive who was sobbing freely. Fury at the pair—who were looking down upon the girl without a single hint of remorse—burned inside me. I was close enough that I could hear them talking, but the words were lost in the echoes off the standing stones.

Time was running out for the girl, and I wasn't going to stand here and watch. However, I had dropped my knife in the loch and was now weaponless. Looking around me, I grabbed a fist-sized rock from beneath my feet and crept forward, wanting to keep my presence hidden for as long as possible. If they hadn't yet completed their twisted ceremony, they weren't witches yet, and I stood a decent chance against the two. I crept forward, cursing the squelching of mucky water in my boots, using the rock monoliths to hide my approach. I could now hear the couple's words over the girl's sobbing pleas.

"Now, acknowledge the moon, Uilleam," the woman was saying to the man, who looked barely a few years older than I.

"Aye, Sheona," the man replied, his voice wavering.

"Now, reach out toward the moon, and the creature that lives in the loch. Feel their essences, and repeat after me," Sheona commanded. "O ghealach, bhana-mhaighstir chumhachdach,"

"O ghealach, bhana-mhaighstir chumhachdach," the man breathed.

"Seall air an tairgse seo le fàbhar," Sheona intoned.

Chills flared over my skin, and I heard a dull ringing in my ears. Magic.

No time, I realized. I was on my own.

I eased out from behind the enormous rock behind the pair, raising the stone clutched in my palm. Upon seeing me, their young victim fell silent, her mouth open mid-cry. I brought the rock cracking down on the head of the young man as he began to repeat the woman's words. The man fell with a strangled yell. The woman, who'd had her face upturned toward the moon, whipped to face me where I stood, breathing hard with rock in hand, over the crumpled form of her friend.

"Am I interrupting something?" I panted.

"Brisidh deas-ghnàth!" the woman shrieked, leveling her arm at me, and fire burst from the tips of her fingers. The flames shot toward me and I dove to the ground. Rolling into the grass, barely missing being singed, I leapt to my feet and ducked into the maze of stones.

"How dare ye interrupt our ritual!" the woman screamed, her words echoing off the silent stone giants. I pressed my damp back against the cool face of a boulder, deep in shadow, stifling my panting. I thought she and the man were trying to become witches together, but now I realized the woman must be a mentor, helping the man become a warlock.

Beside me, the grass burst into flames, and I scrambled away, trying to remain hidden behind the enormous monoliths. I danced back and forth between the stones, trying to confuse the witch as to my location.

"Come out and become part of our terrible rite, lad," the woman shrilled. "Yer sacrifice would give us even greater power!"

I peered out from behind the stone and saw the woman's form stalk by, heading toward the distant trees. Quiet as a whisper, I doubled back toward the young girl, who was whimpering as she struggled against her bonds.

"We must hurry," I said in a hushed tone, coming up behind her. The girl yelped, looking behind her with a wild expression.

"Shh, I'm here to help," I whispered. The girl began crying anew.

"Oh, please, 'elp me, please," she breathed through her tears.

"I will," I soothed. "Don't worry." I had no knife, and the rock I held might have been good for knocking people out, but not much else.

"They want tae sacrifice me," the girl sobbed.

"*Shhhhh*. I won't let them," I insisted in a whisper, trying to quiet the hysterical girl. I scrambled to find a way to release her. The ropes were tied around her body in ridiculous quantities. I was good at knots, but not this good.

Glancing behind me to ensure the witch hadn't come back, I reached for a torch to burn away the bonds.

"Okay, hold still, this might get hot," I instructed, lowering the torch toward the ropes.

With a roar, a gale-force wind picked me up and hurled me into one of the standing stones, nearly knocking me senseless and pinning me several feet above the ground. The young girl screamed as the torch slipped from my hand, landing beside her, the greedy flames licking at the hem of her shift.

I strained against the stone, struggling to fight the blackness that threatened to swallow my consciousness. Shaking my head as it rang from the impact, I wriggled, trying to release myself, but I couldn't escape the force that held me there. From behind the monoliths, the rogue witch emerged, silent as a shadow. A surge of terror paralyzed my lungs. Stepping into the ring of torchlight, she came to stand beneath me, a snarl on her face.

"I'll kill ye first," Sheona hissed. "The price for yer insolen—" The witch paused. After a moment of silence, her eyes widened, and I saw her pupils contract slightly. Her face paled, and she turned toward the darkness of the trees beyond me.

"No, not possible," she breathed. "No mages lives within miles of here."

I craned my neck to see beyond the stone I was pressed against in time to see Eimhir and Rhetta emerge from the darkness, fire crackling in Rhetta's eyes, a malicious smile playing upon Eimhir's lips.

"Hello, dear," Eimhir purred. The force holding me aloft disappeared and I dropped to the ground, falling to a knee, as Sheona turned and sprinted out of the firelight, leaving her unconscious friend behind without a second thought. Eimhir took after her.

"Eimhir!" Rhetta called, "Stop!"

But Eimhir didn't listen as she disappeared beyond the standing stones after the rogue witch.

"Brennan," Rhetta said, hurrying over to me, her expression relieved. "Are you alright?"

I exhaled, wincing as I rubbed my shoulder that had taken the brunt of my meeting with the standing stone. "Yeah, well enough."

"Good. Go after Eimhir, bring her back. I dinnae ken what she means to do; she's not strong enough to fight off that witch on her own. We've scared her off. That's sufficient."

I thought it would've been better for Rhetta to go after the rival witches, but she had already begun to untie the sobbing girl. I turned and charged into the darkness after Eimhir. As I tore through the forest, I saw bursts of light through the trees ahead of me, and I slowed, anxious to not get caught in the fight. Leaving the loch behind, I came into the open moors, where lights flashed and shouts reverberated behind an enormous outcropping of rock. I hesitated, debating whether to move forward, when the night fell silent. The battling lights ceased, and I heard a small, strangled scream that was cut short.

Afraid that Eimhir had been hurt or killed, I ran forward, shouting, "Eimhir? Eimhir!"

A figure emerged from behind the rock, and I exhaled in relief as Eimhir stepped into the moonlight, shaking and trembling.

"Eimhir, are you alright?" I called, hurrying toward her.

Eimhir cursed as she came to meet me, the moon casting us in ivory. "She got away. Disappeared right before my eyes," she spat, her voice quavering.

"Why did you run after her? You could've been killed," I demanded.

Through her quivering anger, Eimhir laughed, high and shaky. "Fighting her, I learned we were actually quite evenly matched."

"Couldn't you just feel how much power she had upon seeing her?" I asked, still a little unsure of how the different nuances of magic worked, despite the months I'd lived and worked with a druid and witch.

"I've not the time to explain the ins and outs of magical battling to you right now, boy," she snapped.

"Why did you—"

"I ran after her to see if it was possible tha' she was the one responsible for me daughter's curse," Eimhir cut across me. "Sadly, there was no way it could have been her. She was too young and weak."

She gave another shaky laugh, her shuddering slowing as she calmed, and she gestured for me to follow. "Come. Rhetta is probably needlessly worried about us."

Stepping back into the torchlight that bathed the monoliths in dancing shadows, we found Rhetta hugging the freed young girl, who was crying into her robe.

"Shhh, there, there, lassie, you're safe now." Rhetta glanced at us as we stepped into the light. "Eimhir, you scared me."

"Your worry was for naught, Rhetta dear. She escaped, though I got what I wanted. Tha' wasn't our prey."

"How is it possible that we were able to catch the loch monster *and* find a witch all in the same time and area?" I asked, looking between the two women.

"The full moon, combined with the power of this place, amplifies magic." Eimhir looked around at the stones with an awed expression. "I should've realized tha' it was a possibility tha' someone would be out here tonight besides us. The magic is flowing strong. No wonder we didn't feel them using magic, Rhetta. It drowned them out."

Rhetta clicked her tongue, then turned her attention back to the young girl. "There, there, lassie. Here, eat this now," Rhetta said, pulling a few flowers off her circlet. "They'll help calm you. There," Rhetta said, as the girl slipped the flowers into her mouth, tears streaming freely down her face. "There, there, dear. All is well. What's your name?"

The girl's sniffling slowed, and she wiped her eyes with the back of her hand. "M-me name's Kristina," the young girl hiccupped.

"Well, Kristina, you're safe."

Kristina nodded, her hiccups the only sound in the quiet night air. She looked between the three of us, her eyes lingering on mine, as she whispered, "Thank ye. I-I cannae thank ye all enough."

"We help where we can, dear," Rhetta said, patting the girl on the back. Eimhir stepped forward.

"Well, now tha' this ordeal is over, can you tell us where you're from? Mayhap we can help you get home? Surely you must've been kidnapped," Eimhir asked, putting a hand on Kristina's shoulder with a soft look.

Kristina dipped her head with a shudder, looking at her feet, then raised her head slowly, as if it was difficult for her.

"Come on, lass, we want to help you," Eimhir said, her tone a little impatient as she gave the young girl a gentle squeeze of her hand, and Rhetta shot Eimhir a quelling look. Kristina shuddered again, her eyes wild for a moment, her breath coming in sudden gasps, then she closed her eyes.

"I'm from north of 'ere," she stammered, her eyes still closed. "The village of Fada gu Tuath."

I glanced at Eimhir, who was watching the young girl with curiosity.

"Fada gu Tuath, you say?" Eimhir asked, and the girl nodded, her eyes still closed. "Tha' far? How'd you get here?"

"I was visiting family near 'ere. Then *they* kidnapped me." A few more tears seeped out from behind Kristina's closed eyelids.

"You haven't happened to have heard about any very powerful witches tha' live up there, have you?" Eimhir asked. Kristina visibly shied away when Eimhir mentioned the word "witches."

"Eimhir," Rhetta snapped. "I'm sure she's had enough talk about witches for the moment—"

"We want to find the witch responsible for kelpies, aye?" Eimhir bit back. "We haven't found a kelpie from tha' far north before. Maybe there are some witches up there. We have to find out!"

Eimhir again placed a comforting hand on Kristina's shoulder. "Have you heard of a powerful witch from around your village?" Eimhir asked, her voice hoarse, and Kristina slowly nodded.

"I 'ave," Kristina whispered. She was quiet for a moment, shuddering softly, then spoke, her voice stronger than it had been moments before. "Me family lives in a village near a cursed loch named Ailsh. There once was a town tha' thrived there on the loch, but no one dares to live there now. Magic," the girl said, her expression still dazed, "runs rampant in tha' whole valley."

"Why?" Rhetta pushed. "What happened there?"

"The legend goes tha' about two 'undred years ago, there was a mighty battle between witches tha' destroyed the village and the village next tae it," the girl muttered. She shuddered once, then went still, looking at her hands, which trembled in her lap. "Nay a soul en the surrounding villages go intae tha' accursed valley, fer fear o' the magician tha' es said tae still reside there. Magic es thick en the air."

As I listened to her story, the hairs on my neck and arms stood on end. I glanced at Eimhir, whose focus was so riveted on the young girl, I don't think she blinked the entire time the girl was speaking. I felt my excitement rise—this could be it. A powerful magical presence, a battle two hundred years ago? It all fit the description of our kelpie-cursing witch.

"Me brother snuck tae go see it once with 'is friends," Kristina continued, goose flesh standing out on her arms. "'E said they got as far as the loch, tae the cottage on the island, but 'e wouldn't say no more. All I know is they came back, shakin' en their boots. They ne'er did talk 'bout what they saw."

Rhetta pressed Kristina for details about where the battle took place and where it was said the magic user resided. The girl didn't know much, but she said her brother claimed that they saw someone moving around on the island in the middle of Loch Ailsh. He and his friends ran away after that.

"No one came after him? No one cast magic at him?" Eimhir pressed when Kristina finished her story.

Kristina shook her head, looking tired and confused. Eimhir bit down on her knuckles and strode away, standing still as she stared out over the megaliths. Rhetta patted Kristina on the back. "Well, I think that's all we need, my dear, unless, do you have any more questions, Eimhir?" Eimhir, in the flickering light, shook her head. "Very well," Rhetta said, clapping her hands together. "Kristina, I think it would be best to get you home."

She nodded, her lip trembling as she eyed Eimhir with some wariness. "Aye, please, I just want tae go 'ome."

Chapter Twenty-Three

Eimhir insisted on wiping Kristina's memory, as we had spoken openly about the kelpies being a witch's curse, and we feared she would spread the word. It was also decided to clear the unconscious man's memory.

"Hopefully it will also remove the desire he had for becoming a warlock," Eimhir sniffed. "But we shan't take him into town. We're leaving him here. Serve him right if he gets eaten by coin-sìth."

Both were administered the memory-clearing potion, and then Rhetta set off in her wagon, taking Kristina to the nearest village, several miles from the loch.

Eimhir and I headed back to our camp, both of us too wrung out and excited to talk much. I mentioned my worries about the possibility of Sheona coming back to find us and enact some revenge, but Eimhir laughed. She doubted Sheona would want to take on her *and* Rhetta, but if it would make me feel better, she would keep watch while I slept.

Her expression softened as she looked at me. "You've been through quite a lot tonight. I'd say you deserve some rest."

I fell asleep the moment we returned to camp—despite still being damp and filthy— exhausted from the night's events. However, it wasn't to last. It seemed that I'd barely closed my eyes before Eimhir was shaking me awake.

"She returns," Eimhir whispered. For a moment my thoughts landed on Sheona, and I jumped to my feet, eyes wild.

Eimhir snickered behind a hand. "I meant Rhetta returns."

With a sigh of relief, I followed Eimhir to stand by the fire as Rhetta's cart came into view. She pulled up to a stop, clambered down, and we all took a seat beside the fire.

We were all silent for a moment.

"Well, I think what Kristina told us was what we've been looking for," Rhetta said, breaking the silence, her voice breathless.

"I should say so," Eimhir replied, unable to keep the smile from her face.

"How do we know it's the right witch?" I asked, leaning in, elbows on my knees.

"We don't, but it's the only lead we have. Ever knows, we're taking it," Eimhir snapped, then quickly took a breath. "I'm sorry. I'm . . . rather excitable right now. If she isn't the correct witch, we may be able to look into her mind, to see if she knows of other witches. She'll be a far deeper well of this kind of knowledge than humans."

"Besides, Kristina said the battle was over two hundred years ago," Rhetta pointed out. "That's about the time the kelpies came into being. The two instances might be connected."

"Will the witch talk to us? What do we need to do to approach her?" I asked, eager to make the next move. Now that we finally had a direction, excitement rippled through me. I felt like I couldn't breathe properly. It was possible I would be seeing my family soon. My *whole* family.

Rhetta and Eimhir looked at each other in silent communication. I hated when they did that; it always meant they were about to tell me something I wouldn't like.

"Well, the first thing we need to do—and this is exciting for you, lad—is send you somewhere safe while we're gone. You could go home for a short visit, if you like," Rhetta replied, smiling at me.

I started upright so fast that I kicked dirt into the fire, gulping in so much air that I began to cough. "Sorry, what?" I rasped, eyes watering.

"You can go home, but we'll need you back after a time, if this isn't the witch we're searching for," Rhetta said, her smile expanding at my shocked expression. "You've been such a help to us, you deserve a bit of a holiday, and I'm sure you're eager to see your sisters again—"

"Now wait just a moment," I began, my voice angrier than I meant it to be, and I saw Rhetta's expression falter at my tone. I looked between the two women. "I thought we agreed that I would only go home if I didn't believe we were heading in the right direction, or that this was all just madness. What we have discovered is beyond anything I'd hoped to find. You—you can't send me home when we're so close!"

Rhetta held up a hand, her tone soothing. "It won't be for long, lad. And this next part in our journey is no place for a boy like you."

I glared at her use of "boy."

I'd had enough of others thinking me useless. I'd tackled kelpies and water tarragons, battled off villagers intent on destroying me, and learned about magic even though it scared me to death. I'd continue on learning about magic if it meant I could see my parents and Maura again. I'd done more to eradicate kelpies than any man in my entire village had ever done. Wasn't that proof enough that I could take the next part in this journey?

Eimhir, seeing my anger, shook back her hair and leaned forward, a small smile on her lips. "She means a *non-magical* boy like you, lad," Eimhir clarified, hiding a laugh. "You'll only be in the way if you come with us."

I sat back on the log and looked away from the flames, at a loss for words. These months with them had changed everything for me. I wasn't just a temporary assistant anymore. This work had lit a fire in me that would not die out until I had seen through to the end of this journey, when everyone was free.

"I cannot leave. I am staying here," I barked, looking between them, making sure I made eye contact. "I have to see this through."

"Lad . . ." Rhetta began.

"I can't quit now, knowing what I know!" I demanded, looking over the fire to her. "I would go mad waiting to hear from you back in Glasgow! There has to be more I can do. I can't quit while my loved ones are still trapped."

Eimhir snorted and leaned her forearms onto her knees, looking at me through the snapping flames. "Lad, I dinnae think you understand. We dinnae need you—"

"Well, I need you!" I stood and shouted, my voice cracking. The two women started, their expressions blank with surprise.

I looked away, face hot as I studied a scar on my right elbow where a pirate had tried to cut my arm off during an attempted boarding on one of my voyages. The memory was a sharp image in my mind, one of the few times I felt truly fearful for my life. The battle had been going badly, and men older than I had reckoned I was too young and untried to help push back the pirates, but I grabbed up a weapon and joined the melee. Though I'd been wounded in the process, I helped turn the tide of victory to our side, and I came out stronger, despite the injury.

The cause I faced now was greater than just protecting my shipmates and our cargo. My family was at the forefront of my mind, but I realized that a whole country was involved. I pushed away the dizzy flush of embarrassment at my outburst. I didn't need to be ashamed about my zeal.

"I need you," I continued, pleased I kept my voice from trembling, "so my family can be whole once again. I chose this path, and I'm going to see it through to the end, even if I have to face a hundred witches and the very mouth of Hell. I just faced a witch not hours ago, and I'm still here. At the very least I can cause a distraction," I asserted when Eimhir opened her mouth to interrupt. "It's the best work I can do in my lifetime, and I won't abandon it." I jabbed my forefinger into my palm for emphasis. "I may not be able to use magic, but I'm a man of the highlands. I don't give up, and I don't turn away when victory is in sight, though the way is perilous. I'm going to stay, and you'll just have to find some use for me." I sat back, arms folded tight across my chest, clenching my hands to hide their trembling.

The night was silent except for my labored breathing, the crickets singing, and the snapping of wood in the fire.

Finally, Eimhir sat up, stretching.

"Very well, lad," Eimhir said, her tone amused. "I say he can stay, although you didnae need to give tha' jolly old speech. You could've just said you wanted to stay." Eimhir smiled, her eyes impish, and I felt my face flush. "The more the merrier, I suppose. What do you say, Rhetta?"

Rhetta's eyes were bright as she looked up at me with a trembling lip, and she nodded. "Perhaps there's some druid in you yet, boy." She gave me a kind smile, but Eimhir exhaled with a laugh.

"Oh, please," Eimhir drawled, "I've seen earthworms with a greater penchant for magical ability than this boy." She cast me another mirthful expression. "Well, if your speech is over, let's get back to the matter at hand."

I released my pent-up breath, relieved they weren't going to leave me behind. I had been serious. At this moment, this discovery was more important than anything else in my life. Well, besides Emilia, but because of her, I would see this through.

I nodded my thanks and quickly sat back down on the log. "So, have you any ideas on how to get close? And what we'll do when we get to them?" I asked, trying to sound matter-of-fact after my outburst.

"Well, Kristina did give us a clue tha' has given me an idea," Eimhir said, sitting forward. "We may just have a use for you yet, lad."

"Oh?" Rhetta asked, frowning.

"Kristina said her brother saw something moving on the island, but it didnae attack him," Eimhir said, her tone excited once more. "I'm certain those boys didnae have any magic or I'll kiss a cù-sith, which is why they were able to walk away alive. If this witch is as powerful as Kristina said, they'll be able to feel our magic, Rhetta, despite any relics we use to shield ourselves. Brennan doesn't have magic. He can go in first. We'll give him an enchanted object to alert us when he's found the witch, and then we'll pop in and take her by surprise with a mental ambush. She'll be far more powerful than us, but we'll have surprise on our side, and it will give us a few seconds to get into her mind and see if she's the right witch. If so, we can root out the spell she has on the kelpies."

"What will Brennan say when the witch sees him?" Rhetta asked.

"He can pretend he's looking for magical help," Eimhir explained, flashing me a smile. "If he flatters her enough, she might not kill him on the spot."

"That's a very dangerous assumption, Eimhir. You have no idea how she'll react," Rhetta argued.

"She may react favorably," Eimhir shrugged.

Rhetta made a strangled noise of disbelief, but Eimhir continued.

"It's the best plan we've come up with yet," Eimhir pointed out. Rhetta didn't argue.

"Besides, we're already halfway up there. We could make a quick trip of it, see if it's her. Not to mention we have all tha' we need. I had a feeling bringing this stuff would come in handy, and I always trust my instincts. One moment." She stood up and went to root around in the back of the wagon. Rhetta and I sat in silence until she came back, holding a glass vial filled with a brown-green liquid.

"I've been brewing something for a long time. It's a potion of compulsion. I started brewing it the moment I learned it might be a witch responsible for the kelpies, in case we ever found her. The longer it's brewed, the more powerful it is, and this has been brewing for three years. 'Twon't last long, because controlling someone completely takes more power than you'd imagine. Not to mention, human beings are harder to control than animals, and a witch will be especially hard. The moment we appear, I can force the potion down her throat, and we'll have some time to get what information we need. If it isn't the witch tha' made the kelpies, we can escape before she's burned through the potion, and we'll be safe. If it is the witch we're lookin' for, we can force her to tell us the countercurse. Then we kill her," Eimhir explained, her tone cold.

"Kill her?" Rhetta gasped.

"She would deserve it, for what she's taken from me!" Eimhir hissed, and flames seemed to rise up in her eyes. "Besides, if we didnae, do you reckon she would let us live, once she knows of us, after we've humiliated and overpowered her like tha'? She could make the kelpie spell even worse or come out of hiding and start killing people herself! She must be destroyed."

"How do we know she's still alive at all?" I interjected.

"She's alive," Eimhir nodded. "If the witch was gone, the magic Kristina described wouldn't still be there. It would be absorbed into the earth and animals."

"If she were dead, would her spells be broken?" I asked. "If we killed her, would the kelpies change back to humans on their own?"

"No, that's not how spells work, unfortunately. They aren't directly tied to the life force of a mage," Rhetta sighed.

"Well, maybe this witch is still alive, but what if the witch who made the kelpie spell *is* already dead? What do we do then?" I asked.

"We pray she isn't. And if she is," Eimhir replied, anticipating my insistence of the question, "then we have more work and study ahead of us. But I say we seize this chance now. We will always regret and wonder if we do not."

Rhetta licked her lips, frowning, and nodded. "I realize you have a point, Eimhir, but I think we should come up with a better plan that won't be so danger—"

"I'm tired of talking about this!" Eimhir snapped. "This is the best idea we've had yet. We can take her by surprise. She'll never see us coming. It's the best chance we've got to get in, get the spell, and make it out alive!"

The fire sputtered at her words, and I saw Rhetta looking at Eimhir with trepidation.

"Well, I don't know about killing the witch," I replied, and Rhetta and Eimhir both whipped to look at me. "But I think Eimhir's plan may be the best idea. I haven't heard your other plans, but if this one is the best, I don't reckon I want to hear the other ones. And it's likely the witch will try to kill us, in which case, though I don't relish the idea, we'd be fools not to be prepared to kill her in self defense."

"Yes!" Eimhir laughed, reaching over and grabbing my hand, giving me an eye-crinkling smile. "The lad is with me! What say you, Rhetta?" Eimhir, still gripping my hand, turned to Rhetta, her tone breathless.

Rhetta's frown softened into something closer to consternation. She looked to me, and I felt strange. For once, it was Eimhir and I against Rhetta. I didn't like the feeling of it.

"If Rhetta doesn't think it's a good idea, I say we don't do it," I said, and Eimhir's smile dropped as she released my hand in exasperation. Rhetta gave me a grateful smile, then looked to Eimhir, who nodded at her.

Rhetta exhaled, closing her eyes. "Yes, let's do it."

Eimhir's smile flared up again, and she quickly stood. "Excellent. I'll check our stores in case we want to prepare anything extra, but then we should get some sleep and head out in the morning. We should continue traveling with the wagon and not use magic to speed our journey, as it might alert the witch to our arrival. We need it to be a complete surprise."

Eimhir hurried to the wagon, a ball of flameless light above her head as she began to rummage through the contents of the wagon again. Rhetta sighed, shaking her head. "I pray we're not rushing forward foolishly," Rhetta said, looking into the fire.

Something splashed far out in the loch. Rhetta and I whipped our heads toward the sound, but the loch was still. Our eyes met, a question in Rhetta's face. I stared back out at the loch once more before turning back to the fire. Rhetta was quiet for a moment, and I could feel her eyes on me.

"So, what happened out there? On the loch? How did you survive?" Rhetta asked, her tone eager. "We thought you had perished. We tried to follow the tarragon as best as we could, but he was so fast, we lost him. The lass's screams are what brought us to you." She smiled, her eyes shiny. "I cannae tell you how happy I was when I saw you alive."

I gave a humorless laugh, then yawned. "I'll tell you in the morning. I will say this, we aren't cutting off any more of that tarragon."

Rhetta nodded. "Aye, I agree. If this lead comes to nothing, we'll have to find another way to change back kelpies." She paused and looked me hard in the eye. "You'll need to prepare yourself, lad. Change is a'comin', for good or ill, I cannae say as yet."

Chapter Twenty-Four

"Ye blasted fools!"

"Nothin' but destruction will meet ye in tha' forsaken land!"

"Ye'll curse us all!"

The villagers' shouts of warning rang in my head as we stood at the mouth of the supposed cursed valley. The trees before us appeared normal, except the hair on my arms stood on end. I felt a strange susurration, as if the air was alive with an energy that tingled along my skin.

Our journey further north had taken us only a few days, following Kristina's instructions, which Eimhir said Kristina had given her while Rhetta and I had gone back to retrieve the wagon to take the young lass to the nearest town.

We made it to a prosperous little village on the fringes of the wilderness that contained the forbidden loch. When the villagers saw us head in the direction of the valley, they begged us to go another way, to not go into those misbegotten lands. When it was apparent that we planned to disregard their warnings, they shouted and scorned us, cursing our folly.

Now that we were on the brink, the air changed dramatically, like a change from a desert to the jungle as we stared across the hilly landscape. We made our way into the copse of trees, the tingling feeling growing stronger with every mile.

Rhetta stopped her cart just before the edge of where the trees ended.

"Right. You ready, lad?" Rhetta asked, her tone worried. Taking several deep breaths, I nodded and hopped out of the cart bed.

"Good," Eimhir tittered. She had been breathless with anticipation the entire trip, her mood rubbing off on all of us. But now that we were here, a solemness had settled upon Rhetta and myself.

"Now, we dinnae ken how far away the witch is, so remember to ring the bell we gave you when you find her, then keep her distracted. Ring the bell a second time for us to come, preferably before she attacks you with magic," Eimhir said, hiding a smile.

"Right. Any other advice to help me escape, should she try to attack me?" I asked, flexing my fists to calm my nerves.

"Run and dodge," Eimhir said, shrugging. "Tha's about all tha' can be done to avoid spells."

I nodded.

"Well, off you trot, lad," Eimhir said, giving me a small smile. "The loch is out there somewhere. Follow the flow of magic you feel on the air, like you've learned. I'm sure she'll be at the thick of it."

Clutching the enchanted bell I carried in my pocket, I gave a small wave and hurried out of the trees into a narrow clearing before diving into another pocket of woods.

I wandered through brush and open field, sensing when I was wandering farther away from the ebb of the strange sensation on the air and correcting my course to find the strong feeling again.

As the sun began to sink toward the horizon, the magic hit me like a brick wall as I came upon a shattered hill. Jagged edges of rock and earth jutted upward from its summit. I made my way around the base, which revealed a large, gaping crater in the hillside. But it wasn't the appearance of the ragged hill that made me realize I was getting close to the source of magic.

Shards of rock, bits of tree trunks, and yellowed clumps of grass drifted in the air above the hill, which looked like it had just been hit with a giant's club, and the bits that flew into the air never came back down. The fragments of nature merely hovered, the smaller masses of dirt and wood drifting in a nonexistent breeze. The breeze of magic.

Goosebumps erupted down my spine, my legs trembling at the sight.

Beyond the mangled hillock, I saw splintered trees, singed bushes, and large globules of river water floating high in the air around the valley.

As I traveled, careful to avoid the floating logs and suspended liquid, I soon saw more than just trees and bushes floating. A cracked door hovered over a large, blackened crater. Pieces of glass and bedding danced in the breeze, roofs and bricks, hay and furniture all floating in the stillness, suspended in the air. Chills continued to race through me as I journeyed deeper and deeper into the splintered place that had once been a village much like the one I'd grown up in.

I left the fractured village behind and came upon a loch, where magic swirled around me, ruffling my hair, a swooping sensation in my stomach. Across the water, a couple ship lengths from the shore, lay a broken island covered in trees, some floating, and some growing from the ground. Through the wreckage of trees, I saw a ruined little cottage from whence the thrum of magic came. Slipping off my boots, I waded through the water, not fearful of kelpies residing here, as the thick magic was sure to have scared off any of the cursed beings. I slogged through the water, the depth rising only to my chest and then dropping again as I neared the island.

Pulling myself onto the bank, I stared through the drifting trees, where the ravaged cottage peeked through the destruction. The hair on my arms stood on end as I eased through the wood and came before the cottage.

Half of the thatched roof was missing, as well as a portion of one wall that looked like it had once contained the chimney. Lumps of clay brick hovered over the dead grass. Without hesitating, knowing I would lose my nerve if I did, I stepped into the sagging doorway, crunching on small animal bones underfoot. The corners of the cottage were shrouded in shadow, even though the missing walls exposed much of the room to the open air.

After a moment, my eyes adjusted, and at first I believed the room was empty.

All that remained of the furniture was a slumped chair and half of a table. The rest of the space was bare. As my eyes scanned the room, the beating of my heart nearly drowning out all other sound, I sensed a hint of movement in a far corner, deep in shadow. I stepped forward and beheld what appeared to be a small child.

Moving closer, I realized it was no child, but rather the oldest woman I'd ever seen, and so diminutive, she only appeared child-like. Her hair was a sickly straw-yellow. Her face so puckered and creased it resembled an old apple left in the sun. If the woman stood beside me, the top of her head would barely reach past my navel.

She stood hunched, stock-still in her corner. Her eyes were glazed and unfocused, looking beyond me as if she didn't even see me enter. A headache sprung behind my eyes, and I blinked at the pain.

"Hello?" I rasped, coughing to clear the cracking of my voice. "My name is Brennan Lennox. Are you the great witch that the villagers in these parts speak of?"

The woman was silent, not moving, her eyes never flicking to me. I waited, breathless, for a reply that never came. I coughed again as I rang the bell in my pocket.

"I've come here to ask for magical help," I continued, striving to keep the tremor from my voice, my nerves alive with tension. Here before me stood a woman that looked every inch a witch, down to what I had imagined a witch would smell like. Every instinct in my body was screaming at me to run from the ravaged cottage, but I forced myself to stay. If this witch was the one who had taken my family from me and cursed us all with the blight of kelpies, I had to make sure our plan was a success or die trying.

The ache behind my eyes seemed to increase, and I took several fortifying breaths to calm my nerves. It appeared as if moving would be difficult for the witch, her shoulders hunched into a hump on her back. I reassured myself that she was so small, I could easily knock her over if she did somehow attack me.

"I was told you may be able to help me. Please, it is of great importance, only someone of your amazing power and intellect can help me."

No movement. No sign she even heard me.

I glanced behind me. The forest outside was just as silent as before, and I wondered if Rhetta and Eimhir would be ready to come when I rang the bell a second time.

I turned back around to see the shriveled woman standing right beside me. Before I could even cry out in alarm, the woman had my hand in her cold, papery one.

My vision blackened, and my head seared in agony as I felt a new presence in my mind trying to shift me into the back of my own head. I fought for the control I felt I was losing over my body, but I was quickly overpowered. Slowly my sight came back, but it flickered occasionally, my head aching.

A voice, cool and young and accented, entered my mind. *"My, what a strange language you have. Simple. Common. Easy enough to learn. Hmm, pity. Currently not a drop of magic in you. But you could, if you desired to learn . . . Ah, I see you know people who do have magic. They came with you. And* she *is with you. How interesting,"* the voice oozed with delight.

I felt my arm that the witch wasn't hanging on to raise of its own accord, and I fought to lower it, but the voice in my mind made a tsking sound.

"You are young and strong. But it will be fruitless to try to resist my command. I shall win out in the end."

With an extended arm, we pointed toward the broken table. A jolt of energy coursed through me, the hair along my arms standing on end, and the table began to rise, wobbling as it climbed into the air.

I watched in horrified amazement as magic erupted from my hand, my arm and palm burning.

The voice was frustrated as the words resounded in my mind *"My physical ability is weak, though my magic is strong. I have been unable to work the forces inside me for centuries, and using a new body is difficult."*

The table, still shuddering as though it was about to fall to the ground, flew across the room and smashed into a tree outside. The heated energy in my arm subsided, and the voice continued, *"It will take much practice."*

I fought for my own voice, my lips struggling to form the words. "Who . . . who are you?"

Memories and images that were not my own streaked through my mind's eye. Flashes of men clad in foreign armor, a destruction laying waste to lands I'd never seen before, sweltering jungles, open plains, ice-tipped peaks, parched deserts. They all faded to reveal a young woman with long blonde hair, her face fair but marred with a brutal, unforgiving mien. She stood, filled with unspeakable magical power, over the kingdoms of ancient Europe. She was nearly worshiped, with the fearful devotion of those who could do nothing to stand against the power she wrought. I realized the young woman was the witch who now stood beside me, a haggard shell of what she once was, though her immense power still resided inside her broken body.

"I am Margund," her voice thundered inside my head. *"I was once the greatest witch the world has ever seen. I brought millions of other magic users to their knees. No, to their graves."*

Tremors wracked my body as I saw thousands of faces flash through my mind.

"Magic itself trembled before me, shrinking into the black. For centuries, only I knew its secrets. I've seen the world, I know it's bar-

barity, what ignorant fools would do with power such as mine. I can keep it in check, can seal away those who threaten. Everyone else is too weak, too primitive, and would let it rule them. Only I deserve to be its keeper."

I struggled to break away again, praying that Rhetta and Eimhir would come, but Margund interrupted my thoughts.

"You think to be saved? Despite being crippled by that upstart, I still have more power than any alive, and I crippled her in return. And now the jackals descend to try and finish the job. But that wench shall not defeat me again."

My mouth opened of its own accord, and my voice was projected out of the cottage, across the water, echoing through the riven landscape.

"I know you are out there," the ancient Margund called through my voice, the words heavily accented. "Come to me. I have your mortal boy. Face me, so that I may finish you and perhaps regain some of my former glory."

The air seemed to ring with silence after her announcement, and I struggled to keep some sense of self amidst the overpowering presence of the foreign mind inside my own. We waited, and I was unable to dwell on who she could be referring to as I wrestled to keep my place inside my own head.

At that moment, Rhetta and Eimhir appeared before us inside the cottage. Both women looked wary as they beheld me towering over the tiny whisper of a woman who clung to my hand.

"Brennan, are you alright?" Rhetta gasped.

I tried to speak, but my mouth moved, forming words different than the ones I tried to say. "The boy is well enough. Though if he continues to fight me, he will end up dead," Margund said through me. I knew she was trying to cow me, but it only stoked my ire.

"Brennan, can you hear me?" Rhetta called, her voice shrill. Fighting against the grip the witch had on my body, I raised a jerky hand, waving to show I heard.

"Let him go!" Rhetta demanded, but she didn't move toward us. I could hear the fear in her voice, and my heart ached as strongly as my head.

"*Yes, she is afraid*," came Margund's smug response in my mind.

"Not yet," she replied aloud with my stolen voice.

My eyes involuntarily went to Eimhir. "Ah, Eimhir," Margund said, "You lived. I would have imagined it to be a pity, but now I see it is a great boon for me. I might be able to make my body whole again yet."

A thought that wasn't mine flashed in my mind's eye: Margund killing all three of us and using our vitality to heal her own wasted body.

"You destroyed me mind, old hag," Eimhir spat, and I saw Rhetta twist toward Eimhir with a bewildered expression.

"And you destroyed my body with that potion of yours," Margund replied, and I felt heated anger flare inside us. "Potions, the weak witch's crutch. But I was foolish to underestimate you."

"And now I can *only* rely on potions, thanks to you," Eimhir seethed. "But I will not be undone again."

"You were powerful once, I admit," Margund said through my mouth, "so much so that even your potions gave off a powerful signature. But you *shall* be undone again. To heal me. Though I admit your creation was ingenious, this time your water horse potion will not save you from me."

Surprise broke me away from the witch's hold on my mind enough for me to gasp aloud, "*What*?"

I didn't understand exactly what Eimhir and this ancient witch were talking about, and by Rhetta's pale, confused face, I wasn't alone. The kelpies were a creation of *Eimhir's*? My mind struggled to grasp the fullness of the implication.

Wasn't this ancient witch responsible for the kelpies?

Margund laughed at my surprised thoughts. "Oh, no, no," she replied aloud to my unasked questions, regaining control over my mouth. "I didn't create the kelpies." I felt Margund's smugness inside my mind as she watched Eimhir squirm. "*I've not had this much entertainment in an age*," she whispered to me.

"What are you saying?" Rhetta asked with a sharp intake of breath.

"Why don't you ask Eimhir?" Margund said, laughing.

All eyes turned to the Eimhir, whose face was drawn up in anger.

"Don't you—" Eimhir sputtered.

"Don't what, Eimhir? Reveal how you created the kelpies?" Margund mocked. "Why don't we show them?"

Darkness fell over my physical eyes, and with a wrenching pain in my head I finally lost all sense of self as my mind merged completely with Margund's. I felt everything she felt, thought what she thought, moved when her body moved. We slipped into a painful memory, remembering the days when we had more power than all the mages of the world combined, all before civilizations across the world even began.

Power had coursed through us, and we reveled at how nothing could stand in our way as we flew over the lands, traveling, searching for any hint of magic. We didn't expect to find any, as we had squashed magic from the face of the Earth.

In the memory passing through our mind, we saw ourselves traveling across a land we knew very well. It wasn't our home-land—it being a rather insignificant isle—but it had been an excellent hunting ground for witch and warlock prey in eons past: the isle of Albion. It hadn't contained any magic of great consequence to bother with over the last several centuries, but now that we had quelled all magic in the east, we desired to travel, checking in on our old hunting grounds to see what could be seen. And what could be conquered.

On the breeze, a familiar pulse came at us, heedless of the wind. *Magic.* A lot of it. How could this be? It was more magic than we had felt in this part of the world for ages. We had been foolish to not visit this isle of peasants sooner, to check on those mucking about in the filth of the earth. There was magic to be had now, hiding from us. Or rather, not hiding. They were fools who did not realize what stalked them.

We followed the blaze of magic across vale and peak, coming upon a woman who stood before a cowering line of people all bound at the wrists and ankles. One by one, the witchling—Eimhir—took a whimpering human from the line and enacted the magic. We kept our distance, not wanting to alert her to our presence, and so we did not see what exactly she was doing, but we could feel another blast of power assault the air. Before our eyes, the human's screams of terror turned into the screeches of a wild beast, a magnificent horse, terrifying and commanding in its beauty. Still shrieking, the horse turned and fled, and the woman turned her attention to the next human in line.

We watched for a time, amused, as one by one this witch turned humans to horses. For what purpose, we did not know and did not care. But soon the witchling would finish her rituals, and it would be diverting to catch her by surprise while she was distracted with her frivolous undertaking.

Commanding the magic that thrummed inside us, millennia of gathered power, we descended upon the witchling with our might.

We had not attempted to read how much power she had, our pride blinding us. She was more powerful than we thought, and our past easy victories had made us complacent. We had not battled with such a power in centuries, and we were caught off guard.

The witchling, whose hair flashed like embers in a fire, danced with us, casting spells and curses in our direction. Our magic blasted houses to bits. Trees imploded. Humans ran and died trying to escape our glorious conflict. The battle raged for nearly half the morn as we tried to rally from our complacency, to take on this unanticipated struggle and rise victorious.

Once we got over our surprise, we bore down on her. As she weakened, we reached inside her mind, cracking it effortlessly, allowing the magic to drain from her like water from a splintered wooden pail. We soaked up every drop, reveling in the power she had held inside her.

But again, complacency was our undoing.

When she had been diminished, we stopped our assault and turned our back, not bothering to kill her, no longer worried about the broken witchling, who would never hold much magic again.

As we turned away, something shattered against our shoulder, and a wet burning began to crawl along our skin. With a wail, we realized too late that she was trying to turn us into one of those equine beasts. We had assumed she had been using spells, not potions, to turn the humans to horses. We struggled against the magic, strong magic, that tried to change us. How could this be? This magic was stronger than what she had held in her body. We had scoffed at potions, thinking them pathetic, but now we suffered for our scorn.

We did not change into the beast we'd seen, but the magic required to keep our form broke our body, leaving us crippled and old. Our mind was still active, still powerful, but without a body that was whole and hale to direct the magic, we were lame. We were unable to take hold of the beloved power that now seeped from us. We could barely move, not without a bumbling human to control. Most of the humans in this village, and the one beyond, had died, fled, or been changed into beasts. The magic taunted us by flying free, suspending the devastation of our battle around us in the air. An ocean of power just out of reach.

Not realizing she had crippled us so completely, the witchling fled for her life, and rightly so. We would have killed her, were we still able.

Here we have remained for the past two hundred years. The remaining walls of this cottage protected us from the wind and rain. Touching the occasional human who wandered into our path allowed us to access a greater portion of our power, but these human bodies were weak and quickly consumed by the flow of power. It had been decades since we'd made use of a body of any merit. Magic sustained our wasted body but could not repair it. We had been damaged by foreign, powerful magic, and nothing could restore us except perhaps the witchling's knowledge and youth. So we waited for her return; we knew she would, given enough time. And here she was, *at last*. We were going to enjoy this.

The memory lifted from our mind's eye. We still stood in the cottage by the loch where two small villages had thrived. The witchling was before us once more, but we were no longer crippled so completely, for now we held a human that was young and strong in mind and body.

We came fully to ourselves, and I wrenched myself free from Margund's identity, returning to the painful pressure in my head as I came into my own self again. Rhetta, paler than a corpse, turned to look at Eimhir.

"*You*?" Rhetta rasped. "*You* created—?"

"They deserved it," Eimhir spat, and the air around her seemed to shimmer with heat. "My husband's progeny didn't deserve to live as humans, but as beasts!"

Rhetta, her face slack in disbelief, said, "I thought you said you wanted your husband back."

Eimhir laughed so shrilly it was a scream. "I didn't become a witch to get me husband back! I did it to *curse* him! But by the time I had come up with a plan and enough power, the old fool had died, leaving his children's children behind. They would have to do. Gawen thought he could find more happiness with someone other than I? It was a sin, a degradation tha' I be forced to watch the happiness of Gawen and tha' harlot Catriona, see them create a family. A family tha' should've been mine! Humans are all the same. They don't deserve the happiness tha' was ripped from me!

"I found me own happiness, me own joy in darkness. I could do what Gawen never could, what tha' wench Catriona never could! I would make them all pay, with a magic so feared and furious that I would rise and scourge the earth! But then, *she* came," Eimhir hissed, looking toward us. "She came and ruined everything I had created.

She broke me so tha' I could no longer hold magic inside me, the one thing tha' gave me purpose. I searched all of the British Isles to kill and steal magic from witches and druids much weaker than me, but it was never enough! The magic would always run out before long."

Shock echoed inside the cottage. I felt Margund's contentment to just sit and watch whatever unfolded, in no hurry to destroy Eimhir once and for all. She would before long. I struggled to break free as Margund reveled in the thought that she would finally be able to heal her body and return, more powerful than before, and I raged at my helplessness to stop her.

"Then who . . ." Rhetta stammered, breaking the silence, her eyes on Eimhir. "Who was that girl? The one you claimed was your daughter? The one I saw taken by the kelpies?"

Eimhir laughed a cold, hard laugh. "I don't rightly know. Some village brat I kidnapped to use in a ruse to gain your trust. I first felt your magic when you were trying to summon a kelpie from the water all those years ago. Then I realized what you were up to, trying to break the curse of the kelpies, and I realized this could be me chance. I knew you wouldn't have me confidence unless I appeared vulnerable, and if I appeared to share your goal of ending the kelpies, I could slowly use you to me own ends."

"You wanted to kill me for my magic?" Rhetta said, anger hardening her voice.

Eimhir laughed again. "I'll admit, tha' was my original goal, but then I realized you were the most powerful creature I'd found in decades, though tha' isn't saying much. You were too strong for me to take by meself, and even if by some miracle I did beat you, the magic I stole from you would be gone in a year or so. But with your help, I could get back at this ancient wench," Eimhir spat, glaring at myself and the ancient witch. "It was me only chance. With your magic, I could overpower the hag, and with her limitless power, I could fix me mind, heal meself, get me magic back."

"You were clever," Margund cut in, even as I struggled in vain to close my mouth, "working these poor fools for months and years, biding your time. Though you're more patient than I could've imagined, I knew you'd come to me one day. But fool that you are, you grew impatient of the tiresome ruse of changing back kelpies. The minute you appeared on my ruined doorstep, I saw enough of your memories before you began fighting to block me out. This mortal boy never understood that you nudged them here, planting my location in the mind of that mortal girl you had rescued at the standing stones, guiding them here to your old abode. But it doesn't matter. Remember I am more powerful than both of you combined," Margund said through my mouth. "Though I may be crippled, I know enough of your plan, Eimhir. You've brought along a potion, no doubt trying to steal the power I've accumulated for more than seven thousand years. Fool! I was more powerful than you are now by the time I was eight years old. I sealed away the Ever with my own two hands! Though you have fresh power in you from that unfortunate witch you recently killed, do not presume you have enough to best me."

Rhetta lunged toward us, and I was suddenly knocked out of the ancient witch's grip, just as a tingling sensation ran over my entire body. I fell to the floor, hitting my head hard on the cottage wall, but I didn't feel any pain. Dazed from my release of contact with the ancient being, I scrabbled to roll myself over, afraid the witch would come for me again. Instead, the witch latched onto Rhetta's elbow and immediately tried to cast a curse at me. Fiery death flew at me, but before I could flinch away from the blazing light, the spell rebounded off of me. Panting, I realized Rhetta must have put some protection over me before she was taken over. My mind went to the tingling sensation I had felt on being released from Margund.

"Ahh, this is better," Rhetta sighed, stretching—but it wasn't Rhetta speaking. Her accent and inflections were different. "This druid woman is quite strong in magic, and is fighting me quite a bit. Now, Eimhir, give me what you have brought." Rhetta flicked a hand toward Eimhir, and a stoppered vial of potion flew out of Eimhir's bosom. Eimhir lunged for it but ducked away as a spell sizzled from Rhetta's hand, striking a small tree that had grown up through the floor. With a sharp crack, the smell of burnt wood filled the ruined cottage.

"Simple Eimhir. Though you continue to fight my mental inspection, you failed to hide your plan from me. So, you thought you could set upon me and finish me, stealing the power from me as I did to you, to steal what is rightfully mine through millennia of work and toil!" Margund laughed, Rhetta catching and holding the vial aloft, shaking it in her hand, a smug smile on her lips. "Are you so pretentious you only bothered to bring one dose?" Rhetta raised the vial high as if to smash it.

"NO!" Eimhir shouted, shards of ice hurtling, not only toward the ancient witch, but at me, fury etched in Eimhir's beautiful face. Rhetta dodged out of the way, deadly ice daggers embedding themselves into the wall behind her, as well as shattering harmlessly against the shield Rhetta had placed around me. The ancient woman was holding onto Rhetta, floating beside her as if she weighed nothing. Eimhir looked to me, where I was still lying stunned on the floor.

A fountain of water shot from Rhetta's hand, and Eimhir held up her arms, trying to hold back the deluge.

"Ahh, it's so exquisite to use magic again!" Rhetta sang.

"Fool boy, why did you let her touch you!" Eimhir screamed as I huddled against the floorboards, terror beating against my ribs as the violent display of magic, the very thing I had feared since childhood, raged before me. "Had you not, we could've overpowered her!"

Rhetta barked an incredulous laugh. "Overpower *me*? You have no idea what I've protected you all from, what lurks in your wildest nightmares that I've locked away. Your gratitude would be boundless! So do not think yourselves able to best my power."

Eimhir's face changed, her tone pleading as fire danced from her hand. "Brennan, we have to stop her!" she cried as she grappled with Rhetta. "She'll destroy us all to get her body whole once more! We must try, together!"

"Child, do not listen to that wretch that calls herself a witch," Margund called back, stumbling as she tried to control Rhetta and shoot stones at Eimhir, which Eimhir blasted away. "I have seen into her mind. This is what she has planned for you and your kind!"

My mind was seized again, and in the agony and darkness, sudden light burst forth. But this light was angry, hateful. Inside the light, I saw Eimhir rising, rising from the ashes of Margund's decimated body as Eimhir stole the depthless magic from the ancient witch's blackened remains. I saw, in my mind's eye, Eimhir turn her magic, the new calamitous, indescribable power within her, onto us, striking Rhetta down as though she were a dry leaf on a dying branch.

Rhetta, the magic and life fleeing out of her eyes, fell to the ground, never to rise again. I watched with mounting horror as

Eimhir turned on me. Within a breath I was gone, my eyes empty, my body still.

Eimhir then rose from the cottage, razing everything before her. I saw Glasgow tumble to rubble in a whirlwind of fire and magic, London burned, followed by every major city of Great Britain. Then, choked on victory and hatred of the human race—a race she felt was responsible for her husband's faithlessness—Eimhir set her eyes to the world. Screams of terror and pain filled the Earth. The kelpies, the sinister prison of her making, ran freely among the people, turning humans into the love-starved beasts of darkness by the millions.

"Stay out of me head!" Eimhir shrieked, a stone wall suddenly blocking out the horrifying vision that had been playing out before my eyes. Horror gripped me as my own vision returned. I gaped at the dueling witches, shuddering with terror as I lay forgotten on the ground. *I was right to fear magic*, I thought. *No person was ever meant to wield such power.*

Where Margund had control, only stamping down those who would oppose or compete with her rise in magic, Eimhir was a wildfire of hate, determined to raze every base human, to inflict her fury at her traitorous husband on every living person.

I shook my head, the last remnants of the horrifying vision leaving my mind, and I saw Eimhir and Rhetta fighting fiercer than ever, magic crackling the air, debris flying from blocked spells.

"Dinnae think she won't kill us either, boy!" Eimhir screeched, as she fought against a white-blue bolt of lightning coming out of Rhetta's hands. "She's been locked in this place for the last two hundred years. She will not leave humanity untouched!"

"Why do you bother to entreat the child? The boy cannot help you, Eimhir. He is a powerless worm," Rhetta said, her body jerking to and fro, as though Rhetta was fighting against Margund's control, as I had. "Oh, I see," she said with a wild laugh, "you're exhausting your recently acquired power—you cannot hold out against me!"

Eimhir gained some ground as I saw Rhetta not only blocking Eimhir's spell but also fighting against Margund's control. Rhetta reached out with her open hand, the other still holding the vial of potion, and tried pushing the old woman away. Rhetta's hand caught the ancient woman's head and pulled some coarse blonde hair free as she tried to wrench out of the haggard witch's grip.

"Not quite yet!" Eimhir shouted. "I have something even you won't be able to escape from! They obey my command!" Outside there was a screech, and a kelpie rammed through a wasted wall of the cottage.

In that moment, when everyone turned to see the kelpie who was bucking and rearing, I saw Rhetta look to me, her eyes sharpened. In that brief span between a breath, Rhetta locked eyes with mine, wrapped something once around the vial in her hand, and flung the glass at me. The moment the vial left her hand, her eyes went dark again as Margund retook control. The fighting between Eimhir, the shrieking kelpie, and the two other women intensified. I caught the glass beaker filled with bile-yellow liquid.

"*Destroy that vial, Brennan!*" Rhetta shouted, and I was unsure if it was Rhetta or the witch speaking. "*We cannot let Eimhir acquire this power!*"

"No!" Eimhir shouted, feinting toward me, then lunging at the wispy form of Margund, but Rhetta battled her away.

I looked at the potion in my hand, the potion Eimhir had created for the very purpose of stealing someone's power.

Keeping one of my fists curled tight around the beaker, I realized that this potion of Eimhir's was one she hoped to use immediately, just like the one we'd used countless times to change kelpies back into humans. A potion to be used as soon as you add the final ingredient. Wrapped around the glass beaker, I saw the four blonde hairs. Rhetta had known.

"Do not destroy tha', Brennan!" Eimhir bellowed with some effort when she saw me holding the vial. Eimhir tried to duck toward me again, but Rhetta blocked her with a powerful blast of wind. Eimhir clapped her hands together, and the wind seemed to pass on either side of her. A second kelpie joined the fray. "If you dump tha' out," Eimhir shouted as she grappled with Rhetta, sending heated shards of glass toward her, "We will be helpless to Margund's power, and she'll kill us all! I cannae hold her off for long! Give me the vial. I can save us!" She ducked away as Rhetta blasted a kelpie backward. The screeching beast flew over Eimhir and landed hard on the grass, unmoving. "I'll spare you! I'll make you richer than your dreams!" Eimhir shrieked.

Two more kelpies burst into the cottage, joining the fight. "I'll get your family back! Just get me the vial!" The mention of my family made me pause. Rhetta's voice came again, but this time I could tell it wasn't Rhetta speaking.

"She's lying, Brennan!" Margund said through Rhetta. "I can see into her mind. Eimhir intends to kill us when she gets my power! Destroy the vial! *Now!*"

I looked between the battling women, who were also fighting against the kelpies that Eimhir kept calling forth. The kelpies roared as they struggled to approach Margund and Rhetta, beaten back by magical barriers and flashes of light. With Margund's attention on both the kelpies and Eimhir, they were evenly matched. For now.

Eimhir summoned a fourth kelpie, and I scrambled to my feet to avoid the legion of sharp hooves, and soon all three women were so engrossed in trying to keep up with one another that I was forgotten for a moment. Despite the urgency of the situation, I stood rooted to the spot, knowing what had to be done, knowing I only had seconds to make a decision.

I didn't fully understand how magic worked, but I knew the great power could not remain in the old witch, and it could not be given to Eimhir. For either to have it would mean death to me and to Rhetta, possibly to hundreds of thousands.

My aunt.

My sisters.

Emilia.

In one movement I uncapped the vial, pulled the coarse hairs from around the glass, and slapped them into my mouth before downing the potion. I felt the hairs dissolve immediately, and my tongue and throat burned as if I had swallowed a white-hot coal. I staggered, falling to my knees as tears began to pour from my eyes, my nose streaming. A roaring sound surged in my ears as the potion slid down my throat. I dropped the empty vial to the ruined, splintery floor, where it shattered.

"*NO!*"

The bellow knocked me off the ground with a blast of energy and I crashed through a crumbling cottage wall, falling with a bone-shaking thud onto dead grass. I blacked out for what felt like a half second, then saw debris explode into the air as another wall of the cottage was blasted from the inside.

My vision swam for a moment, blinding me, and all I could hear from inside the cottage were blasts and shouts and kelpies keening.

All at once, the kelpies' screams fell silent. I tried sitting up, but my body wouldn't respond. My insides began to roil and squirm, but my eyesight cleared.

Rain was just beginning to patter down from the cloud-scattered sky. I raised my head enough to see Eimhir emerging from the ashes of the exploded wall, her eyes murderous as she stalked toward me. Through the clearing dust inside the cottage, I saw the old witch shaking uncontrollably, her wide, glazed eyes focused on me, an incredulous look curling into a knowing smile. Through the chaos, I saw the tiny Margund throw her head back and release a high, loud laugh that seemed to blast outward through the trees. My body began shaking as Eimhir moved toward me, but she was intercepted by a blast of fire from Rhetta, freed at last from Margund's grip. Eimhir turned to confront Rhetta with a burst of icy daggers.

As Rhetta and Eimhir grappled together, blinding flashes of light began shooting from inside the cottage. The ancient witch's laughter turned into a terrible scream, and through the light and dust, I saw the old witch writhing. As her screaming grew to a terrible, piercing pitch, surges of pain began to wash over me like the ocean tide crashing against rocky cliffs. With a final shriek, the ancient witch's screams ceased as she imploded into clouds of darkness, the force collapsing the remains of the roof.

The pain hit me like I'd been bludgeoned by a hundred kelpies. Agony ripped from the top of my head, down my spine, to my feet. I flashed boiling hot and freezing cold, and an immense, blinding energy began to fill my bones, my muscles, my very blood with power. I felt as though I was swelling, and I realized I might have just killed myself.

I could no longer see with my physical eyes, and I no longer cared about the battle between Eimhir and Rhetta. The chaos and agony inside my mind wiped every thought but survival from my head.

My mind retreated inside itself from the ravages of energy and memories and pain and light, fighting against the force that tried to rip me limb from limb, to destroy my sanity at the overwhelming amount of information and sensations. I hunkered down, fighting to keep myself intact.

No, I will not be undone! I shouted inwardly at the onslaught. *I will endure*!

The storm only increased, and increased again, with me howling into the dark, wondering if I would come out of the tempest unscathed. Or even alive.

What had I done?

PART III

Chapter Twenty-Five

The magic roared through me, binding every fiber of my physical being with something vastly more powerful and alien. There was no way to fight the magic melding to my physical form. I was changing from something frail and mortal to something inhuman and enduring. Ripping heat with budding growth, the blaze burned away the old and created something new from the magical fire now flooding through me. In the void my mind had retreated into, I tried to call for help, but no one heard me.

After what seemed like days of darkness, of exquisite lonesomeness and merciless pain, I felt the blackness lift, only to reveal a series of events I couldn't understand. Flashes of light filled my sight with visions no sane person would ever want to behold. Images of Margund's life played before my mind, showing me every facet of her: her creations, her magic, her spells, her curses, her growing power. I couldn't comprehend a single flash of it. My body was aware of every sense, my nerves tingling and twinging with sensations and emotions: ugly emotions of hate, spite, vindictive pleasure, and pain.

Only a few moments of happiness beamed through the swirling, choking hostility of her life, but those were soon lost in the pain and suffering she caused with the murder, torture, and despotic ruling of those she felt were beneath her.

Even as a little girl she had been strong, but the horrible things in her life transformed her into the dark being she had once been. She, and only she, wanted to rule magic, to be its keeper. She stamped out others who tried to make magic grow, who wanted to learn what magic could do. She wiped them out. She was the cause of the loss of all magical knowledge throughout the entire world. I shrank away from the flashes of her that had made her the terrifying woman she had been.

I floundered in the roaring ocean of magic for eons, watching the ages of the world pass. After timeless moments lost in every sense, very slowly every horrid spectacle, every nerve on fire, every color and word began to lose its vibrancy. The raging tides of magic calmed, and everything muted.

I was acutely aware of the silence as it fell like a shroud over my exhausted form. My mind, now free from the torturous landscape of transformation, opened, and I felt myself becoming conscious of the physical world.

Behind my closed eyes, I could hear the crashing of the sea against a nearby shore. Birds twittered and gulls cried. A soft, salt-ridden breeze ruffled my sweat-damp hair. I took a deep breath—the first breath in what felt like years—and relief, sweet and cool, rushed into my lungs, awakening my senses fully. I was lying on something soft, though I was not comfortable. My muscles were frozen and stiff, my back hunched.

I cracked open an eye, which was caked over with a yellow crust, and blinked, trying to clear it away. From my sideways position, I could discern I was inside a large tent made with linen walls. Light spilled through the curtained entrance. The tent was empty except for a dying fire in the middle of the room where the grass had been cleared away. The smoke escaped through a hole in the fabric ceiling.

My spine felt frozen in place as I huddled with my knees pressed against my chest, my fingers curled into claws around my shins.

I tried to uncurl my spine and stretch out my legs, but a shooting pain lanced down my entire body, and my hearing muted as if I was abruptly plunged underwater. My muscles locked, and through my fogged hearing, a shrieking echoed inside my head. The pain flashed red and orange before my eyes, blinding me, the underwater screeching deafening me.

Hands lifted me and a cup was pressed to my lips, some tasteless liquid forced down my throat. The shrill scream stopped, but the pain remained, my hearing still muffled. The cup disappeared from my lips and the howling continued.

Pressure, rhythmic in its tightening and loosening, began on my calves, and the pain flared hot before calming to a dull throbbing. The popping colors in my vision intensified as I felt hands trying to get my bunched and knotted muscles to loosen.

My legs resisted straightening, and I was fed more of the liquid. Soon, the roaring rivers in my ears faded, the unearthly screeching that reverberated in my skull quieted, and I could hear Rhetta's voice, quiet and muffled at first, then growing in volume.

"There now, easy, easy . . . Is that better? Can you hear me, lad? I thought we'd have this problem when you came to. You've been more rigid than a church pew this whole time. I was hoping I'd be here when you woke up, so I suppose it's a good thing I heard you shrieking like a banshee." She worked her hands up to my lower back, rubbing out the hard, knotted muscles.

"Phew, lad, you're tighter than a bowstring, you are." She rubbed a particularly tight muscle, and I cried out.

"Here, drink more of this," Rhetta said, lifting the cup to my lips. I could now taste the brew, and I jerked away, gurgling in protest.

"Oi, none of that now," Rhetta demanded. "I know it tastes strange, but it'll help your muscles relax. Drink it, lad, I cannae ease all of this out by myself."

Working my jaw, which felt like it had been rusted shut, I cracked open my mouth, wincing at the pain in my gums. Why did my *teeth* ache?

I took several long swallows, grimacing at the flavor, but eager to stop the pain.

"There, good."

The recollection of where I had been before the endless pain and torment seared in my mind. I grabbed at Rhetta's hand, pushing the cup away from my lips, sloshing the contents over my shirt.

"What . . . *happened*?" I rasped, every word a struggle as my jaw fluttered with spasms from the unaccustomed movement. "Where . . . are . . . we? Eimhir?" I fell back, pain blooming up through my back and hips, and I ground my twinging teeth to stop from groaning.

"We're safe for now, lad, dinnae worry," Rhetta soothed, the light from the open tent flap wreathing her hair in a warm afternoon glow. "I transported us away, far away, the moment Margund died and you collapsed. Eimhir was trying to kill you to get the power from you." She paused, then forced the cup to my lips again, looking hesitant. "I . . . I hope you dinnae mind, but I siphoned some of your newly acquired power from you and used it myself to help us get away."

She was silent as she stared down at me, and I watched her through half closed eyes as I finished off the tea. Even looking around hurt, my eyes dry and gritty.

Her voice was quiet when she spoke next, setting down the empty cup. "If you dinnae mind me saying, the power you have now, lad . . . it's . . . it's . . . indescribable. The magical well you possess is . . . bottomless. I only had to use a tiny fraction to get everything we needed." She shook her head, coming back to the present, and resumed working over my aching body. "We're far out of Eimhir's reach."

"Where?" I gasped, as Rhetta massaged my upper shoulder.

"A small island north of the mainland. More than a hundred miles from Loch Ailsh. If Eimhir tracked us, it would take her a good while to get here, even if she traveled with magic and knew where we were. If she has less power than I do, she cannae go more than a few miles at a time before having to rest for quite a while."

"H-how . . . long have . . . I . . ."

"Three days, lad," Rhetta replied.

Three days? It had felt like lifetimes. What had happened to me during those lifetimes? I didn't want to think about it. We were safe, but at what cost?

I groaned and tried to sit up, anything to move to a more comfortable position and ease the terrible cramps in my legs.

"Here, lad, let me help you." With great difficulty, even with the help of Rhetta, I rolled onto my back, my legs now uncoiled and resting straightened out. Although I still ached all over, the new posture was a great reprieve.

"There, does that feel better?" Rhetta asked, placing a blanket over my sweat-slicked body.

I gave a sigh of relief in response.

"Very good. I'll get you some food. Just rest. It's a miracle you survived that much power transferring into such a mortal frame. Come to think of it, Margund using you as a conduit likely primed your body for magic, but still . . . it was a great risk. But you're young and sturdy. That probably helped." I felt Rhetta stand and walk away, but she was back in a moment, crouching down beside me again. "Open your mouth. I promise this tastes better than my tea."

I allowed her to slip a shallow wooden spoon into my mouth, and I swallowed the warm broth, savoring the flavors of wild greens, rabbit, and mushroom.

I grunted in surprise, my stomach now grumbling, and opened my mouth wider, despite the popping in my jaw. Rhetta chuckled and continued to ladle the broth into my eager mouth.

I had three more bowls of the broth, as well as another cup of the unpleasant tea, before my stomach un-clenched from hunger pangs.

With the broth warming me from within and my muscles slowly unclenching, I began to doze, even as Rhetta tried to get me to finish off the last few spoonfuls of broth. She clicked her tongue, and I heard her dust off her hands and whisper, "Get some sleep. You haven't been able to rest at all. You've been tossing and turning and magically affecting the things around you for days. I thought I'd die of fright when I saw you sink into the ground *while* unconscious. You even somehow managed to flood our tent with the sea one day.

Crustaceans everywhere." I heard the smile in her voice, and then she sighed. "Well, rest, and we'll try to get you standing in the morning."

She moved away, the movement snapping me awake.

"Rhetta," I slurred, propping myself on an elbow, grimacing at the effort, "I don't know how to thank you. You . . . you saved my life, and I—" My shoulders popped and I lost the remaining strength in my arms. With a grunt of pain, I collapsed back into the mattress, which I just then realized was beneath me. It felt stuffed full of feathers.

"Shh, lad," Rhetta said as she undid the tent's flap and let it fall shut, darkening the room. "I'm a druid. It's what I do. You know, this whole thing has reminded me of the first time we met, and we both got through that. But we'll talk more after you rest." Giving me a smile, she left the tent. I fell asleep almost instantly. A short, pleasant dream about Emilia played behind my eyelids before I dropped into deep unconsciousness.

Chapter Twenty-Six

My eyes snapped open, my heart thundering. My pleasant dreams had turned dark and twisted, waking me. I bolted upright, forgetting about my sore body. My muscles convulsed sharply, and I barked out a grunt.

I heard a sharp gasp of "*Cirein-cròin naomh!*" and looked up to see Rhetta with a hand over her heart as she stirred a small pot over the fire.

"Gracious, lad, you scared me!" she scolded.

"Sorry," I growled, my voice sounding like rocks grinding together. I rolled my shoulders to loosen them, running my tongue over my teeth and grimacing at the sour taste in my mouth.

"Here, let me get you breakfast."

As she busied herself filling bowls with stew, I looked around the dark tent.

"Rhetta, where did you get all of this?" I croaked as Rhetta handed me a bowl and another cup of the brown tea.

She sat beside me, biting her lip. "I . . . may have been dabbling a bit with magic. Not enough that Eimhir could track us, mind you," she assured me in a quick breath. "But I've been drawing it from you. I would never have been able to create this stuff on just my own power. I hope you dinnae mind."

I choked on a humorless laugh. "I haven't even noticed anything being drawn from me. Besides, it's not my magic. Use all you want."

"It *is* your magic now, lad," Rhetta said, her tone serious. "I told you, it was a miracle you survived so much magic entering your mortal body . . . I've never seen anything like this before. Magic has a way of changing everything it touches. It occurred to me, your body isn't mortal anymore. You must be something different, now. The magic saved you."

I had already known that I was something else. The days I was physically unconscious but mentally awake was proof enough for me.

"What if I don't want it?" I asked, not feeling hungry anymore. I didn't want to think about what I had become. Evil. A monster. A magic user. A *witch*.

"Lad . . . Brennan," Rhetta said, setting down her own bowl as I glared into my stew. "I know what you're feeling, and it simply isn't true. Magic is not evil unless you do evil with it."

"But it's like you said, you have to kill someone to become a witch, and I . . . killed Margund. I . . . became a witch. A warlock," I insisted.

"I dinnae ken if you actually killed her, lad," Rhetta soothed. "I think all the magic leaving her body is what killed her. Her body wasn't able to function once magic wasn't in it. Besides, even if you did kill her, you didnae do it for personal gain. You were acting on noble intentions, and in self defense. Magic augments what's already there, and since you didnae mean to take Margund's life, but were trying to protect us, nobly sacrificing yourself, I think you'll find you have naught to worry about. Not to mention, there was no ritualistic aspect to how you acquired the power. The magic is yours, and it's pure and good, like you. You're not a warlock." Rhetta smiled.

I shook my head. I wasn't so sure.

Rhetta sighed. "You're young, lad, but once you get older, you'll realize that it's very hard to change human nature. Humans don't like change because it takes work and dedication. You were already noble and good, lad. It would take more than just an influx of magic to change that. That's why witches are mostly evil: they do evil things to acquire magic, and because their bodies aren't meant to hold magic, the magic warps them, and they stop trying to fight against the darkness. The baser instincts are much easier. But you have *not* been warped. You had magical potential before all this, so the magic isn't inside you unnaturally."

"What? No, I didn't—I was just a normal man."

"Many humans have lived their lives without realizing they have had the breath of magic potential inside them," Rhetta said gently. "They only realize it once it's been activated inside them, like you. Do not fret, lad. You'll be like me. I use magic, and I'm not bad or evil. A little eccentric, perhaps, but not evil." Rhetta gave me a shy smile, and I nodded, looking away to wipe the few stray tears that escaped my eyes. "You've been given a great gift, lad. I have no doubt you will do marvelous things with it. You'll make the magic your own."

I didn't respond. I didn't want to do marvelous things with it. I wanted my old life back, free of magic.

I wanted to be a merchant again. To see my sisters. To marry Emilia, to spend my life with her, to create a family of our own. She wouldn't want me now that I was . . . *this.*

Did they have to know? I wondered, working my sore jaw. Could I hide who I was? Could I go back to my old life, concealing my magic? No one but me, Rhetta, and Eimhir knew what I was, and I doubted Eimhir would be telling it on the mounts. She wanted the magic for herself and wouldn't want competition.

Maybe, just maybe, I could go back, pretend things were the way they were before this terrible transformation.

Rhetta interrupted my thoughts.

"I'm so sorry, lad," Rhetta choked out.

I glanced up at her. "For?"

She was wringing her hands in her lap, the tendons standing out in her neck, an anguished look on her face as she met my eye. "This is all my fault. I . . . I had no idea that Eimhir was so old. And so well versed in magic. I could feel the magic inside her when I first met her, and it was as dim as a spark in a dying fire. I honestly thought she was young, inexperienced. Especially when I saw that girl get taken, the girl she claimed was her daughter. The lengths she went to for her manipulation." Rhetta shuddered. "I had no idea it was even possible to break someone like that so that they couldn't hold magic. Her magic, I honestly thought—"

"We both ignored the cardinal rule," I grunted. "We trusted a witch. She fooled us both."

Rhetta nodded, biting her lip as she watched my face. "I truly am sorry for getting you involved in this."

"I don't blame you, Rhetta. This isn't your fault. Eimhir is all to blame. For *everything.*"

We sat in silence for a few moments, and my anger began to bubble. Eimhir *did* take everything from me. And not just from me, but from everyone in Scotland who had lost a loved one to the kelpies. I lived with that monster for four months of my life. I had thought we were becoming friends, but it was all a lie. Everything I thought she was had been counterfeit. My stomach curdled at the knowledge she had hunted, tortured, and killed for hundreds of years, all because she couldn't forgive. And if she had made the kelpies because she couldn't forgive her husband . . . fear clawed around my lungs at what she was possibly prepared to do to me because I'd stolen magic from her, on top of all she'd already done. *She* made me what I was. *She* caused me all this pain.

I grimaced at every bite of my stew. Everything ached or twinged with pain. Every so often, my chest felt as though a fire erupted behind my ribcage as the new magic flared, causing the grass around me to grow right before our eyes or earthworms to wriggle out of the ground.

"Will it always be like this?" I growled as the earth moved beneath me, shifting me sideways and causing me to slop stew over my hand. I wouldn't be able to hide my magic from my family if the ground shifted at my feet everywhere I went.

Rhetta hid a laugh behind her hand as I tried to right myself. "No, dinnae fret. The magic is running free right now, because you dinnae ken how to rein it in, to control it. But once you learn to master it, you could look like you'd never touched magic in your life."

The thought filled me with hope, and I took a fortifying breath. I could do this. I could spend a few more days learning to keep it hidden, or maybe even find a way to channel it out of me into something or someone else. Maybe I could be normal again. At that moment, the stew tasted more delicious than it had before, and I didn't mind the twinges in my jaw as I began to slurp down my food with gusto.

"More stew, if you please, Rhetta," I said, swallowing my final bite and holding out my bowl with a wince. She gave me a warm smile at my request and stood. "Rhetta, could I rid myself of this magic, somehow?"

She didn't answer right away as she filled my bowl again. When she turned back to hand me my stew, her lips were pursed, her face grave. I grunted as I reached up to take it, then settled back into the mattress.

"You cannae go back. You are not 'Brennan Lennox' now. You never will be again. You are something more, you understand that, dinnae you, lad? You will never *not* have magic. It is who you are, now. You will not age like you once did. Your family will notice that they grow old as you remain the same. It is the gift and curse of magic. Magic is like the thistle," she said, gesturing to the small pile of thistles on her preparation table, their spiny, vivid purple heads cheerful against the tent walls. "Beautiful, but they can sting. You cannae escape it, lad."

As she spoke, the vision of my life in Glasgow seemed to crumble before my eyes. I clenched my jaw and looked away from her. Rhetta knelt beside my bed and put a hand on my knee, peering up into my face.

"I dinnae mean to be cruel; it's just how it is. Magic altered you, yet saved you. Even if you tried to siphon out the magic now harbored within you, it would be a futile attempt. You generate your own magic. You are as the pech or boobrie or selkie; you are a magical creature. You will never be free of it. Your body relies on magic now. It's like the blood within you. If you were to be drained of it, you'd perish."

A sick feeling curled where I had once felt hope blossom. I made my own magic now. My hope dwindled to nothing as I realized the magic wasn't *inside* me; it *was* me.

"Perhaps perishing would be better than what I am now," I snapped, jabbing my spoon into the stew, crushing carrots and potatoes to bits.

"Oh, lad." Rhetta clicked her tongue and stood. She didn't say anything more, no admonishments or rebukes, and so we fell silent again. I shifted into a more comfortable position, wrestling with Rhetta's words. But deep down, I knew she was right. I was changed. I had felt the magic reshape every fiber of me. It must be why I was so sore.

"Lad? How soon will you be able to move?" Rhetta probed, poking at her stew.

I twisted slowly from side to side. "I can move a little now," I grunted. "Still hurts, though."

"I mean, move on from here. Go back."

"Back . . . back to Loch Ailsh? Why?" I asked, my tone more sharp than I meant it to be. I didn't want to face going back to the mainland, confronting my newfound power so soon. I didn't want to think about what my sisters would think or how much my life had changed. I could never go back to that time with them. With Emilia. I bit the insides of my cheeks.

"Because, well, Eimhir is still out there," Rhetta cautioned, setting her bowl aside.

"Yes, and?" I asked, exhaling as my lower back twinged, and I shifted to take the pressure off it.

"Well, she'll be wanting to get this power you have, and—"

"Good, let her take it," I glowered, feeling belligerent. I knew I couldn't let Eimhir have it, wicked and destructive as she was, but I was in a foul mood. Despite Rhetta's assurances that I wasn't evil, I still had magic, and to anyone else, I was wicked, corrupt. Nobody, not in Glasgow or my childhood village, would understand me anymore. In fact, everyone would see my transformation as proof that witchborns were destined for evil. Magic was mischief; that was the end of it. I had sealed my fate. I would no longer be accepted in society.

"Lad, you know she must never be allowed to have control over such power as you have," Rhetta scolded. "You saw what she did with the kelpies before her full strength was taken from her. And that was a drop in the barrel compared to what you have now. We know what she is: ambitious and power hungry. And clever. She won't stop until she gets what she wants, and if she has to tear down the powers of the world to get it, she will. She would use your power to overthrow everything she deems a threat. She cannae be allowed to acquire your magic."

"Alright, alright," I grumbled, tired of the lectures. I picked at my stew, not saying anything. Rhetta was right, of course, but the thought that I had any magic at all made my skin crawl. What would I possibly do with it?

"Anyway, back to the matter at hand," Rhetta said, now sounding impatient and nervous. "As I said, Eimhir is still out there, jealous and angry that you stole Margund's power from her. I think . . . she'll try to get it from you any way she can."

"What do you mean?" I asked, slurping down the stew as aggressively as I could.

"Well, she probably believes that if she applies the right pressure, you'll give in and surrender the magic to her. She knows what is important to you, and I'm afraid she might go after—"

"My sisters," I breathed, "Emilia." The bowl of stew slipped from my grasp at the realization. It stopped a few inches from the ground, great gobs of broth and chunks of meat suspended in midair, trailing from the bowl. Rhetta reached out and plucked my dish from where it floated and gathered the drifting drops back into the bowl as I stared blankly at a spot on the tent wall.

My sisters and Emilia were in danger.

"Aye, that is my fear," Rhetta said, turning her back to me to refresh my stew. "My, you do affect things in the strangest ways, even things just lying around you," Rhetta chattered as if she hadn't just said my sisters were in mortal peril. "You wouldn't believe how many plants sprouted up around you while you slept, you were nearly suffocated by a few—wait, lad, what are you doing?" she demanded as she turned around to see me struggling to stand.

"You asked when I'd be ready to move, and I'm ready to move now!" I snapped, scrambling to right myself as I fell sideways.

"*No*, lad, you need more rest," Rhetta insisted, trying to push me back onto the mattress. I wriggled out of her grip and rolled off the stuffed mattress onto the once-again growing grass, sitting up with a low growl as my backside and legs spasmed in protest at the sudden movement. "You don't need to—"

"Eimhir is going after my sisters. I have to protect them. We have to get to them, *now*. Eimhir has had a head start of several days!" I crawled through the waving grass toward my boots by the entrance, but Rhetta stepped in my way.

"Lad, there is no way you can face off with Eimhir!" she said, shooing away my hands with her foot as I tried to reach around her ankles for my boots. "Even though you have limitless power, you dinnae ken how to use one drop of it! Eimhir has had hundreds of years of practice. Not to mention, she'll be able to draw your power from you as I have! You dinnae ken how to protect yourself or your magic yet! At best, you'll be evenly matched, if not outmatched by her, in your current state!"

"That doesn't matter! You can teach me a few things, and I'll just blast her into oblivion! We are heading out immediately. Now *move*!" I growled, and at that moment, the earth beneath her shifted and moved backward, carrying her outside the tent. With a cry of surprise, she fell over, the lump of earth settling itself back in the ground.

She sat up, glaring at me as I grabbed my first boot and rolled over onto my back to shove my foot into it.

"Boy, you are infuriating! Did you not hear me? You're not *ready* to face her!" Rhetta snapped, getting to her feet and brushing grass and dirt from her dress as she came back inside the tent.

"But if we wait, it will give Eimhir time to exact revenge on my sisters, and I will not allow that! I have to kill her," I panted, reaching for my other boot.

"No, lad, you cannae kill her," Rhetta frowned. "At least not yet."

When I looked up, furious, into Rhetta's face, she held out a hand. "She holds the key to lifting the curse of the kelpies. I know you're angry, but you cannae kill her, at least not until we've gotten the information on how to turn the kelpies back into human beings. Boy, are you hearing me?" Rhetta demanded as I finished getting my boots on.

"Yes, yes, I hear you," I snarled. "Now help me up. Please." I looked to her, holding out my hand. She placed her own hands on her hips, staring down at me. My arms trembled as I tried to hold myself up in that sitting position, and she exhaled.

"Boy, you're weaker than a newborn fawn. How do you expect to fight against Eimhir like this?" Rhetta grunted, grabbing my hand and helping me to my feet. I wobbled for a few slow steps, still clinging to Rhetta's hand for support. The fact that I could stand and move about made hope well up inside me.

"I'm not so weak," I said, taking a few experimental turns around the tent before letting go of her hand completely. "There. You see? Good as new."

My knees gave out, and I fell backward through the flap of the tent, landing on my back in the late summer grass. Above me, the sky was streaked with the colors of the setting sun. Several paces away, the sea crashed onto the rocky shore. Off in the distance, I made out a few gray smudges rising from the sea's horizon: other islands, and farther off, the mainland. Rhetta stepped out of the tent and stood over me.

"There. You see? You aren't," Rhetta huffed, gesturing to my sprawled body. "Lad, give it another day, please," she begged, "There's no point in rushing off to meet your death. It would be much better if you had time to learn a few things first. That way there's at least a small chance you could defeat her, instead of dying and forfeiting millennia of magic to her."

"Yes, it would be better, but we haven't the time! We need to get to my sisters immediately. Maybe if we get there before Eimhir, I can hide them."

Rhetta stared at me as I rolled unsteadily to my feet, then sighed as I collapsed.

Curse this weakened form. I thought I was supposed to be strong in magic! Why wasn't it helping now?

"Lad, I dinnae reckon that Eimhir will hurt them. If she kills them, she knows you won't give yourself over to her."

"If she kills them, yes, but what's to stop her from torturing them first? We have to get to them before she thinks of going after my sisters at all!"

With a snarl, I rolled to my feet, despite the pops and cracks my body made as I stood, determined to stay standing.

Rhetta stared at me, her expression stormy, then shook her head. "Boy, you are something else entirely."

"How do we get off this rock?" I asked, ignoring her and looking out over the coastline.

Rhetta sighed. "While I dinnae agree with you rushing off to face Eimhir, I do think we should move, just in case Eimhir *is* searching for us. But that is it. We're just moving somewhere else. We're not going to Glasgow." I glared back at her, and Rhetta held up a hand. "Not yet. Not until you learn some semblance of magical ability."

Chapter Twenty-Seven

Once we were packed, and after several hours of instruction from Rhetta, I was able to vanish us from the island. We appeared twelve miles to the southeast, as Rhetta had calculated, and not in the sea, as she had feared.

"Not bad for your first go at directing your magic," Rhetta said, her tone grudging. "That's farther than I've ever heard someone travel in one go."

I ignored her compliment, too busy making sure I didn't collapse. My head felt as though it would drift off my shoulders and my body trembled with muscle spasms. I tried to shake off the lightheadedness. I couldn't be weak now. We had to get to Glasgow as soon as possible, and Rhetta wouldn't allow it if I kept collapsing all the time. After my head settled back on my shoulders, I demanded we make another jump. Rhetta looked worried, but before she could stop me, I concentrated hard, and we disappeared. I had no recollection of reappearing.

When I woke up inside the tent, Rhetta explained that we hadn't even made it a half mile when I had passed out, and so she had pitched camp. We had lost another day as I slept.

Rhetta demanded I stay put, even going so far as to magically restrain me to the cot. "You may have more magic than I, but I'm more knowledgeable," she said, exasperated, as I struggled against the magical bonds. "See, this is what I've been trying to tell you. If *I* can tie you down, Eimhir can sweep you away with a flick of her hand, and she can barely hold magic in her. She'll also be able to withdraw the magic from you, just as I'm doing right now."

"You are?" I asked, pausing in my struggle with the bonds and staring up at Rhetta with a blank look.

Rhetta clicked her tongue. "Yes."

With an exhausted sigh, I laid back into my cot. We were silent for a while, Rhetta continuing her supper preparations. I mulled over what Rhetta had said. She was right, and I was acting like a child.

"Rhetta," I began, considering something that I couldn't quite figure out. "How was Eimhir able to hold off Margund for so long? Even with the power she got from killing Sheona, I thought she was practically powerless."

Rhetta sighed. "When Margund had me in her grip, I saw more of Eimhir in those minutes than I'd seen of her in our four years working together. She hid many things from me, one being a relic, similar in power to mine. Since the relic was drawing on the dregs of her magic, I didnae feel it. She had stored the magic she stole from Sheona and what little of her own she makes into the relic, saving up for who knows how long because she cannae hold magic in herself. But even the relic doesn't help much. She's broken, and when she pulled from the relic, she lost a lot of that power as she fought. She was counting on her magic-stealing potion to do the rest." Rhetta gave a wry smile. "But you ruined her plans. Eimhir is very cocky and trusts in herself too much and in humanity too little. She never thought you would drink the potion yourself. I imagine she figured you feared magic too much to take such a leap. She didnae bother to truly get to know you like I have, and therefore, she underestimated you."

Rhetta looked to me, her expression softening "It was a very brave thing you did, lad. You saved our lives. You didnae fully understand the consequences of the risk you took, but I know that when I passed you that vial with Margund's hair, you recognized what I was asking of you. You understood enough, and you still did it. Thank you. For saving my life."

I nodded, embarrassed. If I had understood *more*, would I have done it? I had this power now, yet I felt helpless in every way. Wondering about what might have been would only torture me. I took a deep breath.

"I understand what you meant by not being prepared, and I would like to learn how to use my magic. I'm still anxious to get to my sisters before Eimhir does, but if I knew the basics, it would be enough. Anything would be more useful than just lying here, tied to this cot." I swallowed back the fear thumping in my throat. "Will you teach me how to use magic?"

Rhetta dipped her head. "Of course I shall, but you're eating and resting for a while first."

Once she was satisfied I'd rested and eaten some of the venison she had roasted, she sat down across from me. "First, you must learn how to keep out those that wish to draw magic from you." She explained that it was essential to learn, but I had a feeling it was my first lesson mostly because I could remain resting in bed while we practiced. But two minutes into the practice, when I struggled to deflect her and keep control of the magic that she effortlessly took from me, I was grudgingly glad she insisted on this lesson first. I lost energy quickly, even while laying down. I tried for hours, stopping often to fill my belly again and again as my energy depleted. Meanwhile, Rhetta tidied the tent, made plants grow and bloom around us, levitated stones, and prepared more food—all using my magic. I was unsuccessful the whole evening, falling asleep late into the night, feeling ill-tempered and drained.

The next morning, I again strained to keep Rhetta from siphoning my magic as we sat outside in the grass. I was sick of lying on the cot and was desperate for fresh air and sunshine.

"If you learn anything, learn how to deflect those who would extract from you," Rhetta kept saying. "As long as you keep her from drawing from the power in you, you might be equally matched."

"Why don't you teach me how to, I don't know, throw fire or something at her?" I said through gritted teeth as Rhetta levitated a bowl at her eye level, using only the magic I was failing to keep from her. The bowl didn't waver or wobble one bit as I strained to break off the flow.

"Once you've mastered this, then we'll move on. Besides, you'll need more than just fire to stop her," Rhetta warned, and with a flick, she began to levitate another bowl. I stopped trying to block her, unsure of even how to begin, and wiped my sleeve across my forehead. I couldn't even recognize the magic leaving me.

"Can we at least move further south now?" I gasped, my heart thundering against my ribs at the exertion. I felt like I had been running for miles. "Even if we get just close enough to watch over my sisters?"

Rhetta clicked her tongue. "Once you can stop me drawing from you and move yourself without my help, *then* maybe we'll move. I'm not moving us until you've learned *something* about your new self. Eimhir will get you cornered before you even know what is happening. If she kills you on sight, rushing to your family will all be for nothing. You have to learn to defend yourself before you can help your sisters."

The logic was undeniable, but I didn't like hearing it.

"But I don't know what to do to block you!" I snapped.

The bowls dropped gently to the ground as Rhetta ceased feeding magic to them and turned to me. "Just throwing you into this clearly isn't working." She fell silent, thinking, and I took a long drink of water, contemplating how on earth she would be able to teach a novice mage who had been gifted with a well of power greater than anyone had ever seen.

"Look deep into yourself," Rhetta said, her voice slow with deliberation. "The magic is part of you now. You should take time to learn about it, how you react with it, how the magic feels, how you now feel. When someone draws on your power, you need to recognize that someone is taking a part of you. That might be a place to start. Recognizing the magic as a *part* of you, not just something that is *in* you."

I made a face.

"I know you hold magic in disdain, but it's something you need to reconcile yourself with," Rhetta demanded. "Unless you open your mind to the fact that magic *is* you now, you'll never be able to conquer this side of you. You'll always be weak, never reaching your full potential."

I glowered at the bowls. Such simple objects, but the thought of lifting them with magic felt as impossible as lifting a kelpie with my bare hands.

Rhetta sighed. "I'll give you some time to think on this. We'll try again tomorrow."

She left me lying on the grass, leaving me to ponder about my future. A future I never wanted.

I closed my eyes, enjoying the sunlight and twittering birdsong as I rested in the grass.

I would never be the same as I was.

How did one look inside oneself, see the changes, and use them to their benefit? Where did the magic reside? I felt foolish as I kept my eyes closed, the leaves dappling sunshine onto my face, and I exhaled. As I listened to my breathing, I noticed there was a strange feeling in my chest. Now that I was quiet and actually concentrating on my body, I noticed a difference from before.

Magic thrummed inside me, the sensation similar to the humming beehives my uncle had kept at his estate at Kedlefield Hall, where he used to take us for summer holidays. I remembered my uncle showing me how to collect the comb from the hives. The loud buzzing was muted in my chest. But there was something else about the buzz within me, a slight ebb and flow to the magic, like the waves on the ocean where I'd completed my boyhood aboard ships. Tears rushed to my eyes at the comforting sensation.

The ocean was where I had learned to be truly sure of myself. I'd learned my self-worth there. I wasn't a witchborn or a coward: I was a cabin-boy, then a sailor, then a merchant, then an heir. My uncle had given me that chance to learn about myself. As I got older, I was given greater responsibilities, because he had trusted me. Inheriting the business and his estate was the greatest act of trust he could've given me: trust in my abilities, trust in my responsibility, and trust in my decisions.

He knew I never made a decision hastily when I had the time to think it over. When a decision had to be made rapidly, he trusted me to make the right one. Over time, I had learned to trust myself, too.

So where was that trust now?

Back in that awful cottage, I hadn't fully understood what would happen when I drank the potion. But I knew enough. Though taking the potion had terrified and disgusted me—and though I knew it could kill me—it seemed a far better alternative than Eimhir gaining control of this all-consuming power. In that moment, I accepted the magical responsibility. And even though it turned out to be a greater weight than I could have ever anticipated, I couldn't let go of that responsibility now.

The magic seemed to echo parts of me that were important. It *was* part of me, but I didn't feel any different from who I had been. Maybe it wasn't so bad.

I felt the bright orb inside myself flare, and I looked up to see the two bowls hovering above my head. I cracked a smile. It wasn't what I was trying to accomplish, but it was something.

I spent the rest of the evening trying to picture myself and my magic being one and the same; perhaps from that perspective, I would notice if anyone tried to draw from me.

I went to bed, hopeful that I would be better in the morning.

I wasn't.

When we tried again, I could at least feel Rhetta siphoning from me now, but I didn't know how to break off her contact. I spent the whole day trying to cut it off, but I only succeeded a few times, and only when she wasn't pushing hard.

Rhetta wasn't satisfied when we clambered onto our respective cots for the evening. I was still feeling haggard from the force the magic had on my body. My hands were still half-curled into claws, my face drawn, almost two weeks' worth of a beard hiding my sunken cheeks. I was prone to random cramping as I stretched and worked my body.

I lowered the blanket that draped between our two cots, to respect Rhetta's privacy. Despite our circumstances, Rhetta was still a woman, and I was a respectable young man. I would not jeopardize that, no matter how much Rhetta laughed at me, and no matter how much I didn't feel like a city gentleman anymore. I had values I'd received during my upbringing from a man I respected like a father, and I wasn't about to change them.

When I finally fell asleep that night, my dreams were troubled, full of magic and shadow. My sisters were running down a dark Glasgow alley, but this time it wasn't just a kelpie that chased them. Eimhir, with a legion of her cursed creations, hunted them, cornering them between two brick buildings with no way out.

I finally rose from my cot, unable to handle the horrible scenarios running through my brain. I hobbled over and lifted the flap, exiting into the chilly, drizzly air. Thunder rolled over the hills, and a soft rain sprinkled my face. The wind skirled about, ushering in heavier rain clouds.

If I was to save my sisters, I *needed* the magic to work for me. I took a deep breath and focused my attention on a bush before me. I concentrated on the magic in my chest, taking a shallow scoop out of the well of power. It was still a strange feeling. I didn't think I would ever get used to the bright, endless pool of energy inside my chest, nestled right beside my heart.

I took a deep breath and focused on the bush, working the magic as Rhetta had taught me until it expanded, and I could feel the power running down the lengths of my arms to my palms. I thrust my haggard hands forward toward the bush, trying to release the energy pent up there, but nothing happened except a muscle spasm.

"Brennan, lad? What are you doing?" Rhetta asked from behind me.

I exhaled in frustration and turned to her. "Will using my magic always take this much concentration?" I snapped. "I feel like I have to block everything out just to get the magic to come forth from me, and even then it doesn't work most times. Eimhir will kill me before I even try to *summon* the magic." I fell to my knees, panting.

"When you sailed the first time, were you a master of the seas?" Rhetta asked with crossed arms.

"No," I muttered, ripping up a handful of grass.

"And when you sailed the second time, did you have everything about the winds and the tides memorized?"

I sighed, twiddling a piece of grass between my fingers. "No, it took me years of practice."

"Just so," Rhetta said, "In short order, with plenty of practice, it will be just as easy and natural as breathing, and you will be able to do so many wonderful things you didnae think possible. You just need to learn how *you* use magic."

"I don't need it to be natural, I just need to know how to use it *now*, to protect my sisters."

"And you will. Give it time."

"We don't *have*—"

"We have sufficient," Rhetta interrupted. "Now, try again to do whatever you were about to do with that bush."

I tried several times, and finally, on the fifth try, the bush burst into flames. The rain, which had increased during my failed attempts, immediately doused the fire.

"Make it stop raining above you," Rhetta directed.

"I could *do* that?" I gaped.

"Lad, you're only restricted by your imagination. Try it."

Searching for the same feeling I got when I'd successfully lit the bush on fire, I tried twice, then on the third try, rain poured around me but didn't hit me. Concentrating, I moved the circle of protection to include Rhetta, and she smiled at me, wiping the rain from her face.

"Very good. Magic has been suppressed for so long, only now are we discovering spells and ways to use the magic all over again. Back in the feudal days, they only knew how to do primitive magic, only working with fire, wind, water, and earth. Now the times have changed—we have weapons beyond the sword, we've sailed across the world—we're discovering new things every day, and it is the same with magic. As the world changes, so will how we use magic. It's an exciting and daunting thought."

Rhetta left me to continue training on my own. I practiced until the sun came up, although the gloomy, rain-drenched skies remained dark. By the time Rhetta called me for our midday meal, it only took me two or three tries on every task I focused on, instead of five or six. I felt keenly my lack of skill, but I didn't care. So great was my anxiety for my sisters, I turned to Rhetta with a determined expression.

"Can we *please* move on?" I sighed.

Rhetta looked at me, eyes narrowed. "You're getting better, I'll admit."

"Yes, I suppose knowing my sisters are in grave danger is giving me some motivation," I replied, grim. "I can even block you from drawing my power. You said that was most important, and I can do it."

"But you're still shaky, maybe still a little too—"

"But it's enough to head to Glasgow," I pressed. "It has to be."

Rhetta was still, watching me with an uncertain look.

"Rhetta, *please*. Why are you holding me back?" I demanded.

Rhetta met my gaze, working her jaw. "*I'm* scared, Brennan! Scared of you getting hurt. And . . . I'm scared I'll fail you. Eimhir has already outwitted me once! And she is more powerful than me just by her years of magical experience alone! What if *I'm* not strong enough? What if I cannae—" She cut off, looking away.

I stared, realizing I had been so wrapped up in myself that I hadn't considered Rhetta had fears of her own. She always seemed so sure of herself, so powerful. And I had taken that assumption—that she had all the answers, all the confidence—for granted. She was human, too, full of failings and fears. She just hid it much better than I ever could.

I stepped forward and placed a hand on her shoulder. "We'll be together. Eimhir may be more powerful than the both of us alone, but together, we can overcome her. If we make it there before

Eimhir, perhaps we could move my sisters to a safe location, then I could continue working on my skills. I *need* to know they're safe, and I need you with me. Please."

Rhetta closed her eyes, and with an exhale, replied, "To Glasgow, then. You stubborn, stubborn lad."

Chapter Twenty-Eight

Though I was riddled with anxiety and excitement, my magic seemed to flow more easily than it ever had before as I helped gather the tent.

"*Careful*, lad," Rhetta admonished, ducking as a ladle flew past her face as items zipped to and fro, packing themselves up. "While strong emotions heighten your power considerably, you dinnae want to have to rely on them to work magic. That's a terrible crutch to have. Now take it easy, we'll only be going a few miles at a time."

I raised an eyebrow, but otherwise disregarded her assumption about what distance we'd be traveling. The moment everything was bundled, I focused my energy, honing in on the feeling I got when I successfully worked magic. I fixed my mind on Glasgow, on a specific copse in a park near my home so we wouldn't need a carriage.

I included Rhetta and the tent and all our supplies in my scope of power. Delving into the magic, I willed us to be transported to the park. With a puff of air, I opened my eyes, and saw that Rhetta and the tent were gone, and I was standing alone in the exact same place I'd been, wind tickling my hair.

"No," I growled, turning in place. Had I sent Rhetta alone to Glasgow, or had I banished her to someplace else entirely? Quickly focusing the power inside me, I pictured the place again and willed the magic to move me there.

With a whoosh of wind, I appeared, standing on top of the tent that had tumbled free from its bundle. Rhetta was extracting herself from a bush.

"You sent us all the way to Glasgow?" She blustered when she saw me, and I grimaced. "That was extremely dangerous! I've never heard of anyone going that distance in one go! Well, maybe Margund could've managed it, but she didnae rely on heightened emotions! Dinnae forget you're playing with fire. You could've sent me into someone's hearth!" She brushed stray leaves from her dress. "Though I'll admit that was impressive. Even if you forgot to send yourself along with us." She hid a smile under a sharp exhale.

Ignoring Rhetta's last comment, I helped her gather up the supplies and stow them in some bushes. After stashing away last of it, Rhetta turned to me with a cocked head, tapping a finger on her lips as she scrutinized me.

"Boy, if you go into the city like that, people will think you're back from the dead."

"I am," I muttered.

Without waiting to see if Rhetta would follow, I left the cover of the park and entered the bustling streets of Glasgow. Tears sprang to my eyes as the familiar smells and sounds assaulted my senses. This venture with Rhetta had been much stranger and had felt much longer than any oceanic voyage. The familiar sight of ships' masts jutting into the sky over the tops of buildings made my heart ache with longing. The carriages, the people, the closeness of the buildings . . .

I was finally home.

I couldn't stand and stare, however. This place was now in danger, just like my sisters. I tried to run the entire two blocks to my aunt's home, but was slowed, not only by my hobbled body, but by the crowds clogging the streets; I had to dodge horses, carriages, and people out enjoying the fair summer weather.

I had been so caught up in the world of magic for these last weeks, I had forgotten how mundane and slow real life could be. I had just traveled over two hundred miles in just a few days, which, according to Rhetta, was a feat unheard of even in the magical world.

Turning the corner of my street, I arrived at my aunt's house. I sprang up the steps and barged through the front door. Tabitha, the serving maid, was carrying a tea tray toward the parlor. Upon seeing me, she shrieked and nearly dropped the platter as I stood in the doorway.

"Get out, you vagabond!" she screeched, and as I turned to her, recognition took over her face. "Oh! Wha—Master Brennan? How . . . you look . . . you're back!" she dithered, "We weren't expecting you back so—"

"Where are my sisters?" I demanded, not caring that I had interrupted her. Rhetta came up into the house beside me, panting slightly. As I turned to glance at Rhetta, I caught a glimpse of myself in the entryway mirror. Besides my stormy expression, I looked positively wild: dirt streaked my unshaven face, my frame had grown thin, and I no doubt smelled. I couldn't blame Tabitha for thinking me a street urchin. The maid gave Rhetta a curious look, but addressed me.

"Why, in the parlor, sir. I was just about to take them their—"

Without waiting for her to finish, I ran down the hall to the parlor, Rhetta at my heels. As I reached for the door latch, the double doors flew open.

Norah was stepping out, calling, "Tabitha, are you alright—" She stopped still upon seeing me standing before her.

"Brennan?" Norah asked, pulling back, hand on her mouth.

"Brennan? He's back?" I heard Slaine call from inside the room, and in a moment, she was beside Norah.

"Brennan!" My two sisters cried in unison, and before I could catch my breath, I was overwhelmed as they flung themselves onto me.

I twirled them around, kissing their faces and hair as I squeezed them tightly, my heart hammering in relief. "Oh, my little birds," I breathed.

"Oh, Brennan, what—what has happened to you?" Norah gasped, stepping away to take in my ragged appearance. I noticed Slaine wrinkle her nose as she pulled her face away from my chest.

"No time for that now. How are you both?" I urged, my throat tight. They were alright. I wasn't too late.

"We're wonderful now that you're back so soon! Just as your dear friend Eimhir promised us you would!" Norah laughed, her eyes bright. My heart froze, and my head snapped up to look into the room behind my sisters.

Eimhir, dressed in an immaculate blue dress that would catch the eye of any man, stood from the tea table, her eyes flashing. She wore wickedness well.

Mentally I threw up protections around my magic so Eimhir couldn't draw power from me as we stared each other down. I was still shaky at it, but hopefully I could hold her off if she tried anything.

"She told us she'd met you during your travels, and she was visiting town for the next few weeks, and since she was a dear friend of yours, we insisted she stay with us," Norah chattered happily, but I wasn't listening as I tried to rein in my anger. Seeing *her* there, sitting and chatting with my sisters as if she were their friend, made fury erupt inside me.

"Get *out* of my house," I snarled, stepping into the room.

"Brennan!" Norah gasped as Slaine clapped a hand over her mouth at my rudeness. Eimhir merely smiled as if I had complimented her dress.

"Now, now, Brennan, is tha' any way to speak to such a dear friend?" Eimhir asked, smoothing the front of her dress, her red hair catching the sunlight streaming through the windows. She looked stunning. I shivered.

"Brennan, who is this?" Slaine asked, looking past me toward Rhetta. Instead of answering, I pushed my sisters behind me, ignoring their protests and questions, and glared down at Eimhir.

"Get out. *Now*," I growled.

"Brennan," Rhetta said in warning, coming up behind me, placing a hand on my shoulder. I didn't care.

This *thing* before me was the reason half of my family had been taken away from me, cursed to live in a tortured shape. She had inflicted suffering on thousands of people, and for what? Her own twisted ambition and hatred.

Now she was here, playing with my sisters, encroaching on their hospitality, naivety, and youth, threatening their lives while playing the part of a friend. Rage I had never known burned within me, and the magic nestled in my chest danced in anticipation.

"I said *get out*," I thundered. "Or I will destroy you."

I could feel my sisters tense behind me, and I heard one of them whimper.

"Remember, lad, you may have more power than me, but you have no knowledge of how to use it. I could easily be the one to destroy *you*, and then your sisters would be easily dispatched afterward," Eimhir said with a pleasant expression, running her fingers over a piece of lace on her dress that had begun to curl away from her bosom. She pouted her lips in a frown when the piece of lace wouldn't stay flush against the silk of her dress.

"You will not touch them," I barked.

"I admit, I'm glad you're finally here," Eimhir sighed. "It was getting quite tiresome, all this pretending to be friendly; first with Rhetta, then you, now your sisters. However, the ruse was all worth it to see the shock on your faces. And now, I'll get what I came for."

My chest was burning, the heat traveling down my arms into my hands. "Rhetta, take my sisters out of here."

Eimhir's attention snapped onto Rhetta for the first time since we walked in the door. "Rhetta, dinnae you move those girls, or I will kill all three of you without hesitation," Eimhir commanded, her eyes narrowing.

"Remember, *dear*," Rhetta said, her tone icy. "I, too, have more power than you."

"True," Eimhir sneered. "Even with me relic, you overpower me," she said, gesturing to the ragged white and black stone she had tied around her throat with a ribbon. "But remember, you dinnae know how to use your magic very well either. You druids are so afraid of those of us who use magic to the fullest tha' you've worked your powers as sparingly as you could your whole life. I am more powerful with my knowledge alone. Five hundred years of it. Now, I dinnae want to kill all of you," her voice became a mere hiss, her eyes glinting as she spoke, "and everyone else in this household, but I will, unless I get what I want."

I bit my tongue.

I didn't want this to spiral out of control by setting her off, but I didn't trust a word she was saying about sparing us if I gave up my power. Maybe it *had* been foolish to rush here so quickly.

"All right, let us talk. But without my sisters present," I snapped, beginning to push my sisters into the hall.

Eimhir barked out, "Stop!"

I paused, glaring at her.

"They *do* need to be here," Eimhir insisted. "I have a feeling you won't give up what I want easily, so I want what's at stake for you to be right before your eyes."

"I'm not giving up my sisters!" I growled, and I felt Norah and Slaine press up against my back.

"And yet I suspect tha' you won't give up your magic either," Eimhir said, making a tsking sound with her tongue, and I heard my sisters gasp behind me. I winced. I had a good idea what they were thinking.

"Amazing how quickly magic draws you in, isn't it?" Eimhir smiled, snake-like. "But you have to make a choice, *laddie*."

I stared daggers at Eimhir while she smiled her chilling smile, her eyes flaming bonfires. She was so power-hungry herself that she would never believe that I *didn't* want the magic. My only desire was to keep *her* from having it. Panic threatened to overwhelm me, and all I could think to do was stall until I could come up with a plan to get my sisters to safety.

"How do you intend to take my powers?" I challenged, "I drank the only vial of potion you made."

"Did you?" Eimhir asked, her expression sharp.

I paused. "Margund said . . ."

"Yes, well," Eimhir sighed, inspecting her fingernails. "Margund, despite her power, did *not* know everything." Eimhir sent me a shrewd look. "Making me potion took decades and I couldn't make very much of it, but I had enough. Margund assumed I was cocky, bringing only one vial. What she didn't realize is tha' the flask she took away *was* me backup vial. Or at least one of them. Margund didn't even consider tha' I had already taken some of the potion and tha' all I needed to do was ingest her hair."

She bared her teeth at me. "I tried to keep her focus on you and the vial so tha' in the chaos, she wouldn't notice me stealing a strand or two. But you killed her and took her power before I could get at it. Then I went for your hair, but Rhetta was too quick. So, again, I already have the potion." Eimhir ran a hand over her stomach. "I took it the moment I heard your sisters call your name. Though it would be much easier if you would just hand over your hair now. Taking a physical part of another magic wielder by force can be *very* difficult."

Dread quickened my pulse. I *was* a fool to come! She just needed to get her hands on one strand of my hair, and she'd be the most powerful creature in the world. And I'd be dead.

Slaine broke the silence with a tiny voice. "Brennan? What's going on?"

Not daring to look away from Eimhir in case she chose to strike first, I reached behind me, patting the back of one of my sisters. "It's okay, Slaine. Everything will be well. But this woman is no friend of ours. She's a witch," I snapped, and my sisters gasped, clutching at my arms.

"Why is she here?" Slaine whimpered.

"Why am I here, dear one?" Eimhir asked, her tone mocking.

"Don't you dare speak to them," I snarled.

"I'll do as I please," Eimhir snarled back, the horrific sneer making her look positively rabid. Her expression softened as she looked around me to Slaine. "I'm here to take what's mine. Your dear brother is being very selfish, and I'm afraid I'll have to give him a little incentive to make him give me what I want. I'll have to kill you." Eimhir gave a kind smile to Slaine, then locked her cold eyes to mine. "Time's running out, lad. What will you do?" She lifted a hand with almost casual ease and began pushing up the sleeves on her arms.

"Norah," I commanded, "Where's Aunt?"

"She's on a social call," Norah said, her voice so shaky I could barely understand her. My heart felt like it was breaking anew. My sisters had no idea why they were in the middle of this quarrel, or what it was really about, and I was to blame for that.

I had broken the one rule instilled in us from birth: never trust a witch. Now everyone else was paying for my folly.

"What about Emilia?" I asked, breathless. "Is she here in the city?"

Norah squeaked out a "Yes," as Eimhir cried, "Oh, aye, Emilia! I met her the other day. Beautiful girl. I will have to pay her a visit once everyone here is dead."

I snarled, ignoring the magic that burned down my arm at her baiting, "I cannot give you what you want. Why risk death?"

Eimhir cast me a pleasant smile. "Why will you?"

There were gasping shrieks behind me, and I turned to see both of my sisters rising into the air, clutching their throats.

"Give the power over to me, or they're dead," she called over their choked cries.

With a bellow, I turned to Eimhir, my ears ringing, my vision flashing red, and charged, imbuing my entire body with the heated magic in my chest. Eimhir moved to cast something at me but not before I collided into her.

There was a concussive explosion as we slammed into the wall behind Eimhir, and the brickwork crumbled like it was made of ash. We tumbled into the next room, brick and wood raining down on us. I scrambled to my feet over the debris, dust choking my vision, the ringing dying away. I heard distant screaming and the falling of a few more bricks. I turned, looking for Eimhir, who was also getting to her feet, looking dazed.

I didn't recognize the room, and it hit me: we had crashed through the wall into the house next door. The screaming came from the neighboring boy and girl as they ran from the destroyed room in terror. I turned to see Rhetta lowering my sobbing sisters to the ground. As I whirled back to Eimhir, who was getting her bearings, she cast a silvery cloud of smoke in my direction. I tried to throw up a defense, but I was blinded as the cloud enveloped me.

I swung my arms around, desperately trying to rid the veil over my eyes, tripping over the pile of rubble in the middle of the room and falling to the bricks. Something started constricting me, starting at my ankles, then rushing up my body as I lay among the rubble. Inert, I struggled against my invisible bonds, but to no avail. I felt rough hands grab me and heard Eimhir muttering as she yanked my head.

With a roar, I tried to wiggle away, but she twined her fingers into my hair and began to tug just as I felt another body collide with us. Eimhir lost her grip on my hair, the few strands she had managed to pull free dropping into my open mouth. Spitting, I could suddenly see as Rhetta placed a hand on my forehead and whispered something. The very hairs on my head seemed to shimmer and tingle. Had she placed a protection around my *hair*?

As the tingling stopped, Rhetta rasped, "Get yourself unbound," before she ducked away, barely evading a portion of wall that Eimhir hurled at her. The section of brickwork hit the wall beside me and showered me with brick dust.

I concentrated on my stiff body and called up the magic, trying to find ways to weaken the curse that held me bound as fire and glass roared across the room above me. I soon found a crack in the enchantment, and, using the power inside me, I rammed the weakness with a magical punch that shattered my bonds. Scrambling to my feet, I saw Rhetta and Eimhir facing one another, their hands out, their faces contorted in concentration as they grappled with one another.

Drawing up my magic, I tried recreating the bonding spell Eimhir had put me under, but ended up spouting jets of sand toward her. Eimhir stepped out of the way of the incoming sand and hurled a crackling ball of fire toward me. I flung up a weak shield that barely took the brunt of the searing heat, but it disintegrated on impact, the force of it throwing me back through the hole into my aunt's house. My body slammed onto the dust-riddled carpet. I shook my head, trying to clear the stars that twirled in my vision.

"Come here, dear!" Eimhir called, and Rhetta was thrown across the room, crashing into a chair. "Now, where are your dear sisters?" Eimhir shouted.

"Don't you *dare!*" I roared, leaping to my feet. I shot several bricks at her, the rage rising again. When she deflected my projectiles, I took a deep breath and charged at her a second time.

"Not again, lad!" Eimhir shrieked. Behind her, the entire front of the parlor exploded out into the street. Glass, brick, and iron rained down on those going about their business, throwing the crowds on the street into chaos. The screaming was deafening as Eimhir hopped out to the cobbles, me on her heels. I reached out to grab her with my magic, but she danced away from my efforts and cleared people out of her way with grand sweeps of her arm.

"Do you want the whole city to suffer, lad?" Eimhir shouted over her shoulder. "Because I *will* raze this precious town of yours to the ground if you dinnae give me what I want! This is much more than your sisters, now, isn't it?" To emphasize her point, she lifted two women and a young boy that had been running by into the air, throwing them more than three stories high before they started to plummet back down.

"No, *stop!*" I shouted, concentrating on trying to slow their descent, but Eimhir cast another fiery ball at me, tearing away my focus as I dodged, and all three people hit the street with sickening thuds. I stared, horrified at their bodies lying there motionless, and turned back to Eimhir, who was grinning, her face flushed, breathless. Around us, the screaming and pounding of running feet seemed to dim as I stared at Eimhir, feeling ill. She was enjoying this.

"Who should be next?" she called, tittering. With a wave, she raised an entire carriage—complete with a squealing, terrified horse and occupants inside—and raised it high, higher than the houses, and held it there.

"Give me the magic, boy, and I won't drop them."

I didn't believe her for a moment. She would drop them no matter what, just to show her power.

Instead, I reached up with my own magic and began to struggle with her for the carriage. Eimhir laughed.

"You think you can win? You'll drop them before I do," Eimhir trilled.

I cursed inwardly at the truth of her words. If she let go with her magic, I wasn't trained enough to keep the heavy carriage with a screaming horse in the air. Desperate, I jerked the carriage away from her grip. As she laughed, I threw the carriage, none too gently, over to the nearest roof, where it clattered down, tiles hailing to the street below. The steep roof was precarious, but I had propped the carriage against the chimney, wedging it in place.

The horse, still strapped in the traces, began rearing up, bucking the screaming occupants still inside. Before the horse's flailing could send them careening to the ground below, I reached up to calm the panicked horse's mind. As I struggled to soothe the horse, I felt something tug at my chest: someone drawing upon my power. In horror, I looked to Eimhir, who was grinning madly. Wrenching my eyes back to the carriage, I forced the horse to calm just as a gale-force wind whipped me away, throwing me down the street. Landing hard on the cobbles, I gasped, struggling to bring air back into my lungs.

"You see, lad? You cannae beat me." Eimhir sauntered toward me, the crowds stampeding to get away from us. "You cannae concentrate on more than one thing at a time. And now, you're vulnerable to me." To prove her point, she redoubled her efforts, and people left and right of us went flying into the air while at the same time, an enormous pressure began to bear down on me as she drilled me with her eyes.

I mentally jerked away, trying to break her link with me, but I could feel her delving in deeper, reveling in the inordinate amount of power inside me, her face fierce with amazement and greed. Her expression made my skin grow cold.

I scrambled to my feet, still wheezing from hitting the cobbles so hard, and ran, throwing up a shield around me. Maybe if I got far enough away, her hold on me would break.

"Oh, lad. There's more power there than I could even imagine!" Eimhir cackled, her voice drunk with joy. "You think running will save you? A coward's choice, because I will never stop till what you have is mine!" she called, her voice amplified with a spell as I ducked through the terrified stragglers in the street before dodging around a corner.

Behind me, the cobbles began imploding, a wall of deadly projectiles shooting after me as Eimhir's curses destroyed the street. The panicked screaming around me intensified as I ran faster, my heart searing, my body howling at the torture it had been through the last several days. I struggled to stuff down my growing horror as I watched innocent people struck down by exploding stones as I dashed past. Still trying to hold my mental shield, I cast another spell to protect myself from physical projectiles, hoping I could keep both shields in place.

I glanced back to make sure Eimhir was still following me. I wouldn't be able to reach the house in time if she doubled back to get my sisters. Thankfully, she was in pursuit, throwing people out of her way with impunity as she came.

I ran for a few more blocks before turning onto the street that lined the riverbank, where the citizenry was unaware of our ongoing battle, but the tumult and distant smoke had caused the milling crowds to slow with curiosity.

As I dodged through the street, the familiar smell of the river and the creaking of the ships docked at the wharves washed a new emotion over me: regret.

I had still hoped I would be able to come back to this life, even if only for a little while, but I was slowly destroying it, bit by bit. As I ran through the crowds, I tried breaking Eimhir's contact with me. It was a little weaker than before, but I still couldn't shake her tenacious grip as she drank from the deep ocean that I held within my breast.

As I was trying to stave her off, a building off to my left exploded outward, and the street's normal noise shattered into deafening disarray. People scrambled for cover, while those who were injured from the debris lay helpless in the street. The building beside the ruined one also exploded, showering the street with brick, stone, and horribly, I realized, some unfortunate innocents. The explosions continued, rocking the ships in the river, churning the water with the violent concussions.

I stopped dead still, watching the pandemonium in the street, my ears ringing from the explosions. So many dead. Dread curled around my heart as more screaming pounded in my ears. *I did this. I was destroying this city.*

I couldn't keep running; she would just keep coming, keep hurting.

I turned back to face Eimhir and saw her standing stock-still in the street, dismissive of the chaos and suffering around her. Heartless. Cruel. She would destroy the lives of everyone in the city if it meant she got what she wanted, and then her cruelty would only increase.

She was still drawing from me, I could feel it. She could draw power for the next hundred years and still not make a dent in the power that resided there.

Though she would never be able to drain me fully without taking my hair and using it in her potion, she was getting more and more dangerous the longer she was connected to me. I felt powerless, despite the magic thrumming within me. Why hadn't I listened to Rhetta? I had been foolish to rush in so quickly to meet with Eimhir. The witch hadn't hurt my sisters in the several days she had stayed with them. She had waited until I had arrived to finally show her hand.

I had doomed them all in my haste to save them.

Dismay washed over me. I was not ready to enter this world of magic, where those more cunning than me lurked. Whenever my family was in danger, I was used to charging in head first, without thinking. But now I was dealing with creatures who stalked and planned for years. My tactics of bursting in to save those in danger would not work here; it was a flaw that would get us all killed.

"Feeling overwhelmed yet, lad?" Eimhir called, laughing as a ship behind me exploded. Sailors' howls echoed across the water as timber and shredded, fiery sails crashed down onto the docks. "Overwhelmed by all this death you're causing by your selfishness? I know tha' the power is enticing, but you're causing more suffering than is necessary! All these dead and injured by your unwillingness to end the destruction. Give tha' magic over to me, then I can end your anguish."

I saw the glint in her eye. She would kill me, then kill my sisters for good measure, and I had no doubt that she would then raze the town that had given me my life back after *her* kelpies had taken everything from me. *She* had taken everything from me, and I didn't know how I would stop her.

In a heartbeat, Rhetta appeared behind Eimhir, who was too focused on me to pay heed to the tumult around her. Rhetta, her eyes squeezed shut in exertion, grabbed onto Eimhir's neck. Eimhir seized up with a silent scream on her lips.

Both women jerked and shuddered, and I assumed Rhetta was trying to control Eimhir, as Margund had done to us. I moved toward the women, thinking maybe I could help subdue Eimhir, but Rhetta screamed out as she was blasted backward. I realized that Eimhir was still drawing from me. I cursed. I just couldn't shake her loose.

Fury etched Eimhir's countenance as she looked between me and Rhetta.

"I admit, even with access to your—my—power, it's difficult to fight the both of ye at once. Perhaps it's time I call some help of me own!"

She threw a palm out toward the waterway, and behind us, the river began to roar. I turned and my knees nearly buckled beneath me as all along the waterfront, the river's surface seethed and frothed as kelpies, dozens of them, came bursting from the water and charged toward the heart of the city.

"Better hurry along, there, lad. These kelpies will actually drown their victims, not change them. You wouldn't want tha' on your conscience, would you? Off with you now, since you love trying to save the day!" Eimhir called, shaking with laughter at my pale, horrified expression.

"*Lad, come on*!" Rhetta screamed, getting to her feet and blasting a kelpie away that was charging us. "We have to stop them! Break their legs, bash them in the head, anything!" She lifted bricks and stones into the air with magic, sending the projectiles hurtling off toward the escaping kelpies. I sent several flashes of fire at oncoming beasts, my chest tight, my stomach sick as I realized I was killing humans trapped in their cursed form, but I had to. If I didn't, more people would die.

Reaching up with my magic, hating myself and cursing Eimhir's name, I pulled the remaining half of a crumbling building down, crushing a handful of kelpies as they tried to pick their way through the rubble. I stared, stomach roiling, at the pile of rubble pinning the silent kelpies down, praying that some survived.

I heard something behind me and turned just in time to see Eimhir wave, send me a chilling smile, and disappear with a laugh.

"Rhetta!" I bellowed, "Eimhir's gone!"

"I know!" Rhetta grunted, heaving part of a mast into the air. "Kill her, lad. You have to kill her! She's going to finish your sisters! Go! I can handle this!" she cried, felling several kelpies at once with a swipe of the splintered mast.

Kill her. I grit my teeth, knowing I couldn't dwell on my reservations. Rhetta was right, but I needed to be smart. Eimhir would know I was coming for her. She would block every magic spell I used. Somehow, I would have to draw her attention away from any obvious attacks. My mind whirled. I didn't have enough magical know-how, but it didn't matter right now. I had to stop her, and I *would* think of something. I *had* to.

Concentrating, trying to block out Rhetta's cries and the screams of dying kelpies, I transported myself onto the front steps of my aunt's house. The moment I appeared, I heard screaming, and I burst through the doorway. Eimhir had both of my sisters by the throat, holding them off the ground. Tears streamed down my sisters' faces.

"Careful, laddie," Eimhir called. "You wouldn't want me to *crush*—" she paused, and my sisters' screams choked off into silence, "their pretty little necks, now would you?"

"Eimhir, please," I said, my anger curdling into fear. I held up my hands. "Please, please, don't—"

"You know what you can do to stop me, lad," Eimhir commanded.

I swallowed, mind racing furiously, and before I could reply, I heard a voice that made my heart nearly burst in my chest.

"Norah! Slaine!"

I turned as Emilia, her voice strangled with worry, came stumbling in through the doorway. My throat constricted as I took in her wild hair and ripped dress. "Norah! Slaine! Are you both alright—" She stopped in her tracks as her eyes fell upon me.

"Brennan?" Emilia whispered, eyes widening. I nodded once, then her eyes slid to Eimhir, who was still holding my sisters up by their throats. Emilia gave a confused shriek and charged past me toward Eimhir.

"Put them down!" Emilia screamed as I grabbed her around the waist to stop her, dragging her back into my chest as my sisters clawed at Eimhir's hands.

"Ah, your pretty young lass!" Eimhir crowed, eyes narrowed in delight. "Maybe *she'll* help quicken your decision." Eimhir threw my sisters aside as if they weighed no more than a pair of kittens and gestured toward Emilia.

"NO!" I roared as Emilia was pulled from my arms. I leapt and failed to grab onto her as she was swept to Eimhir as if on a stiff wind. Eimhir caught Emilia around the throat with her hands, then threw her high into the air with magic, where Emilia dangled, her feet jerking beside Eimhir's head.

"The longer you wait, the more you'll regret, lad," Eimhir called as Emilia began screaming. Emilia, struggling high above, kicked out hard, her foot connecting with Eimhir's face. Though Eimhir barely flinched at the blow from Emilia's shoe, she looked up at Emilia with hatred in her eyes.

"Maybe it would be best if this lass forgot everything she's seen. Including you!" Eimhir hissed, her face blotchy red. Emilia made a strangled noise and I desperately flung some white-hot bricks at Eimhir, who shoved them away with a contemptuous flick of her wrist.

"When will you understand tha' you cannae touch me with your magic?" she seethed, "You barely know how to contain the magic inside you—do you really think you have any spells tha' could disarm me?" Above us, Emilia screamed and sputtered. I had no idea what Eimhir was doing to her, but the overwhelming helplessness crashed over me again.

Think, *you fool! Take her by surprise, somehow!* I snatched up an iron bar from the rubble but realized I wouldn't be able to shoot it at Eimhir. I couldn't touch her with any spell.

"You're losing her, lad. The magic inside you will not save her," Eimhir gloated, her expression looking more beast than woman.

The magic inside me.

I knew I couldn't work it into any helpful spell, but perhaps I didn't need to. The power itself would be enough.

Finding the connection Eimhir used to pull magic from me, I drew into myself and opened my mind, allowing a huge wall of power to flood from me into Eimhir. Both of us gasped at the influx of the staggering amount of magic.

Eimhir's eyes rolled up into her head, her body shaking at the overwhelming crush of power now overflowing into her.

I lunged toward her, not bothering to use magic. Instead, my grip tightened on the metal rod still in my hand. Before Eimhir could revel in the power, I drove the twisted metal rod through her heart as I wrenched at our connection, completely cutting off my wave of magic. Eimhir's laugh warped into a rasping shriek, her body arching backward. I felt repulsed as blood spurted from the wound, gushing over my hand. I also felt magic, the magic from her body, begin to fill the room and somehow reel itself into my own magical reserve. Above us, Emilia screamed as the magical noose around her neck disappeared, and she fell to the floor with a cry, then scrambled away, dragging a limp leg.

Eimhir's knees buckled, and she fell into me, her dead weight knocking me to the floor. With a gurgling scream, her mouth opening and closing, she let out a few final frantic breaths before her eyes turned glassy and she fell still.

I was nearly sick all over her dead form, but I kept my stomach and pushed her off me. I had to be sure. I crouched over her and put a hand over her mangled breast, searching for a heartbeat. When I felt none and was certain she was really dead, I felt relief flare up inside me. The relief was quickly smothered by revulsion as I looked down at her body.

Rising, I stared at my blood-soaked hands. They twitched and fluttered like the frantic wings of a bird. I clenched them tight. I had never taken a life in such a way before. Margund, and the kelpies, had been different. This . . . the feeling of someone's life leaving their body was one I was sure would haunt my coming dreams. I never wanted to feel that again.

But what if a situation like this happens again? a cautious voice nagged at me. I shook it away. I was not a killer. I did not relish killing. It had to be done, but even as I stared at the lifeless form of Eimhir, I felt remorse. Remorse and pity that it had to come to that final act. How often would I have to take those final, desperate steps to stop others from hurting the ones I cared for? I raised my head, wanting to avoid those wrenching thoughts, and looked to the rest of the room.

The hall was crowded with servants and my sisters, who had hurried to Emilia's side and crowded around her. All were staring wide-eyed at me.

I stepped toward my family, but they took several hasty steps away from me, their eyes fearful, their jaws slack. I paused and looked down again at my bloody, shaking hands. I knew how I must look to them. They had seen me use magic. They had seen me kill. I could imagine what was going on in their minds. The same would've gone through mine before I learned more about magic. Before I had been transformed by it.

I was a changed creature, now. I could see their terror of me in their eyes. Rhetta had been right: I was no longer Brennan Lennox.

"Emilia, are you hurt?" I asked, my rough voice making her jump. She shied away, clinging to Norah.

"Emilia, please," I whispered.

She looked at me with bewildered eyes. "Wh-who are you?" she panted, trembling. "How do you know my name?" Her voice shrilled in the silent hall.

I stumbled forward, hand outstretched in a pleading gesture. The crowd backed away again. "Emilia, it's me . . . Brennan."

"I don't know you. I don't know you! Norah, who is this?" Emilia gasped, holding on to Norah as if she were a lifeline. "Don't you come near me!"

I pulled back my hand, my stomach curling in horror. No, it couldn't be . . . I cast my mind back to Eimhir's words as she had held Emilia aloft. Eimhir's threat was not just a threat: it had been a spell, wiping me completely from Emilia's memory.

Norah stared at Emilia, chin trembling, before turning back to me, horror evident in her eyes. "What have you *done* to her?"

I heard quick footsteps behind me and then Rhetta gasped, "Lad, you must come. All the kelpies are down, but some not for long. You must help me get them back into the river."

The kelpies . . . With sudden horror, I looked at Eimhir's broken form on the floor. I turned to Rhetta, heartsick.

"I'm sorry, Rhetta," I choked, gripping my hair. "I killed her before I could get the counter-curse from her mind. She had my sisters, Emilia—I had to protect—" Until that moment, I had forgotten that we were to keep Eimhir alive until the counterspell could be withdrawn from her thoughts.

"Dinnae worry yourself, lad. I already got it," Rhetta said, giving me a tired smile. "Back on the riverfront. Come, we must hurry."

My knees turned soft in relief, and I gripped the banister to keep from falling.

"How long will it take to make the antidote for the kelpies?" I asked, elation making my voice shake.

Rhetta shook her head. "We cannae hope to make it right now. It will take months, at the very least. Right now, we can move the kelpies into the water, and since Eimhir—" Rhetta's eyes flicked to the slain form at my feet, "—since she's dead, and not controlling them anymore, we can try a spell to keep them in the water for now. But you must come help me before they wake."

I turned back to the girls, who pressed themselves into the wall behind them. Exhaustion welled up inside me just looking at them. "You're safe now, I promise. Stay here with Emilia. I'll be back. It will all be alright."

With a grimace, I picked up Eimhir's body. As I moved to leave the house, I looked back at their pale, terrified faces staring back at me. Emilia glanced around in confusion. I ground my teeth together.

If only I could take the pain away, make it as if it never happened.

With a sigh, I turned to Rhetta. "We best go sort out those kelpies."

Chapter Twenty-Nine

It took us over an hour to pick our way through the ruined waterfront, searching out every kelpie in the streets and removing them to the water. My heart wrenched at every fallen man, woman, child, and kelpie I passed, their deaths another stone of guilt crushing my soul. I unceremoniously took the stone relic from Eimhir's throat and dumped her body into the river, turning away as she sank out of sight. With the help of Rhetta and my magical store, we cast a barrier over the water to keep the kelpies inside until we could create the cure. I don't know how many kelpies died in our efforts to stop them, and I didn't want to think about it.

As the final words were uttered over the river, I sank onto a half-destroyed wall, my face in my hands. I felt a gentle touch and looked up to see Rhetta staring down at me, her expression twisted in concern.

The crowds were gathering again, now that the commotion had ceased, and I was grateful we had been able to get the remaining, living kelpies back into the water before the masses had all arrived. I didn't want to imagine the chaos and butchering that would have occurred had we not finished our work in time. Now, hundreds of people began to cautiously flood the waterfront, inspecting the ruined ships and houses.

"There!" a voice cried, and we turned to see a man pointing a shaking finger toward us. "The witches who did this!" A rumble ran through the crowd, though no one moved toward us, their faces a mix of rage and fear.

"We best go, lad," Rhetta whispered. "They look ready to riot, they do."

I followed her around a corner, but stopped her before she could transport us.

"Is there any way we can erase their memories of this?" I asked, my heart aching. I had destroyed so much of my town. I didn't mean to hurt them, and I didn't want them thinking an evil warlock had come and caused so much havoc and death.

"I dinnae see how, lad. This level of devastation . . ."

"Can we, I don't know, put it into their heads that it was something natural, like a fire or storm?" I asked. I didn't want to be held accountable in the eyes of all these people, even though I deserved it. Despite trying to save them, I had caused unfathomable damage.

A thought came to me like a bolt from Eimhir's hand. Forgetting about the wreckage of the town wouldn't be enough. Once the kelpies were turned back, people would realize what they'd done to their loved ones. I didn't want to imagine the insanity that would follow. With the knowledge that people had been cursed, the masses would look for someone to blame and come for magic wielders. More bloodshed would occur.

And it was possible more witches and warlocks—perhaps ones even worse than Eimhir had been—would come searching for the mage that had enough power to break a country-wide curse. All the power within me put a bounty on my head. But I couldn't give it to anyone, no matter how much I wished it away. I could trust no one but myself with this terrible burden of eternal magic. No, we had to make more than just Glasgow forget.

I ran a hand through my hair, realizing the scope of what I needed to do. An entire country would need their minds wiped, replaced with other memories. I stumbled backward into the wall, groaning.

"If it's something you want to try, we can," Rhetta said, concerned. "I dinnae ken what's going on in your mind right now, lad, but I think we should head back to your sisters."

That brought me back to the present, and the problems it presented. I shook my head, digging my fingers into the brick behind me. "Please. Don't take me back to my sisters. I cannot bear the way they looked at me." I ducked my head, throat burning, ashamed at my cowardice. I would do anything, even battle Eimhir again, to take the looks of terror and revulsion from their faces.

"Lad, after all you've done to protect and care for them, you cannae abandon them now, when they're so full of fear and questions. Can you imagine what they're feeling?"

Yes, I could imagine it, but my strength was already threatening to give way. The thought of having to explain everything—the kelpies, the power I had received—it would all be too much for them. It was too much for *me*. Not six months ago I had set out to sell my family property, and now I held more power than anyone could imagine in my very being, not to mention that the responsibility of restoring the kelpies was on my shoulders. I had to persevere.

I nodded.

We went back to the house, where my sisters were surrounded by the servants and my aunt. I suspect she had hurried home after hearing about the destruction throughout the city. When I entered, the whole crowd fell silent, glaring eyes on me. Rhetta opted to stay outside while I had it out with my family. Ignoring the scowling faces, I held my hand out to my sisters.

"Norah, Slaine, I must speak with you, privately," I said, careful to keep my tone soft.

"No, you will not!" My aunt Alana stood in front of my sisters, defiance etched where gentleness usually resided. "I don't know what creature you are, but you will leave this house immediately."

"Aunt, I will speak to my sisters," I pressed, feeling more weary about having it out with my aunt than taking down another witch. "Norah, Slaine, *please*. I mean you no harm. I wish to explain some things. I am your brother, I swear."

"I have no doubt you are Brennan. You're just not the Brennan who left us," Alana shot back, her voice trembling.

"No. I'm not," I replied, my tone growing heated. "But that does not mean I wish you harm. If my sisters say they do not desire to speak to me, I will honor their wishes, but you cannot speak for them, Aunt." I turned to look past Alana to my sisters who were holding each other, watching me with terrified eyes.

"Norah, Slaine, will you speak to me?" I avoided looking toward the stairs, where Emilia sat. I couldn't bear to see her blank eyes staring back at me.

Norah shook her head, eyes wide, as Slaine cried into her hands.

"Norah, please," I rasped, "Please, it's me, your brother. Slaine, you sewed me this handkerchief," I urged, digging in my trouser pocket and pulling out the soiled and creased kerchief sewn with the swans and thistles. I thrust it toward them, and all those gathered in the hall flinched backward. "And Norah, you got that scar on your foot when a piece of coal fell into your shoe, and Emilia . . ." I choked, finally looking at her. She shrank back, bewildered. "I love you. I was to ask your father for your hand."

I held my own hand out toward her, and she shrank away from me.

"You're . . . you're a *witch*, Brennan," Norah whispered, eyes filling with tears.

Grief cut through me, sharper even than the anguish I'd felt when Maura and my parents were taken away. My hand dropped to my side, at a loss for what I could do to convince them I wasn't a witch, though I did now have power to wield magic; they hated magic as much as I had. What hurt the most was, while I chose this path, I did it unwillingly. I did it for them, for *more* than them. I did it for the whole of Britain. But no one would understand that. No one knew what Eimhir had been or what I stopped her from being. What stopping her had cost me. I did it all to save them, and they would never, *could* never, understand.

It would've been better, in their eyes, if I had died. If they had never known me, I thought, looking to Emilia. Her beautiful face was twisted in confusion, pain, and fear. I would do anything to wipe that look from her face, from my sisters' faces.

So be it, a voice said in my mind. Despair welled up in me as I raised a hand toward the crowd gathered around the damaged staircase. They shrank back in terror.

"Rhetta," I croaked, "shield yourself."

I turned back to my sisters cowering before me. "I'll always love you," I choked.

Using all my heartache to strengthen the power a hundredfold, I released the magic, the power filling the house, my mind instinctively forming the spell, shaping it to the needs and situation of my family. Pushing through the terrified cries of my loved ones as magic shook the house, I breathed, "Everything's going to be alright."

I expanded my spell's reach to beyond the walls, the neighbors, the people in the street, those on the docks, everyone who was affected by my actions. My power did not wane, didn't even flicker, as tears poured down my face, anguish fueling the magic.

Erasing memories and planting new ones should have been difficult, but somehow, I felt strangely confident. This was how *I* was going to do magic: for the good of others. My mind just flowed, knowing what to do without conscious thought. As the last person was wiped clean, new memories in place, I lowered my hand and turned back to the group by the stairs. They were shaking their heads, their eyes foggy.

I waited until they would look upon me with new eyes.

It didn't take long.

"Who . . . who are you?" Slaine asked, seeing me standing there in the entrance hall. I put a hand over my mouth, gripping my jaw so hard I felt it bruise. She truly didn't know me. Her expression was blank as she stared at me. No recognition, no smile, no joyous shout of my name. I felt like I could collapse right there, but I used the wall to brace myself.

"I just came to see if you're all well," I rasped, swiping the tears off my cheek with my arm. "Many other houses were damaged in that storm. Is everyone here alright?" The huddled group loosened, and several servants stepped into the other room and down the hall, surveying the damage with sorrow and wonder.

"We're fine, sir," Alana said, her tone kind. "Thank you for checking in on us. That was a storm like I've never seen! How fares the rest of the city?"

"There's some damage, but the whirlwind is gone now, so all should be well going forward. I'll send a constable to you as soon as I can, so you can report your damages."

"Thank you, sir," Alana replied, standing beside her nieces. "We'd appreciate that."

"Not at all, happy to oblige." My gaze shifted to my sisters and Emilia. "Are you ladies alright?" I asked, my throat tight.

"Yes, we're fine. Thank you for your kind concern," Norah said, hugging Slaine tightly. My eyes flicked to Emilia, who was looking at me, no recognition in her eyes.

"Miss, are you well?" I asked, my voice cracking as I stared down at her.

"I . . . hurt my leg. In the . . . storm, I think," she whispered.

"I'm terribly sorry," I rasped, heart constricting. I locked eyes with her, part of me desperate for some hint of awareness in her gaze, but she only gave me a small, grimacing smile before looking away.

Keeping my emotions under control, I memorized their faces in my mind. With a final glance, I nodded to the group and ducked out of the doorway.

As I descended the front steps of the house, my legs nearly gave out from under me as the implications of what I had done penetrated my heart.

No one—not the servants, my family, or Emilia—would ever know me again. I had made it so. My darling sisters would never remember that they had an older brother, and Emilia would never remember her betrothed, the man whose heart would never love another. I clapped a hand over my mouth to keep from being sick all over the street.

"Lad?" Rhetta asked as she saw me bent double, taking great gasps. "Lad, what have you done?"

"I would like to leave this place. Please," I choked as I straightened, my throat burning as I reeled from this storm of emotions.

Rhetta peered into the doorway behind me, and comprehension spread over her face at their blank expressions as they murmured over the strength of the storm.

"Very well," Rhetta replied, concern etched on her face as I strode past.

We left the houses behind, retraced our steps back to the bush where we had hidden our items, and without a backward glance at the city I had loved and destroyed, I grasped Rhetta by the arm and willed us away.

Chapter Thirty

Wind and rain whipped at our faces as we appeared on Margund's island, which had once been Eimhir's island. Though the landscape no longer pulsed with magic, I could see a few tree trunks and a wall of the cottage still hovering in the air. Other than a few remaining floating items, the magic didn't seem to have affected the island with any permanence.

In the gloom of the storm, we stared at the ramshackle cottage, which seemed to have caved in even further without the overabundance of magic flowing from Margund to support it.

Now that I had possession of the magic, my strong body and mind could hold it all in, even though I felt like the power would burst from me at any moment. I understood why a frail, broken being like Margund couldn't keep it contained.

"Well, lad," Rhetta said, looking at me through the drenching rain, "shall we get to work?"

The thought of all that had to come—the struggle of it all—pressed down on me, and I sat down hard on my haunches.

The task *still* wasn't done. Yes, Eimhir was gone, my sisters were safe for now, but we had all the remaining kelpies to turn back, and I had to erase the mind of an entire country. How did one wipe clean hundreds of years of darkness, alone?

"It'll be a lot of drudgery," Rhetta said, crouching down beside me. "But we start with one day at a time. It *will* come, lad." She put a hand on my arm. "I'm here with you, you know that, right?" she asked, her voice soft.

I looked over at her, rain clinging to the hair around her gentle face, and my shoulders relaxed. Calm swept through me, soothing my troubles for a brief moment. I *wasn't* totally alone. Rhetta understood everything. She knew I wasn't evil. She knew what I had done, and she understood what had to be done now—and the toil it took to get here. She would help with the burden that was upon me. Upon us. At that moment, I realized I trusted her completely. Together, we could do this.

The going was slow for several months.

When Rhetta had broken into Eimhir's mind to search for the reverse spell, she had discovered that underneath the island loch, Eimhir had carved a cave, similar to the one she'd had back at her cottage, but much larger.

We found the entrance in short order, and underneath the wreckage, we discovered an entire library of Eimhir's journals. Centuries of knowledge that helped clarify what Rhetta had extracted from Eimhir during the Glasgow battle.

In one of the last hand-bound books we searched, Eimhir had written on her studies of making kelpies. Not only did we learn exactly how to reverse the kelpie curse within its pages, but from this and the other journals, we gained a great wealth of magical knowledge.

I had a lot to learn yet about magic and all I could do with it, so Rhetta tasked me with spending several hours a day studying up on magic lore and practice found in Eimhir's journals. In the meantime, she poured through the writings, searching out ideas on how to complete our nearly insurmountable task, focusing on the kelpie antidote and how to combine it with an incredibly powerful memory-wiping spell.

I learned there was so much more to magic than just pointing your finger and willing the magic to follow your whim. Some spells required perfect incantations, others required potions or natural herbs or the bones or blood of mythical beasts. Sometimes emotions and thoughts got in the way, mucking up the spell.

As I studied, I learned that the memory spell I had cast on Glasgow had been so potent and complex because the deep and painful emotions had done most of the shaping and creating. My whims and desires were the creators. But if I were to try it again in a normal state of emotion, I wouldn't be able to create such an intricate and complete enchantment. It would be several decades before I could produce spells that powerful and all-encompassing without those emotions to influence and empower the magic. Rhetta had been right: relying only on emotional influence like that was dangerous, and I had to learn how to strengthen my magic without it.

Not all my education came from Rhetta and the books.

Margund's visions and memories haunted me almost every night. One memory showed a cavern like Eimhir's, but somewhere deep in a mountain range far in northern Europe. I made the decision that I would travel there one day and collect the spellbooks that Margund had acquired and created, not only to keep them safe but to learn from them. However, that journey would have to wait until my task here was completed.

Within a year of defeating Eimhir, we had created the antidote for the kelpie curse. Judging by Eimhir's journals, our process of making the antidote was much faster than Eimhir's method had been when she created the original curse. Her experiments had taken her decades, while we merely reversed the enchantments and tested them on several kelpies.

Because of my enormous amount of magic, catching kelpies became a simple task. They could not withstand the strength of my power, though they tried in vain to flee. After turning them back with the antidote and erasing their memories one by one, we kept a watchful eye on them, making sure they stayed human and that the memory spell stuck.

It took us another year to create a spell that would wipe the minds of all, kelpie and human alike.

Rhetta asked me why I wanted to wipe the minds of the entire country. "People should know what happened," she'd insisted. "They should know what we did to save the kingdom from this terrible plague, and that we that use magic are not to be feared!"

"That's exactly what I do not want," I'd replied with a grim shake of my head.

Even without the knowledge that the kelpies had been a magical curse, humanity feared and despised magic. If people were to learn that the kelpies had been freed by a witch with great power, power-seekers and magic-haters alike would come for me. And if they discovered my family, my aunt and sisters could be shunned, or worse, targeted, just as Eimhir had done.

Not to mention, the paralyzing fear that would enter the hearts of those that didn't use magic; my family's reaction to my powers had been proof of that. The world wasn't ready to believe that magic could be used for good. Magical power would certainly be branded as evil, and more hunts for mages would continue, more brutal than ever before. Mage or non-mage, fear caused people to do horrible things. Margund's fear of being overtaken had caused her to murder thousands upon thousands of people and creatures for her own ends, to become the most powerful being, and that fear had spread to Eimhir. But it would stop with me.

No one could know about the curse, know that it *was* a curse. Those killed by the kelpies would be remembered as succumbing to a famine, while those who had been kelpies would not have any recollection of their time in that cursed state.

The people would then fill in the blanks themselves with rationalizations and justifications. Humans did that when they couldn't really explain what had happened. The people would form their own version of events to make sense of their lives.

When the curse was lifted, there would be no joyful reunions, but no harrowing memories either. It would be as if their loved ones had never spent time as kelpies.

And the world would be safer, because it would be as though I, and this immense magical reservoir, didn't exist. I would disappear, without fanfare and without acknowledgement. Everyone would go on, happy and oblivious, the horrible moment in history nothing more than a faint nightmare that disappears with the return of dawn.

Chapter Thirty-One

Rhetta stepped up to me as I surveyed the darkening sky. We stood at the northernmost shore of Scotland. The sound of waves crashing behind me helped soothe my frantic nerves.

"Are you ready, Brennan?"

Off to my left, the harvest moon was just rising, its large, full face shining golden against a firmament the color of the deepest ocean.

A chill, salty breeze ruffled my hair, scattering dead leaves at my feet, and a shiver not having anything to do with the autumn air raced across my skin.

"I'm ready."

And terrified.

This full moon, closest to the autumnal equinox, would amplify our many years of hard work. Yes, I was ready, but still felt inadequate to the task: to see the fruition of many hard years' work.

The spell we had put over all the waterways in Great Britain three years earlier had stopped kelpies from rising from the depths for all that time. Everyone across the country had been baffled—but hesitantly grateful—at the sudden disappearance of the water demons.

Now, their loved ones would rise, never to be turned again, and the horrors erased.

Apprehension swirled inside me. I tried not to focus on whether my father, mother, Maura, and even Rhetta's husband Daimh were still alive. This was about *all* of Great Britain. But still, a part of me squirmed with breathless excitement for their sakes.

I met Rhetta's eye, and after an encouraging nod from her, I took a deep breath and raised my hands.

I opened my well of magic, allowing Rhetta access to it, and together, we conjured an enormous, roiling stormwall of wind and flashing magic that filled the entire horizon. The storm churned even the clouds in the heavens, leaves whipping past us as we stood at the forefront, cloaked in protections against the memory-wiping spell.

Willing my magic upward, we took to the sky.

Rhetta had gotten the idea of lifting ourselves heavenward to enact the spell. We'd practiced soaring into that starlit expanse for months, realizing it was the only way we could ensure the magical storm never wavered, the only way we could confirm it was working. The clouds were becoming a familiar refuge, but taking flight like the birds in the blue still made my stomach clench as my feet left the ground.

From our vantage point, the mountains were mere hills, the rivers threads of silver in the moonlight as we soared over the waves of magical power, propelling them forward across the entire breadth of Great Britain, touching water, earth, and all creatures great and small. As wave upon wave of the remedy crossed the country over the lochs, we dipped low, undoing the spell that bound the surface of the waters.

I watched with churning emotions as the first kelpies, squealing, burst from the rivers and lochs in droves, their screeching sending a chill of remembrance down my spine, but it was short lived. As kelpies left their watery homes in search of more victims after their long imprisonment, the counter-curse washed over them in a surge of mist and magic. I gasped aloud as I watched the magnificent water horses morph back into humans in varying states of nakedness before we blazed by overhead.

As we flew over, I could see the confusion immediately settle over their eyes as their minds were wiped, and, though they were surely embarrassed about their natural state, we knew they'd find their way back to their homes, unable to account for their unreasonable undress. The magic would nudge the hordes of humans to come to an explanation on their own. The memory spell wouldn't sit well with some, but for nearly all, it would be enough, and I could live with that.

As we sailed ahead, watching more and more kelpies fall to the earth, only to rise as humans once again, I fought back the elation and hope threatening to burst from me.

We soared south ahead of the stormwall of magical power until we reached the southernmost shore of England, ensuring that the stormwall did not waver, and that every leaf, house, thicket, and loch was touched by the spell as we directed it over the length of the land. We had decided to cover all the isle of Great Britain, just to ensure no stray kelpie escaped.

As the last of the kelpies transformed back into their human skins, and the magical wave blew itself into nothing over the ocean, we landed, staring out at the churning magic as it dissipated, and I closed access to my magic. A sob burst from my throat as tears welled in my eyes and streamed down my cheeks. I turned and embraced Rhetta, who was weeping just as hard as I. We clung to each other, icy sea water rushing over our ankles as we stood on the rocky shore.

It was done.

As the sky began to lighten, Rhetta and I broke apart, still gripping hands, and turned to watch the ocean change from midnight ink to deep burgundy, kissed with highlights of gold. Rhetta began laughing, a sound brighter than the sun that was now dawning on a new day, tear trails sparkling on her cheeks.

Throat thick, I couldn't stop myself from smiling back, the first time in three years.

The reign of Eimhir and her water demons was over.

Epilogue

The late summer sun sent bright, dappled sunshine through the trees and onto the blankets spread out onto the grass, casting the family that sat on them in a warm green-and-yellow light.

I stood apart in my dusty traveling cloak, halfway behind a tree. I was far enough away from the group to be hidden, yet close enough to hear their conversations. My beloved family talked and laughed, unaware that I was there watching them enjoy the summer day. A few yards away from the picnic, a large pond glistened in the sunlight. I remembered swimming there during boyhood summers when we visited the estate with my aunt and uncle. This place once held many happy memories for me. Now those memories were bittersweet.

Although all my sisters were younger than me, they now appeared years older. I still looked as young and fresh as I did on my nineteenth birthday, even though thirteen years had passed since that fateful day we had departed for Bòidhchead, to sell our old cottage home.

But I didn't feel nineteen. I didn't even feel thirty-two. I felt the centuries of knowledge inside of me, knowledge I'd used in the last few years trying to stamp out all recollection of the kelpies: where they came from and what they were. As Rhetta and I anticipated, not everyone had been affected by the memory spell we had cast over the Kingdom of Great Britain. We spent the last decade tracking down and erasing the few existing memories of those who retained some idea of the kelpies. No doubt I still missed some people's memories—there had always been that chance—but at least now the kelpies were nothing more than a myth.

I didn't like the thought that I was doing the same thing that Margund had done—stamping out magical knowledge—but it had to be done, for everyone's sake. I wasn't trying to halt magical progression; I just wanted the terrible, terrible nightmare of kelpies to be forgotten.

But now, as I stood behind this tree, I felt tired and stunted. Listless and useless. What else could I do here in my home country, besides watch and pine after my family? Scotland was, for the moment, free of contention—magical and mundane—yet I didn't want to leave.

"Alban, do be careful with the baby!" Norah called to her eight-year-old son as he helped his tiny sister toddle around in the grass.

"Don't worry, Mama!" called Alban II, so named after my father.

With a half-smile, I watched my nephew and niece traipse around the grass before turning my attention back to the three women sitting on the blankets, half-empty platters of finger sandwiches and cake spread before them.

Norah, Maura, and my mother.

Two little girls sat with them, Charlotte and Emily. Maura's daughters.

When I discovered that my mother and Maura had both survived their stint as kelpies, my relief was beyond measure. My heart still twisted in longing as I stared at my mother's aging face. It had been one of the hardest things to do, letting her forget that she had another child: her eldest and only son. But seeing her, living and smiling, helped ease the sting of being forgotten.

"Mama, when are Aunty Slaine and Uncle Robert coming back from Paris?" Charlotte asked as she wove her younger sister's hair into a lopsided braid.

"From Slaine's letter, she should be arriving in Glasgow port on the Royal Oak sometime today, and they'll take a carriage to Robert's estate for a few days before coming here."

A small shout and the wail of a child drew everyone's attention, and I looked to where Alban was hovering over his little sister, who had fallen to the grass.

"Oh, I'm sorry, Brenna!" Alban cried over his sister's wail. Norah stood and hurried to scoop the little girl up. My heart leapt every time I heard them call the lassie by name, thinking for half a moment that they were calling for *me*. Perhaps the memory spell wasn't as tightly knit as I had thought.

"There, there, love," Norah soothed, rocking the baby close.

"I'm sorry, Mama," Alban replied, shamefaced.

"You need to be more careful, dearest," Norah replied, running a hand under her son's chin. Alban bobbed his head, and they moved back to sit on the blankets.

My mother clapped her hands. "Why don't we set up a game of What Time Is It, Mr. Wolf? Your grandfather loved playing it with his daughters," she said, looking between Norah and Maura with a misty expression. There was a clamor of agreement, and my heart twisted. My father had not survived his time as a kelpie; my family believed that my father had died of influenza.

From time spent watching them from afar, I could tell that my family's memories of those years after they'd been turned back into humans were murky, which they attributed to the pain of losing our father and Uncle Douglas. I also had to change my aunt Alana's memory so that she knew my mother was alive, and thankfully, I didn't have to do much tampering to get my mother's and aunt's lives and memories compatible with the rest.

Of her own volition, my aunt gave my mother ownership of Kedlefield Hall, declaring she could never live outside of Glasgow and that it was rightfully my mother's anyway. It brought a sense of peace to my heart. My mother had lost her inheritance due to me, and now that I no longer existed, she had gotten it back. There, at Kedlefield Hall, my mother and sisters were able to live and grow together with their new families as if they'd never been apart.

I had stayed away at first. Though I was grateful they didn't question the blank spaces in their memories and were happy, my own pain at the separation was too great.

I had visited Emilia a few months after we'd freed the kelpies. She had been doing well, courting a gentleman I didn't know. She looked radiant and happy on his arm. She truly didn't remember anything—Eimhir had made it so—but to see her move on with her life, perfectly content without me? That broke something inside me, and I fled, unable to bear the sight.

I resolved to never check in on her again.

Seeing my mother and sisters was easier, because while my future was no longer with them, they would always be my family.

My mother gathered the children and they moved toward me, stopping only a few feet from my tree. She lined her grandchildren up, facing her. "Now, we all remember the rules? I—" She stopped speaking, her eyes straying, incredibly, in my direction. I didn't move to hide but involuntarily gasped. I knew she could not possibly see me—I had cloaked myself magically from sight—and yet . . . she seemed to be looking right at me.

"Grandmother?" Alban asked, glancing behind him. "Are you alright?"

My mother's glazed expression cleared, and she looked at her grandchildren, smiling.

"Yes . . . Yes, I'm fine. I just had the oddest feeling that . . . Are we missing someone?" she asked, looking to where her daughters sat on the grass.

"No, we're all here!" Alban exclaimed as he counted out his siblings and cousins.

"I just had the strangest sensation that . . . that . . ." Again, my mother's eyes grazed the lawn, searching. I raised a hand to my mouth, biting down hard on my knuckles, my eyes burning. It wasn't possible. Was it? Deep down, did my mother remember me? Could she somehow sense my presence?

My mother seemed to shake off her stupor and turned to her grandchildren, her expression lively. "Alright! I'll be the wolf!" She hurried several yards away, then commenced to shout out a random hour of the clock every time my nieces and nephews shouted, "What time is it, Mr. Wolf?"

Eyes stinging, I took in the sight of my beloved family, fixing their faces into my mind as they played and laughed before I turned and fled the park with an aching heart.

I couldn't visit my family again. I couldn't do this to myself anymore, especially if the veil separating my mother and myself was that tenuous. I had made this visit after my final march across Great Britain, searching out any last memories of the kelpies. But now . . .

The emotional bond between us all was too strong, and if I visited again, I feared the spell of forgetfulness I had cast upon all my living relations—to shield them from the fear of magic—would shatter entirely. Or I would break it on purpose, just to be with them, to have them look upon me with remembrance for even a moment. But I couldn't. Not only would I be breaking the promise I made to myself, it would lead to too many questions, questions I couldn't answer without mentioning magic. I didn't want them, or anyone else, to know about my magic. This overwhelming power was still a little frightening even to me, and I imagined it always would be.

As I crossed the road, the urge to run back to my family was almost overpowering.

Before my resolve broke, I sprinted down the road leading toward the small town near Kedlefield Hall, hoping the exertion would take my mind off my family. Entering town, I slowed and stepped into an alley to catch my breath. I gripped my head in my hands as all my anger and sadness swallowed me. I had no new challenges to take my mind off my family. Now that the kelpies were mere myth, I had no reason to stay. No desire to stay.

A realization hit me like a kick from a kelpie: it was time to get away from Scotland.

A sudden breeze lifted my hair and cooled the sweat on my neck. Turning, I felt a faint call on the wind to find undiscovered knowledge in the wide, wild, forgotten world. Surely there were others out there that I could help, and perhaps doing so would make these painful wounds more bearable and take my mind off my lonely future.

I would outlive anyone I came to care for; my family was a constant reminder of that. Norah's oldest son was only a few years shy of the age I had been when we had first arrived in Glasgow. And I could never find a true home in society. Magic was so feared, I would be shunned by all but those of my kind.

Though I still had Rhetta as a friend and confidante, she was busy living her life with Daimh, with whom I'd also become very close over the years. Though they offered me a place at their fire whenever I wanted, I had no desire to stay with the druids, whose happiness was found in plain, simple living. And now that magic had opened up a whole new world for me, I desired more vast horizons than they. I'd seen to the kelpies and to my family's happiness, and I could no longer use Scotland or my family as an excuse against that first step out into the unfamiliar world. Traveling and learning would be the only way I could forget my past, protect my family, and focus on my responsibilities.

Without taking a moment to consider everything, I disappeared from where I stood, reappearing in Glasgow. The smell of the city, with that salty tang to it, was like a salve on my wounded soul. It had been so long since I'd been out on the open ocean. A sea voyage was exactly what I needed at that moment. Though I could travel across the English Channel into Europe in the blink of an eye, something as familiar and nostalgic as sailing sounded invigorating—the wind in my hair, the spray on my face, even the back-breaking work. I could relive a happier time, even if just for a while.

But first, I wanted to see Slaine and her new husband, Robert, for the last time before I left.

Hurrying through the crowds, I made my way to the harbor master's house, sidestepping a group of naval officers as they exited the office. A dowdy man with white hair and spectacles sat at the desk inside, peering at the small script on a ledger book.

"Good morn, sir. Has the Royal Oak arrived in port?" I asked.

"It's been in port for a good hour now, lad," the man replied, not bothering to glance up at me.

Anxiety squeezed my lungs. I might have missed her.

"Thank you, sir," I gasped, hurrying out the door without any other explanation. The port had grown since last I'd been here. The waterfront bustled with sailors, merchants with their cargo, and passengers milling about the wharf. The prospect of missing Slaine, lost in this mess and probably already away, made my chest hurt.

I pulled out my handkerchief in agitation, the stitched swans starting to fray from the many times I drew it out for comfort. As I came around an enormous stack of trunks, a shout caught my attention, and I turned to see two men scuffling before they were pulled apart by a crowd of sailors. Shaking my head, I turned back around, my shoulder shoving into someone standing beside the pile of trunks. The woman gasped, her parasol clattering to the ground, my handkerchief slipping from my hand.

"Oh, I beg your pardon," I murmured, bending low to scoop up the fallen, lacy parasol, then straightened. The bottom dropped out of my stomach.

Slaine stood before me, holding my handkerchief.

She was a beautiful young lady now: twenty-two, fresh-faced, and newly married. She smiled at me, holding out my handkerchief as I clutched her parasol.

"Forgive me," I rasped, my grip tightening around the parasol handle.

"Not to worry." She smiled at me as I held her gaze, her smile turning nervous when I failed to hand her the parasol, and she looked down at my handkerchief in her hands.

"What a lovely design," she said, stroking an embroidered thistle with a dainty finger.

"Thank you," I whispered, my throat thickening. "My youngest sister made it for me."

"She's very talented," Slaine replied, once again holding the handkerchief out for me.

I took it, nodding, and handed back her parasol with a soft, "Here you are, little bird." I froze as her face quirked in question, but then she gave a light laugh.

"Thank you, sir."

I continued to stare, drinking in her face, her nervous smile.

At that moment, Robert, Slaine's towering, blonde-haired, mustachioed husband, came into view, holding a pair of lady's gloves.

"I've found them, love. They were back onboard—" He paused, stopping beside Slaine, glancing between the two of us and putting a protective hand on Slaine's waist. I tucked my handkerchief away and nodded at him. He gave me a curt nod back, though a slight frown pulled on his handsome face.

"Again, forgive me," I said, turning back to Slaine. She gave me a kind, but neutral, smile. The lack of recognition in her eyes cut me to the core again. Before I could stop myself, I grabbed her hand, anguish piercing my soul, and pressed a fervent kiss to the back of her hand.

I broke away and pushed through the crowd, a sob surging up my throat.

"Slaine, who was that? Are you quite alright, darling? *Slaine?*" I heard Robert gasp, his voice edged with sudden panic. I glanced back just as Slaine staggered against the pile of trunks, a hand on her forehead, her face ashen. I froze, heedless of the people bumping into me as I watched Slaine tremble, looking ill. Fear curdled my stomach, my muscles screaming to run back and help her, but I restrained myself. I would only make things worse for her.

"Slaine! Darling?" Robert asked, putting a hand on her shoulder.

"I'm fine, I'm fine, Robert, dear," Slaine panted, straightening and casting him a wan smile. "I just . . . felt very strange. It's nothing, just dizzy for a moment. It's passing, now," she insisted, sitting on a trunk and fanning her face. "I'm fine."

I thought—or maybe wished—I saw her cast a searching look around the milling crowd, but the moment passed, and she was accepting her gloves from a still-worried Robert, laughing at his twisted expression. "I'm fine, dearest. Perhaps it's just a consequence of being fresh off the ship," she said. The color was coming back into her face, though a confused look clung to her expression.

I relaxed. She was alright. I didn't know what I had done, but I wouldn't hurt her anymore. I had to go. Giving her one last wistful look, I hurried through the crowds toward the bobbing ships on the river, intent on catching the next boat out, not caring where it was headed.

Acknowledgements

I'm about to get sappy, so buckle up.

This book has been a major effort for me, the culmination of eleven-plus years and countless tears and many hours throwing down with Imposter Syndrome. It also took so long because I am a very self-conscious person, and showing anything I wrote to anyone—including my husband, who is semi-obsessed with me—was physically painful. Still kind of is.

But I didn't accomplish this feat alone, despite how often it felt that way.

I'm forever grateful to my Heavenly Father and his son Jesus Christ. I know without their help, this book would never have made it out into the world. They helped me break out of my comfort bubble and learn and grow, even if I was ungrateful for it at times.

The same can be said for my husband Bryan, who has been wanting me to be published ever since we started dating over ten years ago. He is my number one fan, my editor, my best friend, my champion, and I one-thousand-percent guarantee I would not have made it this far without him.

Thank you to my alpha readers, Mary Locke Jolley and Sarah Lowe, who told me the hard truths, but kept cheering me on and believing in me, even though they *saw* the first iterations of this book. Like, they *saw* it, and told me to keep writing. Wild.

Thanks to my parents who have always shown their encouragement for my writing by enrolling me in public writing classes that absolutely terrified me, but I got through it alright. Thank you for your support, I love you!

Thank you to all the family and friends who beta read this book; my mother-in-law Gayle, who, like her son, never stopped bugging me to publish, Emily Randall Barker, Meladee Kirton, and all my siblings who have given feedback and suggestions on titles and cover stuff: Candice, Nick (and Paige!) Kyle, Camille, my other inlaws, and my maternal grandma, Sherron Robison, who always encouraged me to do hard things, and who is usually the first person I told my big life decisions to.

Thank you to any other readers who saw this before it was published, you were champs for indulging me: Lynn Lonsdale, Mary's niece and nephew, Alex and Bekah, Nicole Burnham, Veronica Burnham, Shelby Burnham, Beka Williams, and anyone else I missed, I'm sorry—I have sent this out to a plethora of people, it's hard to keep track—but I am so beyond grateful for you!

To my editors, McKell Parsons and Becca Bird, thank you so much for helping me get it polished, you're both incredible, and you made my work shine!

To My Lan Khuc Valle, my cover designer, you made a stunning cover out of my feeble descriptions and I'm still amazed! You truly worked some dazzling magic!

And to you, cherished reader, thank you for taking time to read my book: out of all the hundreds of millions of books out there, I am so grateful you took a chance on mine.

ABOUT THE AUTHOR

Chantel Burnham is a writer of Young Adult Fantasy and Sci-Fi, as well as a movie quoter extraordinaire. After spending some time as a film major, she discovered that her true passion is creating worlds of her own through writing.

When she isn't procrastinating writing her next book, Chantel can be found crafting decorations for Spooky Season, listening to music non-stop, reading from her ever-expanding TBR list, or snuggling her dog, cats, and husband, usually all at the same time.

Chantel lives in Northern Utah even though snow isn't her thing. *Magic Feared and Furious* is her debut novel.

Feel free to check out her website at www.chantelburnham.com or scan the QR code.